MW01139630

LOVE & LEGACY

Amor Eterno

BOOK ONE

KIMBERLY SÁNCHEZ-CAWTHORN

This is a work of fiction. Names, characters, places, and incidents either are the product of the author's imagination or are used fictitiously. Any resemblance to actual persons, living or dead, events, or locales is entirely coincidental.

Copyright © 2019 by Kimberly Sánchez-Cawthorn

All rights reserved. No part of this book may be reproduced or used in any manner without written permission of the copyright owner except for the use of quotations in a book review.

First paperback edition April 2019

Cover art by Jerry Santistevan
Cover design by Logan Cannon
Author Photo by Cindylee Johnson

ISBN: 9781797481753

k_s_sanchez@yahoo.com
@kimsanchezcawthorn on Instagram

Dedication

To my grandmothers, Emma and Jennie, real Proverbs 31 women who are the anchors of our families' culture and history; and to Darien and Kyara, the future of our legacy

Acknowledgements

To God for inspiration and guidance and by whose grace and mercy has made it at all possible to write this book. I am forever grateful for who You are in my life. You consistently show me that You know me, that You love me, and that You are with me every step of the way, proving to me that with You, indeed *all* things are possible—even writing this story in a month and a half in the midst of being a busy stay-at-home mom! To Rozelle, who read the first fifty pages and told me that he really liked the story, which gave me the confidence to continue. Thank you for your support, and for letting me fill your ears as I became more and more consumed with these characters and this story. And to my children, for their tireless patience as I wrote every second I could get. To my son also, for asking me to sit and write with him one evening as he wrote his own stories in a notebook for school. It was because of your prompting that the floodgates were finally opened. To my parents and my brother for listening to me rant and talk your ear off about this story and reading each version. You have always believed in me no matter what adventure I've decided to embark on and/or drag you into. To my primo, Jerry Santistevan, for agreeing to illustrate the cover of this book, enthusiastically, without hesitation. Your support and immediate willingness to be a part of this book has meant the world to me. I also want to thank one of my former students, Emmanuel Barrón, for taking the time to share his expertise in Archaeology. I appreciate your help in shaping those chapters and bringing real life to that work. To my editor, Katelyn Stark, for your acute editing skills and for helping me pull out the emotion and sensory detail that brings more fullness and life to this story. To Logan Cannon, the graphic designer who skillfully brought the artwork and text together to create the beautiful cover.

Finally, to my favorite Chicano authors, Sandra Cisneros, Laura Esquivel, Rudolfo Anaya, and the countless others, who have paved the way for the rest of us to follow our dreams of writing. Your work inspired me to love reading again. Through your writing, I am especially reminded that our history, our stories, and our lives are magical and vital, not only to our heritage as Latinos, but they are integral fibers in the rich cultural fabric of the United States of America as a whole. I would like to particularly thank Victor Villaseñor for sharing the inspirational novel that encouraged me to document my own family's legacy years ago before I even understood the depth of what I would uncover in my genealogical research. I remember flipping through the pages on my own study abroad trip to Spain and reading *Rain of Gold* fervently until the wee hours of the morning, not caring that I had to be up for class in a few hours. I remember finishing the book late one night, buzzing and not being able to sleep, not fully understanding how it would impact my own writing a couple of decades later. I will forever be grateful.

Thank you to Moctezuma Esparza and the team who wrote and produced *Walkout* for your inspiration and for continuing the fight for social justice through your art. To the film makers, poets, musicians, artists, and playwrights who write, document, and perform our stories now and to those yet to come, continue to be inspired to bring our beautiful oral tradition to life, letting the world know that these events indeed happened. That they do matter. And that they do belong in the history books. *¡Que viva la Raza, nuestra cultura, y las historias de nuestros antepasados!*

Chapter 1

Catalina,

Corral de Almaguer, Toledo, España,
Circa 1595

Benjamín's face was imprinted in Catalina's mind as she rushed through the meadow, making the long grasses whistle. The sun was setting, and the warmth of the summer evening hugged her skin. Catalina had snuck out of her home to meet him again at the tree-lined river. She had seen him in the square earlier that day with her parents. He had caught her eye through the masses of people between them and had winked at her. Her heart had skipped a beat, and she had blushed sheepishly back at him. The sparkle in his eyes had told her he was counting the seconds to see her. Later that evening they would be together at their beloved sanctuary next to the river, under their old, large, beautiful tree that was hidden from the sightlines of their homes. They had been meeting there every Sunday evening for months.

When she arrived, he was already waiting. He grabbed her and lifted her into his arms. Each week seemed to get longer in between their visits. The heat of the evening mixed with the passion between them, and, for a moment, they were breathless in each other's embrace. Benjamín wiped his brow. Catalina sighed. The river cooled the air somewhat, and the early evening light danced on the water, welcoming them to come in and cool off. They sat on the cozy blanket she brought, and he looked down at her and stroked her hair. His fingers ran down the side of her cheek. There was an intensity and longing in his dark eyes tonight that she didn't quite understand. He looked away when he saw her watching him. Concerned, she held his face smooth in her hands coercing him to look at her.

"¿Qué pasa, mi amor? ¿En qué piensas? ¿Por qué te ves tan triste?"[1]

"Nada...Aquí te truje algo."[2]

He turned to grab something out of his sack. She noticed him trying to discreetly dry a tear from his eye. She blinked and scratched the back of her head. *¿Qué le pasará?*[3] He pulled out a small, red velvet box and handed it to her.

"¡Mi amor!" Her eyes moved quickly from him to the box. She stared at it in both of her hands, wondering what could fit inside there.

"Anda. Ábrela."[4] He leaned into her and motioned toward the box with his hands.

"Espera...tengo algo para ti también." She reached into her satchel and pulled out a long, thin gift wrapped in cloth and ribbon. *"Y quiero que lo abras primero."*[5]

"¿Qué es esto?" He took the box and tore at the ribbon. Then he paused, tilting his head. *"¿Pero por qué?"*[6]

"Bueno, porque...te vide admirándola en la plaza y...porque te quiero."[7] She shrugged her shoulders and bit a corner of her lower lip.

Benjamín pulled at the cloth and found a wooden box that was etched with a detailed, colorful pattern; inside was an expensive paint brush with several vials of paint fitted alongside the box.

He gasped and kissed Catalina's cheek. He shook his head and chuckled. *"¡Con razón te quiero tanto! Anda...ahora tú."*[8]

She flipped the lid of the box and inside was a delicate gold butterfly brooch. She wrapped her arms around him.

"¡Hermoso, mi amor!"[9] she said in a low voice as she admired the details and the jewels embedded in it. *"Este lo guardaré yo para siempre."*[10] She held it to her heart.

---

[1] What's the matter, my love? What are you thinking about? Why do you look so sad?

[2] Nothing. I brought you something.

[3] What is going on with him?

[4] Come on. Open it.

[5] Wait...I have something for you too...and I want you to open it first.

[6] What is this? Why?

[7] Well, because...I saw you admiring it in the square, and...because I love you.

[8] No wonder I love you so much. Ok...now, it's your turn.

[9] It's beautiful, my love!

[10] I will save this forever!

Catalina couldn't take her eyes off of it. Streaks of sunlight broke through the trees and kissed it, making the colors luminous. Her heart warmed at his thoughtfulness. Not too long ago, she had told Benjamín the story of butterflies reminding her of her grandfather who had recently passed away. One particular butterfly had surprised her grandfather by following him through the meadow and resting on his shoulder as he worked. He had described the black and golden colors in the butterfly's intricately designed wings to Catalina and had shared how he had spoken to it in a kind, child-like voice, asking the butterfly why she had chosen to come to him. Catalina remembered how much her grandfather had loved animals and had always maintained that *'Nomás hablar les falta.'*[11] He had instructed the butterfly to go wait for him by the river at his tree where he had left his knapsack with his lunch. When he had returned to the tree after finishing his work, there was the butterfly fluttering about, waiting for him, and landed on his shoulder again as he drew near. He had passed away soon after that. But ever since, butterflies had held a special meaning in Catalina's heart.

Reminded of this story, she looked at her brooch and a grateful grin took over her face. Her Benjamín was so attentive. He always knew what to do to make things special and show her that he knew what she needed. She lifted it to her heart and thanked him with sweet kisses all over his face. He laughed, holding her and kissing her back. They walked hand in hand toward the river and took off their shoes to cool off. Catalina lifted the long skirt of her dress in her hands and tied it in a knot at her knee, exposing her calves and ankles. She knelt down and cupped some water in her hand and splashed it at Benjamin with a sly grin before running toward the meadow. His mouth fell open in disbelief, making Catalina giggle. He wiped at some drops that had made it into his eyes, even though they had instinctively shut as the water shot towards them. He chased her until he caught her. His arm wrapped around her waist, and they fell to the ground, giggling. They lay there, side-by-side, trying to catch their breath, with his head leaning against hers. When their heartbeats had returned to normal, he kissed her softly, stood up, and reached out his hand to lift her up.

---

[11] All they lacked was the ability to speak

3

"¡Cómo eres atroz! Me pudieras haber quita'o un ojo."[12] He pointed an index finger in her direction as they strolled back to the river.

"¡Ay, escandaloso!"[13] She rolled her eyes and nudged his arm. They waded a while longer, enjoying the last bits of sunlight as it peered through the trees, splashing each other until their clothes were soaking wet.

He took her in his arms and held her, staring deeply into her blue-gray eyes and playing with her long, light brown curly hair that she had let fall loose to just above the small of her back. She felt like he could see right through to her soul with the intensity of his dark eyes. Then he touched his lips to hers. She kissed him back, slipping her fingers through his thick, dark hair. Catalina pulled away quickly. She studied his face, taking in every inch of his olive complexion, strong jaw-line, and thick, dark eyebrows. His hair had fallen to one side of his forehead during their play with the ends almost reaching his eye. She pushed it back with her fingertips.

"Ahí está otra vez, Benjamín. Esto lo que siento de ti no está bien. Me da miedo. Dime por favor, ¿Qué es lo que pasa contigo?"[14]

Barely allowing Catalina to get the words out, he blurted, *"¡Nos vamos!"*[15] His breathing grew heavy as is eyes flooded. He walked toward the meadow where the blanket was, and she followed, still watching him. Her heart began to race.

"¿Qué me dices?"[16]

He fell to his knees with his face in his hands and then rested them at the back of his neck. He looked up at her, wearing his misery on his sleeve.

"Es que…es muy peligroso aquí ya, Catalina. Mi familia se va a Turquía donde nos han dicho que es más seguro."[17]

"¡No!" She kneeled next to him, hugging him. *"No te vayas. Quédate tú aquí conmigo."*[18]

---

[12] You're so mischievous! You could have taken my eye out.

[13] Big baby!

[14] There it is again, Benjamín. The feeling I'm sensing from you isn't right. It's scaring me. Tell me, please. What's going on with you?

[15] We're leaving!

[16] What did you say?

[17] It's just…that it's very dangerous for us here, Catalina. My family is going to Turkey where we've been told it is much safer.

[18] Don't go. Stay here with me.

He was quiet for a moment, watching her body tremble. She was sure her face was red with confusion and fear.

Reaching for her shoulders, he cried, *"¡Cásate conmigo, Catalina! Y te vas tú con nosotros."*[19]

"¡Estás loco!"[20]

She considered his sudden proposal, realizing that once she left, in all likelihood, she would never return. She thought about all that she would leave behind. Her parents. Her family. Her beloved Corral de Almaguer and the tranquility she found at her sanctuary under her tree next to the Rio Riánsares. But what was it all worth without him?

"¡Sí, sí voy!"[21] The tears broke from her eyes as she nodded, grasping for his hands.

"Bueno, mañana vamos mi papá y yo para pedir tu mano...en matrimonio,"[22] he said with glossy eyes and a wide grin. Both of his hands caressed hers before he cupped her face.

He stood, helping her up and pulling her close. He closed his eyes and took a deep breath. She could feel the tension leave his body. He held her head to his heart and kissed her multiple times.

"Estoy contento...calmado, ahora que sé que vienes conmigo."[23]

She nodded and held his hand and gaze until their fingertips parted. They made the trek back home, he to one side of the river and she, across the meadow, to the other.

That night, Catalina couldn't sleep with all that was running through her mind. She would be married soon and traveling to an unfamiliar country with the love of her life. As she lay in her bed, butterflies swarmed through her and anxiety filled her mind's eye. She tossed and turned in and out of sleep when a vision of Benjamín came to her; he was sitting on the back of a horse-drawn wagon, legs dangling from the edge, and a tear rolling down his cheek. Her eyes were forced open from her sleep with a sharp pain in the pit of her stomach.

"Benjamín!"

---

[19] Marry me, Catalina, and you can come with us!

[20] You're crazy!

[21] Yes, yes, I will go!

[22] Ok, then tomorrow, my father and I will come to ask for your hand...in marriage.

[23] I'm happy...content, now that I know you're coming with me.

She sat up in her bed, breathing hard and finding it difficult to swallow. She tip-toed to the window, careful not to wake the family. It was pitch black. Nothing could be seen more than a few feet away. All that was heard were the noises of the night, crickets, the rush of the river, and a horse neighing in the distance. Before long, she awoke once again to the smell of her mother making breakfast. Catalina greeted her and got to her chores. Butterflies continued jabbing wildly at her stomach in anticipation of her engagement when out of nowhere came her younger cousin Eleazar running and screaming down the cobblestone streets and toward the meadow and their house. Everyone rushed to their windows to see what the ruckus was all about.

In between breaths, he yelled, *"¡Se fueron! ¡Se fueron! ¡La familia Carvajal se ha ido a Turquía! Su casa está toda vacía. Llegaron las autoridades de la Inquisición a las 05:00 de la mañana y ya no los hallaron."*[24]

Catalina shivered, feeling the blood drain to her feet. Her vision was real.

No era sueño. Es una verdadera pesadilla.[25]

She became lightheaded, grabbing the doorframe to prevent her fall. Rumors of Inquisitors had invaded Corral de Almaguer months ago. They arrived on horseback everywhere they went, raiding homes, seizing families, trying them in courts, hanging them, torturing or burning at the stake those who committed the crime of practicing Judaism. Since the expulsion of the Jews in 1492, they had all either fled the country or become *conversos*[26] getting baptized and sometimes changing their names just to remain in the land they loved and had lived in for generations. Yet, they continued practicing their traditions and their laws in secret. Inquisition authorities had kept close watch over Benjamín's family, under the suspicion that they were engaging in the customs that had been strictly prohibited. Catalina saw her life unravel right before her eyes. She threw down her apron and the *trapo*[27] she held in her hands, grabbed for her satchel, and ran toward their sanctuary.

---

[24] They're gone! They're gone! The Carvajal family fled to Turkey! Their house is empty. The Inquisition authorities came for them at 5:00 this morning and they had already left.

[25] It wasn't a dream. It is a horrible nightmare.

[26] Jewish converts to Christianity, namely Catholicism

[27] Dishtowel

"*¡Catalina! ¡Catalina! ¿Adónde vas? ¡Ven pa'ca, ahora mismo!*"[28] yelled her mother.

She tore through the thick grass, her chest heaving, and sobs trailing down her cheeks. Her mother's voice floated through her ears as if in a dream as she worked her way toward the tree. She'd be able to see his house from there. She needed to see this for herself. As she reached their tree, she fell to her knees and gasped for air. She wiped at her wet, blurry eyes and squinted, trying to focus. Across the river, his house stood eerily empty. No horses. No belongings. No one tending to the chores. They had disappeared almost as if they had never existed. She sat up against their tree with her knees pulled to her chest and created a river of her own with her tears in the meadow.

Her eyes burned. They were heavy and swollen. She felt for her bag and pulled out her *pluma*[29] and the wooden diary she had made. She felt the texture of the soft cover. She had wrapped it with a fine piece of crushed velvet purple fabric that her aunt had given her from her travels to France years ago. She had made a dress with the fabric, and this is what she had had left over. She pulled the butterfly brooch that Benjamín had given her from her sack and studied it. She sighed as her fingers caressed the thin, delicate, precise golden lines that formed the butterfly's wings and body. She gently shined the brooch on her skirt, wiping a couple of tears that had fallen on it. The tiny emeralds in the wings and the antennae, each adorned with a small red ruby at the top, were brilliant in the sunlight. She knew it had to be worth a fortune. *¿Cómo me pudo comprar esto?*[30] But the monetary value didn't hold a candle to the sentimental value that it represented.

She wiped her nose with her hanky and pinned the brooch to the front cover of her diary. It was a perfect fit for it. Her diary was her most prized possession. Her very heart and soul had been spilled onto its pages. She felt blessed to have been given the gift of reading and writing. It was where she found her solace. *¿Qué voy a hacer ahora, Benjamín?* She cleared her throat, pulled open the book, with the purple ribbon marking her last page, and began to write:

---

[28] Catalina, Catalina! Where are you going? Get back here this instant!
[29] feather pen
[30] How could he have afforded to buy this for me?

7

14 de agosto 1595

Lo que sucedió hoy me ha rompido el corazón en más pedacitos que pueda uno contar. El amor de mi vida me ha dejado para siempre. Todo lo que amo y la vida que conozco se va alejándose más y más como agua entre medio de mis dedos...[31]

When she had finished, she wrapped it in her satchel and attempted the long walk home through the meadow. Every step was heavy as she mustered the strength to push forward. Even more so, her heart wouldn't let her eyes stop dripping with anguish.

As she walked, she lamented at how the Inquisition had gotten progressively worse over the years. For centuries, the Jews had lived side by side peacefully with Christians and Moors alike in thriving communities, contributing to government, mathematics, science, literature, and society in meaningful ways. But over the last two hundred years in particular, the success and carefree lifestyle they once led had increasingly become a secretive and anxious one. They were constantly looking over their shoulder, fearing the Inquisition officers.

They had changed their holy rituals in various ways so that if anyone would come upon them, they wouldn't be found out. Catalina recalled one Friday evening not too long ago when the authorities had come banging on their door, supposedly looking for a friend of her father's. Her parents had anticipated their arrival. They had set up their table with a long table cloth that hid their small lit candle on the floor in the middle of the table underneath. Her parents and aunts and uncles had playing cards set on the table and had begun to play a game. They had hidden their holy scriptures in their laps with the tablecloth covering them.

Inquisition officers had pulled her father outside and questioned him. Catalina had held her breath, watching her father through the window. Another had come in and snooped around every nook and cranny of her home, searching for any glimpse of guilt. She had

---

[31] August 14, 1595
What has occurred today has torn my heart in more pieces than I could count. The love of my life has left me forever. Everything that I love and the only life I have ever known is escaping from me more and more, like water flowing through my fingers...

looked down at the wrinkled cone-shape that she had left in her dress as she had held onto it, squeezing it for dear life, and had tried to smooth it over with her sweaty palms as she waited for them to leave. She had been sure everyone could feel her heart pounding. They had left soon thereafter, having not found anything incriminating. They had been blessed that day. Her best friend from childhood had not been so lucky. They had torn into her home in the middle of the night, dragging her father out as her mother and brothers and sisters screamed in horror. They jailed him and tried him. Then, using him as an example in an *auto de fe,*[32] they had burned him at the stake in the middle of the square in Corral de Almaguer. To the protests of her friend, Catalina had not let her go to the square to watch. Instead, she had taken her to her house and held her while she cried in her arms. The rest of her family had moved soon after that incident, and she had never heard from them again…and now she had lost Benjamín, too.

Since their supposed conversion to Catholicism, Catalina and Benjamín's families, like many others, had previously been lax and believed that Inquisitors had paid closer attention to larger cities like Madrid and Sevilla where there had been more concentrations of Jews and now conversos. But in the past year or so, Inquisition authorities had heard word that there were converso families living in and around Corral de Almaguer that had been guilty of being *Judaizantes,*[33] and they were now coming after them with a vengeance; there was no room now for carelessness. The royals had toughened in their quest to bring Spain together under Christian rule. Anyone who threatened their vision was to be stopped and expelled or annihilated. In parallel, Queen Isabella had also funded several trips to the new world, and people had returned speaking of rich and plentiful lands that they could occupy.

For the royals, this occupation could only further their empire and strength around the world. They sent soldiers, priests, and families out to settle the lands in the name of the Queen and King of *Castilla y Aragón* to ensure their legacy. Now, as the voyages continued, for many conversos making the three-month journey to the new world could be their only hope of having enough distance from the Spanish

---

[32] Literally 'act of faith,' a public display of penance for being found guilty of heretical acts during the Spanish and Portuguese Inquisition
[33] Christian converts who practiced Judaism

9

crown to finally have the freedom to practice the laws of Moses and the traditions of their G-d[34] in peace.

Catalina walked back into her home and was relieved that her family wasn't there. She took a deep breath as she considered her life now as it lay before her. She threw her satchel with her diary in it on her bed and slid to the floor. She was spent. Hollow. In the last six months, the sun had risen and set with Benjamín. And just a few hours ago, she had felt the paradox of a lifetime of love with him and the precarious journey into the unknown. She leaned her head on her bed and stretched out her feet on the rug that covered the stone floor, focusing unsuccessfully on the newly plastered white ceiling. She strained to make out the texture with her eyes, fatigued and blurred, begging for an easier target to focus on. Her mind fought them, not able to bear another second of seeing images of Benjamín and wondering whether or not he would come back for her. The voices of her family returning home startled her. She heard her mother and father speaking of the Carvajals. She shuddered at the thought that it might be their house the Inquisition may attack next. She needed to rest and pray to *El Dio*[35] that when she awoke this would have all been a horrific nightmare.

---

[34] Jewish practice "of avoiding writing a name of G-d, to avoid the risk of the sin of erasing or defacing the Name." http://www.jewfaq.org/defs/g-d.htm

[35] G-d, Ladino. Sephardic Jews referred to God, *Dios* in Spanish, with the article 'el' and without the 's' to distinguish their monotheistic beliefs.

Chapter 2

Ariana,
Present Day

Demi Lovato's *Neon Lights* blared from Ariana's dorm room. It was the last day of school, and her finals were finished. She felt accomplished. She had done pretty well despite her massive workload. She eyed the room and the walls and frowned at how pathetically empty it looked. It had been a good year. A productive one. She was moving forward with her history and Spanish double major, and, so far, graduation would be right on schedule next May, pending the passing of her summer course. The two majors were a lot to pack into four years, but her advisors had assured her it would be doable. Her grades had been her best yet this year, and she could only attribute that to her focus and determination. And now she was a senior! A rush of excitement came over her.

She reached for one of her empty boxes from the floor. The last thing she had to pack was her bookshelf. It had taken her the whole month to get this far. She had written a detailed plan, carefully packing all of her clothes, accessories, trinkets, wall hangings, and toiletries one by one, leaving out only what she thought she might need for her summer course. She had delicately folded each article of clothing, wrapped all of her knickknacks and wall hangings, and labeled each box…and then there had been all of her shoes.

She pulled the books and organized them in the box. Her parents would be here in a few hours, and she hated making anybody wait. They would stay the night at her aunt's house and take her to the airport the next morning. She stood up to stack the last box and stopped for a moment to look out the window of her second-story dorm room. The buildings formed a common square, and students were walking back and forth, hauling their belongings on the green grass. She had learned so much not only academically but also about herself these past three years. And to think that she had just about forfeited this invaluable experience her freshman year.

She froze as her eyes focused on the figure walking across the lawn in front of her building. It was him. As much as she had tried, she just couldn't get him out of her mind, and she didn't understand it. Her heart thumped, causing a warm sensation to flow to the tips of her toes. She almost ran out to catch up with him, but she decided that would be ridiculous. He would probably look at her like she was out of her mind. She couldn't even be sure he would remember her. She laughed, imagining herself as Chandler Bing in the *Friends* episode when he tore after Cathy through the streets of New York, breathless just to say, "Hi," and turn to walk away defeated. She shook her head and giggled to herself. Her phone interrupted her thoughts.

"Hello."

"Ariana, you have to come over here and help me," Liz pleaded, her voice on the edge of hysteria. Ariana stepped away from the window and put the phone closer to her ear.

"Ok, Liz. Don't move. I'll be right there. Are you ok? What's wrong?"

"Gabe is here and…hey! Don't touch that," she yelled.

I'll be right over. Hold on."

She ran across the hall and up the stairs to Liz's dorm room. When she got there, she was out of breath. She flung open the door and gulped, then she bent over in uncontrollable laughter. As Ariana held the doorframe to catch her breath, she saw Liz's huge blue silk blanket in the middle of the room that was filled with a bunch of her stuff thrown in the middle. Gabe had just thrown in another armful of Liz's possessions and was bringing two of the ends together to try to tie them when Liz jumped on his back, trying to grab a little vase out of his hand.

"Give me that! It's going to break if you throw it in here! I got that on our trip to Mexico freshman year, Gabe!" Noticing Ariana in the room, she screamed, "Hey! It's not funny!"

She threw a pillow at Ariana, and it grazed her hair as she had ducked to escape it. Even though all the classes were technically over, Liz had still been glued to her laptop, trying to finish a final paper for her last class. Her brother Gabe had driven all the way from Texas in his massive Ford F350 to help her pack up all her belongings and take her home. Ariana already knew that Liz hadn't even begun to pack when he had arrived, and she knew Gabe well. He was as patient as a raging river and about as stubborn as a mule. It really wasn't funny, but it was *so* funny. It was just so Liz.

"Liz, let me just finish tying this together and throw it in the back of the truck. You'll thank me later."

"Are you kidding me right now?"

"I'm just trying to get you to move!" Gabe threw his hands in the air. "Molasses moves faster than you! Do you realize how long this trip is going to be? I have to get back for work. Aren't classes supposed to be over already? Why are you still writing a paper?"

"Here, let me help," Ariana offered, drying the tears from her eyes from laughing so hard. "Where are your boxes? I'll start with your clothes. You just finish up that paper! Can't believe they actually gave you an extension."

"*I* can't believe you'll be on the other side of the world for the next two weeks," Liz said. "I'm going to miss you."

"I know. Me too. I wish you were coming with me. I don't know anyone." She lifted a stack of clothes on hangers from Liz's closet.

"Girl, you know I'm not into that historical stuff. Besides, I already have my job for the summer lined up. They're expecting me on Monday."

"Right. Oh hey! Guess who I saw finally after all this time walking through the quad outside my window?" A rush of excitement made her face warm as she folded Liz's clothes carefully into cardboard boxes.

Liz rolled her eyes. "Oh no. Not that guy you saw in the bookstore?"

Ariana threw herself on Liz's bed and pressed her hands to her heart. "It was him! "And he looked so good."

"How could you tell? You were two stories above him. Did you at least run out and talk to him? He's all you've been talking about since that day. What if you never see him again?"

"No. Are you kidding? He would've thought I was a freak." Ariana paused and looked down. "I have faith. If we're meant to meet again, we will."

"Just like in the movie Serendipity," roared Liz. Her voice was thick with sarcasm. "Here we go. You're such a hopeless romantic!" Liz put her arm around her best friend and said, "Honey, I want you to have a great time in Spain. Hopefully you'll meet some fine Spanish guy…with a brother…for me…who will sweep you off your feet, and we can finally put *ese fantasma de la librería* to rest!"[36]

They both laughed, Ariana's uneasy as she relived the sparkle in her bookstore guy's eyes, the shape of his mouth, and the tingle she felt in her tummy as their eyes met.

"I better get back to my own mess. My mom and dad will be here pretty soon. Give me a hug." She reached for Liz and they hugged, rocking from side to side. "I'll miss you, amiga. Bye, Gabe! And good luck with all that." Ariana motioned around the room with her finger.

Liz rolled her eyes again.

"Yeah, yeah. I'll miss you too, chica! Have some fun for once in your life! Let go!

"Bye," Gabe yelled, muffled from the back part of the closet.

"Let loose! Go crazy!" Liz continued well after Ariana had already left the room.

"Yeah sure," Ariana murmured to herself, still hearing her down the hall. "Whatever."

When her family arrived, Ariana was stacking the last of her belongings beside the door.

"Hey, *mi'ja!*"[37] her mother shouted as she walked in her room.

"Mom!" Ariana yelled. She grabbed her phone to turn down the music and ran to hug her.

"It's good to see you, baby!"

Right behind her mom in the hall, her dad, younger brother, and sister strolled in.

"Hey, shorty." Carlos gave Ariana a punch to her shoulder.

"Hey!" Ariana reached high to wrap her arm around her brother's neck and pulled him to her level. "Just 'cause you're in high school now and your voice has dropped an octave doesn't mean I still can't beat you up."

"Whatever." Carlos wiggled out of her grasp. "Don't you remember I was first place in wrestling last year?"

"He's really good, Ariana! Is this it?" her father asked in his gruff voice. He pointed to the stack of boxes by the door.

"Hi, Dad!" She gave him a quick squeeze. "Yes, that's all of it."

---

[36] that bookstore ghost.

[37] Affectionate term for my daughter

"Ok. Carlos, come and help me grab a couple of these boxes, and we'll take them to the car."

"Let's all grab a few," her mother said. She waved an arm in front of Karina's face, vying for her attention. "We'll get done a lot faster that way."

Karina was staring at herself in the mirror attached to the wall, pulling at the wisps of hair she had left out of her ponytail and smoothing in her makeup with the tips of her fingers. Sighing, she said, "Fine, I better not break a nail though."

Ariana rolled her eyes and slapped her sister on the shoulder. "Get out of that mirror and give me a hug. You're not running for Santana Queen tonight!"

"Hey, but you never know who you're going to run into," Karina said as she reached to give her sister a hug. "I missed you!"

"Me too." Ariana rolled up her sleeves. "Now let's get to work."

"*Eeeeh, como tiene cosas está muchita,*"[38] her father complained. "How can you accumulate so much stuff in one small dorm room, Ariana?"

"At least she's organized," her mother said.

"Well, I do appreciate that. But my goodness…and I bet all of it is clothes and shoes."

Ariana laughed, knowing he was right.

"Aren't you happy that Tía Juanita will have plenty of sopapillas and chicos for us after this?"

"I'll be so hungry, I could eat a horse." He paused for a minute. "The sooner we get you off on your trip, the sooner you'll be back home to help us at the restaurant."

"Daaad, don't start," Ariana snapped with attitude in her voice. She felt the *chispas*[39] begin to rise within her.

"Ariana!" her mom said sternly, giving her elbow a tight squeeze.

"Sorry, but you guys know that's only for the rest of the summer, right?" Ariana lifted a couple of boxes and walked after them.

"You never know," her dad called back, looking over his shoulder.

Ugh. Why did he have to bring it up now? She didn't want him to get the wrong idea and assume that she would come home for good after graduation. Lately her dad had been slathering the guilt trip of

---

[38] Geez, this girl has so much stuff
[39] Literally sparks. In this case, sparks of anger or frustration.

coming home to help out pretty thick. Her dad and her grandpa had big changes they wanted to make, and they wanted Ariana involved. It was a given that she would be the next in line to take over one day. But she just didn't understand the logic. All her life she had been told that to be successful, she had to get out and get an education. She couldn't imagine herself going back to San Luis.

For Ariana, San Luis was a sort of love-hate relationship. Even though it was but a couple of hours south of Denver, it felt like a different universe. *I mean, the only general store in town closes by 6pm!* She loved being around her immediate and extended families and spending time in the mountains, but going back home made her feel like the walls were closing in on her and that getting educated was a waste of time. A dead end. She was still contemplating grad school, a career in higher education, or maybe traveling some more. She suddenly became nauseous thinking about cooking in the kitchen for the rest of her life.

Whatever the case, she still had a lot of time, the rest of the summer and her senior year, to think about what she wanted to do—and unfortunately for her dad, going back to San Luis was definitely not an option. Still, she couldn't shake the idea of her father's temper and his stubbornness, like Gabe's, could only be likened to that of a mule—*más terco que una mula.*[40] *That conversation is going to be ugly. I am my father's daughter, after all.* She took a deep breath, slowly letting it out and shoving those thoughts quickly aside, replacing them instead with this trip that she had been anticipating for so long. Feeling the excitement rising within her, she skipped down the steps and out to her car.

---

[40] More stubborn than a mule.

Chapter 3

Luke

Luke took a sip of his champagne. He scanned the extravagantly decorated room in honor of his cousin's Bar Mitzvah. The lighting. The blue, orange, and silver balloons. His cousin Adam claimed to be the New York Knicks biggest fan, and Aunt Rachel had taken the theme to the nth degree. The tables were set in Knicks colors, and little jersey place cards with each guest's name written in elegant letters were aligned parallel with each place setting. Luke swore the distance between the place card and plate had been measured to the exact centimeter. The over-the-top centerpieces were long acrylic vases with blue, orange, and silver sea glass fillers. At the top, each boasted a crystal basketball with the Knicks logo. The towering cake sat in the middle of a table that had been constructed to look like a basketball court. It had several thick round layers with the Knicks logo and colors in various patterns and a basketball cake with Adam's name across the front sitting inside a net ultimately landing on top. *Aunt Rachel always goes overboard.* He chuckled.

Luke was going for another sip of his champagne when his father and a tall, slender gentleman with thick gray hair approached him.

"Luke, I want you to meet Henry Wilson," his father said in a tone that screamed *give it chance.*

"Nice to meet you, Mr. Wilson." Luke took his hand.

"Mr. Wilson is interested in getting on board with us for a huge project." Luke's father turned to him and patted his shoulder. "Luke just graduated from the University of Denver. He's one of the brightest members of our team."

Luke laughed nervously. "Not quite yet. I have an internship this summer."

"Well, it's very nice to meet you, Luke. Looking forward to working with you."

Luke nodded, and the two walked away. He took a deep breath and stared into the crowd, feeling the back of his neck heating up.

"He-llooo!" Jake waved his hand in front of him. "What the heck are you thinking about?"

Lifting his glass to take a sip, Luke rolled his eyes and said, "Nothing."

"Dude, what's the matter with you lately? Check out Melissa over there. She's been eyeing you all night, and here you are holding up the walls." He shifted his position from Melissa to face Luke directly and then glared at him. "Wait a minute. You still love-sick over that girl you won't tell us about?" Jake slapped Luke in the chest with the back of his hand.

Annoyed, Luke gulped his champagne, finishing the glass, and said, "I need some air."

He dashed his way through the tables, trying to make a quick exit. He grabbed for his suit coat at the coat check and started for the door.

"Come on, man! I'm just kidding. Luke!"

Luke peered back at Jake from the corner of his eye just as he had smiled and waved at Melissa. He shook his head.

"Seriously, though, Melissa *does* want to talk to you." Jake's volume increased toward the end.

Luke wasn't in the mood for Jake's taunting *or* Melissa. His mind was on his dad. *Can't believe he just did that.* His father already knew he had been accepted into the Cultural Anthropology graduate program at CU Boulder. It was the perfect complement for his BA in Archaeology. He could see himself in the university setting out in the field doing research and maybe teaching. His internship this summer would help him decide whether or not teaching was for him. On the flip side, he could live at home for free and save up some cash. He knew, however, that this meant he would have to apply to law school eventually, and he didn't want that. But, on the other hand, his family was here.

Luke walked toward the other side of the building adjacent to the parking lot, staring through all of the shiny cars that had carried the guests to celebrate Adam. A cool breeze shot through the air. He buttoned his suit coat, lifted the collar around his neck, and stuck his hands in his pockets. For late spring, it was a chilly evening. But, then again, it *was* New York. He looked up at the night sky. The clouds

18

and the street lights covered most of the stars. He did miss everyone. His parents had seemed to age more and more every time he came home during breaks and holidays. His sister and his nieces and new nephew were here. He had already been in Colorado for four years and had missed out on so many of his family's important events. He hated that he had missed his nieces' births. He let out a deep breath. *Maybe it is time to stay home.*

He greeted a couple who were holding hands as they walked past. Jake and Melissa crept into his mind. It seemed as if everyone had someone to fix him up with lately. The last thing he needed was a relationship right now. He didn't want the distraction. He looked down at the sidewalk and kicked aside a battered straw that had been flattened and folded so that it formed a V-shape. *Do I look* that *lonely? Geez.* He hadn't had a relationship since sophomore year, and when he had broken up with her, he had taken the next few years to focus on school, his future career, and what he wanted his life to be. His parents were both lawyers and wanted him to continue the family business. His interests were different. He didn't want the robotics of following in his father's footsteps. He wanted more. His jaws and stomach tightened. The salmon he had eaten was not sitting well with him. *Ugh.* He wanted to make some fresh footsteps of his own. He wanted passion. Purpose. Digging up the past had always intrigued him. It was exciting to uncover what had been hidden, to reveal the layers of life that had led to the present.

Then, there was that girl. "Ariana," he said aloud with a side smile.

He leaned back against the wall of the building and folded his arms in front of him. He took a deep breath and exhaled as he was reminded of that mysterious girl he had bumped into in the bookstore a few weeks ago. Her hazel eyes and long, dark hair. The freckles around her nose. But it was that smile that took his breath away. They had reached for the same book, and their hands touched. The minute she turned around and looked at him, he was captivated. It was as if there were nothing else around them but the sun in that bookstore basement with no windows. For those few seconds, their souls connected and recognized each other's existence. It felt like something bigger had brought them together.

He recalled the instance in his mind's eye like it was merely a few seconds ago.

"I'm Luke," he had introduced himself.

19

"*Ariana,*" she had replied. The "r" rolled off of her tongue sweet and naturally.

Is that Spanish? he had thought without responding.

She must have felt the awkwardness of the pause because she grabbed the book they had both reached for and said, "Excuse me, but I'm late for class."

And just like that, she was gone. *For the best.* He had too much going on anyway. But that short exchange had been etched in his mind ever since, and he couldn't shake it. It bothered him to know that someone, some moment, could make him come so unhinged. He had tried to find her in the directory to no avail. Her photo didn't come up on any clubs or sports sites that he could find, either. Without a last name on such a large campus, it was almost impossible to search for her. *I know she wasn't a figment of my imagination.* He regretted not following her and asking for her number. That day, he was dumbfounded. It was as if some outside force had taken control of his limbs, bolting his legs to the floor. He had just stood there, mouth open, watching her walk out of sight. He sighed. No wonder Jake and his friends wouldn't leave him alone about it. He *was* acting love-sick.

He had never even felt this way with Rebecca, his high school girlfriend, whom he had dated for two years. Sure, he had had feelings for her. Her family was also from New York, and they were Jewish too, so they had a common background and understanding. But they both knew from early on it wasn't meant to be. When he had moved to Colorado for school, he had realized just how different they were. They each saw life in a different way, and after a couple of years in college, he knew they had completely grown apart. He had stayed in Colorado to take some classes in the summer before his sophomore year, and they had barely talked throughout that time. And the little they did was forced small talk.

He looked up at the sky once again. The clouds had parted, and out of nowhere a shooting star whizzed across the sky, followed swiftly by another. He stood watching without moving. He pulled himself from the wall and panned the sky, trying to find them again. Two shooting stars, one right after the other. That had to be rare. Ariana's image shot through his mind again, and his body felt warm. He could still feel her hand on his, and her face was clear in his mind. He tried to shake the images out of his head. *What's wrong with you, man?*

Get it together, Luke. Get over it. She's just a girl. You don't even know her…or if you'll ever even see her again, for that matter.

He looked at his hands. His palms were sweating. He rubbed them together and walked toward the entrance. He knew he had to get his priorities straight and focus on his internship. It would be a great experience that would hopefully lead to something more. Being away from his family for a few weeks had the potential for clarity without pressure. But, more than that, he hoped he could further his personal family research while he was there. If he did, he would have a worthwhile basis for this work he loved, and maybe his dad could finally see its value and get off his back. He turned and opened the door.

Chapter 4

Ariana

I can't believe we ended up on the same flight. Ariana had been seated at the far back of the plane. As she waited in line to get off, she squeezed the upper part of her large brown hobo bag for dear life and tapped her foot unconsciously against the aisle floor. She had felt her stomach in her throat when she saw him at the airport in New York. He had been talking to her professor. She had scurried behind some other passengers when she noticed him and peeked back toward his way from behind a tall sign with airport directions. She didn't think he had seen her, but she couldn't be sure.

She swallowed and felt the blood rushing to her head. Ariana didn't like this feeling. How could this be when they had only spoken a few words to each other? And now here they were on the same study abroad trip. She felt out of control. It wasn't smart to get involved this way now. She had managed to get all the way through to the end of her junior year without the complication of a serious relationship. *Ariana, aren't you getting ahead of yourself? What are you thinking? What makes you think he would even be interested in you anyway?*

She was parched, and her lips were dry. She reached in her bag for her lip gloss. She rummaged through all the stuff she had packed in her backpack purse to try to find it. It felt like an abyss. It had been difficult to figure out how to pack. She had had no idea what to expect. It was only a two-week course, but it was important to have all the essentials for any occasion—class, touring, and nightlife. All accessories were necessary, including jewelry and shoes. *Gosh, am I really that high maintenance? Aha! Here it is.* She applied the gloss and smacked her lips together. *You know what? Liz is right. Relax. Stop thinking about him. You're in Spain. Time to be open to what this place has to offer*. She stood up straight and shifted her bag from one side to the other, just about hitting the elderly lady behind her whose glare let her know she was less than thrilled with her action.

"So sorry!" Her head tilted toward her shoulder like a little girl, and she flashed the lady an apologetic smile.

The woman just sucked the air through her teeth and looked the other way. *Geez.* Ariana sighed, totally wishing she would have checked in that huge, heavy bag that was digging into her shoulders. Maybe she shouldn't have brought half the stuff she had. *Oh well.* Whatever the case, bag aside, she hadn't been able to tell where Bookstore Fantasma was seated on the huge plane because she had boarded first. *Great. The line is finally moving.* She had tried to keep herself from thinking about him, so she slept most of the six long hours from New York into Madrid and read *Rain of Gold* in between. As she walked off of the plane and onto the jet way, she paused, closed her eyes, made the sign of the cross, and said a quick prayer in her mind, thanking God for this once-in-a-lifetime opportunity and for the safe flight. When she opened her eyes, she noticed him standing at the end of the jet way looking in. Her heart fell to her knees, and her eyes jetted to her shoes. As she reached the terminal entrance, she looked toward the other direction, pretending he wasn't there.

He touched her arm and said, "Hey!"

Their eyes met, and she thought she would melt down through the seam of the crack between the terminal and jet way.

She let out a breathy "Hi!" almost forgetting to inhale.

He smiled. His clear blue eyes sparkled. And everything else faded into the background as the sun surrounded them both in the dim lit airport terminal.

"I thought that was you back in New York. Ariana, right? I saw you asleep on the plane, but I didn't want to wake you. You looked so peaceful with your book laid across your lap and the little bit of drool sliding towards your chin."

With a sly grin, he motioned to her chin with his finger. He got so close to her that she could smell his minty breath. She swallowed and commanded her nerves to stop shaking. Her eyes and mouth opened wide as she realized what he had just said.

"Oh my gosh! What? Are you serious?" She wiped at her mouth with the back of her hand.

"I'm just kidding!" He laughed.

"Ha, ha…funny," she said. "What time is it anyway?"

"I think it's like 6:30 in the morning, Spain time."

"This time difference is going to be weird. I think it's like eight hours ahead of Colorado time. So it's like 10:30 at night at home…" She realized she was babbling. She paused, looking down at her new black ballet flats. *He actually remembered my name!* She wanted to scream.

Realizing her excitement, she cleared her throat and added in a calmer tone, "It's just been so crazy with finals this week and packing. Jet lag is going to be tough! Glad I got *some* rest on the plane."

He gazed at her for what seemed like an eternity. She gave him a sideways smile. *Why is he looking at me like that? Do I have something in my teeth? I talk too much!*

"What?" she asked.

"Nothing." He chuckled. "Can I walk with you?"

"Sure. I'm supposed to meet with my group at the McDonalds here in Terminal 4 to find out how we're getting into Toledo." *Ariana, can you just stop talking? Just because he was talking to Ricardo doesn't mean you're both going to the same place.*

"Right," he said. "It's this way."

Is *he going to the same place?* They walked ahead. She looked at him and pulled a piece of her long, black hair from her face and tucked it behind her ear.

"It's Luke, right?"

"Yeah. You remembered." His smile broadened.

"Were you, uh, waiting for me back there?" She looked over her shoulder and pointed with her thumb.

"I hope that's ok. Can I carry your bag?"

She smiled. *Ok, so he has personality* and *he's a gentleman.* She bit her lower lip to keep from exposing a wide, cheesy grin as she handed him her bag.

"Ok, but it's kind of heavy."

The warmth of his hand on hers startled her as they touched in the exchange. His arm fell slightly, and his sky-blue eyes were wide as he took the bag.

"What do you have in here, a person? Wow. How can something this small be so—"

"Yeah," she responded, snickering, "I've got the kitchen sink in there, too."

"You do know it's only two weeks, right?" He moved the bag up and down in his hands.

Ariana rolled her eyes. *Another wise guy.* "I wasn't sure how to pack. I wanted to be prepared for anything."

He placed her bag on his rolling suitcase. She felt so much lighter. She rolled her sore shoulder to massage her muscles. Billy Joel's *She's Got a Way* played through the airport speakers overhead as they continued walking, passing through passport control and customs; they showed their passports and received their stamps. Ariana hesitated, at a pace just a few steps behind Luke as she took a few seconds to admire her stamp…and him. She wondered if others could see the giddiness bursting within her right now. Her hands were shaky, and her palms were sweaty. *You have got to calm down!*

"Are you an archaeology major?" Luke broke the silence as they walked toward the McDonald's. "I've never seen you in any classes."

Breathe. "No. History," she said. "I needed another social science credit outside my major, and what a more perfect way to get it than from this course in Spain? It's always been one of my dreams to come here. Are you?"

"Yes, well, was. I just graduated with my BA in archaeology."

"Congratulations." *He's not in the program then.*

"Luke, there you are!" Ricardo yelled as they approached the airport McDonald's. "I was wondering where you had taken off to." Seeing Ariana, he added, "Hi, Ariana! I'm glad you're here. This is going to be a great course."

All of the other students were already there waiting on them. There were fifteen students total. According to course description paperwork Ariana had read before the trip, she learned that Ricardo had been taking students to Toledo for years. He was a big guy with a commanding, yet calming, presence. He was older and heavier set and had dark, curly black hair that reached his ears and covered his forehead. His green eyes hid under his thick-rimmed glasses. Ricardo raised his arm to get everyone's attention. "Ok, everyone, here's the deal. I've arranged for us to board a bus that will pick us up from the airport and take us to Madrid then from Madrid to Corral de Almaguer where we will be staying. Marisela, or as she prefers to be called, Mari, and her husband, Miguel, are our hosts. They are expecting us around noon. Right now, it's almost 7:00 in the morning. We will head into Madrid, grab some breakfast, and make the hour and a half drive after that."

Ricardo must have noticed everyone staring at Luke and the whispers Ariana could hear around her from the other students. He added, "Oh yeah, this is Luke. He's my instructor assistant for this course. He just graduated with a degree in archaeology. Ariana's mouth opened. *Instructor assistant? This should be interesting.*

Luke smiled, nodded, and waved his hand.

"He is here to further his own research and will be a lead at our excavation site. He will also be providing some help with instruction and light grading. Does anyone have any questions?" *Yes, can I get private tutoring with him, please?*

As they boarded the bus, Ariana looked around. Everyone was paired off and in conversation with one another. She walked the center aisle, looking from side to side, and finally took an empty window seat near the back of the bus and placed her bags underneath. Luke was sitting with Ricardo in front. She could see the fluff of his texturized dark hair above the seat next to Ricardo. She looked out the window and tried to pronounce the words on the road signs as they began their drive out of the enormous and overwhelming airport. It was definitely Spanish, but she had never heard some of these words before. Several terminals, highways, and cars blurred by. Although there were trees, the landscape looked dry, kind of like the desert. It was almost like landing in Albuquerque. It made her feel at home. She had flown into that airport more times than she could count to visit her grandparents on her mom's side.

When they arrived in Madrid, Ariana was astounded at the traffic and the narrow streets. It was her first time in Europe, and the pictures she had seen of the landscape and architecture could not do this vision justice. Their bus stopped, and they all got off to get breakfast. She heard some locals talking to one another as she walked onto the sidewalk and felt a knot in her stomach. She groaned to herself. *What if my Spanish isn't good enough?* Sure, she was a double major, and she did well in her classes and in conversations with other students, even those native to other Latin American countries—most of the time—but being immersed in this culture and the language would be different. And right now, she couldn't catch a word these ladies were saying. They were talking *so* fast. She could hear them using the *vosotros* form that no one paid much attention to in her classes. No one spoke like that where she was from. She continued to observe

26

them, admiring their flawless hair and make-up. They were a little younger than her mother probably and dressed in floral summery dresses and heels.

Her grandmother would have said, *"¡Qué facetas!"*[41]

She laughed to herself. As everyone gathered in front of the bus stop, Ricardo once again motioned for everyone's attention. Ariana checked her reflection in one of the bus windows before walking toward Ricardo. She had pulled her hair into a ponytail when they had boarded the bus. She smoothed her hair, wiped at the corners of her eyes, and reapplied her lip gloss.

"This is the Plaza Mayor. It is the main square here in Madrid," Ricardo said, "You are welcome to grab some breakfast and look around. We have two hours here, then we will meet back at the bus at 10:30 and head to Corral de Almaguer. Enjoy yourselves, but make sure you are on time."

As everyone dispersed toward the square, Ariana fell behind slowly, savoring her surroundings. She let the tips of her fingers run against the rough, arched brick entrance as she peered inside the lively square filled with people, well-dressed and perfectly coifed, laughing, talking, and enjoying their morning treats. Her eyes moved from scene to scene as if capturing each one with a camera. There were tables and umbrellas outside various areas of the square that she assumed indicated a restaurant or café. Smack in the middle stood a stately statue of a man on a horse. There were a couple of brick arched entryways in the corners, allowing people to enter or exit. Windows were aligned in perfect rows all around the four red, brick walls several stories in the air. One appeared to have some sort of mural painted around the windows. *Do people live or work there?* Her eyes trailed up each window to the puffy white clouds sprawled against the deep blue sky. She took a deep breath and closed her eyes. The smells of espresso and fresh baked bread wrapped around her, waking up her senses, and she felt the tension in her shoulders release.

"Ariana?" she heard coming from a faraway place.

Her eyes opened to Luke standing in front of her. Her breath briefly paused, and her heartbeat accelerated.

"Hey."

"Mind if I join you?"

---

[41] How fancy or elegant!

27

"Not at all." She twisted her foot, appreciating his eagerness to spend time with her for the second time. "Should we try that place?"

She pointed to a corner at what looked like a restaurant on the sidewalk level of the square where various tables with red checked table cloths were clustered.

"Sure." Luke followed her toward a few open tables that people had just left. They sat down at one farthest from inside the restaurant under an umbrella. A waitress came over and greeted them.

Handing them a menu, she said, "*¡Buenos días! Estos son los especiales del día. ¿Queréis algo para tomar?*"[42]

Ariana was taken aback by the "*zeta*" and *vosotros* form again. It sounded so foreign yet beautiful at the same time.

Luke replied in perfect Spanish, "*Sí, yo quiero café con leche y una tortilla de patata, por favor.*"[43]

Ariana felt her eyes double in size.

"*¿Y Usted?*"[44] asked the waitress, looking toward Ariana.

"Um...*Todavía no estoy segura. Me da un momento, ¿por favor?*"[45]

"*Sí, como no. Le doy otro ratito. ¿De dónde sois?*"[46]

"*Yo, de Nueva York,*"[47] Luke replied.

"*Y yo soy de Colorado en Estados Unidos también,*"[48] Ariana said.

"*Ahh! El Gran Cañón de Colorado,*"[49] the waitress said, beaming. They laughed.

"*No, ese está en otro estado. Es el nombre de un rio.*"[50]

"*Interesante*," the waitresses responded. She paused, confusion adding to her wide grin. Then she continued, "*Vale, vale, por supuesto. ¡Bienvenidos! Espero que os gusta España.*"[51]

And she left them for Ariana to decide what to order.

"Your Spanish is impressive, Luke! Where did you learn?"

---

[42] Good morning! These are today's specials. Do you want something to drink?
[43] Yes, I'll have a latte and a Spanish tortilla.
[44] And you?
[45] I'm still not sure. Will you give me another moment, please?
[46] Of course. I'll give you another minute. Where are you both from?
[47] I'm from New York.
[48] I'm from Colorado in the US as well.
[49] Oh! The Grand Canyon of Colorado!
[50] No, that's in another state. It's the name of the river.
[51] Interesting. Well, welcome. I hope you enjoy Spain.

"Well, I've taken some Spanish classes, and I've actually been on this trip before when I took Ricardo's class a few years ago."

"Seems like more than just a few classes. Your accent is perfect, like second nature!"

Luke opened his mouth and nothing came out at first. After half a second, he responded, "My mom's side is Sephardic. My grandparents and my great aunts and uncles all speak Ladino. It's similar."

Huh…That's different. Wasn't expecting that. "Oh ok. Sephardic? Those were the Jews who lived in Spain before the Inquisition, right? This may sound completely ignorant, but I didn't realize the Sephardic Jews still existed, let alone had a separate thriving language."

Luke smiled. "It's not as common as Yiddish, but it is a very large community. I don't usually get into it unless I can tell someone is actually interested. My grandmother claims that our family left Spain during the Inquisition and fled to Turkey. Then we migrated from there to New York in the late 1800s. That's where my mom met my dad. His family is Jewish, from Germany and Poland."

"That's so fascinating." Ariana leaned in toward Luke. She began talking fast. "My focus in history has primarily been Southern Colorado and Northern New Mexico, and most of the classes I've taken focus on more recent Mexican and Latin American history." Realizing her intensity, Ariana sat back and finished in a softer voice, "And although I've read about Sephardic Jews, I don't really know much about them."

Ariana blushed. He was watching her closely. She fluffed her ponytail, shifted in her seat, and swallowed. She quickly pulled up the menu in front of her, remembering why they were there in the first place.

"So, uh, what should I order? What did you get?"

"It depends on how hungry you are. All the specials look pretty good. I got a Spanish tortilla, which is the closest thing to an eggs and potatoes breakfast. You can get it with or without meat. It's kind of like a frittata, but it's normally served in a wedge, like a thick piece of pie. And I got a coffee, which is pretty much like a latte. They don't have American coffee here."

"Ok, then. I'll try what you're having. It sounds delicious. I'm starving!" When the waitress returned, Ariana ordered and turned to

29

look around once more. "It looks like there are stores around the square. And that statue is so impressive!"

"It is. Madrid is a magical place. It's a huge city, but you'd never know it with the way it's laid out and with how friendly the people are. Kind of gives you a small town feel wherever you go."

Ariana turned back and was surprised by Luke's gaze. For a minute, her eyes remained fixed on his as well. She couldn't help it. The waitress interrupted the moment with their food.

"This is *so* good!" she said. She devoured the tortilla. "This isn't what I grew up calling a tortilla, but I bet it would taste even better with some of my mom's salsa!"

She wiped her mouth with her napkin and took a drink of her café con leche.

"Oh, this tastes like heaven right now." The warmth of the foamed coffee hit her palette. The strong smell of espresso combined with its smooth, yet full-bodied flavor made watered-down American coffee seem cheap in comparison. Plus, she welcomed all the caffeine she could get right now after that long flight and not knowing how the day ahead would look.

Luke laughed and nodded in agreement. They continued making small talk, tossing in jokes and wit in the mix of their conversation. Ariana saw Ricardo in the distance out of the corner of her eye. He watched them for a minute, put his head down, and walked away, making her uneasy. Before long, it was time to get back on the bus and head to Corral de Almaguer where they were staying. After they left the city, Ariana stared out her window in a daze. The sky was a brilliant blue, and the sun was shining, welcoming the American students to this part of the world with flair. It was just like she and her dad had always imagined Spain would look. There were rolling hills on both sides with acres and acres of neatly-maintained rows of olive trees and small farms and homes scattered about. *He has to come and see this for himself.*

Huge hedges of floral bushes in shades of pink, lavender, and white split the two lanes on each side in the median. The Spanish seemed to make their landscape a priority. She took out her phone to capture what she was sure wouldn't do justice to the naked eye. The colorful hedges took her back to the fresh flowers that had sat in the center of the table where she had just shared breakfast with Luke. A swarm of emotions overwhelmed her. She was still on a cloud. She felt so comfortable with him almost as if they'd known each other all their lives.

The way he looked at her. She wanted to dive into the oceans that were his eyes to explore the depth beyond the surface of clear azure. He was so funny and easygoing. It had been like a dream, yet it had felt so natural. And now, the sight of the spectacular countryside. She wiped at the goosebumps that had formed on her forearms. She sat back in her seat and let her head lean on the head rest unable to remember the last time she had felt so elated.

She literally could still feel the touch of Luke's hand on hers from earlier when he held her hand as they approached the bus to let her know he would see her in Corral de Almaguer. His hands were warm, yet strong and rugged, like he wasn't afraid of a little hard work. Hers had felt so delicate in his. Just as she was enjoying basking in her thoughts, she noticed her reflection in the window. She felt a pang sting her stomach. A warning of sorts. *I look horrible. Exhausted. Ugh. You better pull yourself together when you get to your room.* A vision of Brian came to her mind, her longest real relationship. '*This isn't enough for me, Ariana.*' His words thrashed loudly in her head like he had just said them.

They had dated for a little over a year freshman year through the fall of sophomore year in college. They had met through one of her Aunt Gabi's friends and had hit it off. However, he wasn't exactly college-bound. He was a nice guy and they had fun together, but if she was honest with herself, they just had little in common. She loved talking about history, religion, and politics, and he just hadn't been interested. Rather, he'd change the subject every time she brought up these topics. They had soon drifted apart after school had begun that fall semester, playing phone tag a few times and never seeming to connect. It had been like he resented her. Like he couldn't have understood that she had work to do. At one point, they had argued about her making school a priority over their relationship.

Then, one day she had been running on her morning routine and she had seen him several houses up ahead sitting on the porch with some girl on his lap. He had been holding her and she had giggled loudly, causing Ariana to look their way. *Ow!* She rubbed her stomach as the pang jabbed at her again. Ariana had locked eyes with Brian when the girl had stood up to walk inside. The look of shock on his face had been priceless, and right then it had been over for her. She had paused for a minute, then had turned up her music, and like Forest Gump, kept running, past him, without a word, focused on the trail ahead. He had tried to call her after that, but for her there was nothing left to say. It was too late. She had moved on. If he hadn't had the *cojones* to tell her in person that he had wanted to see someone else, she didn't have time to hear some half-wit excuse for cheating on her.

She swallowed, feeling the emotions and anger rising through her all over again. *I mean, who the heck was he to let someone like* me *go...someone who was getting an education and going places, for some big-haired, thick, heavy eye-lined* chola. She took that thought back immediately, knowing she didn't *particularly* have anything against that girl or how she looked. She didn't even know her. In all her tough exterior, her bruised, delicate ego agreed with Brian—that maybe she just hadn't been enough. *What* did *she have that I didn't?* She rubbed her tummy again and winced. *Maybe I'm just hungry.* She hadn't thought about that relationship in a long time. She knew, however, they weren't right for each other in more ways than one.

Suddenly, she was struck with the thought of how this situation with Luke would work in this particular setting. She wanted to get to know him better and find out where this intriguing connection would lead, but he was also her instructor. Would Ricardo even let her and Luke spend time together? Is that why he had shaken his head at them? What would the other students think? She didn't think anyone had noticed anything, but what if they had? Would they have a problem with it? Would it even be appropriate given the fact that he might be grading some of her work? She was going to have to slow down. Ariana's thoughts were interrupted as the bus slowed down in front of a tall, castle-like building. Its gray stone architecture and towers spoke of centuries past. It was nothing short of charming.

Chapter 5

Luke

Luke's feet danced against the floor of the bus in his seat as they approached El Convento. Thoughts of breakfast with Ariana rolled through his mind. His heart had jumped out of his chest when he had seen her at the airport in New York. What were the odds? After all that searching and here she was in the same class. She was exactly how he had remembered her, almost more captivating today than that day they had met at the bookstore. She was different. Confident, yet she possessed a shy, girlish quality that was adorable and appealing. He had to get to know her better. She was like a mysterious archaeological site that he couldn't wait to uncover. He loved how the English words that rolled off her tongue were peppered with Spanish accent. *There is definitely something about her.* He sighed. He had to get ahold of himself.

He walked off the bus and motioned for everyone to line up at the door when a blonde woman with a thin frame came out smiling and waving at Ricardo. *Mari!* It was good to be back. Luke was drawn to this place. He had only spent one class here, but after those few weeks, it had felt like home.

"Come in! Come in! We've been expecting you!" She welcomed them with a deep accent. Ricardo hugged her and kissed both of her cheeks.

"*¡Hola, Mari! ¡Te ves cada año más guapa!*"[52]

"*¡Ay, pero mira que caballero!*"[53] She chuckled and patted his shoulder.

---

[52] Hi, Mari! You look more beautiful every year!
[53] Wow, well, what a gentleman!

"A ver. ¿Quién tenemos aquí?"[54]

"¡Gusto de verla Mari! Hace mucho tiempo,"[55] Luke said.

"¡Lucas! Qué bien te veo. ¡Hasta más guapo que antes!"[56] Her arms stretched forward, giving him a warm embrace.

"Gracias, Mari. Y Usted más jovencita que nunca."[57]

She paused and held Luke's shoulders, studying his face with a closer look. Leaning into his ear, she asked, *"¿Estás enamorado?"*[58]

His faced flushed, and he laughed. "No, no, Mari, no."

"Vale."[59] She smiled. Her eyes danced with curiosity.

Mari turned to the rest of the group and motioned for them to follow.

"Vamos. Entren. Roberto está adentro. Él les enseñará sus cuartos. Esperamos que os gusta."[60]

Luke followed the crowd to the front desk where a young man with glasses sat with an open book and called out the student names one by one. Roberto handed them their keys with a packet of information as they came forward. Some of them were sharing a room. There were groups of girls and guys who had evidently planned to be here together. Luke took notice as Ariana took her keys. By the looks of things, she had her own room. She thanked Roberto, and Luke watched her hips sashay up the stairs. He grabbed his own key and contemplated the plan for the afternoon and evening ahead, wondering when he could spend some alone time with her.

Ariana

Ariana followed up the stairs to room #7. It was a corner room, and the door creaked a little when she opened it. She gasped as she entered, taking in every inch with a wall-to-wall grin. She had her own bathroom and a queen-size brass four poster bed with a floral bedspread that was accessorized with white lace pillows. She plopped

---

[54] Well, who do we have here?

[55] Great to see you Mari! It's been a long time!

[56] You look great Luke! Even more good-looking than before.

[57] Thank you, Mari. And you look younger than ever.

[58] Are you in love?

[59] Ok

[60] Come on in. Roberto is inside. He will show you to your accommodations. We hope you like them.

her backpack purse and hobo bag on top of the bed and walked around, touching everything with the tips of her fingers. The walls were lined in pale pink paisley wallpaper and dark mahogany trim. The floors were the same throughout the entire place, a light gray marble tile with various oriental rugs placed in strategic places. Her room was no different.

A fireplace trimmed with the same elegant mahogany woodwork sat on the far wall directly across from the bed. She felt like a princess. There was a huge picture window adorned with matching heavy drapery that looked out onto one of those farms she saw on the way up in the distance. Behind that were rolling hills of olive trees. It looked like a picture in a storybook. Now she understood why Ricardo had always brought his students here to the *campo*.[61] El Convento was an old convent that had been converted to a bed and breakfast, which was large enough to accommodate fifteen students with room to spare. The combination of doubles and singles she had seen in the brochure had all displayed a traditional elegance. She was glad that they honored her request for a single.

She threw herself into the beige wing-backed chair with cherry-wood trim next to the window and laid her key on the table next to it. Her body melded into the cushions, and she thought she could fall asleep right there. She opened the packet and read the welcome letter from Mari and Miguel. It detailed the schedule that they would follow at the bed and breakfast for the next couple of weeks. *Breakfast at 7:00, lunch at 2:00, and dinner at 8:00. Hmmm.* Ariana just knew she would be starving by noon. She compared this to her class syllabus. They would leave to the excavation site at 7:45am and work until 1:30pm, then meet back for an evening class and discussion at 5:00pm. This only gave them a couple of hours of down time or study time in the afternoon in between. She guessed they would have the evenings after dinner too, but that didn't seem like much time. *I guess it will be ok. It doesn't look like there's much nightlife here.*

On Friday, whoever was interested could go on an overnight trip to Madrid into Saturday evening. She was definitely doing that. She had to make every moment count on this trip-of-a-lifetime. She wondered if Luke planned to go. Maybe she would ask him at lunch.

---

[61] The countryside

But right now, she needed a shower and a nap. Her clothes were sticky against her skin, and her eyelids were like bricks.

After a quick twenty-minute nap, she showered and changed into a simple, cotton, eggplant summer dress she had found on sale. The soft fabric hugged her tiny frame like a light, comfy blanket and flared right above the knee. The color made her eyes pop. Just the right choice after such a long flight but something that could easily make an impression. Her black ballet flats were casual and went well with the dress. She applied her make-up and lip gloss and let her thick, long, wavy dark hair flow freely, framing her face. It was no use trying to straighten it. She could feel the humidity thick in the air. It made her skin feel soft and dewy after her shower. She grabbed her key and made her way to the dining area where she was meeting the group for lunch. When she got there, Luke was already there sitting with Ricardo. He did a double take as he saw her walking toward them. She blushed.

"Hi, Ricardo!" she said and then turned to Luke. "Hi," she said in a small voice.

"Hi!" He smiled, those clear baby blues still sparkling.

He sat back in his chair and held his hand out to the seat next to him, welcoming her to the table. "You can sit here if you want."

"Thanks."

She sat down and spun her attention back to Ricardo, not wanting to reveal how Luke made her feel.

"This place is like a fairytale! Thanks for organizing the class."

"Sure! It's my pleasure. It's near and dear to my heart. Wait 'till you go to the excavation site tomorrow. It's…extraordinary."

He looked over toward the kitchen where Mari was calling him.

"Will you two excuse me? Looks like I'm being summonsed."

Their laugh was nervous as they shifted in their seats. Ariana stole a glance at Luke. His dark-wash jeans and red polo shirt fit just right, revealing sinewy arms underneath. His dark hair was cut short close to his head on the sides and in the back. The top was longer, particularly in the front, and styled with purpose. His blue eyes and smooth light skin had a glow about them, and his shapely lips were so tempting.

"You clean up well." He sat back in his chair with the same mischievous grin from the airport.

"Well, thanks. Not so bad yourself, *Lucas*!" she said, imitating Mari's greeting.

Just then Mari announced that lunch was being served. Roberto, Ricardo, Mari, and Miguel came out, carrying many little dishes on platters. Each table got one. Everything looked delicious. It certainly smelled delicious.

"¡Buenas tardes! Bienvenidos al Convento Real. Estamos muy contentos de que habéis decidido estar aquí con nosotros. Yo soy Mari, este es mi marido Miguel, y nuestro sobrino Roberto,"[62] Mari said to the group. *"Nosotros somos los dueños y Roberto está encargado de la recepción."* Roberto nodded, greeting the students.

"Encantado de conoceros," added Miguel, extending a hand toward Ricardo and peering his way. *"Ricardo es un amigo muy especial para nosotros. Lo hemos conocido desde hace mucho tiempo—cuando era muy joven en su propia clase como vosotros. Esperamos que habéis encontrado sus cuartos cómodos. Si hay algo que necesitáis, por favor dinos como podemos complaceros."*[63]

"There is dessert, sangria, and water for tea at the server over there. Please help yourselves. *¡Buen provecho!*"[64] Mari finished and pointed to a long, wide, dark sideboard at the far wall of the dining room occupied with pitchers of sangria and water, sliced cake, cookies and chocolate truffles.

"Look at all this stuff! It smells so good! Where do I start?" Ariana asked with her eyes moving from dish to dish.

Before Luke could answer, Ricardo was back standing in front of the group.

"Before you all get started with lunch, I'd like to formally begin our class with a bit of an ice breaker. Luke is going to hand out a random note card to each of you with a number on it. Each table has a number card in the center. When you get your card, please stand and

---

[62] Good afternoon! Welcome to El Convento Real (literally the Royal Convent). We are very happy you have chosen to stay here with us. My name is Mari, this is my husband Miguel, and our nephew Roberto. Roberto is in charge of the front desk.

[63] Nice to meet you all. Ricardo is a very special friend of ours. We have known him for a very long time—since he was just as young as you all in his own class. We hope you have found your accommodations to be comfortable. Please let us know if there is anything you need and we can provide it for you.

[64] Enjoy!

find your table based on the number you have on the card. There should be five of you at each table."

Luke jumped up to grab the notecards and began handing them out. As they received their cards, the students moved about to find their place. Ariana took the card from Luke, lightly brushing hands with him again. She glanced up at him. He swallowed before quickly looking away and finishing his work. She turned her attention to her card and flipped it over. *Ok, number 3.* She saw a group of girls and a guy at her table. *Hopefully, I'll meet some fun people.* Once everyone was seated again, Ricardo got their attention and asked them to introduce themselves.

They ate the tapas and played more ice breakers with Luke leading some of them. Ariana watched him lead the activities in his easygoing style. She turned her attention back to her table, realizing she had begun to daydream. Deana, one of the girls in her group, she learned, was here alone too, but she did have a roommate. She was from Seattle. She and Ariana had become friends right away. It was a nice distraction from Luke, but every once in a while, Ariana let her eyes shift over his way. Just like clockwork, he seemed to be trying to catch a glimpse of her, too.

"I know you all have barely set your bags in your rooms and have been traveling for a million hours, but it's critical that you read this important document outlining the purpose of the dig and its stage in the process before getting to work tomorrow, and this is the only time we have to do it," Ricardo said after the ice breakers. "It clearly lays out the expectations and explains what our work at the site will look like over the next two weeks."

Ariana heard a few groans around the room, but, nevertheless, they worked for several hours straight, only taking short breaks. By the time they were finished, it was nearing 7:00. They had an hour before dinner would be served, then they were free for the rest of the night. She quickly freshened up and walked out to meet Deana for dinner, which was surprisingly light in comparison to the feast that had been laid out before them for lunch. They ate at the same tables they had been assigned during their class time. Deana introduced Ariana to Ashley, her roommate, and they continued their dinner talking about the class and where they were from. Ariana was speechless when Ashley had mentioned that Luke was 'a beautiful man' as she gawked at him. She had let out a nervous laugh and agreed, trying not to let on her feelings for him. *That was awkward.*

38

After dinner, Deana and Ariana were walking toward their rooms when Luke called her name. She turned to see him standing right behind them.

"Hey, can I talk to you for a minute?"

"Sure. Deana, I'll catch up with you later."

"Ok," Deana said as she started toward the stairs.

Ariana turned to Luke. "What's up?"

"Can we take a walk? I want to show you something."

"Ok."

Curiosity danced inside her like a swarm of butterflies. Her steps quickened as Luke led her through a set of stairs behind the front desk. The staircase rattled Ariana a bit. She reached for the smooth wood-paneled wall and slid her fingertips upward. *I could probably touch both sides with my arms stretched out.* The lighting was dim, and Luke was a silhouette in front of her. She could barely make out the color of his clothes. The steps wound around without landings, and every other step groaned as they climbed. *Are we ever going to get to the end?*

"Ok, Luke. This is starting to freak me out. Where are you taking me?"

"You'll see!"

She was relieved when they reached the last few steps and saw a door. He grabbed for her hand as he opened it. When the door opened, Ariana stood motionless and her breath was caught in her throat. Atop the bed and breakfast was a large open patio that stretched almost the entire length of the structure. The night sky was an infinite sheet of black silk splayed with huge, shimmering diamonds.

"Wow!" was all that Ariana could let herself whisper out. The stars seemed so close she could touch them. "You can see the Milky Way!" she exclaimed after a minute.

He came from behind her and held her hand. The electricity between them was unnerving. They found a wrought-iron bench in a corner and sat down. The summer wrapped its warmth around them.

"I knew you would love it," he said. "It's my favorite place in the bed and breakfast. I used to come and study up here all the time when I was in Ricardo's class. At the end of every course, Miguel and Mari host an end-of-class party up here with live music, food, and sangria."

"Sounds like fun!" Ariana responded, still fixated on the sky above. "This is the way the stars look at home." She realized just how far away from home she actually was. "You know, the night before I flew out to New York, I was outside walking into my aunt's house when I looked up and saw two shooting stars fly across the sky, one right after the other. What are the chances of that?"

His head whipped from the sky toward her and his eyes narrowed, making the hue of blue seem to deepen. "What?" she asked.

"Uh, I was just thinking how rare that is."

"Right?" *¡Como hallar un 12-pointer!*[65] Having almost said that out loud, she couldn't help but smile, thinking of her friend Chris from back home who always said that.

"What?"

"Oh nothing." She knew he would never get the reference.

They sat for a few minutes, gazing upwards. She stared at the sky then out over the short, stone patio wall. She could see the lights of some of the houses. She thought for a moment about the infinite sky and the massive earth. It made her feel insignificant in a way. Like she was but a microcosm of an intricately designed and perfectly thriving, beating system that worked together in ways humanity would never fully understand no matter how hard we tried.

"Isn't it amazing?" Ariana asked, breaking the silence.

"What?"

"That we're a million miles away from home, yet we see the same stars here." She looked away for an instant and shook her head. "I just don't know how people can believe that there is no God."

Luke nodded. "Where are you from?"

"Huh?" She was still in deep thought.

"You said the stars look like this at home. Where's home in Colorado?"

"Oh. Yeah." She straightened up. "San Luis…I'm from Southern Colorado. A small town near the New Mexico border. It's the oldest town in Colorado, actually. You're from New York, right?"

"Yeah, that's where all my family has been for generations."

She looked up at him and paused for a second. He lifted his arm and placed his hand on the back of the bench and motioned for her to lay her head on his shoulder with his other hand. Ariana smiled, surprised that he knew what she was thinking. She didn't say anything. She just lay her head on his warm chest and smiled again. His heart was beating fast. They were still for a while, basking in each

---

[65] Like finding a 12-point elk!

other's presence and their serene surroundings, when a car door outside the building slammed, startling them.

"What time is it?" Ariana sat up and reached for her phone.

"It's 9:30," Luke answered after looking at his own phone.

They held each other's gaze for a few seconds. He let his hand run down her cheek, and once again, she felt like warm butter melting through the slats of the bench. She swallowed.

"I, uh, should go let my parents know I'm here," she said under her breath.

"Yeah. That's probably a good idea. I haven't done that yet either."

She stood and he did the same.

"Ariana?"

The way he said her name, rolling the 'r' perfectly, sent a bolt running down her spine.

She closed her eyes and paused before looking back. "Yes?"

"I'm so glad you're here." He glanced at the stone floor then back at her. "I wasn't sure I would ever see you again after that day in the bookstore."

It was the first time either of them had brought up that day. She walked toward him, took his hands in hers, and kissed his cheek. She hadn't been able to contain herself.

"Me either."

He stood there for a minute with his eyes closed and touched his cheek. Ariana smiled and turned to walk away. He followed. They walked down the creaky steps in silence. When they got down to the lobby, it was quiet. All of the students had already left to their rooms for the night. Ariana looked around the area and found a sign pointing to the library.

"Luke," Ricardo called, making Ariana jump out of her skin. "Can I have a word?"

He was in the sitting room facing the stairs, chatting with Mari and Miguel.

"Sure," Luke answered. He turned toward Ariana and said, "See you tomorrow."

"Yeah." She nodded. "Have a good night."

She strolled toward the library in a daze to email her parents and Facebook Liz. Liz was going to flip!

She sat on the chair in front of the first computer set up against the far wall to the right. She looked around. In the middle was a huge bay window that opened to the parking lot. On the left were endless shelves that stretched from one wall to the other and from floor to ceiling, with books of all sizes and colors stuffed in tightly. A rolling ladder sat against the wall of books near the window. She wondered what types of books they were and if she would even understand the writing in them. Positioned in front of the bay window was a couch that looked like someone had plucked it out of the Victorian era and placed it there. Several more wing-backed chairs, just like the one in her room, had been placed around the room, inviting anyone who wanted to sit and study or enjoy a good book. The space was perfect for studying. She could definitely see herself spending lots of time working here. She turned to the computer and looked at the instructions for logging on.

She signed into her email, letting her parents know that they had arrived safely in Madrid and had traveled to their lodging in Corral de Almaguer. She gave them the phone number to the bed and breakfast and her room number just in case they wanted to call her. Each of them had a phone in their rooms, but it was very expensive to call out internationally, and Wi-Fi out here was very spotty. She let them know she would be in touch soon and promised to send pictures as soon as she could. She already had a ton of them from Madrid and from the drive over. She would have to look through them at some point and pick the best ones to send.

In her Facebook message to Liz, Ariana only said.

> *Girlfriend, fairytales are REAL!!! I'm here. I have so much to tell you. This day has been a dream come true.*
>
> *More later...*
>
> *Love ya,*
> *Ana*

She knew Liz was going to be a wreck trying to figure out what she was talking about, but she didn't care. She just didn't have the energy to explain any more. She was still dealing with all of the enormous emotions she felt for this guy she barely knew.

Luke

As Luke approached Ricardo, the warmth of his time with Ariana was replaced by a cool shiver that ran through him. Ricardo's voice rang in his ears again. *What was that tone about?* He was sure Ricardo had seen them walking down the steps from the patio together. Her face as they sat on the bench flashed through his mind. He was glad he had hesitated when he had wanted to lean in and kiss her, thinking what they were doing was probably already inappropriate. But when *she* had kissed him…his body had flooded with emotion. Her soft lips still lingered on his cheek. This girl was clearly getting under his skin. Ricardo cleared his throat, bringing him to the present.

"What's up, Ricardo?"

Ricardo pushed his glasses higher on his nose and peered behind Luke. "Before we review our plan for tomorrow, Luke, I have to ask…" He paused for a minute as if trying to find the right words and then continued, "What's going on with you and Ariana? Are you friends? Did you know each other before the trip?"

Luke sat on the edge of the chair across from Ricardo and wiped his palms on his pants. He hesitated, struggling with how to respond. *She's a student. Of course he's concerned.*

"No, well, uh, yes," he started. "We sort of met in the bookstore on campus, but I had never really talked to her until today…I don't even know her last name."

He chewed on those words for a second. He didn't even know her last name. He was staggered at the thought of how little he knew of Ariana, yet how deeply connected he felt to her.

"Huh." Ricardo sat back in his chair and crossed one leg over the other. He scratched the back of his head. Luke could see the wheels turning in Ricardo's mind. The back of his own neck was getting warmer. "The way you two carry on, I was sure you had something going on."

"Oh?" Luke let out an uncomfortable laugh, shifting in his seat. "Well—"

"Look, Luke, I know you're a responsible guy and you're very talented. I don't want your integrity to be compromised in any way. You don't want anyone to think you're playing favorites. You *will* be grading these students and leading them at the excavation site, and they will need to be fully engaged. They need to be able to trust your guidance and respect your feedback."

Luke nodded and rubbed his palms together.

Ricardo's head dropped down. He smoothed his pants and sat up right. "Listen, after the class, you're welcome to do whatever you want. Heck, the two of you *are* practically the same age." He waved one hand in the air and rubbed the back of his neck with the other. "What it really comes down to, Luke, is whether or not you think you can be objective as her instructor?"

Luke's jaw tightened. He couldn't let on that there was anything between him and Ariana. He had to keep this internship. He nodded and said, "Absolutely. I'm taking this position very seriously, Ricardo. I love this work."

Luke sat back in his chair and put his hand over his mouth. He had to get a grip. He respected Ricardo and was hoping he could give him a promising letter of recommendation for his next endeavor.

"Good. Then we have an understanding."

"Of course."

"I'm off to bed then, we've got an early morning. Do you have any questions about the events for tomorrow?"

"No," Luke murmured. "I'm good."

"Ok, good night then." Ricardo stood up.

Luke stood with him and looked Ricardo square in the eye. He put out his hand and Ricardo shook it.

"Goodnight, Ricardo. And thank you again for this opportunity."

When Ricardo disappeared out of sight, he sat back in the chair again. He let out a long exhale, extending his legs. *Man, I've got to get it together. I've got to use this opportunity as a chance to prove to my dad and myself that this is a viable career and that I deserve to be a part of it.* He stood up to retire to his room just as Ariana was walking out from the library. They both stood still and stared at one another. He started toward her.

"We've got to stop meeting like this," she said.

Her smile was a ray of sunshine. He felt a tugging at his heartstrings. *Focus.*

"Hey, can I talk to you for a minute?"

Her face changed, like she was on her way to the principal's office. The hem of her dress flowed back and forth with each step toward him.

"Sure. Is something wrong? You look worried."

Her tiny, yet surprisingly curvy, physique stood inches in front of him, and she crossed her arms. He took a deep breath. *She smells so good.* Her perfume mixed with the smell of her hair was an inviting blend of fresh air and delicate sweetness. It made her all the more alluring. *No, really. Focus.*

"Well," he began. "You know I really like you, Ariana. But…"

"Ricardo…and the other students, right?"

She pulled her hair behind her ears and turned her face. Her weight shifted to one hip, and she crossed her arms again. His fingertips brushed her chin, urging her face back toward him.

"I wish we were here under different circumstances."

She looked down and back up at him. Disappointment filled her eyes. "I knew this was coming."

He held her face in his hands.

"Look, today has meant more to me than you'll ever know. We just have to…put things on hold for a while."

"I get it. I was wondering how this was going to work anyway."

She took a couple of steps back, and her body twisted toward the stairs. He reached for her hand, making her flip around quickly.

"Hey, but I'm not going to let you go again without getting your information this time."

She smiled and her eyes lit up her face again. He pulled out his phone. "Will you put your number in here for me? Are you on Facebook?"

"Of course." They exchanged phones. "I am, but I don't use it very often."

"I don't either, but friend me and we can talk through Messenger."

"Ok." Her fingers moved quickly on his phone before she returned it and grabbed her own. He looked at it.

"Ariana Romero."

"Luke Cohen."

She held out her hand.

"Nice to formally meet you, Mr. Cohen."

He smiled and took her hand in his. It felt like silk in his hands, and warmth ran through his body.

"Likewise, Ms. Romero." He nodded, raising an eyebrow.

Ah, ha! A lightbulb flashed in his mind, and his voice became more playful.

He sat on the arm of the chair behind him and said, "Well, now that we've formally met, would you like to go out on a date with me some time?"

She giggled.

"Of course, I would love to. But how do you suppose we make such a thing happen in this predicam—"

Before she could get out the words, he interrupted, "Details, details…Just take an extra day in New York when we get back, and I'll take you out."

She threw her head back and laughed. When she looked back at him, his eyes were still fixed on her. She brought her hand to her throat and swallowed. "Oh my gosh. You're serious…Are you serious? That's crazy. How would I even work that out without paying a small fortune?"

"Don't worry about that. Just work it out with your parents and let them know you'll arrive a day later, and I'll take care of the rest." He stood up and leaned into her. "Ariana, just give me one day. It can't happen here…Don't you think we both owe it to ourselves to figure out what this is between us?" He took her hand, pointed first at her then at him.

Then, he gave her hand a gentle squeeze, and brought it to his chest. Their fingers intertwined, moving with each heartbeat.

"Ok," she finally said after a long pause. She closed her eyes and muttered in a screechy whisper, "I can't believe I'm really going to do this." Then, she opened her eyes, grinned, and said, "Let's do it!"

"Perfect! We can work out the details through Messenger."

He hugged her and kissed the top of her forehead. She turned to walk up the stairs.

"In the meantime," he said, "try to control yourself over the next couple of weeks, ok?"

"Ha!" She rolled her eyes and laughed.

"I mean, don't like bump into me on purpose or anything. And try not to sneak a peek at my booty, ok?"

"You wish!" She laughed. "Now, goodnight," she said in a loud voice, shaking her head, "Goofball!"

"Goodnight," he muttered as he watched her walk up the stairs. *This is going to be a long two weeks.* He let out a heavy breath. *I have to make this work.* The last thing he needed was to give his dad any kind of evidence that would strengthen his case against his career choice or question his priorities or work ethic.

Chapter 6

Ariana

Everyone boarded the bus promptly at 7:45 after breakfast. Ariana found a seat and realized she had hardly eaten a thing. Breakfast was light this morning—cereal and milk, fruit, and pastries, along with coffee, water, and juice. She had stood there considering the goods laid out on the server and had plucked a filo dough pastry sprinkled with chocolate shavings from the assortment on the platter, thinking lunch must be the most important meal of the day. She was sure that this breakfast wouldn't carry her through 2:00 pm. The sweet bread had been warm, flakey, and buttery, and the center oozed with chocolate as she bit into it.

The pastry had almost been as delicious as seeing Luke walking toward the dining room—almost. He had smiled and winked at her as their eyes met, making her cheeks flush. Her thoughts had immediately gone to what he had said the night before about his booty. The corners of her mouth had turned up in a sheepish grin as her eyes automatically trailed toward his jeans and how nicely they wrapped around him. She had sighed, unable to take more than a few bites of her pastry. Her thoughts were abruptly interrupted as the bus made a sharp turn around a curve in the road, forcing Ariana into the window and her *Rain of Gold* book to slide out of her bag.

She grabbed the book and studied the cover. She had just started the book, and she loved it so far. Although Ariana had liked much of the literature she had to read for school, she had never felt a personal connection to anything she had read until now. She was enthralled with the writing style of Victor Villaseñor. The imagery and dialogue regarding his mother's childhood deep in the jungles of a mining town called Lluvia de Oro in Mexico and his father's high in the desert of

Los Altos de Jalisco continued to call her to turn the pages. She could envision their childhood homes and their plights and see herself in the landscape.

Ariana was caught up in the adventures and trials of their migration to the US and stunned by the hardships their families had survived. His grandmothers' wisdom and faith introduced her to magical realism that reminded her of her own childhood lore, which drew her in for more. She had devoured several chapters the night before, trying to get her mind on something other than Luke and the way he had said her name in his cool, deep, soft voice. He had rolled the 'r's, making her first and last name harmonize together, tickling her ears, and touching her soul. She couldn't tire of hearing it.

She bit the inside of her cheek at the thought of staying an extra day in New York with him. How could she refuse his offer? She remembered how torturing it had been not knowing whether she would see him again. She was reeling at the thought that he *had* felt what she had felt that day. That he was feeling it *now*. And to think that they would be here together for the next two weeks without being able to be close. She had to do it. She had to take the chance that he wasn't some psychopath that would leave her for dead in that captivating concrete jungle she had always wanted to visit. She was lightheaded. The screeching sound of the bus brakes quickly brought her mind back to the moment as the excavation site drew near. The motion of the stop pushed her forward into the seat in front of her, adding to her dizziness.

They parked the bus near an old, abandoned house in ruins. As Ariana walked down the steps of the bus and took a gander at her surroundings, she realized that the bed and breakfast was actually situated on the outskirts of Corral de Almaguer in the province of Toledo and so was the site. The small city could be seen close in the distance. She reached for her phone to capture the sight as she stepped off the bus. It was just as Ricardo said it would be. The site was roped off with warnings not to trespass as it had been designated an official world heritage archaeological site.

Ricardo gathered them around, and Luke handed them each gloves, vests, and safety hats. There were a couple of huge bins filled with excavation equipment just outside the ropes. The document Ricardo had given them to read described the site with impressive accuracy. Legend had it that it was a home that had belonged to a Sephardic Jewish family who had fled the city around the time of the Inquisition.

Its original construction had been dated to the 16th century when some Conversos had been forced to move to the countryside from their homes in the city. But that hadn't been confirmed. Ariana walked the grounds, taking in the sights as if in a dream. *Incredible.* She moved from room to room, hearing the crunch of debris and dried leaves under her feet and the sounds of the other students far off in the distance. *Who lived here so long ago? What was your life like?*

The roof was completely gone, but some of the walls were still standing at various levels. Yet the divisions of the rooms were visible as were the tiles on the floor, which were weathered and thick with dirt, paint, and building material. Ariana crouched down and wiped the floor with the back of her glove. The tiles, wrought with small stones in between, could still be seen, laid out in curved designs. The lavender, light blue, pale pink, and yellow stones were dull now, but she imagined that they had once shone with brilliant color. The stone edge and white stone walls indicated the foundation of the home. The Northwest corner wall was jagged but was standing higher than the rest with window-framing still intact.

"Gather around, everyone," Ricardo instructed. He motioned everyone over with his hand. "Luke and I are dividing the group in two. Please come forward as we call your name."

He pushed his glasses up higher on his nose and glanced at his clipboard. "Ariana," he called.

She exhaled, a little relieved as she approached Ricardo. *It's probably a safe assignment given the events of the night before.* Ricardo called the rest of the students in his group before Luke called Ashley and Deana. Ariana's stomach tightened as she watched Ashley practically trip over her own feet to catch up to Luke. She shook her head and followed Ricardo to the other side of the building. *Whatever.*

Ariana's assignment was inside the home. Half of the students were inside with Ricardo, and the other half were outside with Luke. Inside, each student was given a one-meter by one-meter space in which to work. She knelt down in her area and began setting up her unit datum relative to the site datum. Her knees immediately felt the rock and debris dig into her skin through her jeans. She shifted and began the surface survey, documenting everything she saw, then she rolled right into excavation. Her job, as was everyone else's, was to try and uncover any treasure or hint of a former life while still trying to maintain the integrity of the structure.

49

Ariana brushed the surface of the floor with a soft brush and collected the material in a small bucket. The outdoor team would sift through it later with a screen and tarp underneath to try to find any artifacts without losing any of the original dirt and debris in the process. Ricardo and Luke stressed that *everything* tells a story—the chemical composition of the soil, for example, Ricardo had said, "Could potentially provide insight into how the site evolved in various climates over time or reveal 'elements' that could be indicators of certain human activity; and any pollen might expose what plants were around at the time and maybe what people would have eaten."

The more Ariana labored, the more she was drawn to the home, feeling a charging yet, comforting energy, like she had been here before. She sat back for a minute, crisscrossing her legs, hugging her knees, and intertwining her fingers around them. She looked around her and up to the sky. The feeling was intense, but she shook it off, knowing that that was impossible.

They worked for a couple of hours in the heat and humidity of the June day before stopping to take a break. Ariana leaned against the bus, felt the sweat on the back of her neck, and refreshed herself with the water she had brought. She fought against the urge to take off her hat and dump the cool water over her head but paused rather to take in the sights of the area. Her eyes squinted and focused on a river and trees up ahead behind the site that had once been a home. The scene was so tempting. They beckoned for her to come over and play. *Oh, how nice it would be to jump into that water*. She amused herself, almost feeling the cool splash of the water between her toes.

Instead, she pulled her notebook from her bag and began taking notes on what she had seen. Later, she would have to answer some questions and write about her experience in a journal she would upload to Luke and Ricardo on the class website. It was Luke's job to respond to the students and forward any major questions or concerns the students had to Ricardo. They continued their work, not finding anything in particular, and soon boarded the bus back to El Convento Real.

When they got back, Ariana was walking toward the stairs through the sitting room when she noticed Ashley following Luke again. She felt her ears heat up as she saw her link her arm in his and ask, "Luke, can you *please* help me clarify this assignment?"

"Sure, Ashley." Luke slid his arm from Ashley's grasp, using it to point in the direction of the library. "Let's work in there."

Ugh…The next couple of weeks are going to be difficult, indeed.

"Ariana."

"Huh?" Ariana whipped around. Her heart pounded as she noticed Mari standing behind the server in the kitchen. "Mari." She let out a giggle and gripped her chest. *"¡Me 'spanté!"*[66]

Mari laughed and walked out from the kitchen. She looked into Ariana's eyes with the tenderness of a mother, touched the side of her cheek, and said, *"Linda."*[67]

Ariana was small by standards; she stood a mere five-foot-two-inches. Yet Mari was still a little shorter than she was. She was older. She had to be in her sixties, but she had a youthful energy that had preserved her pretty features—plus, she was always done with beauty-shop hair and a full face of precise make-up.

"Confía en el amor, hija," she continued with an index finger in the air. *"No te traicionará…Ven… ¿me ayudas en la cocina, por favor?"*[68]

Ariana's eyes widened then narrowed. *What did she mean by that?* She hesitated for a moment. She glanced toward the library and blew out a heavy breath, remembering New York, and said, *"Sí, sí, como no, Mari. ¿En qué le puedo ayudar?"*[69]

She followed Mari to the kitchen where she was preparing lunch.

Taken by the wonderful aroma floating through the kitchen, Ariana sighed. *"Ay Dios mío, ¡como ole rico aquí, Mari!"*[70]

Those smells elicited the familiarity of being with her mom in the kitchen of their own restaurant. An ache rose up to a lump in her throat, making her feel a little guilty. Of course she enjoyed being at the restaurant. It's where she had spent her entire childhood. But she still didn't want to spend the rest of her life working there.

Mari's laugh made Ariana focus her attention back on her.

"Gracias," Mari said as she glanced at Ariana studying her face. *"¿De dónde es tu familia, hija?"*[71]

---

[66] You scared me!

[67] Beautiful

[68] Trust in love, my daughter. It won't betray you. Come, will you help me in the kitchen?

[69] Yes, yes of course, Mari. How can I help?

[70] Oh my gosh, it smells so good in here Mari!

[71] Where is your family from?

"De Colorado en Estados Unidos."[72]
"Sí, pero ¿de cuál país vinieron?"[73]

Ariana was used to these types of questions by now. Throughout her college career, everyone had wondered about her, students and professors alike. No one could figure her out. With her subtle features, pale skin, freckles and hazel eyes, she looked White to her peers until she opened her mouth. Then came the questions about her accent and her background. It had become a bothersome, predictable routine.

She helped Mari serve the tapas into small dishes and place them onto the platters for serving. There were roasted potatoes with chorizo, jamón, various cheeses and vegetables, mussels, and paella. The dishes were visually impressive, and the smell—that wonderful aroma—made her stomach growl. She could already taste it.

"Es que no estoy segura. Mi familia siempre me ha dicho que semos españoles, pero de muchos siglos pasados. Pensamos que los bisabuelos de mis abuelos llegaron a Colorado de Nuevo México, pero no sé."[74]

Mari nodded. *"¿Entonces eres mexicana?"*[75]

"No creo," responded Ariana. *"Mis amigos mexicanos me dicen que no hablo el español bien y que la comida que cocinamos no es comida mexicana. Me dicen que seigo Chicana, o Americanizada, pero no pienso que es tan fácil como eso."*[76]

"Interesante...es que tu acento es muy raro. Usas palabras que son muy antiguas, palabras que leía antes en literatura del pasado en escuela."[77]

Ariana recalled having read similar literature in her college Spanish classes.

---

[72] From Colorado in the United States.

[73] Yes, but from which country did you come from?

[74] Well, I'm not sure. My family has always told me that we are Spanish, but from many centuries ago. We think my great-great-great grandparents came to Colorado from New Mexico, but we're not sure.

[75] You're Mexican then?

[76] I don't think so. My Mexican friends say that I don't speak Spanish right and that the food we cook isn't Mexican food. They say that I'm 'Chicana' or that I'm Americanized, but I don't think it's that simple.

[77] Interesting. It's just that your accent is unique. You use ancient Spanish words, words that I used to read in literature class in school.

"Si quizás trujieron su idioma y munchas de sus tradiciones con ellos de España."[78]

Mari laughed. *"¡Ya ves! Esas palabras 'truje' y 'seigo' vienen del español viejo."*[79]

Ariana chuckled. She was pretty sure her cheeks were pink. She was always careful while speaking her Spanish, taking into consideration what her audience would understand. She constantly went back and forth between the standard Spanish she learned in school, the Mexican Spanish she was around most of the time, and the familiar Spanish from home she grew up hearing from the older generations her whole life. It was nerve-racking! And when she was nervous, some of her home Spanish usually slipped out. She was often told that her words were wrong, but she never understood how it could be possible that her grandparents' first language, the language they grew up speaking, could be wrong.

Mari's words encouraged her, validating her instincts that their language wasn't wrong, just *different*. Ariana watched Mari work, humming with every movement. There was a spunk about her that made Ariana feel at ease and affectionate toward her. She now understood why both Ricardo and Luke had befriended them as family. Mari was meticulous about her work. Her kitchen was immaculate. It was hard to believe all this delicious food had just been prepared here.

It was nearing 2:00 as Miguel walked into the kitchen.

"¡Hola, Ariana! ¿Cómo estás?"[80]

Impressed that Miguel knew her by name, she responded with a smile, *"¡Muy bien, Miguel! Y ¿Usted?"*[81]

"Bien, bien, gracias, hija...les ayudo a servir los platos."[82]

The three of them came out holding the platters for each table. When she walked out of the kitchen, Luke was on his way to the dining room...alone. Ariana smiled and nodded, greeting him.

"So now you're part of the kitchen staff, eh?" he said.

"Yup! I've officially been recruited," she said, winking at Mari.

---

[78] Yes, I guess they must have brought their language and a lot of their traditions with them when they came from Spain.
[79] See! Those words, "to bring" and "I am" come from the old Spanish.
[80] Hi, Ariana! How are you?
[81] Very well, Miguel! And you?
[82] Good, good, thank you. I will help you two serve the platters.

When she looked back at Luke, she was caught off guard that he was still gazing at her. He turned away as quickly as their eyes met, found Ricardo, and sat next to him. Miguel, Ariana, and Mari served the platters to each table, and Mari and Miguel thanked Ariana for her help. Ariana scanned the room for Deana and sat with her. They ate and retreated to their rooms for siesta. She was glad, too. She needed a break.

She lay flat on her bed, her eyes focused on the ceiling, and went over the details of the day in her mind. The heat and the work they had done at the excavation site had drawn energy from her, yet the site itself had been rejuvenating. At the same time, she was learning a lot about archaeology and was beginning to acquire an affinity for it. It seemed to go hand in hand with her love for history. All of that, in addition to Luke and being around Mari today in the kitchen, had brought out a flood of emotions flowing within her. She had begun to miss home, and it was only Tuesday, her second full day here. She got under her covers, pulled them up to her chest, and grabbed her book. Reading would surely take her mind off of everything.

Just as she began to read, the phone in her room rang. Her heart somersaulted. She let it go once more before picking it up.

"Hello?" she said, uncertain of who would be on the other end.

"Hi."

Her heart fluttered at the sound of Luke's cool, soft voice.

"Hey," she said.

"How are you?"

"I'm ok. Just missing home…You?"

"I'm good…thinking about you."

She leaned her head against the headboard delighted to hear his words.

"Me too."

Luke broke the brief silence that followed. "So…I've been thinking about our trip all day. I just sent you a message with some of my ideas. Take a look and let me know what you think."

"Ok. I've been thinking about it, too. I'm excited to see what you have in mind. I just want to spend time with you without—"

"I know."

"On another note," she said, excited to hear the confirmation from him, "I enjoyed spending time with Mari this afternoon in the kitchen. No wonder you like them so much. She's such a nice person. She seems to have a knack for knowing people."

"Yeah…she does," he said.

A knock came to Ariana's door.

"Ariana, are you in there?" called Deana.

"Yeah, one second, Deana!" Ariana looked toward the door. "Hey, I better go. They're outside in the hallway."

"Ok. I'm looking forward to hearing from you about New York soon. Take care."

"You too."

Ariana opened the door to find Deana and Ashley in the hall.

"We're going for a walk to explore the grounds before class starts again at 5:00. Do you want to come with?"

"Sure."

She could use some fresh air. She reached for her key, slipped on her flip-flops, and closed the door behind her. Deana and Ashley stood in front of her, bright-eyed and energetic. Ashley had a silly grin on her face that annoyed Ariana immediately. *Ugh. Let it go. Give it a chance, Ariana.* They made their way outdoors and strolled along a path that led away from the grounds and talked about the day. The three of them giggled about silly things and talked about their families and school. She learned that they were juniors at DU and anthropology majors. They talked about how archaeology complemented all of their chosen majors and how this experience would impact them.

"It's already changed me," Ariana said, feeling herself a million miles away in her thoughts. "The past two days have been like a whirlwind. I can barely remember life before this trip."

"Wow, ok!" Ashley and Deana laughed.

"I don't know about all that, but I'm having a great time so far," Deana said.

"I am too," Ashley added. "And it sure helps that one of our instructors is *so* hot." She pretended to fan herself.

Deana nodded in agreement. Ariana cringed.

Cálmate,[83] *Ariana,* she chastised herself in her mind. *She doesn't even know anything. He wants* you*, remember?* Somehow, though, the thought of Brian and that girl burned through Ariana's mind, and she became acutely aware of where these emotions were coming from. She knew it was immature and that she had to get over it and

---

[83] Calm down

put that experience behind her. She let out a long sigh, and they headed back to El Convento.

Given that there were a few minutes left before class, she excused herself and shuffled quickly to the library to check her messages. She sat down and logged onto Facebook. There was the message from Luke sitting, waiting for her to open. She stared at it and bit her fingernail. As she scrolled down, she laughed aloud, noticing a ton of frantic messages from Liz too. She logged into her email and there was one from her parents. She would read the message from her parents and the ones from Liz later tonight.

"Querida[84] Ariana," she read out loud. She felt weak as she heard his voice saying 'Querida Ariana' in her mind. She could only imagine how that would sound in person coming out of his mouth.

> *I still think it's crazy that we're on this trip together. Have you been to New York before? We won't have much time, but I thought we could have dinner first. Then we could catch a Broadway show afterwards. Is there any place you've always wanted to go? Also, please forward your flight information to me and we'll work on changing it.*
>
> *Hasta Pronto!*

"Wow," she whispered. "Dinner and a Broadway show. Could he *really* be this sweet and romantic?"

She waited for a minute and thought about what she should say before responding:

> *Querido Luke,*
> *I am so excited about our date. I would LOVE to see a Broadway show! I've never been to New York, but I've always wanted to go. What do you think about salsa dancing? Attached is my flight itinerary. Let me know what you find for later flights and how much it will cost. I will pay you back the difference when I get back to Denver.*
>
> *P.S. I'm glad we found each other here too. It's all been like* a dream.

---

[84] Dear…also loved

Ariana looked at the time on the computer. *4:51*. She logged off and hurried to class. She found a seat at the only open table with students she didn't know.

After class let out, they had a break before dinner. Ariana looked at her notes from the day and paused. She had a lot on her mind that she wanted to say in her journal about her experience. She thought she had better get it out before it escaped her. The journals weren't technical or academically-based. It wasn't a graded assignment in the traditional sense. They received credit for doing it and for thoughtful reflection. Ricardo had shared that the work they were doing and being abroad could be challenging in different ways, and it was important to him to provide his students with a venue with which to reflect on each day, ask any questions, or voice any concerns they might have in the process that the instructors could address.

Journal #1:

My heart is filled with gratitude thinking about this unbelievable experience thus far. Today I have a newfound respect and admiration for the field of Archaeology. I was in awe as we arrived at the site today. As I walked the grounds, I could feel the energy of a people of another time. I could almost hear the sounds of their voices in conversation and their laughter. Being on the grounds of that structure in ruins and seeing the dusty stone floors still struggling to maintain their integrity reminded me of life's tender fragility. I could imagine the mason who built the walls, and the artisan (s/he *had* to be an artist with that type of detail) who laid the floor, taking the time to intricately weave in the colorful pattern. I wanted to have seen it in its full glory. I imagined the people who lived there, what their lives were like, and how they interacted with one another in each of the rooms. I am appreciative for this opportunity, and I will treasure this experience forever in more ways than I can express.

She sent it off and logged into her email and into Facebook where she saw a message from Luke and another one from her mom. Her mom was glad to hear Ariana had arrived safely and hoped everything was going well. She said all her family was praying for her and that her grandmother had lit a candle in the church. *Awww!* She brought her hand to her chest. *I love her.* She hadn't seen her grandmother since Easter, and Ariana longed to hear her voice. Her mom asked her to send pictures and stay in touch as much as possible. *Ugh, I forgot the cord to my phone. I'll send them pics later.* Then she finally messaged Liz after reading all of her rants about 'being swept off her feet by a fine *&%$ Spanish guy and his brother for her, blah, blah, blah.' She laughed to herself and wrote:

> *Just for all that, I'm going to keep you in suspense until I get home. ;p Lol!!! Just know you ARE NOT going to believe what's happening. Let me just say that I'm having a ghost of a time! ☺ I'll send pics soon.*

> *Love you, Ana.*

A ping from the computer startled her. *A response to my journal. Which message should I open next?* She panned from one page to the other and exhaled. She clicked on the journal response, thinking it would be better to get that one out the way first. *Hmmm, technical. Just like a teacher. Such a different tone from his other message, but I guess that* is *his job. Ok, let's read the other one.*

> *Ariana,*

> *I hope you know how difficult it's been not being myself around you. I loved reading your journal entry. You're the only one I know besides Ricardo and me that feels the same way about this site. Would be great to have a real conversation with you about it. I checked out some flights and found a few that are doable. We leave Madrid at 7:15am on Saturday and get into New York at 9:35am with the time difference. I found a flight that would leave New York at 7pm Sunday evening. It would get you to Denver around 9pm Mountain Time. Is that too late for your parents? We can have the whole day Saturday and most of the day Sunday. This one would be my first choice. Talk to your parents and let me know if that will work.*

P.S. Don't worry about the money, please. I will take care of it. I just want some time with you. It's more than worth it to me.

P.P.S. Salsa dancing sounds cool! Are you ready for me, though?

P.P.P.S. Did I catch you checking out my booty at dinner tonight?

She rolled her eyes and laughed out loud. She had to turn around to see if anyone had heard her. *What a goofball...and a sweetheart.* She wrote:

Is there a legal limit for how many p's you can have after a p.s.? Just wondering. Yes, the flight time you found is perfect. Let's plan for that. Thank you...I will definitely work it out with my parents. And the more appropriate question regarding salsa, Mr. Cohen, is are you ready for me? *And lastly, my only defense is to answer your last question with a question...what's a girl to do?*

P.S. I'm glad to hear your REAL thoughts about my journal entry. I felt inexplicably drawn to the site. It was just as amazing as Ricardo described it. That whole area...the meadow, the river...I was almost moved beyond words. Can't wait to talk to you about it and to have the chance to spend some time with you too.

"He can't really dance salsa, right?" she mumbled to herself, loving their playful exchange.

Ironically, the vast World Wide Web was the only way to be close to him even though they were merely feet away from one another in the same building. She yawned and rubbed the tears watering from her eyes. The jet lag was starting to take its toll on her. These first few days of the trip had been so full. She had been running on pure adrenaline until now. She stretched her arms up in the air and forced her legs to carry her back to her room to read more of *Rain of Gold* before falling into a deep sleep.

Chapter 7

Luke

Luke stared out of the window in the bus, trying to focus on the calming campo landscape, but the vision of Ariana walking out of the kitchen with Mari at lunch yesterday invaded his thoughts. Her skin had glistened from the heat of the day and the kitchen. Her nose and cheeks had looked like they had been kissed by the sun from their work, and she had a warm glow about her. The words in Ariana's journal had impressed him. It had given him an indication of what was important to her. While other students had some depth to their first journal entries, many complained about the heat and the uncomfortable safety wear; but his querida Ariana saw this work through his eyes. *Maybe I can't be objective.* He was glad he had followed up his cold instructor response with a personal message.

> *Ariana,*
>
> *Thank you for your heartfelt journal entry. I'm struck by all the meaning you've construed from our work today. Glad to hear you're enjoying archaeology!*

Ricardo nudged him into the present when the bus stopped at the site. They split the groups once again in two with Ariana in Luke's group this time. Luke gave instructions as he handed out the equipment and showed his group to the Northwest corner of the house where they would be working. It was still early, and, although it was warm, the heat of the summer hadn't kicked in yet. It was calm and comfortable in the meadow with only birds and the rush of the river in the distance. The breeze brushed against his cheeks, and he closed his eyes for a minute. There was a freedom and peace that Luke loved about working outdoors, especially here, in this place.

He looked around, noting in his mind all of his students' locations, pausing for half a second at Ariana's. He watched her continue her work from yesterday. Their job today was still chasing surface features while preserving the original floor. They were to photograph, map, and catalog everything they saw in each square unit. She suddenly flicked her long ponytail that had fallen forward out of her way. It hung from the bottom of her hard hat down to the small of her back. He smiled, pulled his gloves from his back pocket, and helped some of the students haul buckets of dirt collected from the floor to the tarp area outside of the structure for screening. Luke had just sat some screens down, with various-sized openings for the sifters, when he heard a thud and a scream. *Ariana!*

"What's going on?" He ran towards her, his shoes skidding on some of the rubble on the floor.

"I don't know." Ariana's eyes were a mile wide. She coughed and waved her hand, trying to clear the fog of thick dust and debris that had filled the air from whatever it was that had fallen to the ground.

He placed a hand on her shoulder, his heart hammering in his chest, and asked, "Are you ok?"

"Luke, get Ricardo!" Drew yelled before Ariana could respond. He sat on the floor, a dark form in the haze, near the outer wall where he had been working. He tried to get the words out in between coughs and wiping at his dusty clothes. "I think you guys want to see this!" Drew pointed to a rectangular object next to him. *What is that?* Luke squinted, trying to get a better look at the object.

"Are you ok, Drew?" Ariana asked, blinking the dust out of her eyes and still trying to clear the air with her hands.

"Yeah, I was working right there when out of nowhere this thing fell out of the wall," Drew said, still visibly shaken as he stood up and took a couple of steps away from the object.

"Looks like an old tin box," Ariana offered, glancing at Luke. She stepped forward and kneeled, trying to get a closer look.

"Yeah," began Luke, reaching for her shoulder. "Let's just leave—"

"Wait a minute! Wait a minute!" Ricardo instructed, coming into Luke's periphery. He breathed heavily as he weaved through the students that had gathered around.

The student jabber increased as they continued pressing in, forcing Luke to take a step forward. *This is getting out of control.*

He turned to the crowd with his palms in the air toward them and said, "Why don't you all take your break."

"Yes," Ricardo affirmed. "Luke and I will assess the situation to make sure it's not dangerous to continue our work. And as soon as we figure out what this thing is, we'll let you know."

Luke waited for the students to walk away and then turned to Ricardo. Ricardo motioned to Luke with a wave of his hand to take a closer look. After he had mapped and photographed the area and the box right where it had fallen, Luke knelt down and picked it up, lifting it carefully and studying every angle. Except for some dents it had just received from the fall, it was in relatively good condition. Luke wiped off the top with his glove. Ricardo took the camera and captured each of Luke's actions. There were no inscriptions. The original teal blue paint interrupted the worn, rusty tin in areas where it had been imprinted with an elaborate design. Given its hiding place, it seemed to have been surprisingly protected from the elements.

Noticing a broken latch, Luke pulled it back slowly and lifted the lid. Inside, he found a time-worn sack that revealed faded purple fabric through the tattered threads underneath. Ricardo knelt down beside him.

"What is it?"

"I'm not sure." Luke couldn't break his gaze from the object to look at Ricardo. His heart was pounding. He peeled back the sack with the care of a surgeon and lifted the purple object from the box. "I think it's some kind of book, Ricardo." He held it in his hands without moving it so he wouldn't risk damaging it.

"Wow! Ok, you know the protocol, Luke. Let's take it back to the bed and breakfast and alert the universities of our findings. We can take a closer look at it at El Convento. I will get the students back in the bus if you will finish up here."

Luke placed the book back in the sack and back in the box and then put it into a casing that would keep it safe. He took out a camera and snapped some more shots of the discovery site. He especially took closer pictures of the hole in the wall. It looked as if whoever had hidden the book had deliberately hollowed out a long space in between the thick outer and inner walls with some sort of sharp object until the space was big enough to hold the box.

Once inside the bus, Ricardo shared with them that a discovery had been made and that their work at the site was finished for the day. Later at class he would share their findings. The ride back to El Convento was long and quiet. Luke entertained various scenarios about what was written in the book. Maybe it was poetry or a novel illustrating Spanish Renaissance life. *Why would someone hide it like that?* He wondered how this would change the course of their class. He wanted to push the driver's foot into the accelerator with his own. He glanced at Ricardo next to him whose thumbs were wildly pecking at the keyboard on his smartphone. He twisted his neck behind him. Many of the students were asleep. Ariana stared out her window, her earbud wires dangling from her ears. He smiled, sat back in his seat, and took a deep breath and let it out slowly.

Luke and Ricardo sat at one of the tables in the library at El Convento to survey their findings. Luke's heart was still beating loudly in his ears. He reopened the casing and the tin box. With gloved hands, he gently pulled the book from the sack once again and rested it on the table. While Ricardo looked on, Luke tried to open the pages of the book. They had stuck together over time, assuredly from countless summers and winters that it had endured inside the expanding and contracting wall of the old house. Once the outer edges had come apart, however, the pages separated with ease. He flipped through, observing the delicate paper and ancient writings. The style of the lettering and the faded ink made it difficult to decipher. Despite time and its minor weathering, the book had been astonishingly well-preserved from its wrappings and hiding place.

"Ricardo, does this look like Spanish to you?"

Luke handed the book over to Ricardo, and he looked inside.

"I'm not sure," he said. "Let me take a closer look."

Luke tapped his fingertips against the table as he watched Ricardo push his glasses up higher on his nose and lean forward. He slid his index finger across the page with a gloved hand, trying to interpret the time-worn writing.

"It *looks* like Spanish," Ricardo said. He sat back and rested his palms on his lap.

"Let me see." Luke took the book back and opened it to where the ribbon had marked the last written entry. The faded ink had bled through to the other side in some parts, making it all the more difficult as some of the words overlapped and blended together. He strained his eyes and blinked several times, trying to pick apart the letters.

"Ha! It's Ladino!" he shouted with a huge grin. He jumped up from his seat, grabbed his forehead, and ran his fingers through his thick, dark hair. "This is unbelievable! The person that wrote these pages was Sephardic, Ricardo! I knew it!" He threw his hands in the air and shouted, "Wooo!" slapping his hands on the table. "Here, take a look for yourself. Only someone Sephardic would have said 'Dio' without the *s*."

Ricardo took hold of the book and began to read in silence.

"What did you say your Sephardic grandfather's name was?"

"Benjamín Carvajal. Why?"

"You have to finish the passage. Start from the beginning." Ricardo carefully handed the book back to Luke.

He began to read slowly, trying to make out the words:

7 de Junio 1597

Aquí dejo, yo Catalina López Robledo, mis pensamientos, mis quejares y angustias metidos en las paderes de mi hogar. Que me perdone mi Dio. Pero, que se queden aquí arruinándose al lado de mi querido Corral de Almaguer y con todas las memorias de mi fe y el amor de mi vida, Benjamín Carvajal.[85]

Luke felt like the room had spun for half a second. "There it is…in black and white." He extended his arm toward the book with an open hand. This is my grandfather? That was his name." His voice was soft at the end. He sat back and put his hand over his mouth. *Unbelievable. Could it be?*

He wiped at a tear that had escaped from his eye, realizing that this was the evidence he had been searching for for so long. He stared at the document for a minute, then his heart fell to his knees.

---

[85] Here, I Catalina López Robledo, leave my thoughts, anguish and my pain stuck in between the walls of my home. May my G-d forgive me. But, let them go to ruin alongside my beloved Corral de Almaguer with all of the memories of my faith and the love of my life, Benjamín Carvajal.

"But my grandmother's name was not Catalina."

"Read on." Ricardo nodded and motioned toward the book with his hand. "See if there are more clues that will tell us who she was and how they knew each other. It could also be someone else with the same name."

"That's true." Luke continued to read aloud:

> *En unos días me caso con David Romero un hombre de honor que viene de una familia honrada y me huyo yo también. Voy a un nuevo mundo que me prometa mejor vida. Sé que estoy arriesgándome y dejando todo lo que siempre he amado y conocido. No sé que penas encontraremos, ni si es un viaje seguro. Pero, me tengo que alejar. Ha sido casi dos años que se fue Benjamín sin ninguna palabra y no puedo quedarme miserable esperando en vano su regreso. Aquí sin Benjamín y sin mi fe, mi vida no vale nada. Y aunque dejo estas páginas que he escrito y esta joya preciosa en este pader (de qué me sirven sin mi querido Benjamín), de seguro las llevaré metidas muy dentro de mi corazón. Así te llevo a ti también, Benjamín. Te amaré con toda mi alma y mi ser para la eternidad. Allí te veo, mi amor, un día en las estrellas del cielo.*[86]

Catalina's words crept deep into Luke's heart. He swallowed, feeling his words getting caught in the knot that had formed in his throat. "So my grandfather had a secret love. He sat back and pondered the idea. He must have known this woman before he had

---

[86] In a few days, I will marry David Romero, an honorable man who comes from an honorable family, and I too will flee. I am going to a new world that promises a better life. I know that it is risky and that I'm leaving behind all that I have ever known and loved. I don't know what worries we will encounter nor whether this trip is safe. But, I have to leave. It's been almost two years that Benjamin left without a word, and I can't stay here miserable, waiting in vain for his return. Being here without Benjamín and my faith, my life is worthless. And even though I am leaving these pages that I have written and this precious jewel in between these walls (what are they worth to me without my beloved Benjamín), surely, I am taking them with me within the deepest parts of my heart. I am taking you with me in the same way, Benjamín. I will love you with all of my soul and my being for eternity. I will see you again, my love, one of these days in the stars of the sky.

met my grandmother in Turkey, right? If it *is* my grandfather she's talking about."

Ricardo sat back in his chair and nodded.

"Do you think you can verify his age?"

"I think so. We have record of his age in Turkey when he married my grandmother."

"If they match, you just found what you've been looking for!"

"After all this time!" Luke ran a hand over his mouth. *It has to be him!*

"So, after that last entry, Luke," Ricardo began, "we can assume that Catalina López Robledo must have closed the pages of her book, placed it in the sack and inside this tin box, stuffed it in the hole that she had carved out inside the wall, and then fled to the Americas with her new husband David Romero...and never looked back." He threw a hand in the air. "This is an absolute priceless discovery, one that is going to be of interest to many people, including countless descendants. It's a miracle that this treasure has endured almost five centuries."

Ricardo turned the book over, studying it. "Luke, take a look at this pin. Did you see it?"

Luke was buzzing. He couldn't wait to share this news with his family...and with Ariana. He leaned toward Ricardo.

"I noticed something was attached, but I didn't take a close look." He gently took a wing from the butterfly brooch and lightly caressed the jewels with his gloved hand. "So unique...and delicate. I wonder how much it's worth or how old it is."

"There's definitely a lot of work to be done here. I will call Madrid and DU. They are going to want to examine what we've found and confirm its age and validity. I will take care of the paperwork, Luke." Ricardo patted him on the back. "You go share the wonderful news with your family!"

Luke could barely type the words in the message to his mother and father, his hands were shaking so badly. He couldn't pull the grin from his face. Then he decided to call Ariana. He was aware that he shouldn't, but he just had to share this with her, especially after how she had described the excavation site. He knew she would understand how important this discovery was to him and his family. He skipped up the steps, almost running to his room to make the call. He dialed the number. His shoes tapped against the marbled floors as did his fingertips on his thighs, hoping she was there.

"Hello." Her voice rose at the end of the word, like it was more of a question.

"Hi."

"Hey! Is everything ok? What was in that tin box? Are you allowed to talk about it?"

"Yeah, but don't tell anyone just yet. Ricardo is going to share it with the group after lunch. I'm sure everyone is wondering what happened, but I couldn't wait to tell you about it."

"It sounds serious."

"So, Ricardo told the group at the beginning that I was helping with the class partly to further my own research. Well, this discovery that literally fell into our hands is a huge breakthrough for me."

He paused again, Catalina's words appearing in his mind's eye. *Amazing.* She was quiet. Listening. He had her full attention.

"I think I finally found the evidence that links my family to Corral de Almaguer."

"That's great! But how? What did you find?"

"We found an ancient diary hidden in the box from a woman who lived in that house. Some of the writing is in Ladino—"

"Yes, the language your family speaks that you told me about in Madrid!"

"Exactly!" Luke exclaimed. *She remembered.* "In it she listed my grandfather's name as the love of her life!"

"Are you serious? It's unbelievable that you could actually trace your family back this far and to that house. What an incredible find!"

"Well, I'm not sure he lived there exactly. The woman wasn't my grandmother, and she talked about marrying someone else. But they must have had some sort of love affair from her words and the tone of her writings."

He stopped for a second as the name of Catalina's husband shot into his mind.

"Ariana, the man's last name was Romero. What do you know about your family history?"

"I don't know that much beyond San Luis in the 1850s. We've always been told our ancestry was Spanish, but I have no idea what that means exactly."

"The only way to know for sure is to trace your family line. There's about a two-hundred and fifty-year gap from the diary to what you know. Is it something you're at all interested in finding out?"

"Of course! Yes, I would love to know. For years, since I've been in college, I've had to explain myself and my background to people without really knowing for sure. We've never investigated the genealogy in my family personally, but there is a lady I know from home that has done a ton of research. If she doesn't have the information on hand already, I'm sure she would know where I could look."

She abruptly stopped her train of thought.

"Are you ok?" Luke had been hanging on her every word.

"Yeah," she said. "I'm just thinking about how nice it would be to finally have some evidence that could shed some light on our identity. I could finally say who I am and where I come from with confidence."

Luke liked the fact that Ariana was as interested as he was and enthusiastic about the idea that they *could* have this implausible tie to Spain. It certainly made sense to him.

"Ok, I can help if you want. I have some online tools you can use."

"That would be great, thank you."

"Listen, I better go. Ricardo is probably looking for me and lunch will be ready soon. About New York," he started. His voice took on a livelier tone. "I've taken care of everything. I just hope you can keep up with me *and* the city that never sleeps."

"Oh, you're on!" Ariana fired back.

He laughed, imagining the expression on her face as she said that and said, "I can't wait."

Chapter 8

Ariana

Ariana set her phone down and fell flat on her back on the bed. She was giddy. She had been wondering what had happened since they had left the site. When they had arrived to El Convento, Mari and Miguel were still busy preparing lunch. The fragrance had already begun to fill the lobby, sitting room, and dining area. Ariana's stomach had gnawed, reminding her that she hadn't eaten much that morning either. It had taken extra effort to climb the steps to her room, preoccupied with the dazed expression on Luke's face as he had walked toward the bus, holding the object as if it were fragile glass. Right before Luke's call, she had taken a shower and positioned herself cat-like into her comfy wing-back chair to read *Rain of Gold*. She had needed a distraction from Luke and her hunger pangs.

She had been reading the part where Lupe had seen herself in the mirror for the first time in California. She had initially thought that it was a beautiful woman walking toward her, then Lupe was stunned when she realized it was her own reflection. In that moment, she had understood what people had been saying to her about her beauty since she was a child. Ariana had been so enthralled in the book that hearing the phone had made her jump out of her skin. She sat up at the edge of the bed for a minute. A broad grin overtook her face. She grabbed for her keys and felt grateful that he had included *her* in his miraculous, very personal experience. It had taken their chemistry to a new depth.

As Ariana glided down the stairs toward the dining room, the chatter of the curious students broke her daze. She saw Luke and Ricardo setting up a display of what had to be the treasure they had found in the tin box. She walked over to them and brushed the tips of her fingers across Luke's back. He snapped around, undoubtedly surprised by her touch.

"Hi," she said.

"Hi, Ariana." Ricardo threw a hand up in a quick wave and continued pulling a folded red cloth from a box and snapping it out in front of him. He smoothed it over a wide, round table.

"H-hi!" Luke said, somewhat stammered.

Ariana watched him take an easel and the weathered tin box from a bin and place them on the table. Then he slowly pulled what looked like a book wrapped in purple velvet from a worn sack.

"This is what was in the tin box?" *Whoa.*

"Yes, please take a look. But be careful. We're not allowed to touch it with our bare hands." He had a wide grin like someone who had just won the lottery. With gloved hands, he gently set the book on the easel and laid the worn sack on the weathered tin box next to it.

Ricardo set a red velvet rope barrier with a big 'DO NOT TOUCH' sign attached to it in front of the display, wiped his brow and walked away. Ariana stared at the book and the brooch pinned to the cover. She was entranced by the same familiar energy from the excavation site. It was breathtaking. Enchanting. She swallowed. Mari, Miguel, and Roberto walked out with the lunch platters, and she sat down to eat with Deana, Ashley, and the rest of the students.

"What do you think of that display?" Deana shoveled a bite of tapas into her mouth.

"Is that what they found in the box today?" Ashley asked Deana, a thumb pointing behind her. "I wonder what it is."

Ariana pulled her napkin from her lap and wiped her mouth. "It's so exciting." She sat back like the Cheshire Cat, feeling grateful to have already heard the privileged information.

"Good afternoon, everyone." Ricardo raised his hand above his head to get everyone's attention. "I hope you enjoyed your unexpected free time. Luke and I have some exciting news to share about this extraordinary display that nearly knocked Drew out this morning." His arm aimed first to the display then toward Drew. The class laughed.

"Luke has made an important breakthrough in his research. He has been working to uncover any link that would tie his family to Corral de Almaguer where his grandfather was rumored to have lived. The book we found is a diary written by a woman who lived in the house

that is now our excavation site. The book lists his g[...]
in it. Luke, do you want to share what this means?"

Luke stood to his feet. "Sure. What this discove[...]
most of us already speculated, that this area was [...]
Jewish community during the Inquisition. This is the [...]
I'm hoping will prove that my fourteen times great-grandfather liv[...]
in Corral de Almaguer before escaping to Turkey. We still need to
confirm the age and timeframe. We had no other records before this
discovery.

"The bigger picture is that this diary provides firsthand accounts
of life in late Sixteenth Century Spain and of the Inquisition through
the eyes of a Sephardic woman who eventually succumbed to the
pressures of becoming a Converso or Jewish convert to Catholicism
to avoid trials or worse. She spoke of marrying another Converso and
leaving for the Americas, which many did at the time. It truly is a
blessing to have this in our hands because up to now, the only
accounts we have are through the perspective of the Inquisition
records."

Ariana gazed at Luke, admiring his excitement as he spoke. She
was fascinated with this discovery. Suddenly it occurred to her that
they had discussed a possible tie in her family to *this* woman and her
husband who had been Jewish. She shook her head. *Definitely a
different Romero family.*

"So, before we can continue any more work," Ricardo said, "the
archaeologists from Madrid have to come in to inspect the grounds
and the diary. Basically, what this means for you, unfortunately, is
that *our* work at the site is over, and thus our syllabus has also
changed.

"We have organized several guided tours for you, one for
tomorrow and one for Friday. You are still to continue your journals
every evening through Saturday. Your prompts are listed on the class
site where you will upload your entries upon your return. Sunday is a
free day. Some of you have expressed interested in attending some
sort of church service. You are welcome to do that.

"Your final assignment is a five-page paper tying the theory we
have read with the practice you have participated in and witnessed.
Please use all of the readings we have provided, our class discussions,
and include a bibliography in your work. The final part of your paper
should be your thoughts and opinions. A description of this

...ment and the rubric detailing how you will be graded is already ...our syllabus. It hasn't changed. This paper is due on Thursday by ...pm. Mari and Miguel are organizing a farewell party for us that evening, and we will leave for Madrid after lunch on Friday.

"We will spend the night there and head to the airport bright and early at 4:00am. Our flight leaves at 7:15am, and we don't want to be late."

No we do not. Ariana brought the tip of her index finger to her mouth and she tapped her lips. The thought of her much-anticipated date in New York gave her chills from head to toe.

Ricardo cleared his throat and pushed his glasses higher on his nose. "Please continue with your lunch and come to admire the diary. Let's meet back here promptly tomorrow morning after breakfast at 8:30, and I will introduce you to your guide. Luke and I will be with archaeologists from Madrid over the next few days to work at the site and travel to Madrid if need be. Enjoy your evening."

Ariana, Deana, and Ashley ate and discussed the new schedule for the rest of the course. Ariana chose to get a head start on her paper rather than going out for a walk with them. She walked slowly to the library and pondered the week ahead. As she neared the library, Ricardo was walking out.

"Ariana, can I talk to you for a moment?"

Oh no! He looks serious. Oh my gosh. Oh my gosh. He knows about me and Luke. She stopped in front of Ricardo. Her mouth went dry. "Of course. Is, uh, everything ok?"

"Yes, I just wanted to get your thoughts about the woman who wrote the diary.

Whew! The diary.

"Her name was Catalina Robledo and she married David Romero. Do these names sound familiar? Have you done any research into your ancestry? Think you might be related?"

"I don't know. We haven't done the research. I doubt there is any relation, though. What are the odds? She could have fled anywhere in Latin America where there are tons of other Romeros, right? And, besides, as far as I know, I come from generations of devout Catholics on both sides of my family. I don't think we could be connected to Sephardic Jews."

"Well, you know, Ariana, there exists pockets of what we call Crypto Jews all over Latin America and the American Southwest. Many of them congregated together and continued practicing their religion in secret once they arrived to the Americas. There are many historians and genealogists from New Mexico and Colorado that have already confirmed a relationship. Even though they were Catholic or Christian, some families had speculated this connection for years. Many had Jewish heirlooms in their homes or questioned certain practices, like not eating pork. But now with the development of genetic DNA technology, these speculations are proving what these families had already known. In fact, there was a study done several years ago in Southern Colorado that linked women from the area with a breast cancer gene that up to now had only been seen in Jews. You know, DNA study has opened the doors to ideas we never thought possible. I have found Jewish ties in my own family DNA in Chile. It could be worth looking into for you."

"Thanks, Ricardo," Ariana said. "I'll definitely consider it. Have a good evening."

He nodded, and she walked past him and into the library. She sat at a computer and rested her face in her hands. *Could I actually be a descendant of Sephardic Jews too?* She pulled the hair tie from her wrist and brought her hair up in a ponytail. *Breast cancer? That's scary. If I am Jewish, what does this mean for my health? Or my faith? I can't see myself following any other religion.* She decided she would table her thoughts and call Maria when she got home to see what she knows.

This was all too much to sift through right now. She plugged in her phone and flash drive and queued up her favorite playlist. Ariana loved music of many different kinds. It helped her focus when she worked, and sometimes the words of random songs often spoke to her heart at just the right time. She drew inspiration from it.

She chuckled to herself, thinking about how others would view her playlists. It was a motley combination of Top 40, New Mexican Spanish, Tejano, Salsa, Hip-hop, Old School, Country, and Classic Rock. She put her earbuds in, hit play, and got to work on her paper.

She wrote for a couple of hours until she made what she thought was pretty good progress and decided to send her family some of the pics she had already taken. She pulled up her photos and logged into Facebook. There was a message from Luke.

Mi Querida Ariana,

Thanks for listening today. I'm psyched about where this discovery will lead. I will be leaving to Madrid first thing tomorrow morning while you all are out touring. I won't be back until Saturday afternoon. In the meantime, I'll be thinking of you. Have a great time in Sevilla. You're going to love it.

She sat back in her seat. Her stomach sank at the thought of exploring Sevilla without him. She responded:

Thanks for trusting me enough to share your discovery. It means a lot. This work is really important to you, isn't it? I can see it in your eyes when you talk about it. Enjoy your time in Madrid. Looking forward to hearing all about it when you get back. I will be thinking of you too!

She sighed and switched gears, picking a few of her favorite pictures and sending them to her parents and to Liz. She gave them a short overview of what had happened that day and shared how it had changed the course of their class. She promised to write back soon and went back to her room to pack and get some rest for the tours ahead.

She hung out with Deana and Ashley as they walked the cobblestone streets of Corral de Almaguer. It was a much smaller town than Madrid, boasting only about six thousand inhabitants. Ariana's eyes were fixed on the impressive buildings on both sides of the street. They were whitewashed and looked like apartments attached to one another. Something soft pushed against her shoulder, impeding her steps.

"Hey!" The girl in front of her snapped.

Air caught in her throat and forced her eyes away from the second story wrought-iron balconies filled with overflowing, colorful flowers long enough to realize that she had run into the girl's backpack nearly knocking her into the student in front of *her.*

"Oh my gosh! I'm so sorry!" Ariana placed a hand on the girl's shoulder. "I should have been paying more attention."

"Don't worry about it." The girl was clearly annoyed. "Just be careful next time."

"I will." *So-rry.*

Their next stop was the *Ayuntamiento* or Town Hall, *Plaza de los Mártires* and *La Ermita de la Virgen de La Muela*. In each space, Ariana was struck by its architecture and the beauty it espoused. All the streets and parks were so clean. Her mind returned to the neat, well-maintained rows of olive trees on those rolling hills with which she had become so familiar. Everything was so well-kept, but she never really saw anyone working. *When does it all get done?*

The most notable edifice Ariana had seen that day was that of *Nuestra Señora de la Asunción*. When Ariana walked slowly inside, she held her breath for a second when the grand altar at the front caught her attention. This church was unlike any other she had seen before. For a second, she focused on the enormous Baroque painting behind the altar centered in between huge golden pillars flanked with statues of saints on either side. The painting depicted the Assumption of Mary into heaven. She wiped at the corners of her eyes and swallowed the lump in her throat. *What faith these people must have had to construct all of these buildings dedicated to Catholicism.* She genuflected at the first pew and made the sign of the cross.

Her eyes followed the altar up towards the ceiling and moved about from one stone wall to the other. She stared at the giant curved arches that framed both sides of the pews, and the entire length of the church made her lightheaded. She grabbed onto the smooth top of one of the pews and slid into the seat. She knelt down and cupped her hands against her forehead. There was a peaceful presence here.

She sat back and wondered when the church had been built. All of the statues and images of the *Virgen*[87] and the *santos*[88] reminded her of the ones that adorned the trail climbing the mesa in San Luis. Realizing she was alone, she stood to walk out. She grabbed a bulletin from a stack she found on a table at the back of the church and stuffed it in her backpack, hoping it would have service information in it. This is where she wanted to attend Mass on Sunday.

They drove to Toledo to eat at a restaurant that Ricardo had recommended. He had already made reservations that would accommodate all of the students and the guide. The restaurant was busy, but their table was ready. Inside, the tables were covered in

---

[87] Virgin Mary
[88] Saints

white table cloths and set with breadsticks, bottles of water, and cloth napkins. Everyone took their place and ordered their meals.

Ariana sat with Deana and Ashley, and they compared the souvenirs each had bought and the pictures they had taken. Unsure of what to order, Ariana asked for the *ensalada mixta* and *arroz Toledana*[89]. It seemed to be a safe bet. She wished Luke was here to help her make her decision.

When their food arrived, Ariana was pleasantly surprised. The *calamares* in the arroz melted in her mouth. That had been the ingredient she was least sure about. Everywhere they went, the food had a different taste from home. It had a richness that tickled her taste buds. She slept on the bus ride back to El Convento with her ear buds in her ears and wondered how Sevilla would fare in comparison to the appeal and beauty of Corral de Almaguer.

They arrived in Sevilla around lunchtime the next day. They had made a pit stop in the alluring city of Córdoba to visit *La Mezquita*. Ariana's footsteps and those of the other students had echoed in the giant, airy inner space of the church. She had walked around, letting her fingers glide along one of the tons of marble pillars that were bearing the load of the fantastic red and white striped arches, which were even larger and more intimidating than the ones in the church in Corral de Almaguer. *Absolutely gorgeous! It doesn't even look like a church in here.* The guide had shared that many of the cathedrals in Spain originated as Moorish Mosques, particularly in Southern Spain, and then had been converted to Catholic Cathedrals. Many of them still carried the characteristics of medieval North African culture, including a minaret and grove of orange trees.

The shops around the *Mezquita* were decorated with different souvenirs, including colorful plates each exquisitely hand-painted in unique, complex designs. Ariana chose a few in colors and patterns she thought her mom and grandmother might like and purchased them. The drive to Sevilla was a considerably longer drive than the one from Madrid to El Convento, and the city was a much bigger metropolis than Córdoba and Corral de Almaguer, but as they entered the heart of the city, the familiar narrow cobblestone streets and wrought iron balconies filled with colorful flowers evoked the same flavor of the smaller towns.

---

[89] Mixed salad and Toledo-style rice

The bus stopped in a parking spot off of *La Calle de la Constitución,* and nothing could have prepared Ariana for what she was about to see when she walked out of the bus. Standing before her in all its majesty was *La Catedral de Sevilla,* a massive structure that soared well over the city and spanned at least three square city blocks. Its architecture, worn with age, they were told, had been constructed beginning in the mid-1400s but took over one hundred years to build. It was the largest Gothic structure in the world and the third largest cathedral in Europe with only St. Peter's Basilica in Rome and St. Paul's in England ampler in size.

Ariana blinked several times and rubbed the goose bumps on her arms. She was rooted to her spot as she took in its enormity and its ancient significance. Inside, she was overwhelmed as she tried to contain all of the sights surrounding her. Several small chapels were built in along the inside walls. The main golden altar in the center, with its endless statues of various *santos* and images of the *Virgen,* reached high into the enormously vaulted ceilings.

She knelt down in one of the pews and made the sign of the cross. She closed her eyes and prayed. Ariana concluded that the builders had succeeded in their goal to "have a church of such a kind that those who see it built will think we were mad."[90] Even though it was airy, built of cold, hard stone, and tourists were sprawled throughout, Ariana still felt the sweet presence of the divine enveloping her, like she and God had had a moment in there. A peaceful tranquility made her smile.

The *Giralda* tower, with its never-ending winding incline, was a gigantic over-exaggeration of the staircase at El Convento. At the top, Ariana stood for a minute to try to capture the breathtaking view of the modern, tall buildings, old churches, and rusty-pink Spanish-tiled rooftops that were held up by white-washed walls zig-zagging every which way, blending the ancient with the contemporary. But, as usual, her camera phone fell short of what could be seen with the naked eye.

The official tour ended as the students continued exploring Sevilla on their own for the next few hours until the next scheduled event. Ariana walked through the narrow, curvy cobblestone streets with Deana and Ashley. It was like a maze and had been designed in complete contrast to those she was used to in Denver that paralleled

---

[90] http://www.sacred-destinations.com/spain/seville-cathedral

one another and came together in complete ninety-degree corners. If it weren't for her detailed map, Ariana knew they'd never find their way back to the bus.

"I'm hungry," Ariana said with an open hand against her tummy.

"Me too," Ashley agreed. "But every place I see is closed!"

"They take this siesta thing serious here," added Deana.

Ariana was impressed that even in this huge city, and in this day and age, this time-honored tradition was still golden. They finally came to a place near *La Plaza Nueva* across from the *Ayuntamiento* and a bank that was open. They sat outside on wrought-iron tables and chairs under a green awning and ordered some tapas. Ariana put her hair up in a ponytail and fanned herself with the menu. An older gentleman wearing a fedora caught her attention. He was sweeping the walk of a store front across the street. He tipped his hat, greeting her. She waved back. *I love it here.*

"Look at all the palm trees." Ariana pointed in the vicinity of a cluster with her nose.

"Yeah, it's much more humid here than Corral de Almaguer." Deana wiped her forehead with her cloth napkin. "I can feel it in my skin."

"What's that smell?" Ashley took a deep breath with her eyes closed.

"I think it's the orange blossoms." Ariana twisted her neck toward a row of trees alongside the sidewalk across from them. A light breeze refreshed her face, making her smile. "It smells so good."

"Ok, I need a drink to cool me down." Ashley leaned forward to scan the drink menu.

"What about this *tinto de verano*? It has the word 'summer' in it." Ariana pulled her chair back and fanned herself some more before laying the menu back on the table. "It should be good, right?"

"Can't hurt!" Deana shrugged her shoulders.

When their tapas and tintos de verano came, the drink hit their palate like heaven on that hot day. Ariana wondered if Luke had had this drink before. She had thought about him all day as she witnessed the landscape and impressive, ancient architecture on their tour. She hoped things were going well in Madrid, but more than anything, she wished her phone worked here so she could text him.

The three of them finished their food and drinks, window-shopped, and then walked back toward the bus. They rested in their hotel for a while before meeting their guide again for their evening activity.

Bringing cocktail attire for dinner and a Flamenco show had been in the email about the tours, and this had piqued Ariana's interest. She slipped on her favorite little black cocktail dress, fixed her hair in an up do with strands framing her face, and applied her make-up. She slid on her heels, draped the black lace shawl with the tiny purple tulips that she had bought in a shop in Corral de Almaguer over her shoulders, and walked over to Deana and Ashley's room.

They walked down to the bus together and rode to the show. The meal was delicious, three courses including an appetizer with *jamón*, their choice of entrée, and flan for dessert. The meat was especially tender in its sauce and the potatoes were like butter in her mouth. They drank red wine with their dinner and had mint tea with a leaf still in it with their dessert. Ariana wondered how the women here kept their figures so slim with all of this rich, delicious food. She never saw a diet anything on any menu or in any store they went into.

The show kept Ariana at the edge of her seat. The music of the flamenco guitar was soulful and rhythmic, and the stylistic vocals unique. Most of the dances were of several couples on stage with the women waving their colorful dresses to the beat of the music and making anticipated abrupt steps in synch with their partners. But one of the dances that featured a couple dancing to a slower, more romantic rhythm had Ariana in a trance. They seemed to flow together on air and in union with the music of the guitar. Her eyes began to overflow, and when she looked over, Ashley and Deana had the same look on their faces. They turned to look at her and began to laugh when they saw each other feeling the same thing.

Ariana sniffed and grabbed a tissue from her small purse. She wanted Luke's shoulder to lean on right now. Butterflies tumbled around inside, reminding her that they would be back at El Convento tomorrow and he would be back from Madrid.

After the show, they walked to *La Plaza España*; the half-moon shaped building glowed in the light of the moon and the street lights. The water in the canal that paralleled the building glistened as it flowed through, carrying tourists and locals alike on small boats. Ariana watched the families with small children still out strolling at this time of night with curiosity. It had to be after 10:00. *Such a different lifestyle from home.*

Back at the hotel, Ariana changed to her pajama tank and shorts, washed her face, and brushed her teeth. She had declined an invitation to go down to the bar with the girls and some of the guys from the class. There was too much on her mind right now. She didn't feel like having surface conversations or hearing more of the shallow remarks she had already heard some of the other students making regarding the heat, the changes in the course, and the lack of people in the restaurants and other businesses who spoke English. She didn't feel like drinking either. For that, she could have been in San Luis. She was happier being drunk in her thoughts of Luke and the sights she had seen over the past two days.

Instead, Ariana lay in her bed and flipped through all of her photos. She said a prayer, thanking God for this grand experience. This trip had been nothing like she had predicted it might be. Every day surpassed her expectations. Other than learning more about archaeology, she thought she might get to see a little bit of Spain and maybe practice her Spanish a little. She never thought two short weeks would have been enough time for much to happen, let alone would she have imagined that in only one week her world would be turned upside down.

She stared into nothing for a bit, thinking about that, and then pulled out her *Rain of Gold* book and flipped to the page held by her bookmark. She read about when Lupe and Sal met and fell in love and how Sal kept his lucrative bootlegging business from her as they courted, fearful that he could lose her since she came from such a religious, proper family. She fell into a deep sleep once again, dreaming of her and Luke wading in the surf of Oceanside, California wearing summer attire from the 1920s.

The drive back to Corral de Almaguer from Sevilla the next day had seemed longer than their initial drive there. Ariana was eager to see Luke. She was anxious to hear all about his work and what the next steps were with the diary. Her jitters had the best of her even though she tried to calm herself.

When they arrived at El Convento, Ariana felt a warm sensation through her when she saw the back of Luke's head sitting across from Ricardo at a table in the dining room. Their conversation looked intense at first until Luke began to laugh and then so did Ricardo. The aroma of Mari's lunch overloaded her senses as the dining room got closer. She just knew she had already gained at least five pounds in the last week from all the mouthwatering food that was constantly in her face. Her eyes met with Luke's, making her heart hammer away.

She said hello in passing and made her way to her room to unpack and freshen up for lunch. Some of the other students stopped to share the excitement of what they had done on their excursions and to ask about the diary. She could tell from the look on Luke's face and how his eyes followed her as she passed by that he had missed her, too. She had so much to say to him, and the fact that she couldn't drove her crazy…and small talk was still not an option. A part of her thought that the end of this course couldn't come any faster, yet she was enjoying Spain so much, she didn't want it to end.

After lunch that afternoon, some of the students organized a co-ed soccer game using a ball they had found in the lobby. Ariana played for a while, but after running around for some time, she left to work on her paper. The lack of ready access to technology at hand was frustrating. She wanted to read her email on her phone or scroll through her Facebook newsfeed without having to go down to the library. It was time for a change of scenery. *The patio! I'll take my laptop up there.*

Ariana gathered her things and took the long, winding flight of creaky steps to the patio. *Awesome! No one's here.* She wasn't sure any of the other students even knew the patio existed—a nice secret for the time being. She stood at the patio wall, placed her hands on it, and breathed in the clean, campo air. She closed her eyes. The sound of the river and birds filled her ears, and a slight cool breeze refreshed her. Her eyes opened to the small farms, the hills, and the rows of olive trees in the distance. *So peaceful.* She felt the stiffness in her shoulders release.

The sudden screeches of Deana and Ashley and some of the other girls cheering for certain players on the teams below interrupted the moment. *Ugh.* She found a bench, popped her earbuds in her ears, and continued her writing. She was on a roll, weaving in and out of theory, practice, and her opinion when a warm hand landed on her shoulder. She jumped, feeling the blood drain to her feet as her notebook and pencil fell to the floor. She grabbed for her earbuds that had slipped out of her ears and looked up. The palm of her hand went straight to her forehead then over her heart which was still racing. She shook her head.

"I'm sorry," Luke said. He was clearly amused. "I didn't mean to scare you. You were going to town on that keyboard. It was pretty impressive!"

"How long have you been there?" She was still trying to catch her breath.

"Not too long. Just long enough to hear you singing Hotel California." He sang in a high-pitched voice imitating her. "Nice voice," he added, still chuckling.

Ariana felt her cheeks turn beet red.

"Whatever." She smacked him on the shoulder with the notebook she had picked up from the floor. "I can sing."

"Ok, ok. I believe you…no need to get violent." His laughter only seemed to increase more.

"What are you doing here?" Ariana asked after she had situated herself again.

"I knew you'd be up here."

"What do you mean?"

"Well, I tried to call you, and you didn't answer, so I figured I'd find you here."

"We probably shouldn't be up here together."

He sat next to her on the bench, picked up her pencil that had rolled to the floor again, and handed it to her.

"I know. But I couldn't wait to talk to you."

Dang. Her heartbeat had almost begun to feel normal again until she took the pencil from him. She couldn't help but notice that his ocean-blue eyes were interrupted by intermittent flecks of gold that reflected in the sunlight. On top of that, warmth radiated from his body next to her, and the subtle airiness of his cologne enveloped her senses.

He smiled, and his eyes fell to the patio floor. "How was your trip?" His voice was soft and gentle as his gaze returned to her.

She looked out at the vastness of the campo, and the corners of her own mouth turned up. Her feet crossed and swayed back and forth under the bench as visions of La Mezquita, Plaza España, and La Catedral de Sevilla moved in frames through her mind.

"Oh my gosh, it was amazing."

Somehow, she could still smell the enticing scent of *azahar* as they walked past the orange trees in the square in Sevilla. She saved her work and placed her laptop on the floor next to the bench. She put her feet up and crisscrossed her legs.

"Everywhere we went just got better and better." She picked up her phone, found her camera roll, and scrolled through to the pics from Sevilla. "Take a look at these."

"I knew you would love it." He took her phone.

"I thought of you everywhere we went."

"I like this one." He showed her a picture that Deana had taken of her in front of the Plaza España in her little cocktail dress.

"Thanks." *Has the temperature just increased out here?* "How was Madrid? Do you have any more news about the diary?"

"Well, they kept it to verify its authenticity, and they wanted to analyze and appraise the brooch to find out where it was made, how long ago, and how much it could be worth. It's pretty exciting."

"Sounds like it. Did you tell your family?"

"Yes, they're pretty psyched. This is just more evidence now that we can use to apply for dual citizenship."

"What do you mean?"

"Well, Spain and Portugal have both signed laws into effect that will allow anyone who can prove ancestral ties to Sephardic Judaism during the Inquisition to apply for dual citizenship. It's a way to make amends for what happened."

Ariana sat up straight. She pictured the diary in her mind, and the same enchanting energy she had felt next to it waved over her again. "So, this is serious stuff. It's not just about finding out where your family comes from then. It could actually have major implications for many descendants."

"Yeah, it's a pretty big deal. That's why you should look into it, too." He nudged her with his elbow.

She smiled but didn't say anything.

He waited a second for her to respond. A glimmer of anticipation came across his face. But she didn't know what to say. *I just can't see it.*

"Anyway, I read the whole diary and took pictures of it and the pages. I especially wanted those that had my grandfather's name in it."

"Is that ok? Are you sure it's really him?"

"I'm almost positive it's him. We were always told he was from Toledo. My mom confirmed the age from our records. It has to be. Taking the pictures should be fine. I'm not going to publish them or anything. I just needed to have *something* in case I never get to see the diary again."

"That makes sense. I would have probably done the same thing." She watched him as he continued scrolling through the photos and said, "You know, I was captivated every place we stopped and…I don't know…I found myself getting frustrated with some of the students in the group. I mean, they're fun and everything, but I kept getting irritated with their attitudes and comments."

He put the phone down and gave her his full attention as she continued.

"It was like…no big deal to them. Maybe I'm just a small-town girl with little experience outside of my little world, and I realize that most of them don't have any connection to Spain, and some of them *are* just here to have something to do for the summer, but it means so much more to me than that. I mean, many of my ancestors walked here and played here and fell in love here. Sometimes it was almost like I could feel their presence wherever I went, like I was walking in their footsteps. And all *they* wanted to do was party after the Flamenco show and complain about the heat or other silly things. Don't get me wrong, I like a good drink as much as the next person, but there was so much on my mind…I just wasn't into it."

She stopped when she noticed that he was gazing at her and realized that she was probably babbling again.

"I'm sorry." She lowered her head and flicked an eraser shaving from her lap. "It's just that…I wanted to experience all those things—"

"With someone who appreciates it like you do."

Her head twisted quickly toward him, surprised he knew. "Yes."

"I know. That's why I wanted to see you. I thought you might want someone to talk to." He looked up at the sky, cupped his hands together, and then looked back at her. "Looks like I was right."

He pulled her toward him and held her. His arms were strong and secure. His warmth melted away the tension that had returned to her shoulders. Her eyes closed, and their breathing began to synchronize. A sudden flash of Ricardo's disapproving face swept through Ariana's mind. *What if he comes up here now? What if he sees us?* She shifted and opened her eyes. And just as quickly as the thought came, it left when her eyes met with his. Instead, she focused on his mouth, which was only inches away from her own. *Oh, so tempting!*

84

His hand followed the curve of her face to her shoulder and down to her hand, and he squeezed it.

"Just a few more days and we'll be in New York. I better go."

Ariana nodded, unable to move as he stood up to leave. She watched him open the door.

"Stop checking out my booty," he teased without turning around.

His comments interrupted her gaze and made her laugh out loud. She shook her head and rolled her eyes, letting herself fall back into the bench. She let out a quiet scream as he walked out. She threw her hands in the air and then slapped them on her lap. She sat like that for a minute, without moving, trying to control her own temperature that *she knew* had just risen several notches. Then she took a deep breath, picked up her computer, put her earbuds back in her ears, and continued her work until it started to get dark.

The next day, Miguel and Mari drove Ariana and several other students to Mass at *Nuestra Señora de la Asunción*. Ariana knelt down to pray and make her wish. She had always been told by her aunts that if she made a wish when she entered a new church that it would come true. This time it would be a little tricky. Her biggest wish had already come true. She closed her eyes, and it came to her.

Mass was uplifting. One of the things she loved so much about Mass and her Catholic faith was its steadiness and predictability. It was something on which she could always rely. Aside from the meaning and purpose behind each section of the Mass, she appreciated that she could be anywhere in the world and it would be the same format regardless of the language.

She got back to El Convento feeling at peace. The next few days ahead were spent writing and re-writing her final paper. Most of the students were hard at work. They had breakfast, worked until lunch, and then again until dinner. Luke and Ricardo were busy grading journals, meeting with students, and working with the archaeologists from DU and Madrid.

When she had finished on Wednesday evening, Ariana uploaded her paper to the class site along with her last journal entry and sat back, feeling accomplished and satisfied. She looked for Deana and Ashley to see if they wanted to take a long walk to Corral de Almaguer to have a tinto de verano with her. She felt like she deserved a refreshing drink after all that hard work. But it was late, and they were nowhere to be found. *Rain of Gold is the perfect way to end the evening then.* Once again, she curled up in her wing-backed chair and got lost in Lupe, Sal, and the traditional shrewdness of their mothers.

Chapter 9

Luke

On Thursday evening, Ricardo gathered the students in the dining room to lead them to the rooftop patio. Luke's foot tapped on the marble-tile floors as he waited for the signal from Ricardo to open the patio door. It made him cringe to hear some of the students grumbling about not having a party. They had been whispering loudly to each other about why there were no decorations or food in the dining room. On the other hand, he knew what their reaction would be once they got to the top, and that would make the wait worth it. Ricardo nodded Luke's way, and he walked over to the door behind the front desk that led to the creaky, winding staircase and up to the patio, and the students followed.

Luke opened the patio door and smiled when the décor came into view. He knew Miguel and Mari would go all out, and they didn't disappoint, and neither did the weather, for that matter. It was dusk, but not quite dark yet. Tiki torches and strings of white lights surrounded the perimeter of the patio. At the far end, there was a long table dressed in white linen with Mari's usual spread, and a barrel of sangria sat in the corner. Some tables and chairs had been placed near the buffet. In the middle, against an inner wall, a man and a woman had set up their equipment and began playing flamenco music.

"You look so handsome, hijo." Mari greeted Luke with a hug and a kiss on each cheek.

"*¡Bellísima, Mari, gracias!*" He walked past Miguel and Roberto, shaking their hands, patting them on the back, and giving them a thumbs up as they welcomed the students. Everyone was dressed in cocktail attire for the event. Once everyone had taken a seat, Mari cleared her throat and invited everyone to serve themselves and enjoy the music.

Luke explored the ambience, fixing his eyes on the outstanding guitarist as his fingers worked the guitar. His voice and that of the woman singing with him flowed together in perfect harmony. He made his way to the buffet table and grabbed a plate. He was contemplating his choices when Ariana's melodic voice unexpectedly sung in his ear from behind him. He fumbled his grasp on the spoon he was about to use for the *ensalada de tomate*.

"I love this music," she said.

He flipped around to see her take a glass of sangria from the server.

"Yeah, these two are awesome." He served some of the *ensalada* onto his plate and tried to steady his hand. "They were here the last time I was here. They are a husband and wife team."

"No wonder they harmonize so well together."

His eyes followed her as she walked back toward her table. Her hips swayed in her heels and sundress, and her thick, wavy hair hung long past the middle of her back. He swallowed. In a coy tilt of her head over her shoulder, she glanced back at him and caught him watching her walk away. He smiled, and so did she. He found a seat and took a sip of the sangria he had poured for himself. *Can't wait 'till we get to New York.*

The dance floor began to fill as people finished their dinner. At intermission, the musicians put on *Feel It Still* by Portugal. The Man, and Deana and Ashley were in hysterics over Drew, the guy who had almost been hit by the diary, and some of his friends at their outrageous dance moves. Luke laughed and walked toward the patio wall. The dark expanse of the campo was tranquil and inviting. He leaned forward against the wall and rested his elbows on top. His thoughts trailed back to the night at Adam's Bar Mitzvah and how much things had changed over the course of the past few weeks. He had found his bookstore girl and was more intrigued by her every day. On top of that, he had found the diary that proved his family's ties to Corral de Almaguer. He would remember these two weeks forever.

He sure was going to miss this place—again. And he didn't know when he would be able to come back. Ricardo and the archaeology team from Madrid had shared that there were many projects he could get involved with here if he was interested. His father's voice sobered the thoughts in his mind, *"Luke, you've got to grow up some time. I'm*

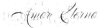

not sure why you even applied to that school in Colorado. NYU is waiting for you and so is the firm'"

On the other hand, he recalled the honest and poetic words Catalina had poured out onto the pages of the diary. It had almost felt like an invasion of privacy to read it, but he had to know. He wanted to feel what she had been feeling at that time. He wanted to imagine himself there at that specific second in history, to witness the lives she and his great-grandfather had lived as she described them with vivid detail. It was an invaluable gift. How could his dad not see that?

He took a deep breath, trying to unloose the knot that had begun to form in his stomach. He didn't want reality to hit just yet. He turned back to the dance floor and found Ariana dancing in step with the group; he had to pull back his cheesy grin. He had just returned his gaze toward the campo when he felt her presence, giving him chills.

"Fun night, eh?" She placed a gentle hand on his upper back. He glanced her way as she stood next to him still trying to catch her breath. Her cheeks and forehead were a pink hue and were shimmering against the patio lights from her dancing.

"Yeah, for sure." He tried to hide the bitter sweetness that had overtaken his mood. He must not have hidden it that well because when her face met with his, she asked, "You ok?" with genuine concern.

"Huh? Um, yeah. Of course." Thoughts of his dad floated away with the breeze as his focus shifted toward her. "You looked great out there."

"Thanks." She quickly looked away and down at her shoes. He smiled. "It's all Deana. She rocks. You know she's in a dance company in Seattle."

"No, I didn't know that." He had been thinking of *her* moves as she had tried to learn the steps to the line dance Deana had taught them.

She definitely had rhythm. He looked out over the patio again. The sky was clear. The stars sparkled above, and they spilled far out onto the horizon. The guitarist began the intro to *Sueño* by the Gypsy Kings, and out of nowhere, a shooting star shot through the sky, followed by another a few seconds later.

Ariana and Luke turned toward one another with their eyes wide. Luke heard some of the other students reacting to the marvel murmuring '*Wow*' and '*Did you see that?*' throughout the patio as many of them had stopped to look at the sky.

Mari stepped over to where Luke and Ariana were standing. Her eyes were shining, and she had a clever grin on her face. "*Maravilloso, ¿no? ¿No sabéis la leyenda de la estrella fugaz?*"[91]

"No," they replied simultaneously. Ariana's mouth gaped open, and her fingers were splayed wide across her chest. Luke crossed his arms and leaned in closer to Mari to hear this 'legend' she was about to share with them. *This can't be happening for the third time.* They had each seen this occurrence on separate occasions, and now they were witnessing it together.

"*Vale, menos mal, menos mal. Se los cuento,*" she began. "*Siglos atrás decían que cuando veía uno a una estrella fugaz es que había algún ser en el cielo que te había escogido para guiarte y ayudarte en todos los esfuerzos de la vida, especialmente el amor. Daba un sentimiento de paz y calma al saber que había seres contigo más allá de lo conocido...Dos estrellas, diría yo, es mucho más significante.*"[92]

She looked at them both and squeezed their shoulders. Then she looked at Luke and pinched his cheek vigorously, saying, "*¡Mi alma! Te quiero como mi propio hijo.*"[93]

Ariana laughed as she watched him wince. The light, mellow notes from the song the musicians were playing tugged at Luke to dance with Ariana, but he needed to make sure he had Ricardo's permission first. He scanned the dim-lit patio and found Ricardo across the dance floor leaning against the buffet table, ankles crossed, like he had been watching the whole time. Luke's heartbeat quickened. He gave Ricardo a plea with his eyes and a tilt of his head. Ricardo pushed his glasses up higher on his nose and ran his hand through his curly hair. He put out his hand toward the dance floor and tilted his head, as if giving in to the significance of the moment. Luke smiled. He had to take advantage of the opportunity.

---

[91] Amazing, right? Do you know the legend of the shooting star?

[92] Ok, good, good. I will tell you. Centuries ago, it was said that when one saw a shooting star it was that someone in the heavens had chosen you to guide you and help you in the struggles of life, especially love. It was peaceful and calming knowing that there was someone out there in the unknown with you...Two stars, I would say is much more significant.

[93] My darling! I love you like my own son!

He reached for Ariana's hand, and she followed him to the middle of the floor while some of the students looked on, including Deana and Ashley. Luke placed one hand on the small of Ariana's back and took the other hand in his. Ariana placed her hand on his shoulder. His gaze met her apprehensive, hazel eyes, and he pulled her close and secure. His insides were trembling. They floated around the patio floor in step with the rhythms of the flamenco guitar, engrossed in one another, and those with the eyes to see watched the sun surrounding them. She leaned her head on his shoulder, and he heard her sigh. She had goosebumps from his warm breathing on her neck. He closed his eyes and folded his arm, bringing her hand to his chest. The heat between them and the warmth of the evening transported him to another world.

When the song ended, he hugged her close and whispered in her ear, "Thank you for the dance, mi querida Ariana."

"Thank *you*."

He smiled as Ariana barely got the words out. Luke glanced at Ricardo as he walked toward the patio door. He was exchanging glances with Mari. With any luck, Luke wouldn't be hearing about this when they were back in the States, but he was grateful Ricardo hadn't had the heart to say no. Ariana had been bliss in his arms. Delicate and soft. The sweet scent of her made him crazy. There would be no way to hide what he was feeling. He had to get out of there fast. He hoped she understood. He exhaled deeply as he trotted down the steps. It was only a matter of hours now before they could be together freely.

Ariana

The next morning was a whirlwind in the halls and in the lobby as the students checked out of their rooms. Ariana pulled out her checklist to ensure she would remember everything. She stood at the door of her princess suite as she walked out and paused, imprinting everything in her mind for the last time. She looked over every nook and cranny, took a deep breath, and held it. The memories from this trip were written on her heart forever. She relived last night once more in her mind. She could still hear his words, '*Mi querida Ariana*', as they tickled her ear, sending massive chills throughout her entire body, and she was butter again, as she knew she would be, upon hearing that sweet name out loud coming straight from his mouth.

He had looked just like a page right out of GQ in his black slacks and purple button-down shirt. She hoped Deana and Ashley hadn't freaked out. She had seen them watching them dance, eyeing one another with eyebrows lifted and smirks on their faces. She ran her fingers through her hair. How would she explain herself if they asked?

With an air of gratitude, she glanced around yet again, took a step into the hall, and closed the creaky door. In the lobby, Mari and Miguel were saying goodbye to the students and wishing them safe travels as they exited El Convento and boarded the bus. Ariana returned her key to Roberto who was checking the students out at the front desk and thanked him for everything.

Then she walked over and looked at Miguel and Mari as she blinked her tears away. She was truly going to miss them and this magical place. She reached over to hug Miguel and say goodbye. Then she stood before Mari.

Mari took her hands and hugged her, saying, *"Bendiciones, bella hija...fue un gran placer de conocerte."*[94]

"Te voy a extrañar muncho."[95] Ariana sniffled and wiped her eyes.

"Vuelva a visitarnos, hija...y trae toda tu familia la próxima vez."[96]

"Sí, de seguro, Mari...Gracias por todo."[97] She pondered the possibility, yet *improbability* of returning with her family as she walked away.

The rocks cracked under the heavy bus as it rolled away on the dirt road with all of the students, Luke, Ricardo, and their luggage heading toward Corral de Almaguer and onto the highway to Madrid. The reality that the trip had ended had set in with all the students, making it uncharacteristically quiet.

Ariana peeked to the front of the bus where Luke and Ricardo sat together and then plopped back in her seat with her earbuds in her ears and looked out the window, savoring the landscape again, not sure when she would ever have the opportunity to come back.

---

[94] Blessings, beautiful daughter...It was a great pleasure meeting you.
[95] I will miss you very much.
[96] Come and visit again...and bring your whole family next time.
[97] Yes, of course...Thank you for everything

They arrived at their hotel in Madrid late in the afternoon. Ariana found a table in the lobby café next to a window and sat down with her lunch. She looked out at the passersby and the ornate detail of the building across the street. *I'll be with Luke in New York tomorrow!* She cleared her throat and scooted her chair in closer to the table, quickly bridling her excitement when Deana and Ashley joined her. The butterflies, however, continued flapping around within her.

"I can't believe it's over already," Deana said. She put her receipt and change back in her purse and set her food down.

"Me either." Ashley sat back in her seat and pulled her knees to her chest. "Feels like we just got here."

"I know," Ariana said. Her voice was soft as she stared blankly at the display of baked goods near the cash register. "I thought this day wouldn't get here fast enough."

"What?" Deana asked.

She broke her gaze and saw them look at each other and then at her with confusion pushing their brows together.

"Oh…I mean, uh, I was hoping this day wouldn't get here this fast."

They nodded, obviously still confused about what she had tried to say. She let it go, knowing it was impossible to clarify.

"Ok…so…that was some dance last night, Ariana." Deana poked at her arm with mischief taking over her face.

"Yeah, what was that all about?" Ashley asked. She leaned toward Ariana and rested her elbows on the table, her expression probing for more info.

Ariana began feeling the back of her neck getting warm. "Uh, yeah…we were in the moment…the shooting stars and all…I was the first person in front of him…you know…someone had to dance to that beautiful song." Her voice trailed off.

They roared with laughter. Deana fell back in her seat, and Ashley let her legs drop before folding over.

"You are so full of it!" Deana yelled in between breaths.

"Yup, you guys were sizzling out there! You could cut the chemistry between you two with a knife!" Ashley added. She scooted toward Ariana again. "Are you blushing?"

Ariana laughed, feeling her hands starting to shake. She lifted her hair and tied it in a knot. The back of her neck was fully sweating now.

"Uh, that's *tension*, Ashley. You could cut the tension with a knife. And, well, what can I say, you did say once that he was a *beautiful man*, right?"

Ricardo lifted his arm high in the air and waved his hand to get their attention. *Saved!* He reiterated how crucial it was for them to be ready to go by 4 am.

"It takes roughly an hour to get there from here, and with an international flight, we don't need any delays. I've already checked the flight information. Everything is on time right now."

On that note, Ariana went to her room to get some rest. She knew she was going to need to reserve some energy for the next few days for her adventure in New York. She wanted to look her best, and jet lag was going to be her enemy.

They left early the next morning before the sun came up, declared their souvenirs, and boarded their flight on time. She located Luke and Ricardo in their seats on the massive airliner, which had three rows of seats and two aisles, and leaned back into her own. Knowing where he was comforted her. Soon they were in the air, and watching the little airplane in the air on the monitor just made Ariana's jitters jab at her all the more. She took out her book from her bag and read for a while before falling asleep. She dreamt of stars in the sky, a flamenco guitar, and she and Luke making vats of whiskey on the patio of El Convento.

When Ariana awoke, they were descending. It would be about hour or so before their arrival. She leaned her head on the glass of her window and out onto the vastness of ocean waves below them. The waves shimmered with an endless array of little diamonds from the summer sun, reminding her of the night sky on the patio with Luke in Corral de Almaguer. She suddenly became aware of how little she did know about him. Her mind became consumed with a million questions. Their connection and chemistry were strong beyond words, sure, but what about his family? What had his childhood been like? Did he have any brothers or sisters…or any pets? When was his birthday for crying out loud?

There were so many things left to uncover. *What about all the stuff he has planned?* She reached for the cup of water that the flight attendant had brought earlier. *Is there going to be enough time to do it all? Just breathe.* She sat back in her seat and finished the last part of the movie that had been playing for the better part of an hour. The monitor showed them approaching the shores of the US in a slow but steady motion. She groaned. What she wouldn't give to get out and push the plane to make it land faster.

They finally arrived at 9:40 am Eastern Time, and Ariana closed her eyes, saying a quick prayer to God for their safe arrival. She didn't mind flying, but she was always grateful when they touched ground. The captain had announced over the loud speaker that it was a balmy seventy-six degrees at the moment and would likely reach eighty-seven later that day.

Ariana stood in line with her things, and when she got through the jet way, Luke was there waiting for her just as he had in Madrid. She walked toward him. *This is the moment we've been waiting for.*

"Let the magic begin, Mr. Cohen."

"And so it finally will, Ms. Romero." He held out his arm for her to take it.

Ariana noticed Deana walking away from the waiting area.

"But before we go," she said, "I want to say bye to Deana. I think she has a connecting flight to Seattle right now."

Deana stopped when she saw Ariana running toward her. Ariana gave her a hug, letting her know that she appreciated her friendship in Spain.

Deana broke away from their hug and said, "Just a dance, huh? You were only in the moment, huh?"

"What?" Ariana followed Deana's eyes toward Luke. She looked down and smiled.

"Well, I guess it was *a little* more than that." She made an inch in the air with her thumb and index finger.

"I knew it!" Deana laughed a hearty laugh and clapped her hands. "Y'all weren't fooling anyone!"

They exchanged information and promised to keep in touch. Then she walked back to Luke, and together they made their way through customs and picked up a curbside cab. Luke gave the driver the address, and they were off. Energy pulsed between them as she sat right next to him in the back seat. She looked behind both of her shoulders. After all that time having to hide their feelings, here they were hip to hip, shoulder to shoulder, and fingers intertwined. She was giddy, like the cat that stole the cream.

"So this is New York! This is finally happening." She leaned her head slightly across his chest to look out the window to take in the sights as they traveled.

"Right?" He lifted their hands and kissed hers. "There's a lot we can do. Just depends on how we want to spend our time."

She looked at him and pursed her lips. She shifted in her seat and folded her leg so she was facing him.

"I was thinking about that…We only have a few hours, and I want to spend them getting to know you better. I'd like to see a play and go dancing, but I was thinking that I don't even know your birthday." Her loose hand was talking with her, emphasizing her words, and her voice rose as she continued, "Do you think we have enough time to do it all? I've got to be back at the airport by five tomorrow evening!"

He watched her babble on intently and chuckled. "Let's play it by ear. We'll have to take a cab to the restaurant, but the show is within walking distance. There's a salsa club not too far away, but we can talk about whether or not you want to go after the show."

His calm demeanor eased her nerves, and her tone became more soft and playful. "Sounds to me like you're scared," she challenged Luke and placed an index finger on his chest.

Luke laughed and sat up straighter. Then he looked down and nodded. "I am. I'm afraid *you* can't hang." He pointed a finger back at her.

"Well, guess we'll just have to see about that." Ariana raised a cocky eyebrow.

"Guess so," he shot back. His face was flirtatious, full of intrigue, and—inches from hers. She fell back into the seat and pulled her hair that she had let loose before getting off the plane around her shoulder.

He put his arm around her, she leaned into his chest, and he played with the hair that fell alongside her face, caressing her cheek. As they drove farther into the city, Ariana put her frustration with the traffic in Denver into perspective, which was nothing compared to this atrocity. It was like a parking lot. Car horns were blaring, and there were masses of people walking briskly through the city sidewalks. It was somewhat of a culture shock after coming from their serene campo in Corral de Almaguer. This city never seemed to end. She could see the buildings towering over the city for miles…and miles. Denver was small in comparison, and to her, *that* had been big city enough.

"A lot of action for a Saturday," she commented. "Where are we going?"

"To my aunt's place in Manhattan. They're out of town in Cabo until next Tuesday. We can stay there. We're getting close."

It was after 11:00 am when they arrived at the apartment. Luke paid the driver, and they grabbed their bags. He took her hobo bag and placed it on his rolling suitcase. She followed him up the steps to the front door of one of the buildings where a doorman stood nearby.

"Morning, Luke," the man said. "Back from your trip, eh? Glad to have you back."

"Thanks, Jim! Yeah, just got in. Good to see you, too." He looked at Ariana and back at the doorman. "This is Ariana."

"Hi." She shook his hand and then glanced around him into the elegant entryway, spying a huge fountain in the center. *Wow!* She made eye contact with Jim again and continued, "Nice to meet you."

"Likewise," Jim said as he tipped his hat. He was an older gentleman with a kind face and gray hair that peeked out from under his hat at the temples.

They walked through the glass door and to the elevators. The floors were a beige marble with black diamonds in each corner, and they shimmered with the overhead lighting.

Luke stuck a card in a slot and pressed the number for their floor, and when they stepped off of the elevator, they walked right into the apartment through a small gallery foyer with shiny, oakwood floors in a herringbone pattern. She saw her reflection in a mirror immediately in front of them that hung above a modern wood table against the wall. She gasped at how tired and disheveled she looked. She walked closer to the mirror, leaned toward it, and wiped at the eyeliner she saw that had bled to the corner of her eye. She licked her lips and fluffed her hair.

She was reaching for her lip gloss when Luke asked, "What are you doing?"

"Oh, I look terrible. I need to freshen up."

He rested the bags against the wall and put his hand on her shoulder. She stopped and turned to him. He took her face in both of his hands. His gaze was intense. She felt her body quiver as she looked back up at him.

"You, mi querida Ariana, are beautiful."

She swallowed, and before she had a chance to say a word, his soft lips touched hers. Her knees went weak. All of the emotion of the bookstore, the airport, and Corral de Almaguer swept through both of them in one remarkable kiss.

Chapter 10

Luke

L uke grabbed the bags and set them by the sofa. "Do you want a tour?"

"Definitely. The place is incredible."

"This way." He placed his hand on the small of Ariana's back as he led her through the apartment. It was just as Aunt Linda and Uncle Al always left it—kind of like a museum in Luke's mind. The walls were stark white, and a bulky white sofa adorned with a cluster of plump plum, red, and silver pillows in various sizes sat in the middle of the room facing a fireplace in the middle of the wall. Two contemporary sofa chairs were arranged precisely facing one another at opposite ends, framing the sitting area. The coffee table and end tables were black with sleek, modern lines. The whole room was accessorized like a show home, including the impressive artwork on the walls. He watched Ariana's eyes as they followed the oak floors through to the living room and scanned the area from top to bottom.

Sunlight poured in from the glass French doors at the back end of the room. Luke took Ariana's hand over a step up that led through the glass French doors and a full terrace that went from one end of the apartment to the other.

"These flowers are gorgeous." Ariana stooped down, held one of the bright red gardenias to her nose, closed her eyes, and breathed in.

"My aunt loves flowers."

"I can see that," Ariana said. Her hand opened to one of several square clay pots filled with colorful floral arrangements and green grasses throughout the space. A comfy outdoor couch with matching chairs and coffee table were positioned right outside the living room.

"Now *this* is a view. It's so relaxing up here. You can barely hear a hum from all that traffic down there. Is…that…Central Park over there?" Ariana pointed to the green canopy of trees at the end of the block."

"It is," Luke said. "It's close. I can take you there tomorrow."

"Ok," she said as a giggle escaped her lips.

"What is it?"

"Nothing." She shook her head and pulled her hair behind her ears.

"No really, what?"

"Well, it's just that…I saw you walking across the quad in front of my room on the last day of school…The whole memory feels like it was light-years away."

What? "Seriously? Why didn't you stop me?" *I really wish she would have.* Luke shifted toward her swiftly. Her cheeks had turned a rosy-pink.

"I was two stories high up in my room. Can you imagine some chick chasing you down, frantically screaming your name? I would have been out of breath trying to catch up to you, and you would have thought I was nuts!"

He laughed at the vision in his mind. "Only…it would have been *you*…" He reached for her hand. "Do you know how much I tried to look for you after that day in the bookstore?"

"Well, *I* had faith that we would meet up again if it was meant to be…and here we are." She threw her palms upwards and looked at him, wearing her sweet, shy smile.

He smiled back, shaking a finger at her. "Risky move, Ms. Romero."

He took a step closer, rested his arms around her shoulders, crossing them behind her, and kissed her again. Her lips were soft and full and tasted like cherries. He could do this all day. They walked through the living area hand in hand as he continued showing her the place.

Outside the living area entrance to the right were two bedrooms, each with their own bath, the master also having access to the terrace. He showed her which one she would be using. Down the hall from the bedrooms, past the living room and foyer, was an open-concept kitchen and dining area with a breakfast server. Four clear, acrylic barstools with high backs sat in front of it. The dining room also had a door with access to the terrace. The kitchen was filled with modern white cabinetry and marble countertops.

"Where did you say your aunt and uncle are? It doesn't look like anyone even lives here." Ariana glanced at her surroundings once more as she ran her hand across the white marble counters.

"They're in Cabo. They usually stay there for a few months in the winter and spring and then come back to New York for the summer."

"Nice." she said. "Kind of get the best of both worlds all year long."

"Yeah, I guess so." Luke remembered the diary and how cool it would be to have dual citizenship in Spain. "Do you want something to drink? Are you hungry?" He walked toward the fridge and opened it.

"I could use some water." She sat at one of the bar stools. "I am kind of hungry, I guess. I hadn't thought about food until you asked just now, and it *has* been a long time since our last meal."

"I don't think there are any groceries here, but we can have something delivered. What do you feel like? There's pizza, Chinese—"

"Oooh, let's do New York style pizza!" she said with a bounce. "I always hear about how great it's supposed to be."

"Oh, you have *no* idea! I know the perfect place." Luke got Ariana some water, made the call for pizza from his favorite pizza place in the area, and poured a glass for himself.

"So, to answer your question, my birthday is July 17th. When is *your* birthday?"

She rested her forehead in her palm. "Sorry. You may as well know that I babble when I'm nervous."

He laughed, reminded of the airport in Madrid. "Yeah, I know. You should really work on that."

"Excuse me?" She smacked his arm.

"I'm kidding!" He laughed. "It's…adorable."

The pink in her cheeks brightened even more. "Well, funny guy, my birthday is August 28th. I'll be twenty-two this year."

"Virgo?"

"Cancer. Interesting. Ok, so, tell me about your family."

"Well, my parents have been married for over twenty-five years. I have one older sister, Nina. She's married to my brother-in-law, Zach. They have twin girls that are three, and I have a new nephew that's two months old."

"Awww! How cute! Do you have pictures? That reminds me, my phone should be working now. Do you mind if I charge it?"

"Not at all. You can plug in right here." He showed her a plug in the backsplash behind the countertop.

He grabbed for his own phone from his pocket and scrolled through his photos to find some of his nieces and new nephew.

"Here they are." He handed her the phone that displayed a photo of his sister's family at his graduation.

"They're adorable! You two have the same eyes. I guess good looks run in the family." She gave him a sideways glance.

She may as well have been batting her eyelashes at him. A wave of warmth permeated his chest.

"Thanks," he said. One side of his mouth curled upwards. "Let's go sit out on the terrace while we wait for the pizza, and you can tell me about *your* family."

They walked outside and sat down next to each other on the small outdoor couch. The warmth of summer and the heat radiating upwards from the concrete and pavement below covered them like a blanket.

"I have one sister and one brother," Ariana began. "I'm the oldest. My sister is a senior in high school, and my brother is a freshman. My parents have also been married a long time—twenty-three years. And we have a dog, a huge chocolate lab named Rufus. All of my family lives in San Luis, including my grandparents on my dad's side and most of my aunts and uncles on both sides of my family."

As Luke listened with his eyes glued to her, they heard a buzz, indicating the pizza had already arrived.

"That was fast," she said, startled.

"Yeah, the place is just right around the corner."

Luke ran back in, paid the pizza guy, and quickly brought it out with some napkins and paper plates that were provided by the pizza place.

"Mmm," Ariana sighed at her first bite. "This is *so* good!"

"It's the best," he said.

They talked while they ate; and when they were finished, they walked back to the kitchen with their leftovers. Ariana reached for her phone.

"Does your aunt have a Bluetooth speaker in here?"

"Yeah, see if it comes up in your settings. What are you doing?" He walked toward her, trying to get a glimpse of her phone screen.

"I want to see, Mr. Cohen, what you've got."

Yo No Se Mañana by Luis Enrique came streaming out through surround sound, engulfing the whole apartment.

"All that big talk," she continued as she salsa-danced her way toward him through the intro to the song, spinning and moving to the music.

Luke threw his head back and laughed as she came toward him swaying those beloved hips and stepping to the beat of the song. He was surprised yet charmed by her dare.

He met her halfway and took her hand in his. They paused to position themselves, and in one swift move, he spun her around, and they twisted and twirled in sync with each other and the music. They moved fluidly back and forth within the open space of the dining room and the kitchen.

With every spin, Ariana's hair tickled his face, and her perfume drifted to his nose, heightening his senses again. The look on Ariana's face was priceless. He was taken by her rhythm and how well their bodies flowed together—like they had been doing this forever.

"Ok, ok, Mr. Cohen…not bad!" Ariana said when the song ended. She fanned herself, trying to catch her breath.

He pulled her toward him, unable to contain himself, and kissed her. He entangled one hand in her hair and the other around her back, gathering a bit of her shirt in his hand. And when they had completely caught their breath, still feeling the passion of the kiss, she leaned forward and lay her head on his chest, and he held her against him.

He had to restrain himself. The heat from the exercise and the sparks between them were lighting a fire within him.

After a minute, he asked, "Do you want to get some rest before we go out?"

"I probably should…but I don't want to move." She groaned.

"I know," he said with a smile. "Me either. But it's already after 2:00." He glanced at the clock in the kitchen. "How long will it take you to get ready?"

"I didn't think it was that late. What time do we have to leave?"

"Well, our dinner reservations are for 6:00, and it'll take about fifteen minutes to get there once we hail down a cab."

"Ok…um, if I nap now, I'll have plenty of time."

"Alright, I'll get your stuff and we can take it to your room."

"Thank you." Ariana sighed, turned off her music and unplugged her phone before asking, "So, how did a nice Jewish boy like you learn to dance salsa like *that*?"

They walked toward the living room where Luke had left the bags. He turned to her and over-exaggerated his struggle to lift her bag. She rolled her eyes.

"Whatever." She shook her head.

"I'm just gifted," he teased.

She glared at him, eyes almost a thin line, saying *c'mon,* with her expression. He laughed.

"I grew up in New York, the birthplace of salsa." Still unsatisfied, her hand went to her hip. "*And* my best friend Jake is Puerto Rican."

"Ok, *now* it makes sense."

"What do you mean? Latin music is in my blood too, remember? Half my family *is* from Spain."

"Riiiight." She laughed.

"What about you? Did you grow up with it?"

"No, not at all. I fell in love with it one night a couple of years ago when my friends took me out. I wasn't sure what to expect. I thought it would be like some hip-hop clubs I had been to…like a meat-market.

"A meat-market?"

"I know, right? But after I watched the older couples moving so well together, I knew it would be different. It was obvious they had been doing it for years and that they were there for the love of dancing and the music."

"It's awesome to watch."

"It is. I love the music. It just—moves you. And the club we went to was so great. The guys would ask me to dance and then go back to where they were. There was never any pressure. It was almost chivalrous…and refreshing. The owners were awesome too. They were always around, making sure we had a good time. We ended up becoming friends with them. Sometimes they'd invite us to stay a while longer after they closed to eat and hang out. I learned the steps from them and how to let your body feel the rhythm of the music. I was hooked from then on!"

Ariana made Luke feel like he had been there at the club with her the way she described it. She had ideals. Morals. *She* was refreshing. Not that the girls he knew didn't have morals or values, but hers were almost old school. Like from a different era. The more he discovered about her, the more he wanted to know.

But, "That's cool," was all that came out of his mouth. He set the bag down on a chair that was in front of a writing desk in her room.

He placed his hands on her shoulders and slid them to her hands. "I'll let you get comfortable."

He kissed her cheek before walking out of the room. He could feel her watching him walk out while he closed the door behind him.

"I'm NOT looking at your booty," she called, lightening the mood and making him laugh out loud.

Luke sat down on the living room sofa, found the remote on the end table next to him, and turned on the flat screen TV housed above the fireplace. He flipped through the channels, focusing on nothing as he fought the urge to go back into Ariana's room. A loud thud came from her room, breaking the tension he was feeling.

"You ok in there?" he asked, amused.

"Yeah," she yelled from inside. "Just dropped my phone."

"Ok," he called back. He let himself sink into the couch and smiled.

"Mi querida Ariana," he whispered as he draped the throw from the couch over him and fell asleep with the TV still on the menu screen.

When Luke awoke, it was 4:00, and he knocked on Ariana's room to check on her.

"Yes?" she responded. "It's open."

He opened the door and found her in a robe with a towel on her head. The air in the room was humid from her shower, and it smelled of cherry blossoms. He resisted coming closer to her, staying at the door instead.

"How'd you sleep?" he asked.

"Great! How about you?"

"Good. I fell asleep on the couch. Guess I was more tired than I thought."

"I'm so excited for tonight!"

"Me too. See you in a bit." And he trotted toward the other bedroom to get dressed.

An hour or so later, Ariana walked out of the room and into the living room where Luke was already sitting, waiting for her. His heart danced. She was gorgeous in the little black dress he remembered from the picture from Sevilla. She had tied her hair back in curls, revealing the curves of her face. Her meticulous make-up brought out her hazel eyes and highlighted her delicate features. Her heels made her toned legs look a mile long.

He leapt to his feet to take her hand. "You look…amazing."

So do you," she said. Her eyes moved from his crisp, white button-down shirt to his charcoal gray slacks and tailored suit jacket.

"Ready?" He gave her his arm.

"Yes." She smiled and slipped her arm through his.

They walked toward the elevator door and rode down to the lobby. Jim led them out the front door.

"Have a great time," he said.

"Thanks," they responded.

The cab came, and they were off. It stopped in front of the restaurant, and Luke paid the driver.

Ariana walked out of the car and looked up. "*El Rincón de Sevilla*,"[98] she read. "It's Spanish."

"I wanted to recreate a Sevilla experience for us to share together."

Ariana's eyes lit up, and a winsome smile took over her face. She rushed to hug him. "It's perfect!"

They walked through the heavy doors, and Luke gave them his name for the reservations. The hostess seated them, and they took a gander at the decor. The walls were filled with paintings and items reminiscent of the city of its namesake. The tables were dressed with white linens and napkins. Ariana took the drink menu in her hands.

"Luke, have you had a tinto de verano?"

"I don't think so," he answered.

"You have to try one. We had it in Sevilla, and it was so good!"

He asked the waitress to bring them two.

They scanned the menu, trying to figure out what to order. It carried a combination of Spanish and American cuisine. They decided on the paella for two, hoping it would be resonant of their recent travels, which, even though they had just arrived that morning, had already begun to become a faint memory in their mind, taking a back seat to being here in New York together.

As they waited, they discussed their childhoods, hobbies, and past relationships. While they ate, they shared their aspirations and talked about their experiences at the University of Denver. Their eyes were

[98] The Corner of Seville

fixed only on one another, and the sun surrounded them in the romantically lit restaurant ambience, just as it always had when they were together in a crowded place.

They ordered a flan for dessert with two forks and shared it. Even though the food was good, they agreed it didn't hold a candle to Mari's cooking. There was something missing. The richness of the food in Spain was somehow lacking here. Maybe it was the love that Mari put into hers that made the difference. Either way, it made them wish they were back there together, just the two of them.

When the check came, Ariana reached for her clutch.

"What are you doing?" Luke asked.

She looked up, wide-eyed and clutch in mid-air.

"Well, I want to help with the check. You've been so good to me by taking care of the cab fare and lunch tod—"

"Hey," he said. "*I* asked you out on this date, remember? I got this. Put that away. Besides, I'm sure there will be plenty of opportunity for you to return the favor."

"Fair enough." She put down her clutch.

They stood up, and Luke waited for Ariana to walk ahead of him. He followed closely behind her and grabbed for her hand as they left the restaurant and made their way down to the theater. The city was pulsating with nightlife. There were limos everywhere they turned.

Luke watched her absorb the sights and window-shop.

"Don't people wear regular clothes here? That dress has to be couture, and those are Louboutin's!" she whispered, leaning into him and looking back at the couple that had just passed them. The city lights flickered in her bright eyes.

Luke smiled. "Yeah, well, that's New York, I guess. We're here."

They reached the Palace Theater early, and Luke gave his phone to the box office attendant to scan for their tickets. The attendant handed them their tickets through the small opening at the bottom of the window. They took their seats inside.

"Luke, it's so beautiful in here!" Ariana marveled, craning her neck to soak in the grand décor.

"It is! This is my first time in this theater as well." The impressive ornate golden ceiling and balconies spoke of times past.

"I can only imagine what this place was like when it first opened."

"I know."

Luke was equally impressed with the play. It was a love story chronicling the lives of an American soldier with a French woman.

Throughout the show, he glanced over at Ariana who was enthralled in the music and the story. He was glad. It seemed to have been the perfect choice.

He grabbed for her hand, and she leaned her head on his shoulder. At intermission, they didn't move. They continued in their seats instead, discussing the artistry in what they had seen and the parts that they had enjoyed the most.

After the play, as they exited the theater, the noise and sea of people rushing through the streets made Luke's steps hesitant. A Statue of Liberty clothed in bikini bottoms and pure paint from head to toe crossed in front of them. *Geez. Really?* He protectively turned to reach for Ariana's hand and pull her towards him, but she had already reached for his arm, intertwining it in her own. Her eyes were glossy when they met with his. Her face was serious, taking him by surprise. All the while, a Spiderman's acrobatics invaded Luke's peripheral vision.

"This day has been..." Her eyes went to her shoes and then to the Spiderman who looked to be headed in their direction. "Well, I just don't want it to end." Her voice cracked as she took a step closer to him and squeezed his hands.

Luke cleared his throat. "I don't either. Ready for the club? It's only about a thirty-minute drive from here."

"Yes, definitely!" Ariana's eyes lit up just as an unexpected hand landed on both of their shoulders, grasping their attention. Spiderman made a heart in the air with his hands, and then he tilted his head and brought his hands to his heart, making them laugh out loud.

"Let's grab a cab," Luke said, and he led her toward the street.

When they reached the club, the music was blaring as they stepped out of the car. A long line had already begun to form. Once inside, they checked in Luke's suit jacket and walked to the bar to observe. There was a live band that night, and the floor was brimming with dancers dressed to impress. Some of them looked studio-skilled, but most of them were just feeling the music and moving to the sounds of their own beat.

Ariana's eyes sparkled, and her enthusiastic energy was contagious standing next to her.

"They're so good!" she said.

"They are! Do you want a drink?"

"How about a mojito?" she asked.

Ariana looked like she was in a daze as she watched the dancers and bobbed to the music when Luke returned shortly with the drinks. They watched for a while until the band began to play a throwback to Eddie Santiago's *Que Locura Fue Enamorarme de ti.*

Luke took her hand and led her to the dance floor. They moved, catching glimpses of each other as they spun around, twisting and turning. Then he brought her close with her back toward him, arms around her waist, still in step, and he whispered the chorus line in her ear, and for a split second their bodies melded together; then he sent her spinning around several times, leading her out again.

Luke was absorbed in the music. The chorus line made his insides tremble. Everything he was feeling *was* crazy. When the song was over, he took her face in his hands on the dance floor and kissed her deeply once again.

They danced all night, taking short breaks until Ariana's feet couldn't take it anymore.

"Are you ready?"

"My feet are." She wiggled her toes under the strap of her shoes.

Luke welcomed the cool breeze that refreshed his face as they walked out of the club. He closed his eyes. *I needed that.* They were quickly forced back open at the sound of Ariana's heels clacking against the concrete as she walked briskly ahead of Luke. *Where is she going?* He watched her stick her fingers in her mouth and whistle loudly at a passing cab. The cab stopped in its tracks and backed up toward them.

"Yes!" she said, kicking up her leg and pulling her fist to her side in victory. "I couldn't resist. I just wanted to see if what I've seen in the movies was real."

Luke laughed and shook his head as they entered the cab. She was in and out of sleep on the hour ride home snug in his arms in the backseat of the cab. He let his fingers slide through her hair and kissed her forehead.

He inhaled slowly. *I could get used to this.*

Ariana showered after arriving at the apartment and met Luke out on the terrace. He was looking down onto the street when he felt her hand glide across his back. He turned to her, feeling goose bumps forming on his arms, and placed his elbows on the balcony. His eyes were glued to her in the pajama tank and shorts that hugged her tiny frame. The soft terrace lighting highlighted the flecks of green in her eyes. *She could probably wear a paper bag and still look incredible.*

"Well, mi querida Ariana, did an evening in New York impress you?"

"No." Her eyes went to her feet, and she shook her head.

"No?" His face twisted, and he swallowed.

"No." Her gaze met square with his and her hand landed gently on his chest. "You did."

Relief overtook his face and an electric current flowed through him. She had a way of awakening emotions in him that he never knew he had.

"Come here," he said, and he grabbed for her hand.

They walked to the outdoor couch and pulled the throw from the living room sofa over both of them. He held her close as they looked at the stars. It almost felt like the patio at El Convento until a loud siren blared beneath them, bringing Luke to reality. His dad's face shot through his mind. He glanced at the top of Ariana's head and breathed in her perfume. *What am I doing?* She rolled into him, put her hand on his chest, and sighed. *Just enjoy the moment, Luke.*

They woke up to faint honks in the street below and noticed it was already 11:30. Ariana helped Luke straighten up the apartment, throwing their trash, cleaning the bathrooms, the kitchen and the living room, leaving no trace that anyone had ever been there.

Luke placed his suitcase near the door. He took a deep breath, trying to control the excitement and uncertainty that kept his heart racing. He walked over to peek into Ariana's room where she was knee-deep into packing. She was making each fold crisp and deliberate and organized every item from top to bottom. He chuckled.

"Are you color-coding those?"

"Ha, ha, ha." She stuck her tongue out at him without making eye contact.

"If you're almost finished, we can grab something to eat and go to Central Park." His voice trailed off as he noticed the expression on her face. He walked over and put his hand on her back. "What's wrong?"

"Nothing." She paused, pulling her hair behind her ears. "I just can't believe I'll be home in a few hours…and you won't be there."

He kissed a tear that slid down her cheek.

"I've been trying not to think about it."

He kissed her, and they clung tightly to one another.

"Ready?" he said when he felt her pulling back.

"As I'll ever be."

He grabbed her bag, and they headed toward the door. Once again, he placed her bag on his. They stepped into the elevator, walked out of the lobby, and greeted Jim on their way out toward Central Park.

"Let's get breakfast here." Luke gestured to a small patisserie with his hand.

Savoring the last few hours together, they sat on a bench and enjoyed their coffee and pastries. Small talk about park life helped them avoid their inevitable parting. When it was around 4:00, they walked toward the street to grab a cab.

At the airport, they held each other, unwilling to let go until the traffic forced the cab driver to prompt Luke.

"I'll call you when I get home, ok?" Her voice was choppy and soft, and her breathing labored.

"Ok." He kissed her softly. "I'll keep the phone right next to me."

"Bye." She squeezed his hand and hugged him tightly one last time. And she turned around and walked into the terminal.

"Bye," he whispered as he watched her walk away.

Chapter 11

Ariana

Ariana sat in an empty seat as she waited to board her plane back to Denver. She sighed and peeled off her backpack purse. She was sweating. The summer heat and the emotion stuck in her chest after leaving Luke made the air thick and her breaths shallow. She fanned herself with her boarding pass and sipped the water she had purchased from an airport gift shop. A young mom with a small child rolling a Barbie suitcase passed in front of her.

Better text my mom that I'm on my way. Her mother replied that they were already in Denver, that she was relieved to hear she had landed safely in New York, and that she couldn't wait to see her. Their exchange brought a welcomed smile to Ariana's face.

When Ariana was comfortable in her window seat and they were zooming into the sky, she peered out onto the New York skyline. She tried to make out where she and Luke had been that night, but it was no use. Everything blended together. Still, a surge of warmth gushed through her as she danced with him in her mind all over again. She considered all of the events since stepping foot on that plane to Spain weeks before. She had experienced more emotions than she probably ever had. Clearly, she was different now. What would she say to her parents? How would she explain all of this to Liz?

She blew out a heavy breath and pulled out her book from her backpack to the part where preparations for Lupe and Sal's wedding were being made and how Sal had decided to stick to a diet of beans to lose weight for the wedding rather than greens and whole grains, thinking that those would fatten him up since that's what they did for horses and cows.

The plane landed in Denver around 9:00 pm. Ariana yawned and stretched her arms up. Her back was stiff and achy. She wiped her watery eyes with the back of her hand. Her legs were still sore from dancing the night before. All she could think about was a warm, soft bed. The train to the main terminal took her to the exit for arrivals, and she had only been waiting outside about five minutes when she saw her parents' red Toyota Sequoia pulling up.

The tears that formed in her eyes when she saw their smiling faces surprised her. Her parents jumped out of the car to give her a tight hug.

"Mi' ja!" cried her mom, wiping her tears. "Oh, it's so good to have you home!"

"How did it go?" Her dad picked up her bag and placed it in the trunk. "¡Eeeeh, esta muchita quizás trujo todo el país de España en este veliz!"[99]

"Not everything, Dad!" Ariana rolled her eyes. *Here we go.* "I left a lot of it over there."

She got in the car, and they drove to her Aunt Juanita and Uncle Tomás's house in Aurora. When they drove up to the house, Ariana noticed a bunch of cars in the driveway, and all of the lights in the house were still on. It was already after 10:00, and she could hear a commotion in the house.

She moaned inside her head as she dragged her feet and belongings across the grass to the sidewalk. Even though she appreciated that everyone had come out to see her, it was just a reminder that she was home now, that her adventures were over and that she would be spending the rest of the summer in San Luis—without Luke.

She struggled to smile as everyone yelled, "Surprise!"

Ariana hugged her family one by one. There were purple balloons and streamers everywhere, and the house smelled of her mother's familiar homemade cooking and fresh roasted green chile. It was a heart-felt welcome home, but she didn't feel like socializing. They walked through the living room and into the kitchen. On the center island was a sheet cake with the words *Welcome Home Ariana!* written across in purple icing. A huge pot of green chile, another of fresh beans, and a mountain of sopapillas sat on the kitchen counter.

---

[99] I guess this girl brought the whole country of Spain in this suitcase!

On the stove was a large cast iron skillet filled with thin slices of elk meat and another with fried potatoes.

The whole spread was a heavenly sight. Ariana's heart warmed. The growl from her stomach reminded her that she hadn't eaten anything substantial since breakfast in Central Park with Luke. *Luke!*

Her hand reached for her mom's shoulder. "Mom, I'll be right back." She rushed to the bathroom to call him.

"Where is she going so fast?" Ariana heard her Aunt Juanita ask as she stepped into the hallway.

"To the bathroom, I guess," replied her mom.

"Ariana," he answered as if he had been watching for the phone to ring.

"Hi." She bit her pinky fingernail as she leaned up against the back of the door. His voice was a glass of fresh-squeezed lemonade on a hot day.

"You're home. What's all that noise?"

Ariana blushed. Her family had turned up the New Mexico music. *Porque* by Ernestine Romero was blaring from the living room, and Uncle Steve had just let out a *grito*.[100] He had already had a couple of drinks, and he was telling animated jokes in the dining room. She could hear the bellowing laughter through the door at her uncle's antics.

"Yes, well, I'm in Aurora at my aunt's house. Sorry about the noise. It's my big, crazy family. They threw a welcome-home party for me."

"Now? It's got to be at least 10:30 over there. But I have to admit, it sounds like a lot of fun," he said with a chuckle. "Aren't you tired?"

"Yeah, but I appreciate the sentiment." She knew they would be looking for her soon, but she couldn't bring herself to end the call. *Ugh.* "How was your drive home?"

"It was fine. I spent some time with my sister and nieces and nephew. My mom is really excited about the diary. She had me explain everything and show her all the pictures."

"I'm sure she's excited. It's fascina—"

"Ariana!" Her mother's voice pierced her eardrums making her jump.

---

[100] A distinctive yell that hangs suspended for several seconds adding deeply heartfelt emotion in a song.

Ariana was sure the neighbors had heard her, too. She had impeccable timing.

"Is that your mom?"

"It is. I better go."

"Ok. I'm glad you're home. Call me when you can."

"Ariana!" she heard her mother again.

"Ok, I will. Be right there, Mom!"

She scrolled through her photos and found the selfies they took in front of the Palace Theater while they waited for a cab. There was one of them smiling at the camera and another with him kissing her cheek. She rested her forehead on the door and sent them to him with a caption saying, 'Missing you already.' A second later he responded with a red heart emoji.

She was in the hall on her way to the kitchen in a daze, and she scanned the room before coming in. Some of them were dancing to the New Mexico music. Some were playing cards or eating. Others were just talking and laughing. She noticed her Aunt Juanita and Uncle Tomás together in front of the island. She was trying to gather some of the dishes and the leftover food, and he was holding her from behind whispering something in her ear. Whatever it was, she burst out laughing. Ariana had always admired their relationship.

Aunt Juanita was her mom's youngest sister. She and Uncle Tomás both grew up in San Luis and were in the same grade. They began dating during their sophomore year of high school and had been together ever since. They were both ambitious. They came to college in Denver after high school, both of them the first in their families to go to college. Their college years had been tough on their relationship, but they rode it out knowing they couldn't live without one another. They got married right after graduation. They were about to celebrate their twelve-year anniversary, and it was still clear that they were meant for one another. And now, they had two young kids, ten and six, and rewarding careers: she was a social worker, and he was a high school math teacher.

They had been a huge support for Ariana while she was at DU, especially her first year. The culture shock she had experienced was so bad that she had wanted to quit school and go back home. But they had not let her do it. She had spent many a weekend at their house, sometimes in tears over comments students and professors alike had made or ignorant questions they had asked. But since they had been through it before, they had already known what she had been dealing with. They had talked her through everything and had encouraged her every step of the way. She would be forever grateful for everything they had done for her. Because of them she knew she couldn't quit. She had to push forward reminded that her education was something no one could ever take away from her.

"There you are, 'jita," said her mom. She put her arm around Ariana as she entered the kitchen. "You haven't even eaten yet. Look at you. Did you lose weight over there? Come here, and let me serve you a plate."

"Mo-om," she groaned. "I think I gained like five pounds over there—at least! There was so much food!"

She walked to the counter with her mom.

"Well, you look too skinny. Do you want a bowl of chile with beans and a sopapilla on the side, or do you want a stuffed sopapilla?"

"Um, a stuffed sopapilla." Ariana felt her *tripas*[101] grumbling at each other as her eyes went from each pot and skillet to the other. Her hand went to her tummy while she watched her mom open one end of a particularly thick and puffy sopapilla and added beans, potatoes, some meat slices, and a little chile. Then she smothered more green chile over the top and tossed on some shredded cheese, making a unique, yet scrumptious stuffed sopapilla with the different ingredients. Ariana sat at one of the stools in front of the long island, grabbed a fork, and dug in.

"Now, *this* is what I call a welcome home." She savored every flavor melding together in her mouth. *Mmm.* She continued shoveling in the chile even though it was making her sniffle. "This chile has some kick, Mom. You must have been mad when you made it!"

"Probably. I was talking to your Tía Gabi. You know how she likes to gossip, and I can only take so much of that!" She rolled her eyes and pulled up a stool next to Ariana. "So anyway, tell me about Spain."

"Who is *that*?" Ariana's brother held her phone with a quizzical look.

Ariana's eyes and mouth fell wide open. "No one! Eeeeh! You're like a ninja! I didn't even know you were there." She snatched the phone out of his hand. "Thank you very much." She couldn't believe she had just laid it carelessly on the counter with one of the photos of

---

[101] Intestines

115

her and Luke that she had just sent him still on display. *OMG! What if my mom saw Luke or the Palace Theater in the background?* Her forehead felt warm and her hands began to sweat.

Her brother giggled. "Geez."

"Anyway," she said, wiping her hands on her shorts. She fired daggers at Carlos and turned her attention to her mom. "Spain was wonderful!"

She looked up at the ceiling, envisioning Luke and El Convento. "I had the best time."

Her mom gave her a mischievous grin and said, "Hmmm, I bet."

"Here, *I* will show you some pictures." Ariana glared at her brother again.

She scrolled through her camera roll, showing them pictures of Sevilla, Córdoba, and Corral de Almaguer. She enlarged some of the pictures that detailed El Convento and the excavation site frame by frame.

"Dad, you would love it there," Ariana said as he approached them.

"Oh yeah?"

"You know how we've always talked about rolling hills and olive trees? Check this out." She showed him her phone.

"Wow!"

"But the pictures don't do it justice, Dad. You'll have to go see it for yourself."

He laughed. "Wouldn't that be nice. One of these days, right?"

"Oh yeah!" Her voice rose as she remembered the diary and the family with the Romero last name. "We found an ancient diary during our dig. Do you know anything about our Romero family and where they came from?"

He looked up and took a deep breath, contemplating her question.

"I don't know, Ariana. As far as I know, we came from Spain and then ended up in New Mexico before we came to San Luis. But I don't know much more than that. Your great, great, great grandfather Solomon Romero was the first one to come to San Luis with the Sangre de Cristo Land Grant, but I'm not sure where his family was from."

"Well, it's crazy because the woman who wrote the diary wrote it in the late 1500s and talked about getting married to a Romero man and moving to the Americas. My professor said I should look into it, but I think it's a long shot."

"You never know," her dad said. His head turned sideways, and he lifted his eyebrows. "We can ask Maria when we get back. She has a wealth of information about all that."

"That's what I said." Ariana threw a pointed finger in the air. "I'll go and talk to her about it when we get back."

They ate cake and talked and laughed until Ariana's eyes were closing on her. She changed to a tank and comfy cotton shorts and threw herself on the bed, staring at the ceiling. Soon she was in Aunt Linda's apartment again, with Luke, reliving that unexpected, first kiss that had left her dizzy. That kiss had lingered on her lips even several minutes after they had stopped kissing. She pictured him from head to toe in that GQ suit that hugged his body, revealing his athletic build. He was about a whole head taller than her when they had gone out that night, even in her five-inch heels. Not a hair was out of place, and his baby blues had her spinning. Aside from all of that, it was his tenderness and gentle spirit that tugged at her heartstrings. She grabbed for the other pillow on the bed, let out a deep breath, and tried to get a grip on her emotions.

On their way home later that next morning, Ariana and her family were getting onto the southbound onramp for the interstate when her dad groaned in a deep, gruff voice. The traffic had become stop and go, and she could see the cars backed up for miles in each of the four lanes on both sides.

"Oh no!" he yelled and banged the steering wheel with his fist. "That's what we get for trying to get back home on a Monday morning."

At the same exact time, Ariana laughed out loud. Her dad glared at her.

"Sorry, Dad!" she said with her cheeks flushed. "I wasn't laughing at that…I just got a text."

Luke had texted her a photo of her little victory dance in front of the cab she had hailed. She hadn't even realized he had taken the picture. He had caught it with perfect timing. She texted back three laughing emojis with tears coming out of their eyes. A second later, she received the one with hearts for eyes. She leaned her head against the window, and a sappy grin spread across her face. Then she pulled her hair behind her ear and casually looked around the car to see if anyone had seen that.

Her brother was sitting in the third seat immersed in a video game. Her parents weren't paying attention, but her sister, who was seated next to her, was watching her closely. Karina was sitting near the other window in the second row of the car, and there was some space between them, but Ariana couldn't be sure if she had seen the picture or the emojis she had exchanged with Luke, but she didn't say anything. She turned to look out her window instead. Ariana shrugged and texted Liz to let her know she was back. When she didn't receive a text back right away, she decided to tease her with the pic of her and Luke in front of the Palace Theater. Suddenly, her phone was buzzing.

Liz responded, *OMG...WHO is that???? Call me.*

Then a second later she added, *wait...don't call me...at work...you have a LOT of explaining to do!*

Followed by, *Is that the Spanish 'fairytale?' Look at those eyes! HE IS GORGEOUS!!!*

And finally, *Ok...back to work...call me later* with a GIF of a girl fainting attached.

Ariana laughed again, and she felt her sister and her mom staring at her.

She blushed and said, "Just Liz...she's glad I'm home."

Once they passed Colorado Springs, they started making better time, but the Denver traffic had delayed them. Ariana's father was annoyed. He had a lot to do at home, and they still had some shopping to do in Pueblo for the restaurant. At this rate, they wouldn't be home until early evening. He had to be back to check on the restaurant and attend a town meeting that evening about organizing the Santiago y Santana fiestas at the end of July. Her mom and dad were part of the steering committee led by the Town Council. The city was ultimately responsible for all of the festivities; however, despite the parties and wild and crazy activities that existed when the town doubled and often tripled in size with extended family during the weekend, at the center of it all was the church. As the largest community celebration of the year, families come back from everywhere to participate. Father Antonio, a pillar of the community, led the organizing. He was innovative and charismatic and had earned the esteem of the community inspiring their religious devotion. The people respected his vision and followed his leadership faithfully.

They got to San Luis with plenty of time, to Ariana's dad's contentment. He dropped off the family at home and left to the restaurant. Ariana got out of the car, and Rufus came running toward her with his tail wagging and leapt up in her arms.

"Rufus! Come here, boy! I missed you," Ariana shouted, hugging and petting her playful dog.

She walked in the house and stood at the door. It felt wonderful yet strange to be home. Ariana had been on campus since Easter. She closed her eyes and took a deep breath. It smelled of fresh flowers from their garden and brisk, fresh air. The windows were open, letting in the breeze from outside, and the house was expectedly spotless. She walked up the stairs toward her room. All of her neat, labeled boxes had been tucked in one of the corners. She loved her house. It was the only home she and her brother and sister had ever lived in. Her mom and dad bought the house after they had been married for a few years. It was in the town of San Luis, the barrio of *Cuba,* as it had been dubbed by the locals for reasons unbeknownst to Ariana.

When her parents had initially bought the house, it was a single story three-bedroom house with a small kitchen, living area, and a bathroom. It had been built at the turn of the century and had thick adobe walls, which kept the main floor cool in summer and warm in winter. When her parents had been pregnant with her, they had decided to renovate the house and add a second floor. They had opened up the main floor, tearing down walls to expand the kitchen, create a dining room, and move all of the bedrooms upstairs, except the master. The home now had four bedrooms and two bathrooms, one on the main floor and one upstairs. There was still an old, working *fogón*[102] in the living room that radiated heat throughout the whole house.

Ariana lay down on her bed and picked up her phone to call Luke. She clicked his number and waited for a response but only got his voice mail.

"Hey," she said. "It's me. I just got home. Call me."

Then she called Liz. It was already after 5:00 Texas time, so she figured she'd be off work.

"Ana!" Liz shouted.

---

[102] Wood fireplace or stove

"Hey, girl!" Ariana laughed, pulling the phone away from her ear, and asked as nonchalant as she could, "What's up?"

"No," Liz said, "the question is…what is up with *you*? And you can start with that fine #$% guy in the picture with you!"

"Oh him? He was just a guy I saw on the street." Ariana pulled her knees up to her chest.

"Shut. Up. Quit playing!" Liz's impatience was seething through the phone.

"Well, that guy, my dear, is none other than *the* Luke, in the flesh. No such fantasma!"

"No way! Are you serious? How the heck did that happen?"

Ariana could picture her at the edge of her seat with her bottom lip hitting the floor.

"Can you believe he was on the trip, too? He was one of the instructors. He just graduated from DU with a degree in archaeology." She paused. "Liz, he felt everything that I felt that day, too! Can you believe it?"

"No!" Liz said. "What are the chances?"

"I don't know, but he actually tried to find me on campus after that."

"See! I told you. You should have run after him on that last day of school!"

"I know, that's what he said…but anyway," she flipped over on her stomach, feet bobbing back and forth in the air, and continued, "we had the best time in Spain and in…" she stopped, unsure of whether she wanted to reveal her trip to New York.

"In *where*, Ariana? Spill it!"

"In New York," she said in a quiet voice. She got up and looked around surreptitiously to see if anyone was around and shut her door. "We couldn't really hang out in Spain too much because he was the assistant instructor, so we had a date in New York."

"New York? Oooooh! You sneaky little—"

"Hey!" Ariana pointed at the phone. "*You* were the one who told me to go wild and live a little, right?"

"Yeah, I did, but I didn't think you were going to seriously take me up on it! What if he would have been a crazy stalker killer or something?"

"I know. Trust me, that thought crossed my mind a time or two. But, Liz, it was so not like that. There's a look in his eyes that's so sweet. The way he just knew things and how we connected when we were together. And you know me, I'm more skeptical than anyone, but I just felt like I had known him forever. I completely felt like I could trust him. He is *so* amazing, brilliant and…such a gentleman."

"I'm sure he is," Liz teased.

"No seriously. We stayed in Manhattan, he took me to dinner, to a *romantic* Broadway show and salsa dancing!"

The memories of their date fluttered through her mind.

"That does sound like a fairytale. Is he Latino?"

"No. Jewish!"

"Jewish?"

"I know! He could dance, too, Liz…*and* he can speak Spanish!"

"Ok, now you *better* tell me he has a brother!"

They both laughed.

"Sorry, just an older sister."

"Too bad," Liz said, the disappointment dripping through the phone from her tone. "My parents would kill me anyway if I met someone who wasn't Catholic. Hey, listen, I have to go. I need to take my little cousin to practice, but I'll call you later. I definitely want to hear more about this Luke guy."

"Alright. Someone's trying to call right now anyway. Talk to you soon,"

"Ok. Bye," Liz said.

"Hello," Ariana said as she clicked over.

"Hey!"

"Hey!" Ariana melted at the unexpected sound of Luke's cool, soft voice.

"So you're *home* home."

"Yeah, just got here a little while ago. I was just unpacking and thinking about—"

"About what?"

"About New York and…I just wanted to say thank you again for *everything*. The dinner, the show, and the dancing. It was all perfect."

"Thank *you* for taking the extra day. I just had to…to see…I wanted to know what it would be like to be around you without restrictions."

"Well?"

"You're everything I thought you'd be and more," he said, his voice trailing off at the end.

"So are you," Ariana said in a quiet voice. "So, what now? You *are* coming back to school in Boulder in the fall, right?" Ariana remembered their brief conversation at dinner about his plans for his Master's program.

"Well," he began, "I'm still not sure yet about going back to Colorado. I uh—"

"Are you ok?"

"Yeah, I'm just thinking about my dad. He...he wants me to stay in New York."

Ariana was quiet. Her stomach knotted at the idea of where this conversation was headed.

"Are you there?"

"Yeah, I'm here." Ariana said.

"Then there's you." His tone changed. "I just want to be around *you*."

Butterflies swarmed, breaking up the knots in her tummy.

"Well then, I guess the choice is clear, Mr. Cohen," she said with confidence. "I'll see you in Boulder in the fall!"

He laughed. "What are *your* plans after graduation?"

"I'm not sure. My parents want me to come back home and run the restaurant, but I know I don't want that. I just have to focus on my last year of school and on both of my senior thesis projects. I don't even know what I want to study yet. After that then maybe I can apply to grad school and possibly get my teaching license or maybe my Ph.D."

"I've thought about that, too." He paused. "I want to see you before summer's over, Ariana. Do you think we can make that happen?"

"I don't know. I'll be here in San Luis working all summer. Maybe we can meet up in Denver some time. Maybe for either one of our birthdays?"

"That would be nice. Let's talk more once you get settled in."

"Ok."

"In the meantime, *estoy pensando en ti*,"[103] he said.

"*Yo también.*"[104]

---

[103] I'm thinking of you
[104] Me too.

Ariana spent the days following her arrival home with her family and visiting her grandparents, extended family, and some of her high school friends that had stayed in San Luis. She began working at the restaurant and helping her parents plan the float they were going to build for the parade during the fiestas. When the 4th of July weekend came, Ariana's family decided to forgo the annual camping trip to the *Poso*[105] with some of her family and instead took a drive to *El Santuario* in Chimayo, New Mexico near Española.

It was always a blast to be at the Poso for the 4th of July. Their family owned a small cabin up there deep in the mountains. But this year, Ariana's dad had bought a new truck for the business, and he wanted it blessed before the fiestas. This was the only weekend that he would be able to do it since they would be working on fiesta planning and their float up until the last day. So they drove the two-hour drive to the small, miraculous church where millions of faithful people visit on an annual basis to fill their vials with the holy dirt from the hole in the little church that is said to be healing and never to empty.

It was just as Ariana had remembered it from her last visit a few years ago. The church and areas around its courtyard were filled with crutches, pictures, letters, rosaries, religious medals, and other items that the faithful had left behind as symbols of having been healed. Ariana's dad wanted to get his truck blessed by the priest and get some of the miraculous dirt to keep in the glove compartment to keep it safe on the roads. After they visited the church and had the truck blessed, Ariana stole a moment alone and took out her phone to take a selfie in front of the little church to send it to Luke when her sister came from out of nowhere, catching her in the middle of the act of texting *Happy 4th*.

"Who are you sending selfies to, Ariana?" she asked. "I've been watching you on that phone over the past few weeks, and I *know* something's up. And don't tell me it's just Liz. She doesn't want a pic of you here!"

"How do you know, Karina? We're really close!"

---

[105] Literally, the hole; in this context, it refers to the given name of a particularly popular camping site for locals high in the Sangre de Cristo mountains at the Rito Seco Park just a few miles northeast of San Luis.

"Whatever, Ariana. Just tell me what the heck is going on. I've seen you blushing and smiling all goofy. That is *not* Liz." She pointed to the phone and landed her hands on her hips.

Ariana hesitated and bit a corner of her lower lip. "Ok fine, Karina. But you have to promise not to tell anyone, ok?"

"Ok." A wily expression took up her whole face as she shuffled closer to Ariana. Her sister couldn't resist any juicy gossip.

Ariana scrolled through her pics and found the one of her and Luke in New York.

"I met someone at school. His name is Luke. He was on the trip to Spain, too."

Karina's eyes opened a mile wide.

"Daaaang! He is fine, Ariana!" She slapped Ariana on her shoulder.

"I know, right?" Ariana said with a silly grin. "I'm going to ask him to come to San Luis for Santana."

"The heat must be making you hallucinate!" Karina's palm went to Ariana's forehead.

Ariana shoved it away, rolled her eyes, and sucked the air through her teeth. "Why? It's probably the best time. There's so many people. Everyone is so busy with all the activities. No one's going to have time to pay attention."

"I don't know about that, Ariana. Think about your cousins. They'll tear him apart!"

"No they won't. I won't let them."

"Well, you better tell Mom first so she could break it to Dad. He's going to hit the roof!"

"That's true," she said. Ideas ran through her mind about how to handle it. "You're right. I will."

A few days before, Ariana had remembered that Luke's birthday was July 17th. Considering the day was fast approaching, she had racked her brain, thinking about what to send him. The best gift, she thought, was for them to be together again. How fun would it be for him to come to San Luis for the fiestas? She had already looked online for plane ticket prices from New York to Denver around the last weekend in July and bought a voucher for him. She knew she might be optimistic that he would come, but he *had* told her he wanted to see her again. Wanting to surprise him, she had asked him for his address, suggesting she might send him a card for his birthday, and he had given it to her without reservation.

When they would get home from Española, she would send a card with the voucher inviting him to come to San Luis with a message written on the envelope not to open it until his birthday. She had also ordered a bouquet of orange and purple sunflowers with blue forget-me-nots and a birthday balloon to be sent to his home on the 17th. Ariana hoped her gift wasn't too over-the-top, but she had appreciated how he took care of her in New York and wanted to reciprocate his generosity. She and her sister walked into the *El Santuario* gift shop and browsed the souvenirs. She found a St. Christopher medal and decided to get it blessed and send it to Luke with the card. He was the patron saint of safe traveling after all.

Luke

Luke took a sip of his drink and sat back in his chair. He and Jake had stopped at a nearby pub to cool off. The warmth of the summer had been beating down on them as they made their way toward the fireworks. He had been in deep thought about his dad and his Master's program when his phone chimed. Ariana had sent him a selfie. He smiled. The knot in his stomach faded and he sent her back a double heart emoji and asked, *Where are you?*

El Santuario de Chimayo in New Mexico, she responded.

"Who are you texting?" Jake asked.

"Ariana." Luke slid his phone over to show Jake her picture. He thought it was about time he shared this experience with *somebody*.

"What?! She is *hot!*" Jake said with his hand covering his mouth. "Where did you meet her?"

"Spain," Luke said.

"She's Spanish? Where is she? That's not Spain, is it?"

"Well…yes, she's Spanish, sort of. And no, that's not Spain. I think it's New Mexico."

"She's Mexican? That looks like an old church behind her."

"No, I don't think so. She's a DU student. She was in our class this summer. I think it *is* a church."

"So you knew her from DU?"

"Not really. I just…kind of bumped into her a few weeks before graduation."

125

"Wait a minute. Is *this* the girl you were all messed up over?" Jake sat up at the edge of his chair.

Luke could see the wheels turning as Jake was trying to put the pieces of the puzzle together. He hesitated to respond.

"Hey, you already started, bruh. You might as well tell me now."

Luke swallowed and shifted in his chair. He gave Jake the goods on how he had met Ariana and their interaction in Spain and New York. He ended his story and felt goosebumps as he reminisced about that last night they spent together.

Jake nodded his head, his eyes fixed on Luke.

"You mean to tell me that you were with *her*," he said as he pointed to the phone, "this beautiful woman here, *and* you were a perfect gentleman."

"Come on, man! Of course. It's not even like that. *That* would've been a waste of time. I wanted to get to know *her* better. And she's...of course she's beautiful, but she's also intelligent and fun. And her heart...the way she thinks about things." He stared into the sky, lost in his images of her and the time they had spent together.

"So Luke's in love with a Latina Catholic girl! I never thought I'd see the day." Jake threw his head back and laughed. "I knew all that time you spent with us would rub off on you at some point!"

Luke sat forward in his chair and laughed. "You should have seen her jaw hit the ground when I took her salsa dancing. She didn't know what hit her. She was already shocked I could speak Spanish."

"I bet! Just be careful. Latinas are...well, you know my sisters."

"What? Fiery, passionate? Those are some of the things I love most about her."

The way Jake's eyes were dancing with mischief and delight annoyed Luke.

"Dude, in the all the years we've been best friends, I've *never* seen you like this over a girl, not even Rebecca. And you know I've known you since we were ten. So what are you going to do? She's a senior. You're obviously going back to Boulder for grad school, right?"

"I don't know yet. My dad wants me to stay and work for him. But, I just...I have to see her again, one more time before I decide."

"Dude, you got it bad!" Jake chuckled and sat back in his seat, drumming his hands on his lap. The mischief in his eyes increased more by the second. "Well, I guess it is about time."

"Whatever, man," Luke said without necessarily denying his assertion.

As they walked over to the East River to watch the Macy's 4th of July celebration, Luke grabbed his phone and scrolled through his photos to find the one of him and Ariana in front of the Palace Theater. He studied the photo, admiring her, awestruck at how far things had come between them in such a short time, yet he was unwilling to promise anything as he thought about his conversation with his father. His stomach tightened again as he relived the encounter in his mind.

"I hope you got that archaeology stuff out of your system now that you found what you and your mom were looking for. I've got a big project coming up, and I want you to run it. Rebecca just graduated from NYU and is starting law school in the fall, and I think you two are the perfect fit to take this project to the next level," he had said.

"Really, Dad? I haven't even been back a full day—"

"Well, you're smart and talented, Luke. What can I say? I just think it's time for you to get a lucrative career going rather than spending more time in school digging up the past."

He kicked a small rock in front of him. He would much rather be in Boulder with Ariana than stuck in some stuffy office with Rebecca. She was a nice person and all, and she and her family had become family friends over the years, so he couldn't totally avoid her, but he just wasn't interested in working with her. His trip to Spain that he had hoped might give him clarity had totally changed his world. But rather than giving him clarity, with Ariana, things were even murkier now. He pictured her leaning against the short wall on the patio at El Convento. Her smile lit up the night sky. *Spain...Dual citizenship.*

The entity issuing citizenship in Spain would review their application and give them word on their acceptance within six to eight weeks. He was planning on gathering all of the materials, filling out the application, and sending it in that week. That would give him until the end of the summer. He was excited. Getting accepted meant that he could go back and do more research. Maybe apply to grad school in Madrid and work on more archaeological projects rather than going back to school in Colorado. Ariana could come after she graduated.

Bursts of fireworks erupted, bringing him back to the moment. He took a deep breath and concluded that that's what he would wait for to help him make his decision.

Chapter 12

Ariana

Music blared from Ariana's speakers as she passed a car on her right, then another, weaving in and out of traffic as she sped to the airport. Luke's plane had already landed. Her fingers tapped to the music against the gear shift just like the butterflies in her stomach. She went over every detail of their time in Spain and New York in her head. It had been over a month since their date in New York, and even though they talked almost every day, she missed seeing his face and feeling his arms around her. The thought of his sweet kisses sent a bolt up and down her spine.

She rounded Peña Boulevard, speeding toward the airport with the infamous blue horse marking the entrance. When she drove through arrivals, her heart skipped a beat when she saw him standing there waiting for her with that breathtaking smile and rolling suitcase in hand. She parked the car and jumped out.

"You're here!" She threw her arms around him.

"I missed you." He held her tight and breathed deeply.

"Me too." She pulled back, and her eyes caught his. Her breath caught in her throat.

He pressed his lips to hers, and for a minute, they were stuck in each other's embrace until they heard the commotion of other cars trying to get through.

"Let's get your bag in the car," she said in a small voice. "How was your flight?"

"Great! I couldn't wait to get here. This is for you." He handed her a gift bag. "I wanted to bring you flowers, but I wasn't sure they would last in the heat of the car during our drive."

Ariana reached for the bag. "You brought me a gift?" She pulled the handles apart and tried to take a peek inside. "You're so sweet! Can I open it now?" she asked with a bounce just as a car honked.

Luke looked over his shoulder. "We should probably get on the road first."

"Right." Ariana ran around to the back of the car and opened the trunk for Luke. He dropped his suitcase in and followed her to the driver's side of the car.

"Do you want to drive?" she asked, confused.

"Ariana, I'm opening the car door for you. When was the last time someone did that for you?" He chuckled as he reached around her for the door handle, slightly brushing her waist with his arm. She swallowed.

"Wow." She slid into the driver's seat, feeling her cheeks warm up. *I don't know that I remember anyone opening the door for me.* "Thank you...I'm sure you're hungry," she said as she fastened her seatbelt. "Let's grab something to eat, and then we can head down to San Luis. We have to be there in time for the pageant. My sister is running for fiesta queen. She's been wanting to do this for years, and she finally got her chance."

"Did you run when you were in school? I can imagine you in a pageant dress with big hair and make-up."

"Who me? Oh no, I wasn't into that...at all. What do you feel like eating?"

"I'm up for anything." He brought a hand to his stomach. "I am pretty hungry."

"Ok, I know where we can go. There's this place in Aurora that my aunt and uncle like to go to. It's off the highway. They have a variety of different types of food there. It's kind of a sports bar environment. It's pretty good." She was talking fast. *Quit babbling! Can't you see how he's looking at you? Don't make him regret he came.*

"Sounds good to me." He smiled attentively until she finished. He straightened himself in his seat and adjusted his seatbelt. *Is he just as nervous as I am?*

When they got to the restaurant, Ariana grabbed her gift and opened it. She pulled out a five-by-seven-inch-framed picture of the two of them in New York that she had texted him. Remembering that night calmed her nerves.

"I love it. Thank you." She studied the photo and then hugged him. "We sure do look great together, don't we?"

He leaned his head on hers to get a better view of the photo. "Perfect." His voice was soft and deliberate.

They found a table, sat next to each other, and ordered. While they ate, Ariana talked to Luke about what he should expect in San Luis. She had already prepared her mom and dad about him. It had been difficult to bring it up at first. Since she had been in college, she had never felt compelled to bring anyone she had dated home to meet the family in San Luis, not even Brian. She told her mom first, who had already suspected something was going on since their drive home from the airport. She told her about how they had met, that he was from New York, and that his parents were both lawyers. Then her mom told her dad, and just as Ariana expected, he had lost his temper. But after talking with her mom, he had reluctantly gone along with the plan, trusting in his daughter's judgment but promising to keep his eye on him.

"So this is the biggest celebration of the year in San Luis," started Ariana. "It's named after *Santiago y Santana* or Saint James and Saint Ann, the parents of the Virgin Mary. They're the patron saints of the town. My mom's name is Lucia and my dad is Joe. My sister is Karina and my brother is Carlos…you'll be staying in his room." She gave him a sideways glance. "Unless you want to stay in your own place. I also reserved a room for you at our own bed and breakfast in town just in case."

"I don't mind." He responded without hesitation, like being apart from her wouldn't do. "I'm looking forward to meeting your family. So how far *is* your brother's room from yours? He can't be much of a light sleeper."

"Luke!" She balled up a napkin and tossed it at him.

"I'm just kidding!" He leaned back and crossed his hands to block the napkin, then he looked at her out of the corner of his eye with a side smile. "Sort of."

Ariana slapped his thigh from her seat.

He laughed and paused for a moment and asked, out of the blue, "So did you really have that medal blessed just for me?"

Ariana glanced at him. "Of course! St. Christopher is the patron saint of safe travels, and I *needed* you to get here safely, Mr. Cohen."

"Is that right?" He turned his body toward her with the look of intrigue all over his face. "And why is that?"

130

"Because there's going to be a lot of dancing to do tomorrow night, and I just couldn't take any chances…and maybe some hiking, too. It's my turn to show you *my* town. You should be prepared, though. It doesn't necessarily have the glamour of New York, but there's a charm and beauty that will take your breath away the same way."

Ariana knew her upbringing was unique. The more she talked to people in the city and people from all over the US and the world, the more she realized she had been blessed, especially by her immediate family.

"Alright then," Luke said. "I'm sure you're right. Now back to the gift you sent. I loved the flowers. No one's ever given me a gift like that, Ariana. But forget-me-nots, really? Not in a million years!"

"Did you *seriously* know they were forget-me-nots?" she asked, pleased that he was still talking about her gift *and* aware that giving a guy flowers could be risky and might have backfired.

"No, my mom was the one home when the flowers came, and she gave me the third degree about who would give me forget-me-nots."

Ariana laughed. "Sorry about that."

"It's ok. She actually thought it was very sweet."

When they finally drove into San Luis, it was dusk and *My House* by Flo Rida was playing in Ariana's car. As soon as they passed the school, the cars were backed up. The town was buzzing. They moved their way at a snail's pace in bumper-to-bumper traffic from the entrance into the town through the main street, past the first gas station, and then to the other end of the town where all of the cars were making U-turns just to make the whole trip back all over again. It took about thirty minutes to make the mile-long ride to the end of town on the two-lane main street. People were dressed to impress and standing around in groups, laughing and talking. Others were walking along the sidewalks on both sides, passing booths with people selling food, t-shirts, and souvenirs. Every car was full of people and playing loud music of all types, bass blaring.

A sudden panic made Ariana gasp and her heart quicken. *Shoot!* She made a right turn out of the traffic and onto a side street. She wanted to see if the pageant was still going on or if it was already over. Guilt tore at her gut when she realized how late it was. *What was I thinking?* She had overlooked the time enthralled in conversation with Luke at the restaurant. Even the unanticipated heavy traffic with the construction in Pueblo hadn't phased her. Now she was going to miss her sister's big night. She passed by the museum where the little theater was housed and stopped on the side of the road.

"They're still in the pageant." Ariana banged the steering wheel and then rested her head against it. "Look at all the cars." She pointed at the parking lot and groaned. "I want to go in, but I don't want to interrupt."

"Are you sure? You should at least try."

"Yeah, I'm sure. You don't understand. It's so small in there. I know it's packed with people. I don't even think they'll let me in now. I could totally cause a huge ruckus or ruin someone's performance." She sucked the air through her teeth and fell back into her seat. "Ugh. Can't believe I missed it." She leaned her head on the steering wheel again and faced Luke. "I just hope they're filming it. I'm praying she wins. She's been rehearsing for over a year for this moment. I don't want her to be disappointed."

"Why don't we go and take my stuff to your house," Luke said, placing his hand on her back, "then we can come back and see if it's over."

"Ok."

When they got to Ariana's house, Rufus ran to them wagging his tail. Luke stooped down to play with him, and Ariana stopped at the front door to watch.

"You must be Rufus," he said in a funny voice, playing with his floppy ears and petting him. "You're too big to be this playful." At that, Rufus lifted his head and licked the length of Luke's cheek. Ariana folded over in laughter.

"Ugh, Rufus! Really?" Luke stood up laughing. He wiped at his cheek with the back of his hand. "I think that was a little too personal for our first meeting!"

"Come on in," Ariana said, still giggling. She walked toward the kitchen to set down her purse and keys on the countertop. "Just set your bag down there by the couch in the front room. I'll show you where Carlos's room is later. There's a bathroom right down the hall to the right if you want to wash your face. The towels are in the hall closet to the left of the bathroom."

"Ok, thanks." He headed for the bathroom.

Ariana met Luke in the hallway after he had walked out of the bathroom. He had stopped to admire some family photos on the walls.

"I have to go freshen up," she said. "I'm going to change and redo my hair and make-up. Everyone back in town is going to be all dressed up for the fiestas, and I'm a mess from the trip."

"Ok."

"But first…" She took his hands in hers and leaned up to kiss his soft lips that had become irresistible to her. "Thanks for being here. I missed you over the past month."

"Me too." The words caught in his throat as he caught his breath, gazing at her as if she had taken him by surprise.

She smiled and stepped slowly toward the stairs, holding on to his hand until their fingers parted. "Stop checking out my booty," she yelled back without looking at him when she had made it halfway up the stairs.

He laughed out loud. "Hey, that's my line!"

Ariana rushed to her room to change. She grabbed the new shorts outfit she had bought just for the fiestas and got herself ready. When she was finished, she walked downstairs and checked herself one more time in the long hallway mirror. She found Luke sitting on one of the kitchen stools focused on his phone. "Are you ready?"

He looked up at her. "Yeah. Whenever you are."

They were just about to walk out the door to go back into town when they heard a commotion outside. The door flew open with what seemed like family members by the dozen filing into the house.

"Mi' ja! You're home!" her mom yelled and ran in to hug her. "I'm glad you're here safely, but you missed it! Karina won! She's the Santiago y Santana Fiesta Queen!"

"Yay! That's awesome!" Ariana jumped up and down with her mother. "Where is she?"

"She's on her way. She's bringing some of her friends over to celebrate. She was disappointed you weren't there. What happened?"

Ariana frowned. She didn't want to say she lost track of time with Luke. "I know. I hate that I missed it. There was horrible construction traffic in Pueblo." *It was true.*

Ariana's mom's eyes moved toward Luke. "Hi! You must be Luke."

"Sorry, Mom. Yes, this is Luke." Ariana held onto Luke's arm. He had stuck his hands in the pockets of his jeans and stood wide-eyed watching all the people coming into the house.

"I'm Lucia."

"Hi." Luke offered his hand. "Nice to meet you."

"Nice to meet you, too. We hug here." She extended her arms and embraced him. "I've heard a lot about you."

"Likewise," Luke said, hugging her back.

Ariana introduced Luke to more of her family members and searched for her dad in the crowd. She looked outside through the screen door. When she didn't see him, she invited Luke to help her and her mom in the kitchen. As they made their way there, Ariana grabbed her mom's arm and leaned into her ear to whisper, "Where's Dad?"

"With your Uncle Steve. He's on his way," she whispered back.

"Ok." She wiped her forehead, pulled her hair in a knot, and washed her hands. Her mom had taken out pots of beans and chile and bags of homemade flour tortillas. Together, they got napkins and silverware and set up the counter in a buffet-style. She heard the front door open and gruff laughter through the noise. A hush came over the crowd as Ariana's dad and her Uncle Steve walked into the living room. Ariana took a deep breath. She threaded her arm around Luke's and held his hand.

"Come on. My dad's here."

You could hear a pin drop as Ariana got closer to her dad.

"Dad, this is Luke, my friend from college."

Ariana's dad had been wiping at his eyes from his laughter when he turned and saw Luke and Ariana standing in front of him. His expression hardened, his mouth a tight line. He shook Luke's hand with a firm grip.

"Joe Romero," he said in a low, gruff voice.

Luke swallowed.

"Luke Cohen. It's a pleasure to meet you, sir. I've heard a lot about you."

Joe nodded and walked into the living room. No one dared to move except Ariana's mom who turned up the New Mexico music with Al Hurricane, Jr. blaring *Flor de las Flores* through the surround sound speakers and called everyone to come and eat. They all spilled into the kitchen. She walked over to Ariana and put her hand on her shoulder.

134

"I'll go check on him."

"Ok," Ariana said, fidgeting with the hem of her top, which had wrinkled from the clutch of her sweaty hands.

She smoothed it over and pushed the loose hair around her face back around her ears.

"I'm sorry," she said to Luke. "I'll be right back."

"It's ok," he said, rubbing her back.

She walked toward the hall and the bathroom to pull herself together. Her face was hot. *That was so rude!*

Her mom and dad were talking in the living room; her dad was blinking and slumped in his living room lounge chair with his hand on his mouth.

She stopped halfway into the hall when she heard her dad say, "I knew this day was coming, Lucia, but I didn't expect it to be this soon."

"She'll be twenty-two in a few weeks, Joe. And she'll graduate from college in a few months."

"I know, but I didn't expect to see her glowing like that either. Did you see them, Lucia?"

"I did," she said, smiling. "He seems like a very nice kid."

"I don't know. We'll see. We don't know anything about him yet. It just took me by surprise, that's all. I need a beer or maybe a shot or both."

Lucia laughed. "I'll go get you something. Now, let's go eat."

Ariana swallowed the lump in her throat and continued to the bathroom to check her make-up and fix her hair.

Karina walked in the house a few minutes later looking like a movie star. everyone whistled and clapped as she made her grand entrance. She walked in still in her gown, crown, sash, and bouquet of flowers. Ariana shook her head as she watched Karina milk the attention and imitate the pageant wave. Her sister was stunning. She was taller than Ariana, even more so now with her five-inch heels, but she was built thin like her. Her gown was long, strapless, and pale pink. It was form-fitting and hugged her as she moved. Her eyes hid behind thick make-up, and her long, sandy blond hair was beauty-shop styled.

"You won! Congratulations! I knew you'd do it!" Ariana ran to her, and they screeched together in some sort of hug slash dance. Karina held her crown so it wouldn't fall.

"Where were you? I can't believe you missed it." Karina pulled away from Ariana and smacked her shoulder.

"I know. Me either. I'm *so* sorry. I hate that I wasn't there." Ariana held on to one of Karina's hands. "It was already a tight timeline, and we ran into some crazy construction traffic in Pueblo. Did you guys film it?"

"Yeah. You're lucky we did, otherwise you'd just have to imagine how amazing I was." She turned her nose up and pressed her hand into her beauty-shop hair."

"Great." Ariana rolled her eyes and threw her hands in the air. "Just what we needed. Now, we're going to have to grease the sides of your head to fit it through the door!"

Luke laughed out loud, making both girls look back at him behind Ariana.

"Is this?" Karina started, looking at Ariana. "Luke?! So nice to meet you. Finally."

"Nice to meet you, too. Congratulations," he said as he reached to hug her.

Karina eyed Ariana while she hugged Luke with her eyes huge and round, and she gave Ariana a thumbs up behind Luke's back.

They all moved to the kitchen to eat, and when everyone was finished, the crowd dispersed. Carlos and his friends went outside, and Karina and her friends had gone back out to town. Some of Ariana's aunts and uncles were still there. Her dad had already had a few drinks and was working on another beer.

"Vamos a jugar a la baraja,"[106] Ariana's dad told her Uncle Steve and Uncle Tomás they sat down at the dining room table. He pulled the cards and began to shuffle them. "Do you play cards, Luke?"

"Sure...yeah," Luke said.

He opened his mouth for a split second but shut it without saying anything. Ariana watched Luke protectively from the kitchen where she helped her mom and aunts clean up. Luke pulled a chair and sat next to Uncle Tomás.

"Mira esta." Aunt Juanita nudged Ariana's mom with her elbow, pointing at Ariana with her lips. *"Anda bien* in love."[107]

"I know," Lucia said, giggling. "I've never seen her like this before."

---

[106] Let's play cards.
[107] Look at her...she's all in love.

"*¡Mira como se le cae la baba!*"[108] joked Aunt Juanita, forcing Lucia to burst out laughing.

"*¡Déjala!*"[109] Lucia wiped her eyes and smacked her sister with a trapo on her thigh.

"You guys! I'm right here!" Ariana broke her gaze from Luke and stomped her foot, making a face at her mom and aunt.

She looked back to find that they had begun their friendly poker game.

When it was Uncle Tomás's turn to shuffle, he said, "Joe, *¿qué no bebe este, o que?*"[110] pointing at Luke with his lips.

"I'll take a beer," Luke said.

"*Oh, ¿hablas en español?*"[111] Uncle Tomás asked, lifting his eyebrows.

"*Sí,*"[112] Luke said.

"*¡Qué frega'o! Ya no puede uno hablar de nadien.*"[113] Ariana's dad grunted and shook his head. He threw his cards to the table face down and stood up to grab a beer for Luke.

Ariana, her mom, and Aunt Juanita soon joined them at the table. Luke pulled out the chair right next to him, and Ariana sat down, trying not to do or say anything that would give her family any more ammunition. And they played cards and laughed until the wee hours of the night. When everyone had already left, Ariana pulled Luke aside to show him where he would be sleeping. They had taken the trundle bed from underneath Karina's day bed and set it up in Carlos's room with fresh linens and blankets.

"That was fun," he said. "Your family is hilarious!"

"I know, right?" She opened a small hall closet and pulled out a pillow.

"Between your Uncle Steve's crazy jokes and your Uncle Tomás's cheating, I didn't know what to pay attention to. One might say I was being swindled."

"Did you win at all?"

"Not even close!"

---

[108] Look at her drooling!
[109] Leave her alone!
[110] Joe, doesn't this guy drink or what?
[111] Oh, you speak Spanish?
[112] Of course
[113] Damn! A person can't talk about anyone anymore.

Ariana laughed. "Well, there you go! Seriously, though, I think you were a hit with them. They were surprised you could speak Spanish."

"That always surprises people."

"Well, you have impressed me once again." She put her arms around his neck. "What *is* a girl to do?"

"I'm sure we can come up with something." Luke kissed her and wrapped his arms around her back.

"I'm sure," she said, kissing him back and pushing the pillow into his chest. "But for now, get some sleep. We have a big day tomorrow. The parade starts promptly at 9:00 am, and my mom and dad are driving the float over at 8:00 to get in line."

Chapter 13

Luke

The aroma of coffee and breakfast cooking downstairs coerced Luke awake. He looked over at Carlos who was still asleep. He found the bathroom, washed up, and went downstairs. Ariana was already there helping her mom. She had showered and was ready to go in a dark green dressy tank, jean shorts, and brown sandals that laced up her calves. *Gorgeous.*

"Good morning," she said with her eyes bright.

"Good morning!" He gave her a hug and kissed her forehead. "It smells good in here."

"Do you want some coffee?"

"Sure."

"Help yourself to breakfast, Luke." Lucia grabbed some keys off a hook on the wall. "There's eggs, bacon, potatoes, and tortillas. Joe and I are headed to the parade to get our float in line. He's already outside hooking it up to the truck. We'll see you all there."

"Thank you, Mrs. Romero."

"Please, call me Lucia," she said with a smile that reminded him of Ariana.

Luke served some eggs and potatoes, grabbed a tortilla, and sat down where Ariana had set his coffee.

"We've got to leave pretty soon. I'll clean up while you get ready."

"Ok, Carlos is still asleep. Is he coming with us?"

"Yeah, I'll go and get him up in a minute."

They got themselves together and were out the door. It wasn't a long walk to the main street, but when they arrived, the sidewalks were already filling up with people several rows deep to watch the parade. The parade started with the sound of a police siren, and the mayor and town council appeared in the first float followed by the Fiesta Queen float with Karina at the center and the other pageant contestants surrounding her. As the parade continued, those who rode the floats threw out candy to the children watching on the sidewalks, and they flocked to pick it all up like a bursting piñata at a birthday party. There were horses, vintage cars, a small marching band, and floats from politicians and local businesses.

"Look! There comes our float!" Ariana nudged Luke and pointed across his chest to Joe and Lucia's float.

"You helped them build that?" he asked Ariana. "You guys did an incredible job!"

The float was an impressive, huge taco with a Mexican hat on top that they had constructed out of chicken wire and stuffed with various colors of napkins. Their restaurant name and logo were prominent in huge bright letters on each side.

"Yeah, it was a lot of fun."

"It's really cool." Luke ducked just in time as candy came flying toward him, and eager kids standing next to him practically knocked him down to grab it. He and Ariana laughed as Luke regained his balance.

After the parade, Ariana's mother reminded her to pick up the pot of green chile from her grandma's house to take it to the cook-off. Luke and Ariana drove to her grandma's house to pick up the chile and introduce Luke to her grandparents. They walked into the small house that sat on the corner of a big lot in town. They entered the living room first. It was spotless but cluttered to capacity with trinkets and photos on side tables and all over the walls. There were plants on top of doilies and knickknacks in curio cabinets and sprawled across the surfaces of all the tables; and every piece of furniture had throw-blankets protecting it.

"Grama, are you here?" Ariana called.

Luke took in the warmth of the home. It was summer warm but cozy warm as well, like a soft blanket wrapped around you—the warmth that Luke could only describe as a grandmother's love. And that wonderful aroma. Luke couldn't quite put his hand on what it was, but it grabbed his senses and wouldn't let go.

"What is that?"

"Mmm." Ariana closed her eyes. "Roasted green chile and tortillas. *My* idea of comfort food."

"Smells good."

"*Sí, mi 'jita. Aquí ando en la cocina,*"[114] her grandma called from the kitchen.

They walked through the dining room and to the kitchen. Luke watched Ariana's grandmother take a small ball of dough from a bunch that were lined up in neat rows on the counter. She formed the ball into a small flat disc with the tips of her fingers, tossed it on the counter, and rolled it flat with a rolling pin. Then she moved swiftly to flip a thick tortilla that had been on a flat, black skillet before giving Ariana a big hug. She picked up her uncooked tortilla and flipped-flopped the disc back and forth in her hand until it was round, flat and ready for the skillet. She piled the cooked one on a tall stack on the other side of the counter. It was evident by her skilled handiwork that she had been doing this a long time.

"*¡Como te miras bonita, 'jita! Van p'al* cook-off?"[115]

"*Sí,* thank you, Grama, you too! It smells so good in here! *Pero, ahora vine a pepenar el chile que hicites pa' llevármelo pa' allá. Mi mom nos está 'sperando.*"[116]

Luke smiled as he listened to Ariana speaking Spanish to her grandmother. Her words and accent were so different from the way she spoke in Spain. He thought about her family the night before. They all sounded the same. Their dialogue was slower and rhythmic, song-like. Their use of archaisms in grammar and some of the words they had used were similar to the Ladino he often heard from his mom's side. He was fascinated and wondered if it was just the same words from the 15th and 16th centuries because of the timeframe their families had both been in Spain or if the Sephardic connection was real. He couldn't wait to find out.

"Grama, I want you to meet Luke."

"Ok," she said, washing her hands and drying them on her apron.

"Luke, this is my Grandma, Aurelia."

"Hi." Luke offered his hand to her. "*Mucho gusto de conocerla.*"

---

[114] Yes, my daughter! I'm here in the kitchen.
[115] You look beautiful, my daughter! Are you going to the cook-off?
[116] Yes...but I came to pick up the chile that you made to take it over there with me. My mom is already over there waiting for us.

141

"Ah! *Habla en mexicano. ¡Míralo!*"[117] She took his hand excitedly and then glared at Ariana. "*¿De 'ónde es tu familia, hijo?*"[118] She turned her attention back to Luke.

"*Mi familia es de Nueva York.*"[119]

"*Oh, pero ¿cómo aprendites a hablar en español tan bien asina?*"[120]

"*En escuela...y luego fui a España por un tiempo también.*"[121]

"*Oh que bueno. Pues, aquí, la plebecita ya no sabe hablar en su idioma... ¡es muy triste!*" she said, piercing at Ariana again. "*Ariana sí sabe un poco, pero lo habla mocha. La Karina menos, y el Carlos...ya no sabe nada.*"[122] She threw up her hands.

The phone rang, taking Grandma Aurelia from the conversation and to the phone station at the other side of the kitchen. She was an older Mari with her spunk, short, strawberry-blond beauty-shop hairstyle, make-up, and apron. Luke nudged Ariana with his elbow. "I think you're in trouble."

"You better watch it, Mr. Funny Man," she pushed back, pointing her index finger at him. He might have believed her had it not been for the smile she was trying to hide behind her hand.

"What are you going to do?" he asked, taking on her challenge. He smiled, folding his arms and narrowing his eyes.

"Huh? Oh, you don't want to know," Ariana answered like she hadn't expected the question.

Before Luke could respond, Grandma Aurelia shared that it was Ariana's mom calling to see if they had already picked up the chile. The cook-off was going to begin soon, and she wanted to make sure that it made it over there. As Luke waited for Ariana to help her grandmother gather the items to take over to the cook-off, he headed for the front door through the dining room, surveying all that the little room held. Much of the furniture was made of dark wood and was heavy, solid, and looked to be antique. He wondered how old the pieces might be. He noticed Joe in a family picture that sat in the

---

[117] Ah, he speaks Spanish! Look at him!

[118] Where is your family from?

[119] My family is from New York

[120] Oh, but how did you learn to speak Spanish so well?

[121] In school...and I went to Spain for a while too.

[122] Oh good. Well, here the young people don't know how to speak in their language anymore...it's very sad. Ariana knows a little bit, but she speaks it choppy. Karina even less, and Carlos...he doesn't know any of it.

middle of a buffet table against the wall next to him. It was Ariana's family. He picked it up to take a closer look and chuckled to himself admiring how cute Ariana was in ponytails, freckles, and a puffy, dark blue dress. He was about to put it back when he saw an old candle holder that had been behind the framed photo. He held the photo in mid-air and squinted his eyes to get a better look.

"Luke," Ariana called.

"Yeah?" He turned her way, back at the tarnished brass candle holder, and carefully placed the photo back on the buffet. He scratched the back of his head.

"Can you help me take this pot to the car, please?"

"Sure." He pulled himself away from what he had just seen and moved quickly to the kitchen to help.

"Grama," Ariana called, "*¿en 'onde 'stán los* pot holders?"[123]

"Allí deberían de 'star," she said. *"Yo los vide 'horita en ese cajoncito junto a la estufa."*[124]

Ariana found the potholders and gave them to Luke. He was caught off guard as he saw her eyes trail to his arms as he lifted the pot. He smiled.

"Be careful," Grandma Aurelia said with a heavy accent. "It's very heavy…and hot. You don't want to burn yourself."

"Ok," Luke said, still grinning.

He walked out to the car and placed the pot on the floor of the passenger side in the car, thinking he would hold on to it while Ariana drove to make sure it wouldn't spill. He was headed back in the house when an older gentleman wearing a Broncos cap with wisps of gray, curly hair peeking out from underneath came from around the back of the house whistling, holding a paper grocery bag and some wood.

"He-llo," he said. "¡Me 'spante!" The older man let out a gruff laugh that held suspended in the air for a couple of seconds. Luke couldn't help but laugh with him.

"Hi." Luke waved and walked toward him.

"You're Ariana's friend?"

"Yes, *mucho gusto de conocerlo.*" Luke extended his hand, figuring he had to be Ariana's grandfather.

---

[123] Where are the pot holders?

[124] They should be right there…I saw them a bit ago in that little drawer next to the stove.

143

The older gentleman took his hand with a twinkle in his blue-gray eyes and said, *"Muncho gusto…Moisés Romero, a sus órdenes."*[125]

"Lucas Cohen," Luke said, enjoying his lightheartedness, *"a su servicio."*[126]

Moisés's eyes narrowed, and his head twisted as he slowly took Luke's hand and shook it firmly. It was a skeptical gesture, like he didn't believe Luke had just spoken to him in Spanish. He shook his head and sat down on the porch swing with his items.

"¿Usted está haciendo algo de madera?"[127] Luke asked.

"Sí, estoy haciéndoles juguetes a mis nietos."[128]

"¿Juguetes?"[129]

"Sí, real toys." Moisés paused and looked Luke straight in the eye. *"Estos muchitos de hoy en día se la pasan metidos en la casa cociéndose los sesos jugando todo el día en esos telefones y ya no saben como jugar…allá afuera en el aire fresco como jugábanos nosotros más antes."*[130]

Luke realized he was still grinning. He sat back on the step up to the porch and crossed his arms to listen to Moisés more intently. He was spirited and his tone song-like as he expressed his angst with this technologically-driven generation, throwing his hands in the air in frustration.

Luke cleared his throat and said, *"Entiendo…es verdad."*[131]

Moisés pulled out the toys he had already made. He had some marbles and an old wooden spool with rubber bands and toothpicks attached to it.

"Mira."[132] He showed Luke how it used the sticks and rubber band to roll on its own like a tire. "This one is going to be a top." He reached back into the bag for another item. "When I was a kid, we used to play a game called *Pon.* You write letters on each side. Then you would have a bowl of marbles or pennies or something like that and you

---

[125] Pleasure…Moises Romero, at your service.

[126] …at *your* service.

[127] You're making something out of wood?

[128] Yes, I'm making toys for my grandkids.

[129] Toys?

[130] Yes…these kids today spend their time boiling their brains inside the house all day playing on those phones and they don't know how to play anymore… outside in the fresh air like we use to play before.

[131] I understand…it's true.

[132] Look

would spin the top. Whatever letter it landed on, you would have to do what it said. So, if it landed on the 'p,' that was *pon*, and you would put a penny back in the bowl. I don't know if they're going to appreciate it," he turned to Luke and continued with the same accent as Aurelia, "but I'm going to try anyway."

Luke put a hand on the man's shoulder. "I hope they do appreciate it. You're putting a lot of thought and hard work into this."

Ariana walked out of the house holding a clear plastic bin with bags of homemade flour tortillas, bowls, napkins, and other items Luke could only assume were for the cook-off.

"Here you are!" she said. "I was wondering what happened to you. I see you've met my grandpa. Hi, Grampo!" She hugged him and kissed him on the cheek.

"Hi, mi'jita!" Moisés said, setting aside his woodwork.

"We better go, Luke. My mom is waiting for us at the park."

"Ok." Luke turned to Moisés and said, *"Fue un placer hablar contigo."*[133]

"Igualmente,"[134] Moisés said with a smile.

"Ariana, can we go back inside just for a second? I want to ask your grandma about one of the candleholders she has in the dining room."

"Ok, but let's hurry. My mom is already like a lion."

They walked inside to find Aurelia still at it in the kitchen.

"Grama, Luke wants to ask you about this candleholder before we go. Which one?" Ariana turned toward Luke.

"This one, here." Luke pointed to the old, timeworn candelabra on the antique buffet.

"Oh," Aurelia said. *"Ese, me lo dio mi suegra.*[135] She didn't have any daughters, and Ariana's grandpa is the oldest in the family. She told me her mother-in-law had given it to her. It's been in the family for many generations. I don't know where it came from first, but it was very special to her."

"Well, it's very beautiful. We have one at home that's similar." Luke eyed Ariana. "I was just curious about where it had come from."

---

[133] It was a pleasure talking with you.
[134] Likewise
[135] My mother-in-law gave that one to me.

nk you," Aurelia said, winking at Ariana. "Maybe it will
_g to Ariana when she gets married one day. Her grandpa and I
didn't have any daughters either."

Luke's cheeks felt warm and Ariana's were blush pink, too.

"Ok, Grama, we have to go. I think I got everything. I'll see you later." Ariana hugged her grandmother and kissed her cheek.

"Ok, 'jita...Have a good time. God be with you." Aurelia stretched her arms toward Luke and kissed his cheek."

Luke was touched by the kindness of Ariana's grandparents. When he got in the car, he caught Ariana staring at him.

"What?"

"Well, you just charmed the heck out of my grandparents. My grandma was totally surprised at your Spanish...and mad at the rest of us for not learning." She nudged him and rolled her eyes.

He laughed.

"Ariana, you seriously have to research your ancestry and do that genetic DNA test we talked about on the phone."

"What do you mean? Why?"

"Well, for starters, your grandma has a menorah in her dining room, *and* your grandpa was whittling a dreidel out of wood!"

"What are you talking about?"

"Seriously. That candleholder your grandma has is a menorah. You know, what Jews light during Hanukkah? And your grandpa is making a spinning top toy for your cousins that he used to play with as a kid. He described the way you play it, and it was just like how I played with it as a kid." Luke's voice was raising at the end, and his heart was beating fast.

"What toy? That's crazy!" Ariana replied. "It doesn't make any sense. We're Catholic, Luke. We've *always* been Catholic. It has to be some kind of weird coincidence."

Her response was a wet blanket on his excitement. He was surprised that she almost sounded annoyed.

"I thought you'd be more excited about this. Why are you so opposed to the possibility?" *Why is this bothering me so much?*

He leaned an elbow on the opened window of the car door and scratched his head.

"I'm not...it's just...I just don't see it. I never even knew anyone Jewish until college."

"But it's so clear," he said, throwing his opened hands up in front of him. "The game. The menorah. The way you speak Spanish—"

146

"Look," she took her eyes off the road briefly to meet his, "when I talked to the genealogy lady from here, we were only able to go so far in her database with the information she had for the Romero side of the family. I know that my grandfather Solomon Romero was the first person to come to San Luis from New Mexico with Carlos Beubién and the Sangre De Cristo Land Grant. That was my Grandpa Moisés's great-grandfather. *His* great, great, great grandfather was born in the early 1700s in New Mexico. His name was Pablo Romero, and his wife was a Mascareñas woman from the same area. We're already in the early 1700s and still haven't been able to get past New Mexico...and *all* of the records are from baptism and marriage records from the Catholic Church."

Ariana finished just as they reached the parking lot of an old building where Luke could see people congregating outside in a grassy area. Her voice was even, and her tone was matter-of-fact. He took a deep breath and rubbed his hands against his denim shorts.

"Ok, I get it."

There was an awkward pause as they got out of the car with the box of goods and Grandma Aurelia's chile. They walked in silence toward Lucia's table. Luke took notice of all the goods that had been set up at various tables as they passed by. There were green and red salsas and chiles of all types of flavors and spiciness with chips and tortillas to eat with it. Luke glanced at Ariana walking in front of him. Her long, wavy hair swung back and forth, brushing the small of her back with every step. He hadn't meant to make her upset. He took a deep breath, and the spicy scents took his senses by surprise. It smelled hot. He could only imagine how they would feel on his tongue—which was now thirsting for a cool drink. He needed to wipe the sweat that had begun to form on his forehead. He looked up at the clear, blue sky. The heat was dry, but the sun was intense. His hands were heating up from the hot pot of chile, too. He could see Lucia up ahead. *Just a few more steps.*

When they arrived, he greeted Lucia and sighed, relieved to drop off the pot. He wiped at his forehead and set the pot holders on the table. Ariana's hand grabbed his, and a cool breeze washed over his face. She led him to the side of the building where they were alone. Her eyes were apologetic. She pulled her hair behind her ears and looked at her sandals before kicking a small rock out of place in the green grass. Finally, her eyes met with his again.

147

"Luke, so you said when we were in Spain that you had some online tools I could use to do more research. Can we look into it while you're here?"

"Of course!" Luke was happy to hear that she was interested.

"I'm sorry. The whole religious thing just freaks me out, but I am curious."

"It's ok. Whenever you want, we can log in and check it out."

"Ok…there will be a break after the cook-off before the family goes to the carnival. We'll miss the battle of the bands, but we can go back to the house and check it out then."

"Great!"

He was excited to see what they would find in their search and grateful for her change of heart. He pulled her toward him and threaded one hand through the hair behind her head and the other around her lower back. The smell of her hair and her heart vibrating against him sent him to the rooftops. They walked around, hand in hand, as the cook-off began, and the judges began tasting the delicacies that had been set before them. When the judges had retreated to discuss their favorites and pick winners from the various categories, the food was opened up to the crowd, and everyone dug in.

Ariana and Luke tasted each of the salsas and some of the different chiles and had a contest of their own. They chose their favorites and argued good-humoredly about which of them had the best flavors. Luke scoffed when Ariana challenged him about not being able to hang with her with the heat. He didn't want to let on that she might be right. But by the time they were finished, they were both red in the face, laughing and gasping for water or soda or some other cool drink that could put out the fire. In the end, Grandma Aurelia took second place for her green chile, and Lucia took first for her salsa.

They drove back to the house after that to do the research. Ariana took out her laptop and placed it on the kitchen table and opened it slowly, like she still wasn't quite ready. She slid it toward him, and he opened the genealogy account that housed the database for his family research. He watched Ariana pull her hair back into a knot and reach into her backpack for a notebook. He could see the apprehension in her expression while she flipped through the pages.

"These are the notes from my meeting with Maria. The oldest ancestors I know are Pablo Romero born in 1719 in New Mexico and his wife Francisca Mascareñas born in 1724.

"Ok," he said as he plugged in the names. "Huh. Nothing." *I guess I shouldn't be surprised. This database is Sephardic.* "Let's look at this other site. If there was any recorded information in the census, this site will have it."

The tension was exuding from her body, and her foot was rap-tapping on the floor next to him. Butterflies began to swarm in his gut.

"Ok. There are several Pablo Romeros born around the same time frame in New Mexico. What was his wife's name again?"

Ariana's eyes were glued to the screen, and her fingernail was in her mouth. "What?" She looked at him and swallowed.

"What was your great-grandmother's name?

"Oh...uh...Francisca Mascareñas." She picked up her notebook and set it back down.

Luke added the name to the search, and they came up together in the 1750 census as married and living in Taos County, New Mexico.

"That's him!" Ariana shouted.

"Awesome! Let's see what else we can find out." Luke shifted in his seat, a surge of energy running through him.

He clicked on Pablo's name, and it listed his parents as Diego Romero and Maria Josefa Trujillo, born in 1696 and 1698. He clicked on Diego Romero and found his parents as well.

He glanced over at Ariana who was sitting at the edge of her seat with her eyes fixed on the screen. With every click, they found more parents until they came to David Romero and Catalina Romero both born in Corral de Almaguer, Toledo, España. They looked at each other. Ariana took a deep breath and held it for a second, biting a corner of her lip.

"We'll get her maiden name if her parents are listed."

"Here, let me," Ariana said. She let out her breath and clicked on Catalina's name, her hand slightly trembling as it hit the mouse.

Her mouth opened and she clasped her cheeks with her hands. "Luis Robledo and Juliana Beatrice López."

They let themselves rest against the high back of their chairs and Luke reached for Ariana's hand that she had rested on her lap. She was still shaking. He was too.

"Catalina López Robledo."

Luke watched Ariana's mouth read the name on the computer screen slowly in a whisper. He grabbed for her other hand. "Ariana, it's her. Catalina is your great-grandmother. Look! I knew it!"

"No way!" Ariana said, shaking her head. Her cheeks were pink, and her eyes were large saucers. "So, let me get this straight…this woman," she pointed at the computer screen, "is my great-grandmother? *And* she was the one who wrote the diary? You've got to be kidding me! How can we be sure it's the same person?" Ariana stood up and paced around with one hand on her head and the other on her hip.

"It all lines up. The names. The dates. Where she was born and when she arrived in the Americas."

"Ok, but Luke, in the diary, Catalina was talking about Benjamín…this means that *your* great-grandfather and *my* great-grand—"

"Were in love over 400 years ago," Luke finished her sentence. He stood up in front of her and took her chin in his hand, caressing her cheek with his thumb. Her eyes were filling with tears. "Are you ok?"

"It's just that…what I felt at the excavation site…and when I approached the diary…oh my gosh…look at my arms." She tried to rub the goosebumps on her forearms away.

"I know. Ariana, it makes complete sense to me. It explains everything. Now it's clear why I have felt such a connection to you from the moment our hands touched and our eyes met in that bookstore. Now I understand why I felt like I already knew you even though I didn't even know your last name."

Ariana took Luke's hands in hers and opened her mouth just as the front door flung open, making his heart rate accelerate more than it already had been. Ariana gasped.

"What are you guys doing?" Ariana's brother asked standing in the doorway. "Aren't you going to the carnival? Everybody's wondering where you took off to. You missed the battle of the bands. Joaquin's band won."

"Uh, yeah, Carlos we're on our way," Ariana said with a quiver in her voice.

"Great timing, buddy!" Luke remarked with an air of sarcasm in his voice, which he knew could have been taken a couple of different ways.

He walked toward Carlos and roughed up his hair. Carlos ducked.

"Does anybody else need a ride?" Ariana glanced at Luke and shook her head, smiling. Her cheeks were still flushed, and there was a radiance in her eyes that clutched his heartstrings tighter.

"Just me," Carlos said. "Karina is going with her friends, and Mom and Dad are taking Tía Juanita, Tío Tomás, and the kids."

"Ok, let's go then." Ariana threaded her arm around Luke's and leaned into him. "We'll finish this conversation later," she whispered.

"For sure." Luke changed his tone and addressed Carlos. "Let's go get on some rides!"

"I want cotton candy," Carlos said.

Luke laughed. "Well, you better wait until after you ride for that."

They rode rides, played carnival games, and ate too much junk food into the evening until it was starting to get dark. Ariana and Luke stole a few moments alone and walked over to a bench that was outside the carnival perimeter and sat down.

"That was so much fun." Ariana sunk into the bench.

"It was! But I am so full. I don't think I've eaten so much in a day in my life."

"Me either." Ariana rubbed her stomach and stuck her tongue out. "Look at the stars." She pointed up to the sky. "I told you the stars were the same here...I love it."

It was a pleasant evening. The air was crisp, and there wasn't a cloud in the sky.

"So close you can almost touch them. Just like Corral de Almaguer." He gazed at her, remembering their interrupted conversation from before. "Beautiful." *Just like you.*

Ariana pulled her hair back behind her ears.

"Luke," she started, "thanks for helping me do the search. I'm sorry I was so skeptical. I didn't see how there could have been a chance...I mean...It's so unbelievable...I'm still shocked."

"I knew."

She took his hand. "I'm still in awe that you...are my Benjamín," she said in a small voice.

"And you, querida Ariana...are my Catalina."

He held her face and lifted her chin to him. He kissed her deeply and held her, trying to soak in the significance of the moment. Then, as if pulled straight from some clichéd movie script, fireworks began to erupt behind them from the school parking lot in the distance. He looked back at the fireworks, and they laughed at the coincidence.

When people began to exit the carnival, Luke asked her, "Do you want to meet up with your family?"

"We should. We need to go get Carlos and go home to get ready for the dance." He hesitated to get up, especially after she leaned her head on his shoulder. He put his arm around her and rested his head against hers.

Back at the house, Ariana came downstairs in a strappy, plum-printed sun dress and some wedge heels that laced up her calves that she had saved just for this occasion. He was casual in his jeans and short-sleeve buttoned down shirt. *Maybe too casual?* He didn't know what to expect. Her hair was even longer when it was straightened. She bent down to fix a lace on her shoes, and her hair fell to one side, exposing the tags still on the dress. He chuckled and reached for them, brushing his hand against the smooth bare skin on her back and making her gasp.

"Your tags."

"Ha! Oops. I'll get them." She pulled off the tags and threw them in the trash.

When they arrived in town for the dance, the main street of the little town with no street lights was still buzzing. There were people everywhere. Some of the booths from earlier that day were still open and selling food, t-shirts, or souvenirs. Cars were bumper-to-bumper and blaring all different types of music. Everyone was dressed to impress, and so were their vehicles. Some of the shiny low riders and vintage cars from the car show earlier were cruising back and forth without a speck of dusk showing off their art work and their hydraulics. The atmosphere was light and fun, just as it had been all day. Ariana found a parking spot about a block away from the main street and they walked over to the dance.

There were cars parked everywhere, including a row of shiny, immaculate Harleys sitting in front of the dance hall, which seemed to be packing up to capacity. Luke walked behind Ariana, holding her hand to make sure he wouldn't lose her in the crowd. The live band was just finishing up a Spanish song that blared loudly from outside as they walked along the sidewalk toward the entrance. The abrupt rhythms of the lead guitar, bass, and trumpets clamored in sync, ending the last notes of the song. One of the musicians let out a *grito* that took Luke by surprise and began singing a ballad beginning with the words '*Qué Casualidad*' as they walked in.

Luke focused his attention on the music and environment around him. He compared the various Latino cultures in which he had known and considered how different each of them were but also how much they really had in common. The language and the love of family, food, music, and dancing were each distinctive to their particular history and country of origin; yet, all of these things were a thread that united them all.

Ariana excused herself to the bathroom, and Luke continued watching the people dancing and the crowd carrying on at the bar. A tall figure walked over to him, and he looked up. The guy stood almost a head taller than everyone in the place, and he had a long beard and red hair that was held back in a braid that hung to the middle of his back.

"You're Ariana's friend." The way his brows met together, it almost seemed like an accusation. He waited for Luke to respond with his fists clenched at his waist.

"Yeah, I'm Luke." He extended his hand.

"I'm Joaquin, her *primo*.[136] Let's go to the bar."

What the? Luke pulled his hand back and hesitated. He didn't like how this "cousin" had approached him. But he wondered where all the antagonism was coming from, so he followed anyway. They found an open spot and sat down. Luke eyed him curiously. Joaquin looked like he belonged in some biker movie in his Levi's jeans and black Harley Davidson t-shirt. He thought about the varying features between all of Ariana's family members he had met so far. Ariana's mom's complexion was dark. Her hair was thick and black, which she wore parted on one side and neatly curled. She had high cheekbones and when she smiled, her slanted eyes turned to thin slits. On top of being nice, she was a beautiful lady, and he could see where Ariana got some of her features and her ways. Her dad, on the other hand, was pale-skinned with sandy blond curly hair, like Karina, and he had the same eyes as Ariana. Carlos had dark, curly hair, and looked more like his mom only his eyes were blue-gray. *And now this tall red-headed cousin. Genetics, are an interesting thing.*

---

[136] Cousin

"Look, man," Joaquin began, still staring him down, "I need to know what's up with you and my prima."

Luke had begun to open his mouth when two other guys approached them. They were big and burly, but not as tall as Joaquin.

"Hey, what's up, man? Who's this guy?" asked one of them.

"This is Ariana's friend from college." Joaquin gestured quotation marks with his hands.

"Luke," he said, a little intimidated.

"What's up, bro? I'm Alejandro, and this is Andrés. We're Ariana's primos, too." He pointed at the other guy with his thumb as they both crowded in closer in between Luke and Joaquin.

Luke nodded. "Hey." Different scenarios ran through his mind about how he would fend off this brood that had just surrounded him.

"Hey, Sam, bring us a round of Patrón," Joaquin said to the bartender. "So, anyway," Joaquin pointed a large finger at Luke's face. "You need to know that Ariana means the world to us, and *nobody* is going to mess with her." He finished by putting a heavy hand on Luke's shoulder.

Luke looked at the large hand, feeling his jaws and muscles tighten and his fists clench. He met Joaquin's glare and said straight-faced, "She means the world to me, too…she's…"

Sam set the drinks down in front of them. All three guys leaned in, fixed on Luke's response and waiting for him to finish.

"She's," his eyes went to his shoes, and he remembered that she had called him 'her Benjamín,' and he couldn't help his cheesy grin, "amazing."

Joaquin's glare softened, and he removed his hand from Luke's shoulder.

"That goofy smile is all I needed to see. The family network already told me everything else."

"Look at him!" Alejandro pointed at Luke and laughed.

"He's *all* in love!" Andrés agreed, landing a fist to Alejandro's gut.

"Salud!" Joaquin picked up his shot and clanged Luke's shot glass, spilling a little on the counter. The rest of them grabbed theirs and repeated the cheers, and they swallowed the vicious liquid, grimacing as it hit their taste buds.

"Right on! Bring us another round." Joaquin chuckled and threw up his glass to Sam.

Luke knew they had broken him down. It was alright, though. He did care about Ariana, and it didn't matter to him who knew it.

Besides, it was endearing that they cared about her that much to check in on who was interested in her. It said a lot to him about Ariana's character and how he wasn't the only one that appreciated her incredible heart.

They were laughing at something Andrés had said and Luke had just finished the third round that he had bought when he saw Ariana walking out of the bathroom.

"What the heck is going on over here?" she asked as she got closer.

"Hey! There she is!" Luke stood up and stumbled, feeling the effects of the tequila that had already begun to sneak up on him. He grabbed for her waist and kissed her cheek. "I just met some of your cousins."

Ariana's eyes narrowed. "How long *was* I in the bathroom, geez! What the heck did you guys do?" She smacked each of her cousins in the chest with a closed fist.

"It's all good, Ariana! *¡Cálmate!*" Joaquin said. "This guy is cool."

Ariana's eyes met with Luke's. He shrugged his shoulders. She sucked the air through her teeth and shook her head.

"What am I going to do with you?"

It may have been the tequila talking, but he could think of a few things. The way the dim light highlighted her cheekbones and her hazel eyes sent him to the moon. The band announced that they were taking a fifteen-minute break and would be back in half an hour to the crowd's laughter. A DJ took over and said, "This is for all the lovers out there." Tim McGraw's *It's Your Love* came over the speakers, and people began flocking to the dance floor.

Luke took Ariana's hand, and they walked to the edge of the floor. He placed his hands around her tiny waist, and she lifted hers around his neck. He leaned his forehead on hers and kissed her softly. She leaned her head on his chest as they slow-danced, lost in the romantic words.

"Los 'friends'." Alejandro laughed, poking Joaquin in the ribs with his elbow and pointing at Luke and Ariana with his lips.

"I know," Joaquin said, rolling his eyes as he chugged a beer.

"*I* want a 'friend' like that!" Andrés said.

Luke heard the comments and chuckled to himself, and then he squeezed Ariana and kissed the top of her head. *There's no place else I'd rather be.*

Chapter 14

Luke

Luke buttoned his short-sleeve shirt, slipped on his shoes, and pondered what this experience would be like. Sure, he had been inside many Catholic churches before when he was in Spain and one time when Jake's oldest sister baptized her first child. But that had only been a short ceremony, not an entire Catholic service. This would be his first. It would actually be his first religious service since, well, a very long time. He took a deep breath. *Just observe and stand when she stands and sit when she sits.* He looked down at his clothes and wondered if he was dressed up enough. Ariana had reassured him several times that his dark-wash jeans would be fine. He smoothed his shirt and hurried down the stairs to meet Ariana and her family.

When they got to the church, there were droves of cars and people gathered around the stone half-wall perimeter of the church courtyard. They walked through a gate and onto some grass where two aisles with several rows of seating led up to an alter dressed in white linens. To the right of the altar, Luke saw what he thought might be a mariachi choir at the front near the altar. There were trumpets, guitars, and violins, and the musicians were all dressed in the same black ornate attire with white trim.

He followed Ariana's family to one of the last pews that had been set up on the grass. The ones in front had filled up pretty fast. Joe and Lucia had filed in first, followed by Karina, Carlos, and Ariana. He was at the end of the row next to Ariana. From the corner of his eye, he could see lots of heads turned in his direction. He thought it was the heat, but maybe it was the eyes of curiosity, or accusation maybe, glaring at him. *Just like all small towns, I'm sure they're either wondering who I am or they already know all about me.* He wiped the sweat from his hand on his jeans and reached for Ariana's. She took it and readily threaded her fingers through his.

In front of them, some of the older ladies wore large wide-brimmed hats, and some of them and families with children held umbrellas over their heads. It was getting warm for 10:00 in the morning. And this heat was even more intense than summers in Denver. The sun felt like it was only several feet away. Thankfully, a cool breeze brushed through every now and then.

The trumpets began playing, and everyone stood up. The guitars and violins chimed in, blending with the voices in English and Spanish. It was harmonious, floating through the air and into the depths of Luke's soul. He swallowed and touched his hand to his throat and cleared it. Was the music giving him a lump in his throat? He hadn't even been paying attention to the lyrics! His eyes followed a couple kids in white robes walking single-file up the center aisle, the one in front holding a large golden cross on a pole. A priest, dressed in a colorful robe followed the children to the altar.

Ariana was completely engaged during Mass, reciting every word, singing all of the songs, and following every action. If anyone in her family was once Sephardic, any trace of its religious roots were now completely non-existent. It occurred to him how efficient the Inquisition had been throughout the centuries in annihilating any tie to Judaism, save for a few remnants like language, games, and family heirlooms. *Maybe that's why she was so hesitant to finding out if there was a connection to Catalina. How would she negotiate this spirituality in her mind?*

After Mass, there was a buffet-style barbecue set up under some tents in an outdoor space across the church. Ariana and Luke took their place in the long line with her family. Several men and women collected payment and served everyone who came through the line. Ariana had explained to Luke that the whole community came together for this barbecue. The families who raised cattle, sheep, and pigs donated the meat, wrapped it in packages, and smoked it under ground. Luke's eyes went from each shredded meat buffet tray to the other. *Which is which?* As if Ariana had read his mind, she asked, "Can I have some of the lamb, please?"

"Sure," the lady said, serving a spoonful onto her plate.

"I'll have the same," Luke said. Next in line were mashed potatoes, gravy, salad, and homemade bread. All of the cooking and the other food items had also been made and provided by volunteers. Ariana's family had brought some of the mashed potatoes, gravy, and homemade bread for the event from the restaurant.

Luke was savoring each bite of the food. The meat was well-seasoned and tender from the way it had been prepared. Ariana put a hand on Luke's knee and whispered, "We have to come back to watch Karina perform at 2:00, but I want to show you something first. Let's go back to the house and change to something more comfortable."

He looked at Joe who was still talking about how his Grandfather Solomon never ate pork because he was allergic to it.

"I'm glad I didn't that gene!" He let out a grunt-like laugh and wiped his mouth with his napkin.

"Ok," he said finally. Her hand on his thigh had taken him by surprise. *Something more comfortable?*

At the house, Ariana instructed him to get his sneakers and shorts on. He laughed to himself as he changed. *Right. Something more comfortable.* When they returned to town, they parked the car near the church, and Ariana led Luke across the street that was still laden with tons of cars to a path through an archway and toward a mesa with the words *San Luis Oldest Town in Colo* written in white rocks up ahead.

"What is this place?" Luke asked.

"It's called the Stations of the Cross Shrine. Years ago, one of our priests had this vision of placing statues of each of the stations along a path that would lead to a small chapel at the top. He wanted people to be able to come and meditate on what Jesus went through leading up to his crucifixion. Then they could come into the chapel and pray. One of our local artists designed and made the three-quarter life-size statues."

Luke took notice of the first statue and its detail, particularly the anguish he saw in the faces. "The artwork is impressive."

They walked slowly along the dirt path, hand in hand, admiring each statue as they continued. Luke sucked in his breath as they reached the top and he caught sight of a large cross rising up from the ground.

"Out of breath already?" Ariana joked.

He looked at her from the corner of his eye and twisted his mouth. "Are you kidding? I could've climbed another thousand feet, especially at your pace."

"Yeah, I'm sure," she said playfully, nudging him in the ribs. "It's amazing, isn't it?"

He followed her eyes back to the cross and stared at it for a minute. It wasn't the familiar Christian image Luke had seen in other churches and paintings of a suffering Jesus nailed to the cross in agony. This Jesus was triumphant, unattached to the cross, and rising from it instead. His head was inclined upward toward the heavens with an arm extended in the air, reaching for it. With the mountains and the clouds draped across the blue sky as the backdrop, it was easy to see how this image could be an inspiration. *Huh. Fascinating.*

Ariana's fingertips along Luke's arm broke his gaze. He looked back at her and put his arm around her shoulder. Behind her, Luke saw a small chapel that looked like it had been lifted out of rural Spain and placed on top of this hill. Ariana led him past the church toward the edge of the mesa.

"Look at this." She pointed to the view.

She sat down on one of the rocks, and Luke sat next to her. His foot pushed a rock loose from its place, and he watched it roll down the steep hill of rock and small brush, giving him vertigo. He situated himself and lifted his head to a spectacular view. "Whoa," he muttered under his breath. The little town was still sprawling with activity, but the noise was quiet from the top of the hill. *So peaceful here.* As he looked past the town out farther east, it was green, open, and grassy. A road divided the expanse and curved upward toward a majestic mountain range with a small snow patch still grasping its hold near the peak.

"How tall is that peak?" He extended an arm toward the mountain.

"It's over 14,000 feet. It's called Culebra Peak, named after the windy river that comes from the top like a snake down through the town." She leaned in and motioned downward from the top of the mountain with her finger. Her hair brushed against his face, making the air even sweeter around him. *Focus.* "See that snow patch near the top? It looks kind of like a bird, and if it's still visible in the summer, it lets us know that the watershed will be enough for irrigation. The grassy area you see on both sides of that road over there is actually

159

one of only two common lands in the country. It's called *La Vega*. The other is Boston Common."

"What makes it a common?"

"The land is not privately or publicly owned. There's a board that governs it. Farmers and ranchers who still follow the ways of the old Spanish agricultural practices use it mostly for grazing their cattle. There used to be many more in New Mexico, but over the years they were bought and sold, legally and mostly illegally, until it dwindled to what we have here now."

Luke watched Ariana as she talked about the land where she had grown up and reached for her hand, intertwining his fingers with hers, and she looked at him before resting her head on his chest.

"I used to come here a lot as a kid, especially when I was upset with my family or friends or hurt by some childhood crush."

Luke chuckled and kissed the top of Ariana's head.

"I used to pray, take in the view, and focus on its beauty. I'd stay here for a while then walk home feeling better…lighter somehow."

"I could see how being here could be meditative...healing. What did you do for fun here, though? Doesn't seem like there was a whole lot to do."

"Oh my gosh." Ariana sat up straight, her eyes lighting up. "We had a blast as kids. We would pack a lunch and ride horses up to the mesas in the summer. We'd go swimming and tubing in the river and arrowhead hunting. We rode our bikes *everywhere*. Everyone knew each other or was family, so we could literally be anywhere and it always felt safe. In the winters, we'd go up to the hills and go snow tubing. There was *always* something to do."

Luke imagined all of those things and smiled, thinking about how infinitely different his childhood had been. Ariana looked at her watch.

"What time do you have to be back at the airport?"

"I tried to take the latest flight. It leaves at 8:30 tonight."

"Ok," she said. "Let's go watch Karina, and then we should probably get on the road."

"Yeah," Luke said. He was surprised at how unexpectedly glum he felt about leaving San Luis.

They walked down the mesa and toward the museum's outdoor amphitheater across the street to watch Karina perform. The crowd had already begun to form in front of the little stage. Luke and Ariana found a spot standing near the wall on the left side, allowing the older

generation to take a seat instead. He stood behind her and held her waist, locking his hands with hers. Her familiar perfume tickled his senses, and he sighed. She leaned her head back against his chest, and he rested his chin on the top of her head.

Some local talent sang, recited poetry, and danced to all types of music. Then each of the pageant contestants presented their talents on stage one by one until Karina took the stage. She stood up there in a long, dark blue satin gown with her fiesta queen sash and crown and heavy make-up. She picked up her violin and began her solo of *Samba Pa Ti* by Carlos Santana, accompanied by Joaquin on the guitar. Ariana explained that she had heard it at a play that Uncle Tomás and Aunt Juanita had taken them to in Denver when they were kids and she never forgot it. When she got the chance, she began violin lessons and learned and perfected the song for this moment. Each note was on point—confident, delicate, and deliberate. The crowd couldn't help but dance, including Luke and Ariana. Their rhythm was effortless. She was warm against him, and her skin was so soft. Every interaction with her was unfamiliar territory but continued to dig deeper into his heart.

When Karina's performance was finished, they found Ariana's family and gave them hugs, saying goodbye. Ariana was going to stay the night at her Aunt Juanita's house so that she wouldn't have to come back home so late.

Luke shook Ariana's father's hand. "Thank you so much for everything," he said. "It was a great time."

Ariana's dad nodded his head. "Make sure she doesn't drive that car or *you* crazy," he said. Then he pulled Luke aside in a loud whispering voice that everyone could hear. "Hey, and don't let her sucker you into carrying that bag of hers. You might throw out your back!"

"Right?" Luke said, laughing. "I don't know *what* she carries in there!"

Ariana glared in their direction. "Da-ad, I can hear you! Is this how it's going to be? You're supposed to be on *my* side, Luke!"

"Of course I am," he said, pulling her close but still laughing.

Lucia, giggling at the exchange, hugged Luke and kissed his cheek. "Come back to visit soon."

"I will. Thank you again."

"Bye, 'jita," Lucia said, hugging Ariana and kissing her. "Be careful. Drive safe and call us when you get there. Love you."

"Ok, Mom. Love you too."

"Please say goodbye to Moisés and Aurelia for me, too. I thought I saw them here a minute ago."

"They were here to watch Karina, but my dad had some things to do back at the house, so they left." Joe said.

"Ok, well, I enjoyed meeting them yesterday."

"I'll tell them. It's nice of you to say that."

They found Karina and Carlos and said goodbye to them as well and went back to the house to gather their belongings. Soon they were back on the road to Ft. Garland and through La Veta Pass.

"Thanks for inviting me to come out here, Ariana. I can see how this place means so much to you. Your whole family is amazing…wild but amazing."

"Thanks." Ariana giggled. She briefly turned his way and nodded in agreement. "I'm glad you had fun."

"I just learned so much more about you. It gave me a deeper view into your heart."

She gave him a grin that squeezed his own heart.

"I can also understand why you were doubtful about being related to Catalina."

"What do you mean?"

"Well, it's just that…I can see how much your faith means to you and how rooted it is into your culture." He angled his body toward her in his seat. "I can imagine how it must have felt to think that your family might have been Jewish."

"It was…is," she said. "I'm just not sure how to process it right now. I mean, all I've ever known is the Catholic faith, and to think that our family may have been stripped from a religion and culture that we are now foreign to is kind of overwhelming. I don't even know what to do with that or what that would mean for my faith, if anything at all."

"I know. I was thinking about that at church today and while we were up on the hill." His mind wandered to the St. Christopher medal she had innocently given him from the heart.

"I *am* going to take that DNA test, though. I'm very curious to see what it will show."

"Me too." He smiled.

They continued their drive, reminiscing about all the fun they had over the weekend and their time in Spain and New York. The time passed rapidly as they traveled, flirting, laughing, and listening to music. Soon the Denver skyline was in sight, and reality set in that it wouldn't be long before they were apart again. The car was silent for a few minutes.

"I'm really going to miss you, Luke."

"Me too." He squeezed her hand that she had rested on the gear shift.

"Have you decided yet if you're coming back to Boulder for school or not?"

"No," he said honestly. "I need to talk to my dad and find out if our application for dual citizenship is accepted before I decide for sure."

"Ok," she said. "Well, I'm here for you if you want to sort through any of that stuff."

"Thanks," he said. "You're the best."

He meant it. He had never known anyone so caring and so…real. There was no pretending with Ariana. What you saw was what you got. She was honest, almost to a fault, and she wore her emotions on her sleeve. He loved that about her.

"Are you hungry?" she asked. "I think we have time to stop and grab something to eat before your flight."

"No, are you kidding? I ate so much this weekend it was ridiculous!" He was serious about the food, but his mind was also so full right now that eating did not seem appealing in the least.

"I know, right? Me too. I don't think I'm going to eat for the rest of the week."

Ariana drove through the tolls to Peña Boulevard toward the airport and exited at the cell phone lot next to a gas station. They still had thirty minutes before he had to go, and she didn't want to spend it circling the airport. She found a spot to park at the far end of the lot away from the other cars, and they got out. The air was still thick with the heat of the day. It had been a particularly hot summer in Colorado. They leaned against the car, and he held her. Ironically, *Already Missing You* by Prince Royce featuring Selena Gómez was next on Ariana's playlist. She rested her head against him, and he kissed her, running his fingers through her hair.

"I think I'm going to kidnap you, Mr. Cohen," she teased.

"It can't be kidnapping if I'm willing."

"I guess it would be more like aiding and abetting, then?"

They smiled and kissed. Their hearts beat in sequence as they watched the sun beginning to hide behind the clouds, making them dark purple and creating blue-gray, orange, and dark yellow lines that outlined the edges of the mountain range. There was nothing like a Colorado sunset. They stood there in each other's arms up until the very last second Luke would have to get through security on time, then she drove him to the airport. She got out of the car to open the trunk for him to grab his suitcase. They held hands on the curb, and he kissed her once more.

"Call me when you get there."

"I will. Let's plan to see each other again soon. Maybe you can come out there before school starts?"

"Maybe."

"Ok…I better go."

"Ok." She squeezed his hand and held onto it until the tips of their fingers let go.

"Bye, querida Ariana," he said before turning to walk into the terminal.

"Bye," he heard her say in a whisper.

Luke found a seat and waited to board the plane. His stomach was knotted, and his jaws tightened. He hated leaving Ariana. He pulled out his phone and scrolled through the photos he had taken in San Luis. He paused at the one of the Culebra Peak he took from atop the Stations of the Cross Shrine. It really was magnificent. He found one of Ariana on a carnival ride with her brother. Her hair was blowing back with the wind from the motion of the ride. She had a huge smile on her face, and he could tell she was laughing out loud. He let out a little laugh, remembering the moment, and studied the curves of her face, the shape of her lips, and the sparkle in her eyes.

He wondered what Benjamín and Catalina looked like and if their features had been passed down through the centuries to them. He wondered if Benjamín felt for Catalina the way he was feeling for Ariana right now, and if he did, how could he have left her knowing he would never see her again? The loudspeaker announced that they would be boarding his row, and he walked onto the plane. He slept most of the way to New York and texted her when he arrived, sending her the carnival pic with the message, *I'm here. Call me if you're still up.*

The next morning, Luke held back a yawn and looked out of the wall of windows and the cluster of skyscrapers in front of him. He had had to be up early for this meeting with his dad. His phone buzzed, waking him up from his daze. *A text.* He shot up from his seat and said, "Excuse me. I've got to take this."

"Luke!" his father said, squeezing a pen with his fist. "What could be so imp…I apologize," he said, addressing the gentlemen seated at the table with them.

"I'm sorry," Luke said. "I'll be right back." And he walked out of the conference room and into the hallway.

Chapter 15

Ariana

Ariana sat on Tía Juanita's couch and stared at the picture of her and Luke that he had given her. She traced his face with her finger and held the picture against her chest. Her fingers tapped against the back of the frame. She picked up her phone again to make sure the ringer was on. *Nothing.* When she had awoken that morning, she had found her book still on her lap and her phone was on the floor. At first she had been a little disoriented, not remembering where she was. She had been dreaming of playing pool with Luke at a pool hall, selling bootlegged whiskey, and dancing at a huge baptism celebration.

I've got to stop reading Rain of Gold *before bed!*

She had picked up her phone and had noticed that Luke had sent her a message.

"What the heck!" she had said aloud, stomping her feet on the ground. "I didn't hear the message last night. I can't believe I missed him. Stupid phone." She had quickly found his name and called him back. It had gone straight to voicemail and she had left him a message.

"Hi! It's me. I didn't get your message until this morning. My ringer was off for some reason. I'm glad you're home. Call me when you can. Pensando en ti."

While she waited, she reminisced about the events of the weekend. His baby blues shining in the sun. His arms and how his muscles had tightened, peeking from under his shirt as he had picked up the pot at Grandma Aurelia's. How her head seemed to fit perfectly against his chest. It had become her favorite spot.

She sighed and shook her head. She was feeling like a lovesick teenager. At this rate, it might not be good for him to come back to

Boulder in September. She might not be able to concentrate with him here and focus on all the work she had ahead of her before graduation. She grabbed her phone again and found the picture he had sent last night and sent him a crazy-faced emoji in response. A few minutes later the phone rang, and she picked it up before it finished ringing.

"Hey!"

"Hi," he said.

"How was your flight?"

"It was good...long." He paused and cleared his throat. "Are you, uh, driving back home yet?"

"Not yet. But I will be pretty soon." She furrowed her brows. His voice was tense and abrupt.

"Can I call you back? I'm kind of in the middle of a...meeting with my dad...but I just had to hear your voice."

"Sure." *What kind of meeting?* "I'll be on the road for a few hours, so call me when you can. Is," her legs stretched out in front of her and she pulled on the stray hair tickling her neck that hadn't quite made it into her messy bun, "is everything ok?"

"I will...yeah. It's just a meeting with some clients."

"Ok. I'll be waiting for your call." *Clients?*

Ariana peeled off her track jacket and tied it around her waist. She was still trying to catch her breath. This walk toward the bookstore was the perfect cool down. The huge campus trees shaded her from the warm August sun, and the fall breeze brushed against her face, cooling her off after her run. School had begun, and it had been several weeks since Luke's visit to San Luis. *I'll call him after I buy the books for my classes.*

"Here. You. Are!" A voice shrilled in between breaths. Ariana flipped around to see Liz trying to grab for her shoulder with one hand and bent over, placing the other one on her knee.

"What's wrong?" Ariana's hand went to her heart. "You scared the heck out of me."

"I, uh, need the shoes you borrowed the other day," she said before swallowing, still trying to catch her breath.

"What?" Ariana scrunched her face watching Liz's dramatics.

"Yeah." One of Liz's hands went to her hip and the other palm to her chest. "It's just that, uh, my feet *are killing* me right now and I...need the ones I lent you. Where are you going?"

"Well, I was on my way to the bookstore." *She hates those shoes.* "What's going on, Liz?"

"Nothing! Your books can wait," she shouted. "I me-ean..." she finished in a softer, more calm tone, "I *really* need those shoes, Ana, *please*?"

"Fine," she said. "I don't see the urgency, but I guess if you *really* need them. I can go to the bookstore later."

"Thanks, Ana!" Liz jumped up and down with a huge grin on her face. "I *really* do."

They walked back to Ariana's dorm room and she opened the door and turned on the light. Luke was lying sideways on her bed with a rose in his mouth. She gasped and blinked to make sure what she was seeing was real.

"Oh my gosh! I can't believe you're here!" He stood up, and she ran to him, her emotions trying to sneak out of her eyes. He picked her up in his arms.

"I couldn't miss your birthday," he said as he planted a kiss on her.

Ariana looked back at Liz and shook her head. Liz smiled and gave Luke a thumbs up, satisfied with her work, and closed the door.

"How did you guys...pull *this* off? I didn't know you even knew each other."

"Well, I do have a ton of tricks up my sleeve."

"Is that right?" She tilted her head upwards and kissed him. "This one, Mr. Cohen, was a pretty cool trick."

He was a sight to see in his dark wash jeans and dark blue checked, short-sleeve, button down shirt. The color of the shirt complemented his skin color, making his eyes even more of a brilliant blue. Behind him, she saw two dozen long-stem red roses already in a vase with water sitting on her dresser next to the framed picture of the two of them. She let go of him and ran to the flowers.

"Luke! These are gorgeous!" She closed her eyes and breathed in their wonderful scent.

"So are you."

"Whatever!" She grabbed the top of her head. *OMG! My hair. I'm in running clothes. No make-up. I must reek! Ugh.* "I just got done running!" She tried to sneak a peek at herself in the mirror.

"Trust me." He walked toward her, took her hands, and said, "I know we talk every day, but…it just isn't the same as being here with you."

The knots in her shoulders released from the touch of his hands. "I know. I've missed you. I can't believe you're here. What should we do?"

"All of that, querida Ariana, has already been taken care of." He held her waist and kissed her forehead. "All *I* need is for you to get yourself ready."

"O-k. For what occasion?"

"Well," he began, "let me ask *you* what *you* want for your birthday first."

"My wish already came true." Her voice was breathy and she put her hand on his chest.

He smiled and kissed her softly.

"Ok, what was your second wish?"

"Honestly?"

"Honestly."

"Well, I wanted to go to the Charlie Puth and Meghan Trainor concert at Red Rocks, but it's sold out. Both Liz and I tried to find tickets and nothing was available."

Luke reached into his back pocket and waved two of them out in front of her.

"Your wish is my command." A grin of satisfaction took over his face.

Her eyes grew wide.

"Do you have a genie and a lamp in there somewhere?" She grabbed them and jumped up and down. "*How* did you get those? How did you know?"

"I got them a while ago when I heard you singing," he said the word *singing* while motioning quotation marks in the air, "to *One Call Away* on our way back from San Luis. I figured it would be a cool birthday present."

"Hey, I can sing!" She smacked his arm with the back of her hand.

"Ok, ok. So you keep saying…just like Hotel California, right?"

"I love that song," she said, giggling. "Anyway… I'm going to forget you said that because I love how perceptive you are." She kissed his cheek. "It's a perfect birthday present. Thank you. I can't believe you did that! I'm going to run and get ready!"

She grabbed some clothes from her closet and ran to the bathroom, dancing and singing *One Call Away*. He laughed.

Luke had the TV on when she walked out; she was wearing an above-the-knee, navy blue a-lined sun dress and wedge sandals. He stood up to meet her halfway.

"Wow, I love that color on you."

"Thanks." Her eyes fell to the carpet.

He lifted her chin with his fingers. "Your eyes look just like your grandpa's." But his gaze was almost as if he were somewhere else.

"Is there something wrong?"

"No, why?"

"It's just something in your eyes. That's all."

"I'm ok. Let's go eat first and then head over to the concert."

"Ok," she agreed, even though she wasn't completely convinced by his answer.

"Should we have sushi?" he asked. "Ready to try it?"

He looked so optimistic and hopeful, but the thought of raw fish and rice didn't seem appetizing to her at all.

"I don't know. What if I don't like it?"

"Then we'll go somewhere else."

"Ok, fine…I'll try it."

They found the sushi place near downtown Denver that Luke and his DU friends had frequented, and he ordered several different types of sushi for her to try. It was not what she had expected at all. The fish was delicious, and the different flavors were very good, especially the spicy ones.

Ariana picked up a roll with her chopsticks and studied it. "None of this is shellfish is it?" When Luke didn't respond right away, she looked at him. He was staring out of the restaurant window.

"Luke?" She wiped her mouth and put her napkin down.

"Huh?" He flipped back to her. "Sorry. What did you say?"

"The sushi. Is any of it shellfish?"

"Oh. No. I don't eat shellfish," he said.

"Good. I don't either."

"Are you allergic?"

Ariana followed his eyes towards the city street and the cars zooming by.

"No. I just think it's gross."

He looked down at his plate, nodded, and rubbed his hands against his jeans. His feet were tapping against the floor.

She put her chopsticks down and pulled her hair behind her ears. "Ok. What's going on, Luke?"

"What do you mean?"

"There's just something about you tonight. Is there something you want to talk about?"

Luke looked down at his food and then back up at her.

"Luke? Seriously. You're starting to freak me out."

"Ok, Ariana," he began, "I do have something to tell you."

She got a pain in the pit of her stomach. "What is it?"

"Well, I have some good news and bad news. The good news is that we got word from the institute in Madrid that our application for dual citizenship was approved."

"That's great!" Then she sat back and crossed her arms in front of her. "So what's the bad news? Do I really want to know?"

He put his chopsticks down and sat back, resting his hands on his lap.

"I've decided to stay in New York and work for my dad until next May."

Ariana looked down at the floor. "I knew you were going to say that." A lump was forming in her throat.

"Ariana, I want to be here with you more than anything. You're all I think about when we're not together. But...I think the right thing for both of us is for me to stay over there."

"Both of us?" Frustration had begun to rise from her chest to the tips of her ears.

"I know you have so much work to do this year. I don't want to be a distraction."

"Shouldn't *I* be the one to make that decision? What about the program at Boulder? Isn't it still a perfect fit?"

Her voice was snappy and loud, rising with each sentence—partly because she wanted him here and partly because she knew he was right.

"It is still a good fit, I think, but dual citizenship means that I can go back to Spain to do the real research I want to do instead of jumping through hoops in some program that may or may not lead me to the career I actually want."

"You want to go back to Spain? Are you serious? What about us?"

She threw her hands up and landed them at her side. Her voice had become even more forceful as she thought of him being not only across the country but halfway across the world from her. She swallowed hard to force back the tears from falling.

"I want you to meet me in Spain after you graduate."

"What?"

"Well, you said you didn't want to run the restaurant in San Luis, right? Come to Spain after graduation, and stay with me for a while until you decide what you want to do. I want to be with you, Ariana. You have no idea how badly." He placed a hand on her upper arm. She looked down at it and back up at him. "But you still have so much to do here, and I also owe it to my dad to help out at least this once."

Her eyes focused on the glossy woodgrain in the table for a minute. "We should get going to the concert." She wiped her mouth, threw her napkin on her plate, and stood up. Her chair screeched on the hardwood floor of the restaurant.

"Ok."

The drive to Red Rocks was quiet. Ariana couldn't talk. His words muddled through her brain. She thought about his rationale for not coming back to school here and that he didn't want to be a distraction to her. She wanted to finish her senior year strong and maybe graduate with honors. She loved the idea of being back in Spain with him without the restrictions they had before. She also needed to be sensitive to his relationship with his dad, but she couldn't let go of the idea that they would be so far apart for such a long time. What would this do to their relationship? She didn't see how it could make it stronger that's for sure.

They got to the amphitheater early as the rows of seats began to fill. They found their seats and watched the opening band finish their set. This was Ariana's first concert at Red Rocks. The sun was beginning its descent on the horizon and the rocks on either side of them. Behind the stage, the sky shone bright orange as did the puffy clouds against the deeper blue sky. *What a view! These are great seats. I don't know how he did this.*

Another couple slid into their seats next to them, slightly pushing Ariana into Luke. She pulled up the blanket she had brought and her hand nudged his. He opened his hand and looked at her. She swallowed and took it.

"Luke, I'm sorry about how emotional I got back there. It's just that I was just getting used to you being back in New York, and now you're here and you're not staying in Boulder—" `

"I know. I'm sorry I laid it all out that way."

"It's ok. You're right. I thought about it the other day. I know I wouldn't be fully focused if you're here. You're all I think about, too," she admitted, looking at him in the eyes. "And I do understand about you wanting to work with your dad. Family is everything. But what's going to happen if you're there and I'm here and then you go to Spain and—" Her fingers pointed in the direction of her words.

"Hey," he said. He pulled her face toward him. "I'm not going anywhere."

"Just New York and Spain," she snapped.

"You know what I mean." He put an arm around her. "You mean the world to me. I'm just a phone call away."

"Ok," she said, "then get rid of that Android you call a phone and get an iPhone so we could FaceTime."

He laughed. "You got it."

The concert began, and they stood up to enjoy the music. They danced, and Ariana sang every song. The last song of the night was *One Call Away*, and Luke led her up above the seating to a grassy area. He put one hand on her waist and took her right hand in the other and pulled her close. She leaned into his chest and listened to the lyrics. Then Luke pulled back and looked at her in the eye, mouthing the words in time with the song, 'Superman got nothin' on me'. He pointed at his chest with his thumb with her hand still in his. She laughed.

"You better be right, Mr. Cohen. You don't want me to have to come out there."

"What are you going to do?" he asked.

"I keep telling you, you don't want to know. Just know that…you're not going to like it," she said, not wanting to admit she really didn't know what she would do *exactly*.

He looked up at the sky and smiled. "Hmmm, about 5'2" and 100 pounds or so coming after me with a vengeance, eh? Now, I'm curious. I may just have to push my luck."

She laughed and smacked him in the chest. "You better not."

He chuckled and held her close before leaning in to kiss her. "What do you want to do now?"

She pulled back and placed her hand on his chest. "You know, in all the excitement, I didn't even ask you how long you're staying."

"I have to leave tomorrow. We get started on the project on Monday."

Kimberly Sánchez-Cawthorn

"Oh," she said, disappointed. "Better make the best of it then. What time is your flight?"

"I have to be at the airport by 7:15 tomorrow night."

"Ok." She tapped her chin with her index finger. "There's a party on campus tonight, but I'd much rather spend the time only with you. I know where we could go."

They drove into the parking lot of a twenty-four-hour superstore where they could get some snacks and maybe something to drink. Then Ariana drove them west, deeper into the mountains, to one of her favorite hiking spots where they could overlook the city, gaze at the stars, and, hopefully, watch the sunrise if they didn't fall asleep first. She pulled out the blanket she had taken to the concert and another one that she kept in the trunk just in case. He helped her set it up on a grassy knoll near the car that was perfect for viewing the city lights in the distance. They ate their snacks and opened the coolers they had bought.

"This is an awesome view," he said.

"I know. I've never been here at night, but during the day the view is amazing. I figured it could only be better under the stars."

He held her face and parted her lips with his. They kissed deeply, letting their hands flow freely around each other in the darkness. Their hearts began to race, and their breathing grew heavy, feeling the passion growing between them. Luke paused for a second to look at her in the eye, and then his gaze followed her body to her feet. His hand moved from her thigh up alongside her body to her face, eliciting chills all over her body. He kissed her softly at first. Ariana reached under his loose shirt and rubbed his back with her fingertips, allowing her hands to explore his chest, his six pack, and his muscular arms. Then she wrapped her arms around him and pulled him close to her, intensifying their kisses.

Luke stopped and looked at her.

"What?" she whispered.

"Nothing."

He pressed his lips to hers again and held her close to him. Her body tingled, melding so naturally into his in a way she had never experienced. She quivered. He leaned back on one elbow and held his head with his hand. He looked up at the stars and took a deep breath. *Whew!* She was elated yet uncomfortable at her vulnerability. They lay there on the blanket and looked at the mass sprinkling of stars

174

glittering in the sky. Ariana tried not to think about the fact that they only had a few more precious hours to spend together.

"We can go to my aunt and uncle's house if you want. They're in San Luis this weekend, and it's closer to the airport from there," Ariana said, finally breaking the silence. She thought that they might need to get *some* sleep if she was going to drive him to the airport and back to DU after that.

"Ok, but later. I want to watch the sunrise with you."

Then, as if it couldn't be timed any better, there were their shooting stars again. One followed by the other in the immense dark sky. They sat up and looked at each other in complete awe that this was happening again.

"What do you think this means?" Ariana asked. "Do you believe what Mari said is true?"

"You mean about celestial beings out there somewhere watching over us?"

"Yeah."

"I don't know. But it seems like more than just a coincidence that this is the fourth time we've seen them."

"Fourth time?" Ariana asked, thinking it was just the ones she had seen before she had left for Spain and the ones they had seen together at El Convento.

"Yes," Luke said. "I never told you. I also saw them in New York the night before we flew out to Spain."

"Unbelievable. What is the likelihood of that? Four times?" She thought about it for a second and replied, "You know, I wonder if it's Catalina and Benjamín looking out for us."

He whipped around toward her. "I hadn't thought of it that way. You're probably right. Maybe they're trying to make sure *we* get it right." He nudged her with his elbow.

Ariana smiled and leaned into her favorite spot. She liked to think that they were 'getting it right', but she wasn't sure how the next few months would play out.

"So, speaking of Spain, I took the ancestry DNA test…I ordered it after I brought you back to the airport from San Luis. I got it about a week later and sent it back right away. I should be getting the results within a few more weeks."

"That's great!"

"I have to know. I don't even know what the test will reveal exactly, but I'm excited to find out how it might confirm what we found in our search and what my family has always known about our ancestry in Spain. Maybe *I* can apply for dual citizenship, too."

Luke smiled. "*That* would be cool."

And he pulled her close, and they lay in each other's embrace, engulfed in the validity of their centuries-past connection and in the belief that somewhere out in the universe there might be beings looking out for them, guiding them, and leading them toward one another. The laughter and sweet little nothings they spoke to each other rose and faded into the crisp mountain air as the vast star-lit night surrounded them. The city lights twinkled in the distance until the deep orange, purple, red, pink and yellow hues began rising up in streaks from the endless horizon of the plains.

Chapter 16

Ariana

Ariana sat at a computer in the library and massaged her calf, trying to make the blood flow back into her foot, which had fallen asleep from sitting in the same position for so long. Thoughts of Luke jumbled with the sentences she was writing for her senior project proposals. On top of studying for mid-terms this week, her advisors had begun sending her reminder emails that they were due by the end of next week. She tapped her feet against the floor and exhaled. She was running out of time. Once she submitted her proposals, she could spend the last part of the semester compiling her bibliographies, reading through her material, and researching her topics in more depth. Spring semester would be senior seminars and the actual writing of her work. She stared at the computer screen blankly and deleted what she had just typed. She had just put her head in her hands and was running her fingers through her hair to her neck when Liz came from behind her and touched her shoulder.

"Hey!"

"Hey." Ariana exhaled without looking up.

"What's wrong?"

"I don't know what to do for my History and Spanish projects."

"Don't worry, it'll come to you."

Easy for you to say! She looked over her shoulder at her friend.

"For now, let's go grab a drink to celebrate," Liz said with a bounce and gleam in her eye that matched her smile.

"Celebrate what?"

"I got my results for my MCATs, and I killed it!"

"Seriously?" Ariana stood up, hugged her friend, and sat back down. "That's awesome! Now you can start applying for med school!" She was quiet for a second before continuing, "Ok...let's go. I guess I could use some down time. I've been studying and trying to finish up work for my other classes, too...and," she pulled her hair behind her ears and rubbed her forehead, "I just can't get Luke out of my mind."

Liz rolled her eyes. "That boy ain't going nowhere, Ana! Don't you know it's so obvious how much he's into you. I was floored that he called me to set up the surprise for your birthday. That was *so* romantic, by the way. *Nobody* does stuff like that!"

"I know. I just miss him, and I don't know when we're going to get to see each other again. He's so busy, and so am I. We haven't talked in two days." She held up two fingers. Liz's eyes crossed as the fingers came at her.

"Oh wow." Liz slapped her palms to her cheeks. "The world is coming to an end." She put her hands on Ariana's shoulders and shook her lightly. "We have to get your mind off all this stuff. Let's go!"

"Alright." Ariana logged off, dragged herself off of her seat, and grabbed her books and bag. It was the right thing to do to celebrate Liz's hard work.

They went to a sports bar down the street from campus, and Ariana bought Liz the first round of drinks. Some of their other friends were already there letting off steam from mid-terms. There was live music, and everyone in the place was dancing, laughing, and talking. The vibrant atmosphere was polar opposite of Ariana's mood. She tried to hang for a while, but she was just not feeling it. Her neck was stiff and her shoulders were tight. She rolled her neck to relieve some of the tension and found Liz.

"Congratulations again, girl! Proud of you." She hugged her and excused herself.

She walked back to her dorm hall and sat on a bench outside, looking at the stars. She put her ear buds in her ears and queued up her music, wondering if Luke was thinking about her, too. He had told her that he would be working nonstop for the next few days on his dad's project. They were meeting with clients and taking them out in the evening, and he was doing research during the day. They had texted each other a couple of times, but she didn't want to bother him. She sat there hugging her knees and rested her head on them, fighting the urge to call him.

Her phone buzzed. She fumbled in her pocket, trying to pull it out.

Pensando en ti…*call me if you're up.* She smiled.

"Hello," he answered, after she called back right away.

"Hey!" She got up from the bench and started for her dorm room. "It's so good to hear your voice. I was just thinking about you."

"I was hoping to catch you. It's been crazy busy over here. I miss you."

"Me too."

"How are classes going?"

"Ok. We're in the middle of mid-terms, but my proposals are due pretty soon." She reached her room, unlocked her door, and threw the keys on her desk. "And I'm still not sure what I'm going to do."

"It'll come to you."

"That's what Liz said."

"She's a smart girl."

Ariana smiled. "I just want my projects to be…good."

"They will be, don't worry. It'll all come together when you least expect it."

"I appreciate your vote of confidence, Mr. Cohen, but I'm afraid you're biased."

"What do you mean?"

"It's understandable," she said, twirling a strand of hair in her fingers. Her tone suddenly became more playful.

"Is that right?" he said, matching her tone.

"I have become so irresistible to you that it has blinded your judgment."

He was quiet for a minute. Her stomach dropped and she bit the inside of her cheek. *Why did I just say that?*

"Are you there?" She bit a fingernail.

"Yeah, I'm here."

Whew! "Well?" She threw an open hand out from her side and lifted the hair from her neck which had begun to warm up.

"FaceTime me."

"What?"

"You're the one who made me get this new iPhone so we could talk through FaceTime, now I feel like we *have* to get some good use out of it. Call me back through FaceTime."

"Ok!" She smiled and threw herself on the bed. Her face warmed as his words registered in her mind.

179

She felt a little guilty for opening her big mouth about the phone. He hadn't had to switch it out, but he did. It made Ariana feel special and a little badly that he would do that just for her. She shrugged and clicked his number, and he answered right away. *Wow!* Even through the phone screen that can sometimes make faces awkward, he looked amazing. *His eyes. His smile.* The corners of her mouth turned up.

"Hi!"

"Hi. Now isn't this better?" she asked.

"I don't know yet," he said. "Now that I see you…I mean, I love hearing your voice on the phone, but…not sure it's making me miss you any less."

She flipped around on her back and put her knees up, holding the phone in front of her face. "Me either…so…tell me about your work then."

"It's pretty boring but important to my dad," he started. "We've just finished the busiest part. Now that we have the big picture in mind of what our clients are looking for, the next step is to put the pieces into place to make it all happen."

"O-k," she said. "Sounds like a lot of work but a little vague."

"Well, we, I mean my dad and the firm provide companies with legal advice to help them leverage their assets for maximum profits."

"Interesting."

"Not really. There's actually a lot more to it than that, but I'd much rather be doing the work we were doing in Spain."

"I can tell."

"What do you mean?"

She turned on her side and rested her hand on her head. "Your voice and your expression are flat when you talk about your dad's work, but when you talk about archaeology and the work you did in Spain—" She paused, recalling how smitten she was watching him lead the groups and talk enthusiastically about their work. "I wish I would have video-taped you talking about the diary to the group or recorded our conversation when you called me when you first found out about it. Then we could have compared it to what you just said, and you would see the difference."

"Oh, I know…it's just…complicated."

"Well, it's good to know what you want, that's for sure."

"And I do know what I want, querida Ariana."

She narrowed her eyes and tilted her head. "Are we still talking about the same thing?"

"I think we've just switched back to your irresistibility," he said, his eyes shining.

"See, this is why FaceTime is so good." She pointed a finger at him. "Now I can witness that sly grin on your face rather than imagining what it looks like from your voice."

"Now you're the one blinded by my charm."

"Possibly. Or maybe it's just the blue light from my phone."

He laughed.

"Thank you," she whispered.

"For what?"

"For making my day."

He smiled. "Can't wait to be with you again. I can't stop thinking about that night in the mountains."

"Me either. It was...amazing." She sat back against her headboard and pulled her knees up. Chills ran up her spine as she thought about how his arms had felt around her and the passion in his kiss.

"Now, get some rest and get a fresh start tomorrow. I'll call you."

"Ok...goodnight."

"Goodnight."

They hung up their phones and Ariana sat for a minute, feeling so far apart from him yet so close to him in spirit. *Ahhh! The things that man makes me feel!* She plugged her phone into her charger and extended her limbs. She stayed like that for a minute before grabbing *Rain of Gold* from her shelf and burrowing herself under the covers of her bed. *I have to do something to get my mind off of him.*

She had put off reading it since school had started, busy with her classes, but she was now determined to finish it. She read all the way through to the end without caring that she needed to be up early in the morning. She just had to keep turning the pages. And when she finally finished, she lay flat in her bed, staring at the ceiling wide awake.

Her mind was full. She had never read a book that touched her in such a way. It was a beautiful love story interwoven with her side and then his until they brought their stories together. And the magical realism aligned with historical fiction was the perfect blend of was-that-really-true and I-can't-believe-that-really-happened. She had learned about the Chinese working the railroads and about the Great Depression and Prohibition. She had also gotten a glimpse into what Mexicans had endured during and after their Revolutionary War through the firsthand accounts of both sides of his family. She loved how Victor Villaseñor had chronicled his family's history. *What a wonderful legacy to leave to generations of family members.*

She sat up, folded her legs, and leaned back against her wall. Her mind trailed to Benjamín and Catalina and how her diary was a legacy for her own family and for Luke's…and countless others she was sure. She thought about Catalina's anguish leaving the only country and lifestyle she had ever known to travel to a new world that she had known nothing about. What fear she must have felt. And the three-month voyage it took to get to the new world was an adventure in and of itself. Many of them, she knew from her studies, didn't make the voyage alive.

Ariana's head was spinning. Her heart was racing with the thoughts and images that were coming to her mind about her own family's legacy.

Catalina and her new husband had not only survived the Inquisition, but they had survived the voyage to Mexico and then had left Mexico to go north into New Mexico to settle yet another ambiguous, foreign land with uncertainties all its own. She wasn't sure of the timeline and how it had all transpired, but it fascinated her to know they had eventually made it to New Mexico only for their descendants to make yet another move north to San Luis generations later. *What bold and resilient people.* She knew that they had sacrificed their lives, facing many dangers they had encountered in their travels, including fighting the indigenous as they had encroached upon them and their land, weather, terrain, and disease. She let herself stew in their endurance and bravery for a moment, then she sat at the edge of her bed.

"That's the blood that runs through *my* veins," she said in her dorm room to no one at all.

Then she thought about her own faith and spirituality and realized that even in the face of their determination and perseverance to live a life free of religious persecution, in the end it had proven futile since any traces of their religion, except for some language, a few heirlooms, and games that Luke had pointed out, had been completely obliterated over time. She walked toward her dresser and picked up a framed photo of her family. *What would Catalina think about our family? Would she be proud of what they had accomplished?*

Her family had done pretty well, she thought in terms of settling and establishing themselves as successful in San Luis. Her family had owned that restaurant for three generations. Her great-grandfather had

182

started the business, and her Grandpa Moisés was still involved, along with her mom and dad. It was supposed to be her turn next. She sat at her desk and rested her hand against her head. *Is that what I want, though? How can I honor Catalina and her husband, my fourteen times great grandparents' struggles, sacrifice, and legacy? What will I do with my life after graduation to make their immense sacrifices worth their unnoticed efforts?*

She wiped at her face and sniffled. The only reason anyone knew about Catalina's struggles was because of her diary, and no one would have even known about it if they hadn't been digging. And then it hit her—she was reminded of a movie she had seen in one of her classes called *Walkout*. She stood up walked toward her desk and slammed her hand against it.

"If it isn't written, it never happened," she said aloud, recalling the words of the teacher at the beginning of the film that had so deeply impressed her. She spun around and a huge grin spread across her face. "I know exactly what I'm going to write about for both proposals!"

Chapter 17

Luke

Luke let out a heavy sigh as he flipped through the stack of files in front of him. *At least I have a window.* He pulled his shade up and stared outside a minute. The Empire State building stared back at him, towering over the other buildings surrounding it, and the street below was flooded with cars and people. His mind blurred and took him back to the colorful sunrise he had witnessed with Ariana, and he sat back in his chair, bouncing the back of his pen off his desk. He saw her clearly in her navy dress. Her tiny frame and long, dark wavy hair. *Those eyes and that smile.* A surge of warmth filled his chest.

She had felt like heaven in his arms that night. And the way her hands had tightened around his back had made him crazy. When he had felt her pull him close, he had known he needed to stop at that moment. To slow down. Be careful about his actions. He wanted to do things right with her. She deserved all the respect in the world.

His thoughts were interrupted by Rebecca's cockatoo laugh from the next room. He closed his eyes and tightened his jaws. *What am I doing here?* His phone buzzed against the sleek, translucent acrylic desk. *Ariana.* He smiled, and his heartbeat quickened.

Luke, I don't want to interrupt. But just couldn't wait to tell you that I figured out what I'm doing for my projects! On my way to the library. Call me when you have a minute!

He glanced at the clock. *Man, I wish I could call her right now.*

"Lu-uke." Rebecca knocked on the doorframe and peeked in from outside the door. "Are you ready?"

"Uh, yeah," Luke said, fixed on his phone as he finished up his text to Ariana.

"I'll wait for you."

"No need. I'll be right there."

"Alright then. See you there."

"Uh huh," Luke said without looking up.

Told you it would come to you! ☺ Excited to hear about your plans. I have a meeting until noon your time, I'll call you then.

He took another gander at the picture of her from *El Santuario* that he had made his screensaver, grabbed the files, and walked out to the meeting. When he got there, Luke's dad looked at his watch and glared back at him. The only spot available was right next to Rebecca. He pulled the chair, sat down, and straightened his tie.

"I told your dad you had gone to the bathroom," she leaned in and whispered behind her hand as he sat down.

"Thanks." *I think.*

Throughout the meeting, Luke's mind went in and out of the fog of Ariana's face and smile, wondering what she had decided to do for her projects. At one point, Rebecca had to kick him under the table to let him know his dad was talking to him.

"Luke? So, what do you think?" his dad asked. He scratched his curly salt and pepper hair and stared at Luke, waiting for him to respond.

"Uh, I, uh…I think we should offer the Wilsons Contract A exactly the way it's written. Maybe tweak the first line to include negotiations with the seller. According to the files," he said, flipping through one of the open folders, "it's the most sensible."

His dad smiled as he twirled his pen in his hand. "Right. Makes sense to me. I'll have Louise draw it up that way."

He pulled at the knot at his tie and smiled a 'thank you' at Rebecca.

As 2:00 drew near, Luke fidgeted in his seat, counting down the minutes until he could break away.

"Well, that was productive." Luke's dad placed his pen on top of his notepad as the rest of the team walked out of the office. "Luke, we're going to grab some coffee at the café down the street. Are you coming?"

"It's still your favorite, right?" Rebecca lifted her hand to Luke's shoulder.

"Sorry, not this time. I've got something to do." He looked at his phone and took a few steps back, barely noticing that it had made Rebecca's hand drop.

"Ok, then. See you back here in an hour." His dad's voice was faint in his ear as he sprinted back to his office and closed the door to call Ariana.

"Hey!"

"Hey! Glad to hear you found your topics. Tell me about them."

"Well, you actually called just in time," she said, in her sweet, melodic voice.

Just what I needed after such a long day! "Why is that?"

"I just got my DNA test results." He could hear the rifling of papers.

"You did? What does it say?" He sat up straight in his chair and switched the phone from one ear to the other.

"I wish you were here to help me figure out what I'm looking at. It's kind of overwhelming." *I wish I was there, too.* "There's a stack of papers, graphs, and brochures that I'm trying to make sense of."

"I'm going to FaceTime you so I could see."

"Ok, great!"

When she answered the call, he felt his face soften and his mouth slip into a soppy smile as he saw her sifting through a pile of paperwork. He leaned back into his seat.

"I can barely see you under all that stuff," he said, chuckling.

"I know! I'm totally buried, literally and figuratively." She threw some of the papers in the air and let them fall, feather-like, back onto her bed. "So, this pie chart says that I'm 71% European and of that I think is 4% Jewish."

"I knew it!" Luke said with a fist in the air.

"That is so weird to me! I just don't understand how it's never come up before."

"You have to understand how serious the Inquisition was, Ariana. Revealing your identity was a matter of life or death. I think the Sephardic Jews who fled to the Americas thought they were getting away from the Inquisition, but it followed them. So they still had to continue practicing their traditions in secret. To give you an example, when I was in San Luis with you, your dad said '*barajas*' to mean playing cards, but that word actually means prayer or blessing in

Hebrew...*baraha*, with an 'h.' I'm not sure what the story is behind that, but it might mean that they used playing cards as a cover for praying. In the case of your family, though, it looks like they ultimately surrendered to Christianity and the Catholic faith."

"Huh. That's where that word comes from?" She looked pensive, like her mind was picturing her family playing cards. "I have been thinking about how the religion was lost over time. It's kind of sad...but anyway..." She lifted the paper she was holding. "It also says I am 28% Native American, which didn't surprise me, especially from my mom's side, but it also shows that I am French, Irish and 1% African! Can you believe that?"

"Yeah, well, given the history of slavery, it's understandable."

"I guess so. It just caught me off guard. There are also all these other words and acronyms that I've never heard before, like haplogroup—Did I say that right? And M-T-D-N-A. Do you know what these things mean?"

"Well, haplogroup just describes the strand of DNA that you share with another group of people from the same line, and MtDNA, I'm pretty sure, refers to the DNA in your mother's lineage, from mother to daughter to daughter and so on."

"Ok. This is so interesting. I really want to learn more." She looked up from her work and flashed him a smile that made his elbow slip from the desk. He felt his face warm up. "Thank you. I knew you'd help me figure this out. I love hearing you talk about this stuff."

"No problem." He readjusted himself in his seat. "You know it's fascinating to me, too. It's partly why I got into archaeology in the first place. My mom's side of the family always intrigued me because it was so different from my dad's. It was mysterious, especially the language. Most other Jewish families I knew spoke Yiddish, and my mom's side spoke Ladino. I was always very curious about that as a kid."

Her eyes were fixed on him like she was hanging on his every word.

"So cool. Well, the more I learn, the more I want to uncover." Her focus went back to organizing the excess of paperwork surrounding her. "I was at the library trying to find information for my thesis, and even in DU's extensive library, I couldn't find too many books. But online was a different story. I was so surprised to find out how much information is actually out there about New Mexico and the Inquisition."

"So that's what you decided to study? That's great!"

She looked into the phone, her face lighting up as she put some papers down. "Oh yeah! I forgot to tell you. I was so excited about the DNA results. I'm going to study the relationship between the Inquisition and the people of New Mexico and Colorado for my history major. *And* I'm kind of hoping you could help me with my Spanish thesis." Her voice raised slightly in the end like a child asking for candy.

He smiled. "O-k. How so?"

"Well, I want to write a short story in Spanish about Benjamín and Catalina and their unfulfilled love."

He sat up straight. "That's an amazing idea! How can I help?"

"I'd like to use the diary as a source. Is that even possible? If it is, I would definitely need help translating it."

"I think so. Let me look into it, and I'll let you know." He spun his chair toward his desk. His eyes landed on his calendar with a note from last week to return a call from Ricardo. "Is Ricardo there this semester? He actually might have more information about it than I do."

"Oh yeah, right. I'll ask him. Thanks for reminding me of Ricardo."

"No problem," Luke said, returning his gaze back to Ariana.

Her hair was up and her face had a glow about it. This conversation with Ariana had invigorated him. He was lighter. More energetic.

"You know, Ariana," he started, "if you do use the diary, I will help you translate it, but I'll send you the pictures of the pages. You'll be surprised at how much you'll actually understand. It's a lot like how you speak. There might a few different words you don't understand, but it's very similar."

"Ok, thanks for all your help, Luke. I appreciate it."

"Any time. I'm looking forward to reading everything when you're done."

"Really?"

"Of course," he said, surprised she would even ask. He heard voices out in the hallway and looked up, catching a glimpse at the clock. He was so caught up in his conversation with Ariana, he had forgotten about the next meeting. *Three minutes to get there.* "Hey, listen, I have to go. I have another meeting coming up. Call me after you talk to Ricardo, and we'll go from there."

"Ok, I will. I'll talk to you later. Thanks again!"

Luke gathered his things and headed for the door. He walked toward his meeting in the clouds. Everything he had felt for Ariana from the beginning was evolving into something more deep and meaningful than he could have ever imagined. They could laugh together, dance together, discuss music and theater, and now they had just shared a passion of his—and of hers too, it turned out. Then there was his sheer attraction to her on top of all of that. He was spinning. When he walked into the meeting room, everyone was already waiting. His smile faded, and he was sure his face was red. The back of his neck was definitely hot. He cleared his throat, pulled himself back from his thoughts, and tried to refocus on why they were gathered there in the first place. His dad's expression was hard. His mouth a tight, thin line. Luke swallowed and sat down. His dad shook his head and got the meeting started.

Chapter 18

Ariana

Ariana lay on her bed on her side and held her head with her one hand while flipping through her collected material with the other, staring through the papers without focus. *He really is brilliant…and a breath of fresh air.* She remembered Brian and how he would change the subject every time she brought up anything remotely close to her studies at school. She rolled her eyes and leaned back into her headboard. The way Luke had talked about her research with her and how he was actually interested in reading her work meant the world to her. Everything about him was perfect for her. Sure there were the undeniable sparks, but they were connected on a level that she couldn't describe. It was the way he knew things. The way he went out of his way for her. How he held her, and the way he looked at her with such sweet gentleness. She sighed.

She sat up and crisscrossed her legs, staring at the paperwork and the plethora of articles she had printed from the library. It still amazed her that these ideas had already been floating around for such a long time. Why hadn't she ever heard about it? Why hadn't anyone ever talked about it at home? *Home.* In all the excitement and conversation with Luke, she had forgotten that there was a note from her mom in the package she had sent. She sifted through the pile, pulled the card from the envelope, and read:

Hi Hita,

 I hope you're doing good and that your studies are going well. Everything is good over here. The restaurant is keeping us busy. Your brother got straight A's on his first report card in high school, and Karina has started to apply for scholarships and to colleges too. We all miss you. You haven't been home in a while, but we know that your last year is very important to you, so keep up your hard work. We are all so proud of you.

We got this package in the mail for you a couple of weeks ago, and I've been meaning to send it to you, but I kept forgetting. I had to fill in for your Tía Dianne for a few weeks at the restaurant because she had to go be with her mom in Albuquerque for her surgery. But, anyway, it looks important, so I hope it's ok that you're just getting it now.

Call us soon to let us know how you're doing. I'm counting the days to see you for Thanksgiving! We love you very much.

Mom

Ariana felt a lump creep into her throat. She loved her mom so much. She was always so supportive, and she hadn't realized just how much she missed home until she read her mom's words. She set the note aside and pulled the certificate congratulating her on beginning her journey of discovery into her ancestry and family lineage and then examined the colorful pie graph with a map that said, 'Genetic Ethnicity' that showed a breakdown of her DNA results: 71% European, 56% Iberian Peninsula, 4% European Jewish, 4% France, 7% Italian/Greek; 28% American Native American from New Mexico; 1% Sub Saharan African. *Italian and Greek? I've got to find out what that's about.*

Ariana was curious about the 28% Native American finding, too. Her mom's side was obviously Native American, but she didn't know anything about that side either. They had never talked about a grandmother or grandfather who was full-blooded Native American. She would love to know what tribal nation or nations her family came from and wondered if Luke could help her with that, too.

Several days later, Luke was reading Catalina's diary and Ariana sat at her desk in her dorm room, listening and reading along to every word. They were engulfed in Catalina's words through FaceTime, and Ariana sniffed and reached for her tissues. Luke broke his gaze from the words he was reading and looked at her.

"She's really profound, isn't she?"

"She was a remarkable person." Ariana wiped at her eyes.

"It's no wonder my grandfather fell for her."

"Well, the way she describes him, he wasn't so bad himself."

"True." He shrugged and his gaze drew upward toward the ceiling. "But what I don't understand is how he could have left without her."

She sat at the edge of her bed. "I know. It must have been the biggest regret of his life. Can you imagine?"

"No…I can't imagine."

Luke's expression looked like he was miles away. Ariana was quiet, thinking about the thoughts behind Luke's words. She got butterflies. She stood up and walked toward the window.

"Thanks for sharing this with me. I'm glad Ricardo gave me the approval to use it as a source."

"Don't thank me," he said. "These words belong to you. The diary is your family legacy. You need to have a copy of your own."

"Wouldn't that be cool?" she said, dreaming of that for a minute. The clock on the tower in the quad bellowed, interrupting her thoughts. She looked back into her phone and into the curves of his gorgeous face, noticing his eyes were red and sleepy. Luke yawned. She giggled.

"Well, I guess I better go then. Are you bored?"

He laughed. "Totally."

She smirked, and her eyes narrowed.

He rubbed his eyes. "I'm kidding! Sorry. I had an early meeting this morning."

"I know. It is getting late, and I need to be up early tomorrow to work on all this stuff some more. I'll let you get some rest."

"Ok, I'll call you tomorrow."

After her initial discussion with Luke, Ariana had filled out the thesis proposal templates for each of her majors. Ariana's advisors had enthusiastically approved her proposals, excited that her projects had so much substance and were so personal at the same time. She and Luke had spent several nights together reading the pages that he had photographed of Catalina's diary, and each time they read it, Ariana was blown away by her ancestor. She had been a very intelligent, spirited person who was living a vibrant life at the time of the Inquisition. Her relationship with Benjamín was sweet and magical. Ariana longed to have known them in person. Reading her words, however, had to substitute for the next best thing. Her mind went to Corral de Almaguer and the feeling she got walking through

Catalina's home. *Wouldn't it be great to see it again, this time through this new lens?*

She sighed after thinking about Luke's offer to take some time to be with him in Spain after graduation and bit her lip. *I would love that.* At the same time, there was a twinge in the pit of her stomach as she wondered about the distance that would most certainly be between them for an unspecified amount of time *and* the uncertainty of her own future after college. *Dad, Grandpa Moisés, and the restaurant.* She wasn't going to think about that right now. But she definitely wanted to share Catalina and Benjamín's story with them when she was finished. She knew they would want to know Catalina the way she was getting to know her.

The next day, Ariana was at the library when she got a call from her mom with some amazing news. She couldn't wait to tell Luke. She ran to her dorm room to FaceTime him immediately after hanging up with her.

"Hey!"

"Hi!" Ariana could hardly contain her excitement. She couldn't wipe the smile off of her face. "I just got the best news. I know you're at work, but I couldn't wait to share it with you."

"Lu-uke, here are the files for the case we just looked at," a woman's voice interrupted.

Ariana saw a young, blond-haired woman walk in the door. Even from the awkward view of the phone, she could tell that the woman was striking in her light gray, tailored skirt suit.

"Thanks, Rebecca," he said without looking back. "Just set them on the table. I'll look at them in a minute."

Ariana waited for the woman to walk out and then asked, "Who is that?"

"Rebecca. She and I are working on the project together."

Ariana's eyes jetted toward the ceiling, wondering why the name sounded so familiar. Then it hit her, and she felt a blow to the pit of her stomach, and her heart sank to the ground.

"Is that your ex-girlfriend Rebecca?" She scratched her head. Her face was hot. The excitement in her tone switched night and day from the one she had started out with.

Luke hesitated, and his expression changed when he saw her face. "Yeah...that's her."

Tears welled up in Ariana's eyes. "All this time, Luke? Why didn't you tell me you were working with her?" Her voice rose with every word.

"I didn't think—"

"You didn't think?" Her voice caught in the back of her throat. She turned her head and blinked back her tears. Visions of Brian and that girl rushed through her mind. She glared back at him. "You're right. You didn't. I have to go."

"Ariana, wait a minute," Luke pleaded. "It's not like—"

She clicked off the phone before he could finish, threw it on her desk, and looked at the ceiling from her bed. She couldn't dry her eyes quickly enough. How could this have just happened to her? Her wonderful Luke. She felt like a fool. How could she have let herself become so vulnerable?

Lu-uke. Rebecca's high-pitched voice made her cringe, and her face and that designer suit shot through her mind. She looked like a model in that suit. And her flawless hair...glamorous, like a perfectly made-up actress from *Law & Order*. *I have to get out of here.*

She stood up and the petite reflection in the mirror glared back at her accusingly, in her faded, torn skinny jeans and a fitted Tweety Bird t-shirt, without make-up and her hair up in a high messy bun. *Ugh.* She changed to her running clothes and queued up her music. Luke had called her several times and had sent several text messages. She looked at them and traced his name with her finger; then she deleted them all, one by one.

She ran out the door and took to her path.

After her run, she was still a wreck. Her lungs, laboring from her run, made her chest ache more, and on top of that, now she had a headache. She called Liz. Liz came over as soon as she could. She brought wine.

"Liz, I can't believe he did this."

Liz sat next to her at the edge of her bed and put her arm around her.

Ariana bawled into her arms, her eyes beginning to feel raw. "He's been so wonderful in *every other way*. Why didn't he tell me?"

"I don't know, Ana. Boys are idiots when it comes to stuff like this. He probably didn't give it a second thought."

"He should have thought about that, Liz. That's a major detail to leave out, don't you think?" Ariana asked, sniffling and putting her head on Liz's lap.

"I guess," Liz said. "There are two ways you can look at it," she continued, pushing Ariana's hair away from her face. "Either he was trying to hide it from you *or* it actually wasn't a major detail to him."

Ariana sat up straight and wiped her eyes with a tissue. "You should see her, Liz...she's stunning."

"That doesn't matter, though," Liz said. "You know relationships are *not* skin-deep. Don't you think if he was really into her that he would still be with her?"

"He chose to go back to New York, didn't he? He's working with her, isn't he? Don't you think he just wants his cake and eat it too? They're all the same!" Ariana felt her hurt turning to anger all over again.

"Maybe, but what about everything you two did together? Your birthday? All that you two have felt for one another? The diary. Don't you think all of that means something to him?"

"I don't know." Ariana stared into space and reached for her wine and took a sip. "I thought it did." She wanted to believe everything they had felt and everything they had shared hadn't been in vain. She looked down at her feet and shook her head. "You know what? I don't need this." She tossed her wadded-up tissue into the trash can, sat back farther into her bed, and crisscrossed her legs. "This is why I was fine without a relationship, especially a long distance one!" She looked Liz in the eye. "I don't need the drama. I don't need to worry about what the heck he's doing...with her...thousands of miles away from here." She flung an arm aimlessly through the air. "I'm done. I have too much work to do this year."

#

Luke put his head in his hands and ran his fingers through his dark hair.

"What the heck just happened?" he said aloud to himself.

He felt like he had just been hit by a wrecking ball. He had no idea where all of that had come from. He tried to call her back, but she didn't answer. He texted her. Nothing. Rebecca came back in to ask if he had looked at the files yet.

"Are you ok?" she asked.

"No," he said. "I need some air…will you cover for me for a minute?"

"Of course," she said. "I'll be here. Is there anything I can—"

"Thanks." He rushed past her and into the hallway. Everything was blurred around him. He found the elevator and took a long walk to Central Park. He sat on a bench, stretched out his legs, and exhaled. He felt the fall air surround him. In all the excitement, he had forgotten to grab his jacket. It didn't matter, though. The adrenaline was pumping hard through his veins, keeping him from feeling the cold.

He couldn't believe he had messed this thing up without even realizing what he had done. He had tried to be so careful and attentive to her. She had made it so easy. How could she not know? Everything they had experienced and shared together. Rebecca meant nothing to him in that way. How could she not know how he felt for her and that he would never hurt her like that? He wiped at a tear that burned his cheek and called his dad. There was no way he could go back to work now, not like this. He needed some time to get himself together.

"Hello," his dad answered.

"Hi, Dad."

"Luke, where are you? Why are you calling from your cell phone?"

"I had to leave. I'm not feeling well."

"I told you not to eat that chili dog at lunch today."

Luke smiled. "Right. I know. I'm going home for the day. I'll be back tomorrow."

"Ok. But don't forget we're meeting with the Wilsons tomorrow bright and early at 8 am."

"I'll be there. Hey, will you let Rebecca know I'm not coming back?"

"Sure, son, I'll let her know," his dad said. "Get better."

"Thanks."

He sat there, staring into nothing, trying to figure out what to do. He called Ariana again, but she didn't answer. He looked at his messages, and she still hadn't responded to them either. Waiting for her to get back to him was gnawing at his bones. He let out a heavy breath and threw his phone on the bench. What he wouldn't give to be in Denver right now.

A couple of weeks had passed, and Luke was playing basketball with Jake at the gym after work. He had been working and working out nonstop since that day, trying to keep himself from letting his emotions overtake him. All he could think about was Ariana's last text.

Luke, I'm really sorry, but I think I just need some time to focus on school right now.

"Dude, did you miss that shot on purpose?" Jake's head moved with his shot that flew across the court a foot away from the hoop. "It wasn't even close."

Luke stepped off to the side to towel off the sweat from his face and neck. He sat down on a bench on the sidelines.

"She still hasn't called, eh?"

He threw the towel around his neck, holding the ends, and shook his head. His jaw tightened as he stared at the woodgrain on the court floor. Images of her face on FaceTime kept haunting his mind, and his stomach ached.

"I told you about Latinas, man. Give her some time to think things through. You two have experienced enough for her to come to her senses, Luke. I know it…hey," he said, hitting his arm, "you're lucky she's not here. There's no telling how it would have gone down if she had actually *walked into* the office and seen Rebecca."

Luke entertained Jake's words. He watched the last thing he said play out in his mind. His fiery Ariana. One of the corners of his mouth turned up.

"Look, man," continued Jake, "*I* know and everybody who knows you, including Rebecca, knows that you weren't trying to hide anything from her. But *she* doesn't know that. All she's seeing in her mind is your ex in that office with you and that you should have told her. She's going to need you to do something big to make this right."

"Like what?" Luke put his head in his hands. "I don't know what else I can do aside from going over there. Flowers and candy are hardly going to cut it. I just need her to let me talk to her…to hear me out."

"Think about how you can speak to her heart in a way that she knows you know her. Remind her of what you have together." Jake paused, shaking his head. "Man, you two have something special.

When you told me about the diary and how she was the descendant of the woman your great-grandfather was in love with…and now, centuries later…you two…I thought, *wow, that's deep*."

Luke looked at his friend, thinking about Benjamín and Catalina, and said, "I have to go. Thanks for the talk."

He got up and tapped Jake's shoulder with the palm of his hand before walking off.

"Anytime. Let me know what happens." Jake paused and yelled, "Hey, and if this doesn't work out, there's always Melissa!"

Luke glanced back at Jake and couldn't help but laugh. He pictured the card with the phone number that she had snuck into his coat pocket at Adam's Bar Mitzvah. *Hmmm…nah.* He showered and drove home in a daze. It was eating him alive that Ariana wasn't returning his calls. His heart was aching like he had never experienced in his life. He wanted to hear her voice badly. He wanted to smell her sweet perfume and run his fingers through her thick, dark wavy hair. He wanted to hold her close and feel her heart beating in sync with his. He saw her eyes and her smile in his mind. His stomach tightened. Hearing Jake talk about Benjamín and Catalina made him think even more that he couldn't lose her like his grandfather had lost Catalina. His heart sank to his feet. He was at a loss at how to make this right with her.

Ariana

Ariana was walking home from her National Spanish Honor Society Induction. She was all dressed up, and her heels were sinking into the grass with every step. There was a chill in the air; but it was a calm, clear night for November. She sat down on the steps in front of her dorm hall and took off her shoes. She plopped her earbuds in and set her playlist. She pulled her knees up into her chest and covered her legs with her long coat. *Luna Llena* by Elida y Avante, ironically, was playing as she stared at the huge gray moon high in the night sky. She felt the tears creeping out from the corners of her eyes and wiped at them, trying to keep them at bay. Visions of her time with Luke were running like slides right before her eyes as she heard the lyrics to that song and watched the bright moon taunting her.

She remembered the day he had waited for her at the airport in Madrid. She heard the first time he had said her name, rolling the r's

perfectly, and how when he had whispered 'querida Ariana' in her ear it had given her massive chills. She thought about how he had unexpectedly found her on the patio of El Convento, how they had held each other and danced under the stars. The shooting stars and their spicy salsa dancing in New York. And his kiss. Oh how she remembered that first kiss. His soft lips on hers and the electricity that had shot through the both of them. She could feel his arms around her…and her head leaning on her favorite spot. She danced to *It's Your Love* with him all over again in her mind. The depth of their conversations. Their playfulness. She missed him more than she had missed anyone in her entire life.

She wiped at her eyes with her ring fingers wishing she had tissues. She wondered if he saw the same moon she was looking at or if he was thinking about her, too. Nothing she had tried to do to move on had worked. She had focused on her work. But the more she read her articles and her books, the more she wanted to share what she was learning. She wanted his thoughts. His opinions. She had opened and closed her books and taken out and put her articles away countless times trying to concentrate. She ran, listened to music, and tried retail therapy, buying several more pairs of boots and an outfit. She prayed. But, it had been no use. He was engraved on her heart. He had become a part of her. She took out her phone and, for a split second, she thought about calling him. Then she put it back in her purse, wiped the tears from her eyes again, put her shoes back on, and walked up to her dorm room.

"Hi, Luke!" his mom said as she mixed some sort of batter in a bowl. "You're home early."

His steps were heavy walking toward her as he hung his keys on the ring. "Yeah, I didn't go to dinner with dad. I left work early and went to the gym with Jake.

"Are you ok?"

"Yeah…I think so." He gave his mom a kiss on the cheek. "How are you?"

"I'm fine. I spent some time with Nina and the kids today. The twins are growing so fast, and the baby is so big! Have you seen him lately? He's already crawling around all over the place. He's babbling trying to say some words. He is *so* cute. I mean, it feels like he was just born—"

Luke was hearing her speak, but she may as well have been the teacher from Charlie Brown.

"What is it, honey? I don't think you heard a word I just said." She sat next to him on a bar stool in front of the breakfast bar. She put her arm around his shoulder.

"I think I messed it up badly, Mom." Luke looked up at his mom and saw the concern in her face. He sat backwards on the chair, resting his chin on his arms he had folded on the back of the chair.

"Oh, honey," she said, hugging him. "Whatever it is, I'm sure it's all going to work out. Is this about the girl who sent you flowers? The one who is Catalina's great-granddaughter?"

He nodded.

"She seems like such a nice girl, Luke. Give her some time. She'll come around."

"How do you know? She hasn't returned my calls. It's been weeks."

"I know if she doesn't, she'll lose the best thing that's ever happened to her. Luke, sweetheart, you are such a great guy. Look at me. I've never seen you happier than when you were on your way to see her or when you came home from being with her. I know she must feel the same way. Trust me…a mother knows these things."

"I hope you're right, Mom," he said. He got up to walk to his room.

"By the way, you know your father's holiday party is coming up. I would sure love to meet the girl that's stolen my son's heart."

He smiled at his mom as he walked away and thought she was being overly optimistic.

Ariana

"Where are you going?" Liz asked, her steps crunching the dry leaves as they synced up with Ariana's.

"To the library." Ariana shifted her book bag from one shoulder to the other.

"I'll walk with you. I'm going there, too."

"Be my guest."

They had walked for minute in silence when Liz stopped.

"Ariana," she started.

Ariana stopped and looked at her. She never called her by her full name unless it was serious.

"Have you called him?"

"No," Ariana said, her voice cracking.

"You know, I could shake the heck out of you right now!" she yelled at her.

"What?" Ariana said, annoyed at her friend's strong tone. "Look, *he* was the one who messed up. He should have told me about her."

Liz grabbed her by the shoulders and looked into her eyes.

"Ariana, I came to check on you. I knew you'd still be a hot mess. Look at you." She sucked the air through her teeth. "You have to quit trying to sweep it all under the rug and stuff your feelings deep down in there," she snapped, pointing at her chest. "You've got to deal with it. You are going to lose the most wonderful person in the world if you don't open your eyes and at least give him a chance to explain. You owe him that much. After everything you shared and experienced together. After everything he's done for you. You just cut him off like you do anyone who crosses you." She paused. "Ariana, *he's not Brian!*" she finished shaking her shoulders.

The blood drained from Ariana's face. Is this what she had been doing? Had she been doing to Luke what she had done to Brian after she saw him with that girl? She was right. Luke was the kindest person she had ever known, and he had been nothing but good to her. But after she saw Rebecca in that office, none of that had seemed to matter.

"You're right, Liz." Ariana pulled her hair behind her ears and sat on the steps of a building next to them. She put her head in her hands and looked back up at Liz. "Luke doesn't deserve this."

"That's my girl." Liz sat next to her and put her arm around her. "I knew you'd come to your senses...eventually. You can be *really* freakin' stubborn sometimes."

"Freakin'?"

"Yeah, I'm trying to clean up my language." She chuckled.

"Good," Ariana replied, smiling. "It's about time." She pointed a finger at her friend. "Hey, and I might be stubborn, but I don't cut people off."

"Yes, you do," Liz said. "I'm lucky *I've* made it this far!"

201

"Whatever." Ariana rolled her eyes and elbowed Liz. "Thanks for caring about me."

"You're my girl!" Liz said. "If I don't look out for you, who will?"

$\mathscr{L}uke$

Luke sat at a restaurant table across from his father. His dad had requested to have lunch with him that morning, saying it was critical that they meet. Luke felt his dad's eyes burning into him as he stared blankly into the menu.

"Luke, what has been with you the past couple of weeks?"

"Nothing, Dad. I'm ok."

"Well, you're certainly not ok." He made quotation marks in the air. "You have been completely preoccupied. You left work not feeling well a few weeks ago, and you've been in and out ever since. And when you're there, you're not really there, if you know what I mean."

"It's fine, Dad. Honest." Luke was trying to convince himself as much as he was trying to convince his dad. He exhaled and sat back in his chair. He folded his arms and stretched his legs out in front of him, crossing them at the ankles. A breeze brushed his face, and the smell of sizzling steak overwhelmed his senses as a waiter zoomed past them. Luke's eyes followed the waiter to a table behind him.

"Luke..." His dad paused. He was clearly annoyed. Out of the corner of his eye, Luke saw him lean forward and extend his arm across the table. "Is this about that girl from Colorado you've been seeing all summer and fall?"

Luke whipped his attention back to his dad. *I didn't even think he knew I had been gone much less know that I was in Colorado with Ariana.*

"Don't look surprised, Luke. I may be driven and a workaholic, but I do know my son."

"Then why don't you know that I don't want to work at the firm?" Luke raised his voice and looked his father in the eye.

"I *do* know, son." His tone softened and he rested his hand on the back of his neck. "I don't know. I guess I've been hoping all this time that the work we do would eventually grow on you like it did me when I took over from your grandfather. I thought after you got the dual citizenship for you and your mom that you had finally put the desire for that type of work behind you." His dad put a hand on his lap, with his elbow in the air, and leaned forward toward Luke again. "You're my only son, Luke. Is it so crazy for a father to want his son to follow in his footsteps and maybe take over one day?"

Luke smiled. "No, Dad, it's not. Thanks for finally being honest with me."

"About this girl, though, there's still a lot of work to be finished before May, Luke." He sat back in his chair, shook his head, and opened his arms. "I mean, I don't understand how you could be so distracted over someone you've only spent a few times with. I have been watching you since you returned from Spain. I need you to be focused now." He leaned forward again and pointed a full hand in Luke's direction. "I need you to be able to finish up the work and the project. There's a lot at stake. The clients are counting on you and so is the firm."

"I will, Dad. I promise. I'll do whatever it takes to get the job done." His jaw tightened. It irritated him that his dad had made reference to how little time he had known Ariana. But he resisted debating it. He knew his father would never understand.

The Nathan Syke's song with Ariana Grande, *Over and Over Again* began to play over the speakers of the restaurant, catching Luke's attention.

"The Wilsons want to meet again tomorrow, and the case Rebecca's been working on is coming to a close. She's going to need some help getting the files together."

"Uh, huh," Luke said. His ear was angled toward the ceiling, trying to hear the lyrics to the song.

"And next week, I want to take Mr. Johnson to dinner to discuss his idea."

"Right."

"There's an elephant sitting at the next table."

"What?" Luke said. He looked at his dad, smiling, finally hearing the absurdity of his statement.

His dad had always done something obnoxious or made some silly remark to get Luke's attention ever since he was a kid.

"Look, Dad, I promise I'll finish up all the work I said I would do through the end of May. I will. But right now, I *have* to do something."

"Go on," his dad said, shaking his head and throwing his napkin on his plate. "Go get her."

Luke flew back to his office. He Google-searched the song and listened to it one more time before he downloaded the file to his phone. It was perfect. It said *exactly* what he was feeling. It said everything he wanted her to know. He knew how much she loved music, and he was hoping this would be the thing that would finally catch her attention and get her to call him back. He attached the link to a text message saying:

Ariana, listen to this and call me, PLEASE!

Ariana

Ariana and Liz had just reached the library when Luke's text came through. She began to tremble. She showed Liz the message on her phone.

"Call him, Ana!"

She clicked on the link to hear the song. When it started playing, she got a lump in her throat and paused it.

"Liz, I can't do this here. I have to go."

She hugged her friend and ran back to her room. She plugged her phone into the charger and set up the Bluetooth. She clicked on the link again and threw herself on her bed to listen to the song, uninterrupted. Everything they had done in Spain and over the summer played like movie clips through her mind again. She saw his face singing 'Superman got nothing on me' at Red Rocks and got chills remembering watching the sunrise with him. She lay there on her bed and felt him get closer to her with every word. With every lyric she heard, his voice dropped the words deep into her soul. When the song finished, she knew she had to hear his voice.

He had found a way to speak to her heart when she had been too stubborn to hear it directly from him. He was just as miserable as she was. How could she not know that he would be? Her past had blinded her from trusting what she knew to be true about him. She scrolled through her screens to find his message and call him.

She lifted her thumb to click on his name. Her thumb stopped halfway and hung in midair. *'Confía en el amor'*, she saw Mari telling her in her mind. Blood was racing through her veins, and she had to wipe her hands on her jeans. *Just do it already.* She sat at the edge of her bed and held her breath. Her thumb finally made contact with his name. A second later he answered.

"Ariana, I'm sorry—"

"I'm sorry, Luke," they both blurted at the same time.

They chuckled. Ariana was teary-eyed, and it was quiet for a minute.

"Ariana, I should've told you that I was working with Rebecca. It's just that I honestly didn't think it was a big deal."

"You didn't think it was a big deal?" Ariana asked, starting to raise her voice.

"Calm down. Let me finish," he said. "It's not like that *at all.* There's nothing between Rebecca and me. There hasn't been in years. It was over way before I met you. Our families have become friends over the years, but that is it. I never even gave it a second thought that I should tell you because I don't see her that way. My dad offered her a job because she *is* going to law school, and he wanted to give her a chance in a familiar place." He paused as Ariana hung on every word. "Ariana, you have to know that I would never hurt you. You've got to trust me...and everything there is between us. You're my...Catalina."

Tears streamed down Ariana's face.

"Ariana?" he asked. "Are you still there?"

"Did you mean the words in that song?" She sat back against her headboard and grabbed her tissues from her nightstand.

"Every word. When I heard that song, I had to...it described everything...it was...the perfect way to tell you *exactly* how I feel."

"Good," she said, "because, Mr. Cohen, I was this close to coming out there." She motioned an inch with her fingers even though he couldn't see.

"I wish you would have," he muttered.

"I'm sorry," she said again. "You have no idea how much I've missed you."

"Yes, I do. It's been...miserable not being able to talk to you or know what was going on in your mind. I was sick that I had messed this up."

"It was my fault," she said. "I should have at least let you explain. Liz pointed out that apparently I have some...let's just say...issues... to deal with."

"Like stubbornness? I told you she's a smart girl."

"Hey, watch it! You didn't have to agree so quickly."

He laughed.

"I missed you so much."

"There's a lot that's happened that I've wanted to share with you."

"Like what?"

"Well, I got inducted into the National Spanish Honor Society the other day."

"Congratulations!"

"Thank you," she continued, "and…the biggest news…what I had originally called you about that day was that my Grandpa got an invitation to receive a copy of the diary in Spain next summer."

"I had no idea they would do something like that."

"Apparently, they translated the diary into Spanish and English and made printed copies in multiple languages. They extended the offer to all of the oldest known of Catalina's descendants to come to a reception and honor them with a copy."

"That's incredible news! Is your family going?"

"Yes, they're saving up right now to take the whole family."

"Where is it taking place?"

"In Madrid, I think."

"Maybe you can stay at El Convento."

"That's a great idea." Mari's invitation to come back with her family flashed through her mind. "It's definitely big enough to accommodate everyone, that's for sure."

"Speaking of family," he said, "my family wants to meet *you*."

"They do?" She felt her heart thump.

"Yes, especially my mom," he said. "They want to know who I've been traveling to Colorado to see…and to find out who's had me so distracted all summer and fall."

She let out an uneasy laugh. *What is that supposed to mean?*

"Seriously, though, can you come out after Thanksgiving around the beginning of December?"

"I think so. It depends on the day. Winter break starts…let me see." She pulled out her planner and sat at her desk. "It starts December 12th, which means our last day is the 9th."

"Ok, well, my dad hosts this holiday party for the firm every year. I'll find out the date and hopefully you can come out and meet everyone then."

"Ok." She pulled her hair behind her ears and imagined what a holiday party would look like in New York City. *I'm definitely going to have to go shopping.*

As if reading her thoughts, Luke said, "Don't worry about buying anything to wear. We can go shopping when you get here."

"Are you sure?" Ariana loved the idea of shopping in New York but was afraid that it might not be enough time to find something. She knew how she could be when trying to find just the right thing.

"We'll have plenty of time," Luke said. "Don't worry."

"Ok, I'm trusting you."

"It's about time."

She smiled, realizing the double meaning in that statement.

Chapter 19

Ariana

Ariana worked fervently up through Thanksgiving, reading through her research, setting up her outlines, and jotting down ideas for the spring semester when she would begin her writing. She read through sources that reminded her of the conversation she had had with Ricardo in Spain about Crypto Jews. She had even found several articles referencing the breast cancer gene that he had mentioned that day, one from her hometown in particular. The more she uncovered and learned, the more excited she became about her final papers.

At Thanksgiving, Ariana broke the news to her family that she was going to New York for a few days to meet Luke's family at the start of winter break rather than coming home right away. Coincidentally, Martin's holiday party was the exact weekend that Ariana would be out of school for break. As expected, her dad had hit the roof. He hadn't even budged when she had told him she would be getting their Christmas presents in New York.

"You know anything can happen in that huge city, Ariana. You have to be careful! And know your surroundings at all times. Your head is always in the clouds."

Ariana had resisted pulling her hoodie over her head as he ranted and raved, pacing back and forth.

No matter that she was the oldest or that she would graduate from college in a few months, she knew he always saw her as his baby. If only he knew she had already had an adventure there. *Ha!*

"And another thing, Luke was respectful, yes, but, we don't even know his family."

Ariana had kept assuring him that everything would be fine. That his family was great and totally normal.

I hope so, she had thought. *Geez. How did he even let me go to Spain?*

And after a long pause, a couple of beers, and a huge sigh, he had said, "If anything happens, I'll be on the next flight. Ok?"

Luke drove to pick up Ariana from JFK airport in his parents' Range Rover Sport. Her heart pounded in her chest when she saw him driving up, and she began to quiver. *Calm down. Breathe.* She looked down at her black double-breasted wool coat with a lavender scarf. She adjusted the matching knitted cap and smoothed her hair that hung in front of her. She hoped she had picked the right outfit. She was wearing light washed torn skinny jeans and short gray boots with heels.

She dropped her huge brown hobo bag and ran to his arms when she saw him rush out of the car.

"I can't believe I'm finally here!" she said, eying him. "You look...really good!"

She was still shaky from the anticipation of seeing him after all the months that they had been apart. FaceTime had at least given her the opportunity to see his face when they talked, but there was nothing like feeling his arms around her and kissing his soft lips. She breathed, and the tension in her body fled, content that she was finally here with him again, even if it would only be for a few days.

"So do you," he said, holding her and breathing her in.

His hand slid down her cheek. She watched his eyes going over every feature of her face. She swallowed and shifted her feet. He pressed his lips to hers, and she closed her eyes. She felt his heart beat and the warmth exude from him as he held her close.

"I'm so glad you're here. I missed you so much these past few months," he said.

"Me too."

A car honked, reminding them of where they were. Luke jumped, turning to see the car, and grabbed for her bag, lifting it swiftly into the air like when you anticipate a brick and it turns out to be a feather. He bounced it up and down in the air.

"Hmmm. Looks like you've unloaded some baggage," he joked.

"Very funny. I'm trying to save room to buy gifts. Lucky for you, it's not going to take out your back." She made a face at him and walked toward the passenger door.

He laughed. They left the airport and made the long drive to Luke's house outside the heart of the city. On the way, Luke gave Ariana the lowdown on his family.

"I can't wait for you to meet everyone. I've already told them all about how we met and about Catalina and Benjamín. My mom's name is Sofia, and my dad is Martin. I think I told you my sister's name is Nina, and my brother-in-law is Zach. The girls are Olivia and Emma, and my nephew is Ethan."

"Ok, I remember your sister's family from the picture you showed me of your graduation."

"The kids have grown so much since then, especially Ethan," Luke said, smiling.

Ariana could tell from how he talked about them that his family meant everything to him.

"My grandparents, my mom's mom and dad are Isaac and Sara. So we can go home and eat and rest, if you want to, then we come back into town to shop for tomorrow."

"That sounds good to me," she said. "I am a little hungry. My aunt and uncle dropped me off at the airport pretty early this morning."

"I think my mom is putting something together."

"Ok," she said, suddenly worrying about what kind of food they would have and if she would like it.

When they got to the house, Nina and the kids were already there, anticipating Ariana's arrival. They walked into the house through the kitchen, and Luke's mother was finishing up setting a brunch buffet.

"Hi, Mom," Luke said, walking in the door.

Ariana felt her stomach grumble. "It smells so good in here!"

She walked in and looked around the luxurious home. All the décor was dressed in white and gray tones. The counters were marble, and everything was very contemporary. There were plum and yellow accents throughout the space, warming up the cool color palette and solid finishes. It reminded her of Aunt Linda's apartment in Manhattan.

"You're here!" Luke's mom said from behind the kitchen's huge center island.

Luke walked Ariana over to his mom by the hand and said, "Mom, this is Ariana."

"Ariana, it is so wonderful to finally meet you!" She smiled with her eyes shining—bright blue, just like Luke's. She grabbed her hands and gave her a light but genuine hug. "I'm Sofia. We have heard *so* much about you!"

"So nice to meet you, too!" Ariana hugged her back.

"I hope you're hungry. Luke has to be. He rushed off so quickly to the airport without eating."

"Starving!" Ariana said with a hand on her tummy. She looked back at Luke's mom. *What a kind face. So sincere.*

Luke set down her bags with a huge grin and said, "Come on. Let's go meet the kids. Where are they, Mom?"

"They're in the living room."

Luke led her to the huge family room where Nina was sitting on a thick cushy blanket that had been laid on the floor for Ethan and the girls to play on. They had spread toys and books on it, and Ethan was crawling around, trying to grab the girl's toys. Nina stood up and walked toward Ariana with her arms open ready to give her a hug.

"Ariana, it is so nice to meet you. Luke has said nothing but wonderful things about you."

"I hope so." She eyed Luke. "It's a pleasure to meet you as well."

They hugged. When the girls noticed Luke, they ran to him, screaming, "Uncle Luke! Uncle Luke!" Ariana looked down at the pink flashes that zoomed by her as they ran towards him, arms flailing in the air. *So cute!*

"Hey!" he said, bending down to kiss them both on the cheek. "I've missed you two."

Ariana walked over to them and bent down to them as well.

"Well, who do we have here?" They both had shoulder length wavy blond hair that curled up at the bottom, and their faces were so pretty and strikingly identical.

"My name is Livia," one of the twins said. She twisted back and forth with a book in her little hands.

"I a princess," said the other, pointing to her crown and tutu, which sparked laughter from everyone.

"Yes, you most certainly are!" confirmed Ariana, taking her chin in her hands.

"She won't let me take them off," Nina said.

Ariana laughed. "She's adorable…they both are. Wow, they look *so* much alike! How do you tell them apart?"

"Well, at first it was difficult," she said. "I used to do it through clothes, but now that they can talk pretty well, and their personalities are coming through, it's made it easier. Olivia loves to read, and she's always carrying books around, and Emma is our little princess who loves everything pink and frilly."

"They remind me of my sister and me when we were little," Ariana said. "I was the one with books, and she was the one in crowns and tutus."

Ariana looked past Nina and saw the baby crawling on the blanket, gnawing on one of the books that was on the floor. She walked over to him and sat on the floor with her knees to one side.

"And you, handsome boy, must be Ethan!"

He crawled over to her. She picked him up, surprised at how fast he had come to her.

"Look at you!" She straightened up and picked him up to her face. "You are adorable, too! You have eyes just like your uncle!" She gave Luke a sideways glance.

He gave her a gummy grin and grabbed onto her hair, trying to put it in his mouth.

"Oh oh," she said. "What do you have there?"

"Sorry about that," Nina said. "He grabs anything within his reach."

"It's ok. I'm used to it. I have a ton of cousins at home."

She could feel Luke and Nina watching her as she picked him up and sat on a couch with him, tickling his tummy with one hand and gently trying to pry her hair out of his hand with the other. He let out a giggle, exposing the only two teeth in his mouth.

"Oh my goodness, you are *so cute*!" she said to him, finally getting him to let go of his tight grip on her hair.

She found a toy on the blanket on the floor and gave it to him.

"Here. This is much better than my yucky hair," she said.

He grabbed it and stuck it in his mouth immediately. She stood up and walked him over to Nina.

"Your children are beautiful," she said.

"Thank you! You're great with kids," Nina said, taking Ethan from her.

"They're so much fun," Ariana said.

She had been nervous to meet them, on her way there. She hadn't known what to expect. But they were so friendly. It was no wonder Luke was so easygoing and kind.

212

"Come and eat, everyone," Luke's mom called from the kitchen.

Among the delicacies were hard boiled eggs, lox and bagels with cream cheese, and coffee. Ariana smiled when she saw the rice pudding with cinnamon. It reminded her of home. They ate the brunch that Sofia had prepared for them and talked about Spain and DU and how Luke and Ariana had met. When Ethan began to get fussy, Nina excused herself to take care of him and then decided it was best for them to go home. The girls had ballet in a couple of hours, and Ethan needed to take a nap before that. Luke left with Nina to help her get them buckled into their car seats, and Ariana watched how attentive he was to his sister and her children. She was so happy and thankful that Liz had smacked her around and that she had called him when he sent her that song.

What an incredible guy. She watched him walk out the door with his sister, holding Olivia in his arms and taking Emma by the hand.

"So, Ariana, *you* are Catalina's great-granddaughter from the diary, right?" Sofia asked.

"Yes!" Ariana answered, bringing her thoughts from Luke back to the kitchen. "Luke helped me do the search, and we found out that she is my 16x great-grandmother."

"That's just amazing," Sofia said. "Have you had a chance to read the diary?"

"I have," she started. "I'm writing a sort of fictional story about her and Benjamín for my Spanish senior thesis based on her writings. We're supposed to create some sort of literature…well, there's more to it in the requirements, but, basically, we have to do a creative writing piece all in Spanish. I couldn't think of anything more perfect than writing about them. Luke and I read through the pages he had photographed together. She was…such an incredible person. So profound. I had to keep a box of tissues next to me every time we read together!"

"I agree! She was extraordinary. Luke helped me read through the pages. I don't read or speak Ladino. My parents and aunts and uncles do, but my sister and I never learned. You know, Luke took it upon himself to learn when he was a kid. I think it always fascinated him. I'm glad the language will continue on through him."

Ariana was listening to his mother and still thinking about her thesis at the same time. She looked down and pulled her hair behind her ears, taking in what Sofia had said. When she looked up, Sofia's focus was behind her. Ariana turned around, realizing Luke had come back into the room.

"So, you didn't grow up speaking Ladino?"

"No, I *had* to learn on my own." Luke glanced accusingly at his mom. He pulled up a stool next to Ariana. "I would make my grandparents speak to me, and I would try to figure out what they were saying. When I started taking Spanish in school, it was much easier to understand after that."

"The language just seems to come so naturally to you. I would have thought—"

"No," Sofia said. "I thought he would outgrow his curiosity, but it seems to have increased instead…to his dad's dismay, of course."

Ariana smiled, thinking of the conversations Luke had told her regarding working with his father.

"Where is your dad, Luke?"

"Working. You'll get to meet him tomorrow morning probably. I'm not sure we'll be back home in time for you to see him tonight."

"Where are you going?" his mom asked. "You two just got here."

"I'm taking Ariana into the city to get something to wear for tomorrow night."

"Oh ok. You should take her to that little boutique Nina loves."

"Great minds think alike, Mom." Luke pointed a finger from his temple toward her. "That's where we're headed first."

"Good!"

Luke turned to Ariana. "Let's take your bag up to the room you're staying in, and we can leave after that."

"Ok. But first let's help your mom clean up. She went to a lot trouble to prepare this meal for us."

"Ok, sure."

"You don't have to do that, Ariana. I can manage. Besides, you'll need some time out there to make sure you find just the right thing for tomorrow."

"Are you sure?" Ariana asked, feeling badly about leaving the mess.

"Totally sure."

"Ok, well, at least let me help clear the dishes from the table."

"Thank you."

Ariana and Luke helped his mom clear the dishes and get the kitchen to a manageable state before heading for the stairs.

214

"Thank you again, Mrs. Cohen, for the delicious brunch. I really appreciate it."

"Oh, please, call me Sofia."

Ariana smiled, and she and Luke went upstairs to the room where she would be staying for the next couple of days. When they got into the room, Luke put down her bag and took her hand. He leaned into her up against the wall and eagerly parted her lips with his, expressing the exhilaration he felt in one long, sweet kiss that left her breathless. She welcomed him by running her fingers through his hair.

"I missed you, too," she said in a soft voice when he broke away.

"Have I told you how amazing you are?" he asked, gazing at her.

"No, but keep it coming."

"I knew they'd love you. I'm so glad you called me back that day," he said as he touched her face. His jaws tightened as he stared into her eyes. "What would I have done if—"

"You would have had to come out and get me," she said, filling in the blank for him.

"I thought about it. Believe me! If I hadn't heard that song that day, I'm sure I would have."

He kissed her again, and they stood there holding each other, happy that the incident was ancient history and that they were now together again.

"Go ahead and freshen up. I'll wait for you downstairs. Hey," he pointed down the hall with his thumb from the door, "my room is two doors down this hall to the left, just in case you get a little cold tonight."

"Get outta here!" She laughed and pushed him out the door.

She rushed to check her hair and clean her face with her make-up wipes where her make-up had smudged and reapply it where it had faded. She looked herself over in the mirror and went back downstairs to meet Luke. She stopped a few steps shy of the bottom of the stairs when she heard him talking with his mom and helping her finish up the kitchen.

"She's wonderful, Luke," his mom said. "I knew she would be. From the flowers to the way you talk about her, I knew she had to be something special. I watched her for a minute with Ethan, too. She was great with him."

"She means a lot to me, Mom," Luke said. "More than anything."

Whoa...I feel the same way.

215

"Well, I can certainly tell that," Sofia said as Ariana walked in the room, blushing.

"Tell what?"

"That it's going to be a fun shopping day for you! Let's go."

Sofia glanced at Luke, shaking her head, and said, "Have fun you two!"

"We will," Luke said. "We might meet up with Jake later, so don't wait up."

"Ok, be careful."

And they grabbed their coats and walked out the door hand in hand.

They arrived in Manhattan and found the boutique that Sofia had told them about. Ariana walked inside and she swallowed. Her eyes went from garment to garment; each one seemed more glamorous than the other. She felt the fine fabrics in her hands as she passed by them. An attendant came to them, and they explained what they were looking for. Luke had told Ariana on the way over that he loved how the navy blue sundress she wore to the concert made her eyes look blue-gray, so Ariana agreed to look at dresses in that color scheme. They walked around the place, pulling dresses in her size that they thought might be flattering, short and long. When they had pulled enough, she went into the dressing room to try them all on. Luke sat on a sofa chair in front of the mirrors, and one by one, she put them on and walked out for Luke's opinion.

They were a little more than halfway into the stack when she walked out again and he said, "That's the one."

"You're joking. I haven't even tried them all on yet." She looked down and smoothed over the dress with her hands.

He sat forward, resting his elbows on his knees. "I know, but you are absolutely stunning in that one right there," he said. He pointed his finger toward her. His eyes were wide and glued to her.

"Are you sure, Luke?" She studied herself from all angles of the multiple mirrors.

"Yes, I'm sure."

She stood still in front of the mirror again. The dress was exquisite. It was long, which they were going to have to fix since it was probably made for women who were six feet tall. It was a navy form-fitted column gown with a V-neckline and strappy shoulders. The delicate diagonal lace overlay with tiny bands of silk threaded in between made a striped effect that went from top to bottom. The low back was flattering, and he was right. The color did make her eyes look just like

Grandpa Moisés's eyes. She loved it. She had never felt so elegant and sophisticated.

"Ok," she said, finally with a smile on her face. "I don't think I have *ever* shopped for a dress and found one this fast!"

"That's because you've never shopped in New York…with me." He stood up and walked toward her.

"I guess you're right, because if I would have been back in Denver, alone, I'm sure it would have taken me weeks to find anything I would have remotely liked at all."

She looked down at herself and smiled, lifting the dress with her hands again to expose her feet. She caught a glimpse of the tag, poking at her arm—then, the price. She picked it up and blinked to make sure she had read it right. She gasped.

"Don't look at that." Luke called the attendant. "We've found the one we want. Can you have it ready for tomorrow afternoon?"

The woman looked Ariana over and folded the hemline. She pinned it in place and looked at everything else. The rest fit her like a glove.

"Sure," she said. "We can have it ready for you by," she moved her head side-to-side and looked up at the ceiling, "around 3:00. Is that ok?"

"Yes, definitely. Thank you."

"Let me bring some shoes that will go with it to make sure we're hemming it at the right place. What size are you?"

"6 ½," Ariana said.

"Do you have a heel preference?"

"Five inches, if you have them. I'm going to need all the height I can get with this dress." She lifted the sides of the dress again.

"Luke, I can't let you pay for this." Ariana swallowed hard when the lady left. Her eyes were still huge with that price tag fixed in her mind.

He took her hands and looked at her. "I want to."

"But—"

"Look," he said, holding her shoulders, "the internship in Spain was paid. I've been working nonstop since August, and I'm getting a bonus next week. Let me do this for you, please."

"Ok," she said, still not convinced it was the right thing to do.

The woman returned with several styles of shoes matching the dress. Ariana chose a strappy pair that buckled at the ankle.

"I'll take those," she told the lady.

"Awesome," he said. "Now, get changed so we could go have some fun."

"Ok!"

Ariana still couldn't believe what had just happened. Maybe she could get him to let her pay for half. But who was she kidding, even with what she still had saved up from working this summer and through her work study job, it wasn't going be much help. She wasn't about to ask her parents either. She changed back into her jeans and boots while Luke paid for the dress and shoes, and they walked out the door hand in hand again. It was mid-afternoon, and they had already finished shopping. Ariana couldn't believe it. They left the store and walked around some more. It was a cool day, and the clouds had set in. The forecast had called for snow that day.

"Do you still want to do some Christmas shopping?" Luke asked.

"I do. Just for my parents and my brother and sister. Where can we go?"

"Let's go to Macy's," he suggested. "For a first-time visitor during the holidays, it's definitely a must see."

"I totally agree," Ariana said, adding a little skip to her step.

When they got there, the store was all dressed up for the holidays. Ariana was in shopper's paradise. It was sensory overload. She looked every which way at the holiday décor. Its gigantic toy displays and holiday decoration made her feel like she was at the North Pole in Santa's giant toy workshop. The line to see Santa was miles long with parents trying to still fidgety and fussy kids by threatening that Santa wouldn't come if they didn't behave. Just past the Santa line, Luke found a store directory that they could browse.

"There are several stories to this store and a bunch of different departments. Take a look and see what you're interested in, and we can go from there."

"Let's get started!" Ariana rubbed her hands together.

They walked throughout the infamous store boasting an entire city-block's worth of space, looking at various items in several departments. Ariana chose clothes for her sister and her mom, a Jets jersey for her brother, and a tie for her dad. She was thinking he could wear it at the reception in Spain, so she decided to get her grandpa one as well. They found a restaurant inside the store that served pizza and ate. As they approached the door to leave, the snow was drifting down lightly in big, puffy flakes. Ariana wrapped her lavender scarf

218

around her neck. Luke did the same thing and put his beanie on. He called Jake before they walked out to see if he was still going to meet up with them. Apparently, he wasn't going to be able to make the holiday party because of a family function, so Luke had arranged for him to meet Ariana then.

Jake was already in the city when Luke called, asking him to meet them at a coffee shop nearby. They ordered some coffee to warm up and waited for Jake to get there. Luke sat close to Ariana and put his arm around her to help her warm up.

"Luke, thank you again for today. I seriously can't believe you did that."

"I want you to dazzle everyone like you do me." He kissed her cheek.

"By all means, don't let *me* interrupt," a voice said from the door.

Luke stood up and gave his friend a hug with a pat on the back.

"Hey!" he said. "Jake, this is Ariana."

Ariana stood up to greet Jake. "Nice to meet you." She extended her hand.

Jake was a good-looking guy. He wasn't as tall as Luke, but he had an athletic build as well. He was olive-skinned with dark eyes, and when he took off his beanie, his short, black hair was curly. He wore a thin well-trimmed beard and had long eyelashes.

"Put that away," he said, referring to her hand. "Give me a hug. It's nice to finally meet you, Ariana. Luke has told me so much about you."

"He's told me a lot about you, too," Ariana said. "It's good to finally put a face with a name."

They sat at the table, first talking about DU and how weird it was that they had never crossed paths. Then Luke and Jake reminisced about when they were kids, giving Ariana plenty of black mailing ammunition for later. She looked at both of them talking and imagined the commotion they caused together everywhere they went.

"Now, I have to ask," Ariana started. "Did you really teach Luke how to dance salsa?"

Jake and Luke looked at each other and laughed.

"Yeah. He was always at my house. And when you're at my house, the music is *always* on. So he learned just like the rest of us." He turned to Luke and slapped him on the back. "This guy's been like a brother to me. He has seen me through everything. He's been a part of our family forever. I've always said he's Boricua *de corazón*, with his Spanish-speaking self." He slapped Luke in the chest. "*I* can't even speak Spanish like he can. He always gets me in trouble with my grandma."

"You too?" Ariana said, laughing. "I'm pretty sure all the younger generation of San Luis got in trouble with *my* grandma when he was there, especially my brother and sister and me."

"I think my shoulder's permanently scarred from her smacking me whenever he's around."

"You two just need to step up," Luke said.

Jake turned his head toward Ariana fast and blinked his eyes in disbelief. "What? No he didn't just. Ariana, do you want to get him or should I?"

"Let me at him." She leaned in toward Luke and narrowed her eyes.

"I'll take my chances with the lady," Luke said, kissing her.

Jake looked down, shook his head, and smirked.

"Ariana, that's not exactly what I had in mind."

"I know," she said without taking her eyes off of Luke. "But look at him. I couldn't help it." She took a deep breath and turned her attention back to Jake. "Well, anyway, the dancing was sure impressive. Thank you *and* your family."

Jake smiled.

"Why are you looking at me like that?" Ariana asked.

"Nothing. It's just cool," Jake said. "I'm sitting right here and you guys are acting like there's no one else in the room."

"He gets jealous," chimed in Luke.

They laughed.

"Right, right. That's it." Jake made a face at Ariana, put his elbows on the table, and his fingertips together. "Anyway...Luke, have you taken her to Rockefeller Center yet?"

"No. We got her dress for the holiday party. We went to Macy's and then we came here. Let's go."

They took a cab to Rockefeller Center since it was already dark and the snow was still coming down. When they arrived, Ariana was amazed at the crowd and the view. The tree was gigantic, as were the fantastic decorations surrounding the area. Any show she had seen on TV did no justice to being right there in front of it. Ariana took tons of pictures and filmed the acapella group singing Christmas carols on a stage under the tree with her phone. Jake took pictures of them together with the tree in the background, and then they took some selfies of the three of them. After they had tried ice-skating for a minute and parted ways with Jake, who had given Luke an approving eye before he left; they found the subway and took it to the parking garage where Luke had left the Range Rover.

"I had an amazing time today, Luke," Ariana said as they were driving. "Jake is fun."

"He's the best. I spent more time with him and his family growing up than my own sometimes. My mom worked a lot when I was a kid. His mom would come pick us up after our sports camps and practices...and sometimes our games, too. His mom's a nurse, and her schedule was much more flexible than my mom's. My parents would pick me up from there. I was either with him or at my grandparents' house."

When they arrived at Luke's house, there had to be over a foot of snow that had piled on the ground in that short time. Their drive over had been cautious and slow. They walked in the house, and everything was quiet and dark. Ariana dropped off the bags from Macy's upstairs, in her room with Luke right behind her.

"Are you tired?" he asked.

"Kind of...but not really. Are you?"

"No," he said. "I could make us some drinks, and we could put on a movie?"

"Ok. Are you sure we won't wake your parents?"

"No. Their room is on the main floor on the other side of the house. Meet me in the loft at the end of this hall. You can get comfortable while I get the drinks."

"Ok. I'll meet you out here in a few."

She changed to a fitted t-shirt and loungers, brushed her teeth, washed her face, and put her hair up. Then she walked out into the hall and toward the loft. There was a media center in the loft with a flat screen TV and a huge comfy couch in the middle of the room facing the TV. Against the wall behind the couch was a small wet bar and a fridge near the sink. Luke had served them both a couple of drinks and had brought a blanket from the linen closet. He found the remote and started flipping through the movie channels.

"Furious 7! Let's watch that."

"Cool."

"I know it's old, but I love this movie." She sat up and sang a line from the last song in the movie.

Luke chuckled. She brought the blanket over both of them and leaned into him with her head on her favorite spot.

"You're wearing it!" She took the St. Christopher medal she had given him in her fingers. It hung loosely over his t-shirt.

"Yeah. I got a chain for it and haven't taken it off since."

Ariana's heart warmed. He pulled her close and kissed the top of her head. They cuddled on the couch and watched the movie until they were both asleep. When Ariana awoke, the TV was still on.

"Luke." She nudged him.

"Huh?" he said, his eyes still closed.

"It's 2:00am."

"What?"

"We fell asleep."

He sat up and rubbed his eyes, trying to focus, and finally fully waking up to her in front of him.

"I better go lie down in the room," she said.

"Wait." He pulled her close, sitting her on his lap sideways. "Come here first."

He gave her a soft kiss and looked into her eyes. He swallowed.

"I…" he stopped himself.

"You what?" she whispered. She felt the palms of his hands getting sweaty.

"I, uh, hope you sleep well," he finished.

"I will." She got up to leave. "You too. Goodnight."

She squeezed his hand, feeling its warmth, kissed his cheek, and walked down the hall to her room.

"Goodnight." After she had walked several steps in the hallway, he continued, "I'm not looking at your booty."

"Yes you are." She glanced back at him and smiled before walking into her room.

Ariana lay down on her bed and covered herself. She heard the glasses clanging in the sink and the TV turn off. She stared up at the ceiling into the darkness and wondered what he had stopped himself from saying. If it was what she was thinking…she did too. She wanted to scream.

Chapter 20

Ariana

The next morning, Ariana woke up later than normal. She tip-toed out of her room and heard faint voices downstairs. Down the hall, Luke's door was open. She showered, dressed, and went downstairs where Luke's dad was making pancakes in the kitchen.

"Good morning!" Luke got up from his seat to hug her and kiss her cheek. "How'd you sleep?"

"Wonderful," she said, remembering their time together.

"Dad, this is Ariana," Luke said with his arm around her shoulder.

"Well, good morning, Ms. Colorado," he said.

"Good morning. It's nice to finally meet you. I've heard so much about you. But *I* am actually not the beauty queen. That would be my sister."

Luke laughed out loud.

"I see," he said. "Well, I hope you're hungry because there are enough pancakes here to fill a stadium."

"Awesome." She pulled a bar stool next to Luke at the breakfast bar with a hand on her tummy. "I am *so* hungry right now. Thank you."

Martin lifted his eyebrows. "Not just a salad and coconut water girl, eh?"

"Not at all." She piled a stack of pancakes high on her plate.

Martin smiled.

"Do you want coffee?" Luke asked.

"Yes, please."

He stood up, filled a coffee cup, and slid the cream and sugar closer to her.

"Anyhow, as I was saying, Luke, Mr. Wilson will be there tonight with his wife. I'd like for you and Rebecca to meet her and answer any questions she might have about the project."

Ariana's hand shook at the mention of Rebecca's name, making her sip of coffee turn into a gulp which burned the roof of her mouth. *Ow!* She tried to cringe without anyone noticing. *She's going to be there.*

"Dad, come on. I thought tonight was about celebrating, not work."

"Well, she's having some doubts, and she just needs some…reassurance."

"Whatever."

Ariana cleared her throat and tried to nurse the roof of her mouth with her tongue. "Where's your mom, Luke?" she asked, sort of trying to ease the tension.

"She and Nina are off getting prim and proper for tonight," Martin said.

"She wanted you to come, but I told her we had to go back and pick up your dress."

"That would have been fun."

He rubbed her back and said, "I know you wouldn't have been back in time to get your dress, though. You're just going to have to come back and visit again to have some have girl-time with them."

She smiled. "Maybe I will."

"Alright, all of this fuzzy, touchy, feely stuff is a bit much." Martin scowled, making Luke and Ariana laugh out loud. "Well, I hope you enjoy the pancakes."

"Thank you, Mr. Co…" Ariana was about to say when she felt her cheeks flush, remembering that Mr. Cohen is what she called Luke. She coughed hard, put a napkin to her mouth, and took a sip of her coffee to wash down the pancakes.

"Oh, just call me Martin." He furrowed his brows at Luke. He was blushing, too.

"Ok. Thank you so much for the pancakes. They totally hit the spot," Ariana said.

"You're welcome. Now, I'll leave you two love birds alone. I'm off to meet with a client before tonight," he said as he walked out of the kitchen.

"Ok, Dad," Luke said, still smiling.

"Thanks again!" Ariana yelled.

They leaned back in their chairs, watching to make sure he was out of sight. When the door shut, they both laughed out loud at the awkward exchange. They cleaned up the kitchen and finished getting ready to go back into the city for Ariana's dress.

The snow had subsided, and the sun was shining, but it was still cold as they drove out of the driveway. They arrived at the boutique, and Ariana tried on the dress with the shoes, and, thankfully, she was no longer swimming in its length.

Ariana spread out all of the jewelry she had brought with her on the dresser. She tried on each set with her dress. She settled on the diamonds that her mom and dad had given her when she graduated from high school. The earrings were a long string of tiny diamonds that dangled from her ears, and the necklace was made of a white gold chain that held a diamond journey pendant, which was just the right length for the V-neck dress. It was a delicate set that held particular sentimental value for Ariana. Her mom had told her that she had chosen the necklace for her as a reminder to celebrate her journey through high school and all her accomplishments, but to look ahead to yet another amazing journey that would lie ahead of her in college.

What a journey it has turned out to be. She looked at her reflection in the mirror. The unexpected journey since last May had created more memorable events than her last three years in college combined—Luke and the bookstore. Spain and the diary. New York and San Luis with Luke. Her senior projects, and now…this party.

She pulled her hair to one side and pinned it with a comb that shimmered with crystals and rhinestones and secured it with bobby pins, making sure that they weren't visible to the eye. She curled her long hair in huge ringlets, ran her fingers through them, and sprayed the whole thing to make sure it wouldn't move an inch. She had already applied her make-up and added glossy lipstick to finish off the look. She stood up and studied herself in the mirror again. Now she could see why Karina loved dressing up this way. It made her feel like a princess. She grabbed her clutch, took a deep breath, and went downstairs to meet Luke. When she got to the kitchen, Luke and his parents were already there waiting for her. She felt a little badly that she had taken so much time to get ready. As all eyes fell on her, she felt the back of her neck heat up.

225

"Well, you look absolutely lovely." Sofia took her hands. "You two did a great job shopping yesterday. That dress is stunning on you."

"Thank you," Ariana said. "I love your dress as well. It's gorgeous!"

Sofia was wearing a long, red, off the shoulder silk gown with delicate white trim that flared slightly in an A-line toward the bottom. It had a belt with rhinestones that emphasized her waist. Her figure was slim, and she looked elegant and regal.

"Shall we, Romeo?" Martin elbowed Luke in the ribs. He hadn't moved an inch.

"Uh, yeah," Luke said when he finally shifted his eyes from Ariana to his dad.

When they walked out the door, a car was waiting for them to take them to the party. Ariana sat next to Luke, and he linked his fingers in hers. Ariana stole a glance at him as they drove off. He was striking in his tailored tux. His neatly-trimmed short dark hair was styled to perfection. She had felt his intense energy when their eyes locked as she walked down the stairs. His smooth skin and baby blues had given Ariana chills when she had seen him waiting for her.

"You're...gorgeous," Luke whispered in her ear. "Exactly as I thought you'd look."

"Thanks. So are you." She closed her eyes and bit her lower lip. She wasn't sure if it was the compliment or his warm breathing against her ear and neck that gave her goosebumps. *Maybe both.*

The holiday party was held in a ballroom on the top floor of one of the skyscrapers in Manhattan. When they arrived, the ballroom was sparsely filled with only a few clusters of people mingling. While Luke's dad took him to talk with some clients, Ariana walked around the room, taking in the elegant holiday décor. Her insides were trembling a little as her fingertips glided across the white table linens. She wanted to make a good impression on these people that were important to Luke's family's business. The long, thin glass centerpieces topped with a mountain of white roses and florals reflected the white lights twinkling throughout. Each gold-trimmed place setting was precise with its flatware, glassware, and stack of plates.

A small jazz band played in a corner. Ariana stood by one of the walls of windows and sighed. The spectacular New York City skyline was all dressed up for Christmas with white and colored lights and fantastic outdoor decorations. As the guests arrived steadily, Ariana noticed their chic formal wear. Her jitters only intensified.

No wonder Luke wanted to take me shopping. He knew what was going to be expected.

Not long after, Ariana felt a presence come from behind her that said, "Ariana, is it?"

"Yes?" She flipped around toward a woman and extended her hand.

The woman took her hand and observed her dress and manicure. Then she gave Ariana a wide smile and said, "Hi! I'm Luke's Aunt Linda. It's so very nice to meet you." Ariana swallowed and shifted from one foot to the other. "I have heard so much about you. You're Catalina's great-granddaughter from the diary, right?"

"Oh, hi." Ariana smiled back. "Yes, I am. It's nice to meet you, too." Aunt Linda's black and gold couture cocktail dress was exquisite, and her flawlessly coifed bob haircut with a side part reminded her of Luke's mom.

"My sister Sofia and I were thrilled with the news about the diary. It's just wonderful to meet one of her descendants. I mean, the whole story is so unbelievable."

"It is." Ariana took notice of the similar facial features that Aunt Linda shared with Sofia and Luke. "It took me a while to comprehend the magnitude of finding the diary and all of its implications."

"Right. You know," Aunt Linda continued with a mischievous grin, "this summer Luke stayed over at the apartment in the city right before we came home from Cabo. His uncle and I don't mind. He and his friends *always* clean up after themselves. But *this* time, I noticed that my bath towels had been rolled, and the containers in the linen closet were arranged by color and size. I always wondered about that."

Ariana felt the blood rush to her head. Her eyes widened as it occurred to her that it was *Aunt Linda's* apartment she and Luke had stayed in when they got back from Spain. She cleared her throat, suddenly feeling parched. She reached for the rhinestone and crystal comb in her hair as if it might fall. Her face had to be beet red. She let out a nervous laugh as Aunt Linda reached in and gave her a light hug.

She pulled back, squeezed Ariana's shoulders, and said, with her eyes shining, "It *really* is nice to meet you. I hope we can talk more later." She winked at her and stole away to mingle with the other guests.

A second later, Luke was at Ariana's side asking, "Are you ok?"

"Yes." She bit at a fingernail. "Your Aunt Linda totally knows I was with you at her house in June."

"How do you know?"

"She noticed I rolled the towels and…organized her linen closet."

The last part of her words trailed off. She was mad at herself for having fallen prey to the cleaning obsession trait she had inherited from her mom's side of the family. Luke laughed out loud.

"I love you," he blurted, squeezing her toward him.

And they looked at each other, stunned at the words that had just fallen out of Luke's mouth. At that same moment, behind Luke, Ariana saw a blonde woman walking toward them as if on a cat walk. Her head snaked slightly to the side to get a better look. She felt a pang in the pit of her stomach. The woman stood at least six-feet tall in her heels, and her long blond hair was pinned back in perfect curls. Her make-up was meticulous, and she looked like a super model in her red, fitted couture gown, white fur wrap, and dazzling diamond accessories. *Rebecca.* She wanted to crawl in a hole. She swallowed hard with all of the memories of those awful weeks less than a month ago rushing back to her.

"Luke, where are your manners?" Rebecca said before turning her attention toward Ariana. "I don't believe we've met." She extended a ruby and diamond-clad hand toward Ariana. "You must be the famous Airy-ana. I'm Rebecca."

"Nice to meet you." Ariana took her hand.

"So nice to meet you as well. Gosh, I feel like I already know you, Luke talks about you so much."

Well, that was pleasant…I think.

Luke let out a nervous laugh. The band began playing their instrumental rendition of *Wonderful Tonight* by Eric Clapton. Luke and Ariana gazed at each other. Luke's words still dangled in her mind. And the three of them stood there in awkward silence. The expression on Luke's face was telling Ariana he had something important to say.

Rebecca must have sensed that she was interrupting something. She suddenly looked from one to the other and said, "Well, it's nice to finally meet you, Airy-ana. Take care, Luke," and she walked away.

228

"Take care," Luke said.

"Bye." Ariana felt sort of relieved at the encounter.

Her mind was going a hundred miles an hour. She had made a huge ordeal about Luke not telling her that the two of them were working together, and he had been talking about *her* the entire time. Once again, she felt horrible about how she had behaved. Moreover, she was still fixed on the words that Luke had just said to her. She didn't know how he had meant them exactly, because of how they had come shooting out of his mouth—like when you're talking to a friend or family member after they make you laugh. But based on what had happened the night before, she couldn't be certain that was the case.

She knew they had strong feelings for each other, and he *had* said it to her in not so many words in the song he texted her. And the implication had always been there from the beginning with the electricity in the touch of their hands, the sizzle in their dance, the depth and complexity of their conversations, and their pure chemistry and connection; but they had never uttered those loaded words before that instant. Nonetheless, just as Ariana opened her mouth to respond to him, Luke's father rang his glass to get everyone's attention.

"Good evening, everyone," Martin began. "I want to express my gratitude to each and every one of you for your hard work and dedication to this firm. We are only successful because of all that you do on a daily basis. Please enjoy the music, the hors d'oeuvres, the food, and the drinks. Have a wonderful evening. Cheers!" He finished to the applause of the guests who had all gathered around him.

Luke took Ariana's hand and walked out onto the terrace of the ballroom immediately after his father's short speech before they could be interrupted by anything else.

"Ariana," he said as he took her hands. "I'm sorry about what happened earlier. I didn't mean to say what I said like that."

"It's ok." She looked out at the city lights. Her mouth twisted. *Well, I feel like a goof.* "I figured it was just—"

"You don't understand." He brought her face toward him to meet him in the eye. "Don't you know? I love you."

Ariana felt her knees go weak as he continued.

"I am so *in* love with you. I knew it from the moment I saw you, and it just…keeps getting deeper every time I'm with you. I've been waiting for the right time to tell you. I wanted it to be special…not haphazard like—" His voice cracked and he paused. He placed his

229

hand on her cheek. "You are so beautiful, Ariana, in every way. I love everything about you. I love your heart. Your spirit. Your mind. You are everything I could have ever asked for and more."

"I'm in love with *you*," she said, her voice caught with her breath as the words he had finally poured out from his heart echoed her own. She took his face in her hands and kissed him.

He held her close for a moment and then reached into the pocket of his suit coat and pulled out a small box.

"I have had this with me waiting for the right moment, and I don't know that there will be a better one."

And he got down on one knee. Ariana's heart pounded so loudly, she felt it vibrating in her ears. Her mouth dropped open wide. She felt like she was on a cloud watching what was happening from above.

"Ariana," he started, gazing up at her, "my life changed the day I met you." He paused looked down, then up at the sky, and finally back at her. She was choking the life out of her clutch as she shifted from one foot to the other. *Oh my gosh. Oh my gosh. Is he* really *doing this?* "I don't want to make the same mistake my great-grandfather did centuries ago. If he even felt half as much as I do for you…I just don't know how he could have…and when I thought I had lost you…and now that I have you here…I just…I don't ever want to let you go." He paused, taking the ring out from the box. "Mi querida Ariana, will you marry me?"

Her eyes were like two rivers now, her legs were noodles, and her heart was a big bass drum beating out of her chest.

"Yes! Absolutely, yes!" she shouted and threw her arms around him.

She had been hoping for 'I love you', but this…this was more than she could have ever imagined. She wiped at her eyes and recalled the day she realized that he had become a part of her. She couldn't see herself without him. And he placed the ring on her shaky finger with his shaky hand. She was astounded. She had never seen anything like it. He stood up and held her face in his hands, and he kissed her with a profound love that she felt at the core of her being. He closed his eyes as he held her close. And for a second, there was the sun again surrounding them under the starry night of the terrace.

Then he pulled away from her, touched his lips to hers, and said, "I love you so much."

"I love *you*, Mr. Cohen. I can't wait to be your wife."

Luke wiped his eyes and his forehead with the back of his hand. Then he took her hand and they walked back into the ballroom. He found a glass at a table near his parents and rang it with a butter knife he had found next to it.

"Everyone, I want you all to know…that this amazing woman standing next to me," he lifted her hand and looked at her, glossy-eyed, "has agreed to be my wife!"

The crowd applauded and cheered for them as they kissed. Ariana overhead Luke's mom say to her husband, "Did you see them, Martin?"

"You can't help but."

"Let's go congratulate them," she said.

They walked over to Ariana and Luke. Sofia hugged her son and said, "Congratulations! I am *so* excited for you!" She took his face in her hands, kissed his cheek, and said, "I love you."

"Congratulations!" Martin opened his arms to hug Ariana. "I don't know about your sister, but tonight you are every bit a beauty queen, and don't forget that."

"Thank you, Martin." Ariana let out a giggle.

"Sweet Ariana," Sofia began as she hugged her. "Welcome to our family! We are *so* very happy for the two of you."

"Thank you both, so much for everything." Ariana squeezed both of their hands.

Aunt Linda rushed over and hugged them both. As she held both of their hands, she said, "This is a treasured moment…for both of our families…and for Benjamín and Catalina. Congratulations!"

Her words brought a warm sensation to Ariana's chest. They stood there for what seemed like an hour accepting congratulation hugs and wishes from everyone, including Rebecca. Ariana excused herself as soon as she could break away to check her eyes and make-up. She was sure she looked like a raccoon. She walked into the bathroom, greeting the attendant as she entered. She found the mirror and examined herself, surprised to see that aside from having to re-do her eyeliner at the corners of her eyes and some foundation, her make-up had held up ok throughout all the emotion.

Before anything, though, she needed the bathroom. In all her nervous energy she had chugged two elegant flutes of champagne and three glasses of water. She made her way to the very last stall, thinking it would be the least likely used. Even in such a luxurious place as this, she still found public restrooms revolting. She entered the stall just as she heard voices and clacking heels walking in. She couldn't help but recognize the shimmering Manolo pumps Rebecca was wearing as she talked with someone in front of the mirror.

She kept quiet as she heard the other woman, whose ostentatious blue pumps were all Ariana could see from that angle, address Rebecca in a scything tone, "Rebecca, you don't actually think Luke is serious about that girl, do you? I mean, really…I'd say she just stomped *all over* your territory."

Ariana's fists clenched. It was all she could do to bust the door down and confront this snooty, tacky, blue pump wench, whoever she was. But she wanted to hear what Rebecca had to say, so she stood still and remained quiet.

"Patience is a virtue, Sylvia. Not to worry. If that little Mexican girl thinks she can fit into Luke's world, she's got another thing coming. Sure, she sort of looks the part in her dress up clothes, but I assure you, he *will* tire of her…I mean, come on. What could they possibly have to talk about? Can she even speak proper English? Did you hear her accent? Besides, Martin loves me, and I'm sure he'll offer me a position in the firm before the project is over. And after that, it'll just be a matter of time before Luke sees what a mistake he made when we broke up."

"Rebecca, aren't you getting a bit ahead of yourself? Did you see that ring?"

"It was his grandmother's…whatever…Syl, look, honey, he *will* come around. He likes digging up the past, right? I'll just keep…reminding him."

Ariana watched Rebecca's hand smooth her platinum blond hair and her form fitting gown through the space in between the door and the stall wall. Her lips and jaws were tight. She felt like a pressure cooker. *I knew it! Backstabbing little princess. Bet she had that dress hand made by Vera Wang.*

"Let's just say, the more time we spend in that close office space, the more he'll remember how great we were together. We just fit. We're cut from the same cloth. That second-class Cinderella can come all dressed up to the ball, but she'll never be royalty."

Ariana's face felt as if it was stuck in a wasp nest as Tacky Blue Pumps snorted out loud and remarked, "Don't worry…she's probably an illegal alien! Maybe Trump will do you a favor and deport her!" They both laughed out loud, cackling and clacking out the door.

Ariana slowly walked out of the stall, making sure they were out of sight. Her eyes met with the attendant who tilted her head and gave her a sympathetic look.

"¡No te preocupas, hija...que les vaya bien y que les trampe'l tren!"[137]

She let out a laugh that jerked her body forward at the same time a tear burned her cheek. She eyed herself in the mirror, forcing her courage and confidence to show up. She took a deep breath and let out a long sigh. She grabbed for the make-up in her clutch and made herself fabulous again, giving herself a pep talk in her mind.

He loves you. *He wants to marry* you. You're *the one with the gorgeous, priceless ring on your finger. This is* your *night. Walk out of here, enjoy your fiancé and his family, and don't waste a brain cell giving her a second thought.*

And with that, she was on her way out the door, pausing to give the attendant a squeeze on her shoulder, *"Gracias. Muy amable."*[138]

She suddenly thought about her parents. Her dad. Rebecca was the least of her worries. How was she going to tell him? How would her dad take the news? She was going to come home engaged! She had to tell Liz ASAP. She took a deep breath and exhaled. *It can wait until tomorrow.* Ariana found Luke standing and talking to a gentleman with salt and pepper hair near a table where his mom and dad were sitting. She walked toward him with Rebecca and Tacky Blue Pumps in the corner of her eye and said loud enough for them to hear, "There's my prince charming!" And she leaned into him, kissing him on the cheek as he grabbed her hand. He took one hand and put the other on the small of her back as she sat down in the seat he had pulled out for her and sat next to her. She glanced over and smiled at Rebecca who was glaring at them. She knew she was being petty, but she had to let Rebecca know she was on to her. She turned her attention back to Luke, and one look in his baby blues had her lost in him and their engagement again with Rebecca but a tiny, faint splinter in her side.

"Luke, wow, this is...this has to be the most gorgeous ring I have ever seen." She held up her fourth finger and examined the rock as it

---

[137] Don't worry, daughter...may things go well with them and may the train trample them!

[138] Thank you. You're very kind.

233

shimmered in the ballroom lighting. "I don't think I have ever seen anything like it."

The ring shone like a bright star, and if it wouldn't have been on her finger, you could have seen right through to the floor with its clarity. It was a huge princess cut halo diamond ring with two layers of smaller diamonds surrounding the large one raised in the center. Two strands of tiny diamonds on each side of the band intertwined to meet the halo layers. In the front and back, holding up the center diamond, two strands of tiny diamonds swirled from each side to meet each other with one small diamond in the middle. It's rare antique quality and intricate design spoke of generations past and was an absolute dream to Ariana.

He took her hand and said, "This was my great-great grandmother's ring. It was given to her by my great-great grandfather, the first person in my family to come to the US from Turkey in the late 1800s. He came with very little, and when he had earned enough, he had it made for her because he thought she deserved a jewel as precious as she was. And now, it's yours."

"I'm honored." She flashed the ring some more in the light. "I absolutely love it. Thank you. And I can't believe it fits!"

Luke's sister Nina and her husband Zach came up from behind them. Ariana hadn't seen them all evening.

"Sorry we're late," Nina said. "The kids wouldn't stay with the sitter. Oh my gosh! Congratulations! They told us the news when we came in, and we rushed over right away. Welcome to our family, Ariana!" Nina screeched and squeezed her in a tight hug. "We are beyond the moon thrilled for you two. Now, let me see." She bounced motioning to Ariana's hand.

Ariana held her hand out and she looked at Luke. "You gave her great-grandma's ring! Wow, Ariana, it suits you *very* well...and that dress...you are a vision in that color! Oh, where are my manners?" she said without giving Ariana time to respond to her compliment.

"Honey, this is Luke's fiancé, Ariana. Ariana, this is my husband, Zach."

"So nice to meet you, Zach," Ariana said. "I met your children yesterday. They are adorable."

"Thank you." Zach smiled. "Very nice to meet you as well. Congrats, Luke!" He hugged his brother-in-law and gave him a slap to the back.

"Thanks," Luke said, grinning.

A photographer hired for the event came over to take their picture. They posed standing together and then with just their hands showing off the ring and then took more pictures with their phones. They danced a little to the jazz music and mingled with the guests, Luke introducing Ariana to everyone he knew. When the evening was over, Ariana and Luke walked toward the elevators and out of the building and bid everyone adieu. Rebecca found them just as they walked out of the heavy doors to the sidewalk.

"Congratulations again, Luke!" She hugged him lightly.

"Thanks, Rebecca. Have a good night."

Then she leaned into Ariana and squeezed her shoulders with her glove-covered hands. "Congratulations. So nice to meet you, Airy-ana."

"Thanks," Ariana said, through gritted teeth. And then, before she could stop herself, it happened like the flash of a light, she whispered in Rebecca's ear, "And by the way, I'm not Mexican."

Rebecca pulled back, and the shock on her face blended in with the blistering winter cold, creating cherry-red blotches on her porcelain cheeks and turned up nose. Luke led Ariana toward the car, waiting for them with his hand on the small of her back. Ariana couldn't help but look back at her as they entered the car. Rebecca's jaw was still grazing the sidewalk. Ariana smiled and waved at her as the door closed.

When Luke and Ariana got home, they got comfortable and met in the loft on the couch again, this time with only music playing in the background.

"I'm still waiting for someone to pinch me and wake me up." She looked up at her ring from her favorite spot and back at Luke.

"It's real, querida Ariana." He let out a contented sigh. He kissed her forehead and ran his fingers alongside her cheek and then through her hair. "I love you. I can't say it enough."

"Me either." She kissed him and cuddled deeper into him. "I love you, too. I'm the luckiest girl alive."

Chapter 21

Luke

Luke and Ariana talked and giggled hand in hand as they trotted down the steps to the kitchen for breakfast the next morning. "Well, good morning, love birds!" Luke's dad said. "How are the future Mr. and Mrs.?"

"Good morning! Doing well. Thanks!" Ariana took a deep breath with her eyes closed. "It smells wonderful in here."

"Morning, Dad, Mom." Luke kissed his mother on the cheek and patted his dad on the back.

"Good morning!" Luke's mom said, her eyes shining bright. "Help yourselves to some coffee. I have some news."

Next thing they knew, Luke and Ariana were on their way to a restaurant for lunch with his mom and dad. Luke's mom and Aunt Linda had resourcefully organized an impromptu lunch for all of their family to announce their engagement. Luke was glad. He wanted his entire family to meet Ariana, especially his grandmother. Aunt Linda, his dad's sister Rachel, and their respective families would be there as well. Luke pulled Ariana to sit next to him in the second row of the car.

"What are you thinking about?" Luke asked. She was focused beyond him on the blurring landscaping out of his window, like her mind was miles away.

"The wedding," she said.

"Already?"

"Yeah. There are just so many options." She broke her gaze from the window to look at him. "We could do New York, San Luis, or Denver, where we met. There is so much to consider."

"What about the synagogue?" Luke's dad asked unexpectedly.

Luke laughed. "Really, Dad? When was the last time you set foot in there? My Bar Mitzvah?"

"Just saying...it's an option. And we could get a good deal at the club if we book soon. Mr. Winters owes me a favor."

"What are *you* thinking, Ariana?" Luke's mom rolled her eyes at his dad and turned around to Luke and Ariana.

"Well, I haven't thought about what kind of wedding I wanted since I was twelve and going to marry Channing Tatum."

Luke laughed, and his mom chuckled.

"Channing Tatum? So that's my competition, huh?"

"Yeah, you better watch out."

He folded his arms and shook his head. "I'm not worried."

"Why not?"

"I'm a better salsa dancer than he is!"

She laughed and kissed his cheek. "I love you."

"We can have the wedding anywhere. It just depends on what *you* want."

"What do you mean?" Ariana asked. "What about what you want?"

"I want you to plan your dream wedding. I just want to spend the rest of my life with you," Luke said, kissing her.

"All of this has *already* been a dream."

He put his arm around her, and she leaned her head into his chest and smiled.

Luke saw his parents through the rearview mirror. His mom couldn't wipe the grin off her face. His dad rolled his eyes. Luke smiled.

"You two are laying on the mushy junk a little thick, don't you think?" his dad teased.

"Martin!" shouted Luke's mom, nudging his arm with the back of her hand. "It's sweet!"

"Whatever you say," he commented dryly, making Ariana and Luke giggle as they snuggled more into each other.

They had been traveling for about thirty minutes through a backcountry road full of hills, thick with tall trees and charming homes on large lots scattered about. Snow still carpeted the banks and the landscape.

"This area of New York is so pretty in winter, so serene. I can only imagine how lush it is in summer," Ariana said. "Look how cute that cottage is!" She pointed toward a structure nestled deep in the trees on the right side of the road. Luke followed her finger to the two-story stone cottage that sat near a small pond that had been frozen over. The whole scene was picturesque with snow atop its roof and on the ground surrounding it. It had a red door, and there was smoke coming out of its chimney. It wasn't a grand building, but its presence was idyllic and alluring.

"I've got it." She snapped her fingers.

"What?" Luke asked.

"I know where we can get married. You're going to love it." She clasped her hands together and shifted in her seat toward him.

"Where?"

"Spain."

"Spain?"

"Yes. Corral de Almaguer." Her eyes shined as if she could see the whole thing in her mind. "That cottage reminds me of El Convento. We can do it there! It's where we found each other after the bookstore. Where we first held each other and danced under the stars. It's where we saw our shooting stars together for the first time. It's where Benjamín and Catalina fell in love." She grabbed his hand. "Can you imagine getting married outside in the meadow near the river in Benjamín and Catalina's sanctuary?"

"Yeah, I *can* imagine that. I *love* that idea." Everything Ariana listed moved through his mind. He paused, glancing and grinning at her. "It's like our families would be bringing Benjamín and Catalina back together after 400 years, exactly where they had spent their last hours together! We have to make it happen. It's the most perfect idea I would have never thought of."

"We can do it in June after you're already there and while all of my family is there for the diary reception." Ariana pointed at her chest in a high-pitched voice. Then she sat back. Her face changed, and her mouth twisted. "But wait, how would that work out for your family? I didn't think it through."

Luke's mom turned to them, cupping her hands with impressive enthusiasm before they could even say anything, saying. "Ariana, that is a remarkable idea! I can already see it all in my mind. I know our family would love to see where Benjamín lived and worked."

"Are you sure?" Ariana's face had a glow about it, and she began talking fast. "This is so great! But, do you think six months is enough time to plan a wedding…overseas?" She counted the months on her hand. "And with my senior projects—"

"I don't know," Luke said.

"Don't you worry about a thing," Luke's mom interjected. "Luke's Aunt Rachel is a party-planning extraordinaire. She and I will help you with every detail!"

"Ok. I appreciate that so much. I'm sure my mom and aunts will want to be involved, too." Ariana danced in her seat and held up her hand, admiring her ring.

"I'm so glad it fits." Luke took her hand and kissed it.

He had asked his mother about it and had taken it to a jeweler well over a month ago before their falling out, knowing that he eventually wanted to propose. He had guesstimated her ring size, remembering her thin and delicate her fingers. He sat back and let it all sink in. Warmth gushed through him as he was reminded of waking up with her in the middle of the night the other night. Even without a lick of make-up, she was radiant. It had always been her from the moment he had seen her, and with every experience after that, he had known that there would never be anyone who could ever measure up to everything they had together. Their love had transcended time and distance. All of this had sealed the deal as far as he was concerned.

A few minutes later, they arrived at the restaurant. All of Luke's family was already there waiting for them, including Nina, Zach, and the kids. They had reserved a couple of long tables in a room at the back of the restaurant to accommodate the whole family. Ariana and Luke walked into the room, hand in hand, behind his parents as they greeted everyone. Then Luke took Ariana to meet his grandparents where they were seated.

"*Avuelo, Avuela, esta es Ariana, mi novia,*"[139] Luke said. "Ariana, these are my grandparents, Isaac and Sara."

"*Enkantada,*" Grandma Sara took Ariana's hand in both of hers.

"*Muncho gusto de conocerlos,*" Ariana gave Grandma Sara's hand a light squeeze.

---

[139] Grandpa, Grandma, this is my fiancé.

"Muncho plazer."[140] Grandpa Isaac placed a hand on his chest and nodded.

"Ella es la nieta de Catalina...el amor de Avuelo Benjamín antes de que se fuera a Turquía... ¿se acuerda del diario?"[141]

"Sí, Sí. How could I forget? Ariana, you can't imagine how important your union with my Luke is to our family." Grandma Sara held onto one of Ariana's hands and said, "Sit, both of you." She motioned to the seats next to her. Luke and Ariana sat and gave her their full attention. "Since I was a little girl, I had heard stories, legends, that my grandfather, Benjamín from many centuries ago had lived an unfulfilled love before he went to Turkey. The story goes that he couldn't marry the love of his life because he had left her in Spain. He didn't want to leave her, no." She lifted a finger and shook it in front of Ariana. "He had planned to ask for her hand in marriage, but before he could, they received notice in the middle of the night that the authorities from the Inquisition were already very close to their house. They already had the horse and carriage full of their belongings ready to leave at a moment's notice." She snapped her fingers.

"They hurried to put the rest of what remained in the house in the carriage, and they were about to leave when Benjamín ran off, sprinting, toward Catalina's house to steal her away with him. A strong wind was blowing that night, making the river more tumultuous than ever. Benjamín slipped on a smooth rock, trying to cross, and fell into the water. His father and older brother jumped in to save him. But it was so dark that they couldn't see a thing. On top of that, Benjamín fought them, screaming Catalina's name in between breaths and rushes of water that filled his mouth.

"His father and his older brother fought hard to get him out of the water, but Benjamín continued to fight them, even after they got him out. He wasn't going to leave without his Catalina. Finally, his dad and brother were able to calm him enough to show him the deep wound he had sustained on his leg." Grandma Sara stretched her leg and pointed to it and shook her head. "But that didn't matter to Benjamín. The pain he had in his heart," she said, as she splayed her palm across her own heart, "was much deeper. He tried to escape them

---

[140]It's a pleasure.

[141] She is Catalina's great-granddaughter...Grandpa Benjamín's love before he fled to Turkey...do you remember the diary?

again and run toward the river, but his bloody leg gave way and he fell again.

"His father yelled at him, 'Benjamín, *¡Ya vámonos! ¡Que ya están por llegar!*'[142]

What could he do? With his wounded leg he couldn't even cross the river let alone the distance of the meadow to get to Catalina's house. The authorities would have abducted him and tortured him or worse. He rolled to his knees and hit the hard dirt with his fists and grabbed the hair behind his head. His father and brother picked him up and carried him to the carriage, wrapping his leg with a fragment from a ripped sheet. He sat at the back of the carriage with his wounded leg covered with a blanket, devastated. They said he had screamed Catalina's name at the same time that one of the horses had neighed loudly, drowning out his voice. At that moment, his heart had shattered into a million pieces like a glass crashing against a rock. As they traveled farther and farther away from his beloved Corral de Almaguer and his beloved Catalina, a tear slowly slid down the side of his cheek." She paused and looked down before continuing.

"As if that weren't enough, the officials from the Inquisition eventually found them anyway. They detained them and jailed them for a long time. We don't know how long it was before they were finally escorted to a ship that was on its way to Turkey." She let go of Ariana's hand and wiped her eyes with a hanky she had taken out from her purse.

"And, now, with Catalina's diary…and seeing you here with Luke, I know now that it was a true story and not just a legend or a myth that was passed down through the generations." She grabbed Luke's hand. *"Lo syento, hijiko,* for not telling you before. The truth is that I never believed it until now." Then she returned her attention to Ariana. *"Sí, mi avuelo Benjamín amó a mi avuela Eva decían, y la cuidó con muncho cariño. Pero nunca se olvidó de su Catalina y tenía ese lamento, esa angustia de haberla dejado en España muy dentro de su corazón toda su vida. Ahora con el matrimonio de tú y Luke en munchos sentidos, van a reunir a mi avuelo con su querida."*[143]

---

[142] Benjamín, let's go! They're almost here!

[143] Forgive me, son…Yes, my grandfather Benjamín loved my Grandmother Eva, they said, and he cared for her with love. But, he never forgot about his Catalina and he lived with the regret and anguish that he had left her in Spain deep

She pulled Luke's hand toward Ariana's and held them both together, finishing her story with her voice cracking at the end. Ariana wiped a tear at the corner of her eye and so did Luke.

"Gracias, por compartir conmigo la otra mitad de lo que pasó con Catalina y Benjamín," Ariana said in between sniffles. *"Esa historia la guardaré en mi corazón para siempre. Sí, el cuento de ellos es muy triste. Pero, es igual de importante para mí y para mi familia también."* She turned to Luke. *"Quiero muncho a Luke. Es el amor de mi vida. Estoy muy agradecida por haberlo conocido y bendecida por tener está profunda conexión con él."*[144]

"Miren, tengo algo más."[145] She held up a finger, reached into her purse, and pulled out an old, worn, wooden box and handed it to Luke.

"What's this?" He took the box and studied its faded pattern that had to have shone brightly at one time.

Ariana's eyes opened widely. "Luke! It's the paint box that Catalina gave to Benjamín! Let me see." She leaned in and pulled his hand toward her.

"No, it can't be." He couldn't move. His heart was pounding. He slid his fingertips across the smooth box, admiring the pattern. He rotated it carefully in his hands and noted the places where it had been chipped and cracked. "This is incredible, Grandma! How?" He opened the box and found only a folded piece of paper.

"It has been passed down a long time," his grandmother said. *"Ya no hay nada adentro. Solo el papel en donde escribió el maasé mi avuela. Ahora es tuyo. Guárdalo, hijiko."*[146]

Sí, lo hago. Este es un tesoro. ¡Es increíble! Munchas gracias.[147]

"Luke! Look at the pattern." Ariana's finger traced the faded colors. "It's exactly as Catalina described it in her diary!"

Luke shook his head. "Amazing."

---

in his heart all of his life. Now with your and Luke's marriage, in a way, you will reunite my grandfather with his love.

[144] Thank you for sharing the other half of Catalina and Benjamín's story with me. I will keep that story in my heart forever. Yes, theirs is a sad story. But, it's just as important to me and my family as it is to yours. I love Luke very much. He is the love of my life. I am grateful to have met him, and I am blessed to have this profound connection with him.

[145] Look, I have something else.

[146] There's nothing in there anymore. Just the paper my grandmother wrote the story on. It's yours now. Take care of it, son.

[147] I will. This is a treasure. It's incredible! Thank you so much.

"Come," Luke's grandmother said as she hugged Ariana and kissed her cheek. *"Welcome to our family, hijika."*[148]

Luke's grandfather hugged her, welcoming her to the family as well.

Words like blessed or exhilarated hardly felt enough to describe what was happening right now. It meant everything to Luke to watch his family embrace Ariana. On top of that, he finally had the answer to the question that had been nagging at him since reading Catalina's diary. He stared at the box that represented the love between Catalina and Benjamín once more, the box that they both had held in their own hands.

"Now we have a piece of them." He tried to hold back the tears that filled his eyes.

"Yeah." Ariana caressed his back and kissed his cheek. She wiped at her eyes again. He looked at her and smiled. He was on cloud nine. The rest of the family had watched them patiently, listening to the story. They all sat down at the table to eat the family-style meal that had been prepared for them. The waiters were serving champagne, and his dad stood.

"I'd like to make a toast," he began, and everyone looked on.

Luke sat back in his chair, especially curious about what he would say. Ariana threaded her arm through his. He leaned his head on hers.

"Anyone who can see can tell that that these two are a match made in heaven. It's almost appalling to be around them for an extended period of time, I'm telling you." Laughter erupted. "Seriously, though, the extraordinary story that they share is unlike any other, and they glow with happiness, reminding the world of what love is supposed to look like. So, if you would please join me in lifting your glass," he said, as he lifted his own. "Luke and Ms. Colorado, may your life together overflow with more love and happiness than you can ever contain. To Ariana and Luke!"

"Cheers," everyone responded.

Ariana and Luke smiled at each other and kissed. He was grateful for his dad's unexpected, kind words.

---

[148] Welcome to our family, Daughter.

By the time they were back at the house, the sun was on its way toward the horizon, making navy and deep plum streaks across the blue-gray winter sky. Luke's dad got the fireplace going, and his mom made some hot cocoa. Luke and Ariana settled into the large, comfy cream-colored sofa set right in front of the fireplace.

"So, what does your family do in Colorado?" Luke's dad asked Ariana, closing the screen of the fireplace.

The crackling fire escaped from the pieces of firewood that were laid in a neat pile on the hearth in trails of dark orange and deep yellow flashes, creating the perfect winter ambience. Ariana leaned into Luke and took a sip from her mug of hot cocoa.

"We own a restaurant," she said. "It's been in our family for several generations."

"Well that's impressive." He sank into a plush, fat accent chair.

"Yeah, my dad wants me to help them run it. I'm supposed to be the next in line to continue the legacy," she said in a small voice.

"And you're not sure about that."

"Well, no, I'm not," she said. "I don't think the restaurant business is for me."

"Well, apparently, you've got to follow your heart these days," he said, glancing at Luke.

"I guess so." She got up to put her mug in the sink, and Luke followed her to the kitchen to fill his mug.

"Your dad is a big 'ol softy under that rough and tough exterior, isn't he?"

Luke sighed. "Yeah, he can be. He's really funny too when you least expect it."

Ariana took a deep breath.

"What's wrong?"

"I'm nervous. I have to call my parents. I don't know what my dad is going to say."

"Don't worry," he said, hugging her. "It'll be ok."

They walked out onto the patio together to make the call. She breathed in the cool outdoor air, and her breath escaped her mouth as a puff of smoke. She rubbed her arm with her free hand.

"I should have grabbed my jacket." She faced the huge trees and the remaining snow that had fallen a couple of days ago in their backyard. Her voice began to shake, and her body shivered.

"I'll get it." Luke ran into the house to the coat closet, grabbed it, and placed it on her shoulders. He stood next to her, rubbing her back. The phone began ringing loudly through the speakerphone.

"I just hope my mom answers," she said right before Lucia's voice came through the phone.

Lucia shouted, "Mi' ja, that's wonderful news! Congratulations! I knew it!" after Ariana shared the news.

They suddenly heard Joe, who must have heard all the commotion, ask, "What's going on, Lucia? Is that Ariana? Is she ok?"

"She's engaged, Joe!"

"Engaged? Give me that phone. What did your mom just tell me, Ariana?"

"Hi, Dad! Uh, Luke just asked me to marry him," she said in the voice of a little girl.

He was quiet for a moment.

"¿Y no me pidió tu mano primero?"[149] he yelled. "Doesn't anyone have the decency to do that anymore?"

Ariana's eyes met with Luke's. His heart was beating fast, and his jaw tightened.

"Joe! What did you do?" Lucia scolded Ariana's dad in the background.

"Dad?"

Joe was quiet. Luke could almost feel his blood boiling through the phone. His heavy boots were stomping through the house, and the fridge slammed, which meant he had undoubtedly grabbed a beer from the fridge.

"Hold on, Ariana," he said. The voices coming from the phone were muffled, like Joe had cupped the phone trying to drown out his conversation with Lucia, which they could still hear.

"You *know* he loves her," Lucia said. "You could see it the whole time they were here. She's grown up, Joe. They're great kids. They're older than we were when we got married."

"This isn't about Luke. I know he's a good kid. But she barely knows him! And we don't even know anything about his family, Lucia."

Ariana rolled her eyes. "Dad, are you still there?"

---

[149] And he didn't ask me for your hand first?

245

They heard a swallow and the crushing of his can of beer, and he finally said, "I knew we shouldn't have let you go over there, Ariana! You tell him to call me."

Ariana squeezed her phone with both hands, and she shook her head. She banged a fist on the deck railing and turned to Luke. Her cheeks were pink, and her eyes glossy. She threw her hands in the air.

Luke blinked, and his jaw tightened again, then he said, "He's right. I should have asked him first. Call him back. I'll talk to him."

Ariana smiled.

"Hello," answered Joe, brusquely in his rough, gruff voice.

"Hi, Mr. Romero. It's Luke." After Joe didn't say anything, Luke continued, "I, um…want to apologize for not asking for your permission to propose to Ariana first. You have to know I never meant any disrespect. But I just had to ask her at that very moment. I couldn't let another minute pass by…I love your daughter more than anything. Will you give me your blessing to marry Ariana…please?"

Joe still hadn't said a word. Beads of sweat had begun to form on Luke's forehead. Ariana sat down on an outdoor chair next to a side table with a small ceramic pot. She put her head in her hands and exhaled, scaring off a squirrel that had scampered by.

"Look," Joe said, after some time, making Luke jump out of his skin. "You were respectful to us and all of our family when you were here, and I could see that you care about her. I watched you guys together. But you're both so young. What's the rush? She hasn't even graduated from school yet."

"I know. We'll wait until after she graduates for sure." Luke leaned against the railing of the deck. "Mr. Romero, Ariana and I have spent most of our relationship apart from one another, and we know it's only been a few months. But in that time we've been together, we've learned so much about each other and from each other. She's the most beautiful person I've ever known. I love her. She means the world to me."

The sudden crushing of another beer can made Luke's heart race even more just as another voice stormed into Ariana's house.

"Joe!" yelled the man's voice in between breaths. "It's Dad! Let's go now. He fell."

"*¿Qué?* What the hell happened? Luke, look I can't deal with this right now. I'm sorry. The answer is no. Tell Ariana to come home. We need her here, now!"

Luke put the phone on the table. He gave Ariana an apologetic look. His throat was tightening, and he blinked, swallowing hard.

Ariana stood up. "What's wrong? What happened?"

"It's your grandpa."

"Is he ok?" She leaned forward toward him looking for answers in his face.

Luke scratched the back of his neck, let his hand fall to his side, and shrugged. "I don't know. He fell. Your dad said he wants you home now."

She grabbed her phone without looking at him in the eye and said, "I have to go. I'm sorry." Her words were choking in her breath. "As much as I love you and want to spend the rest of my life with you, I just don't think this is going to work." She took off the ring and put it in his hands gently, sniffling and she stormed through the kitchen past his mom and dad and up the stairs.

Luke followed her.

"What just happened out there?" his dad asked.

His mom stood up. "Luke, honey, what's the matter?"

All Luke could say as his feet hit the stairs is, "I just need to talk to her." He was out of breath when he reached her room. Ariana was flinging her belongings aimlessly into her bag when Luke came in after her.

"Ariana, what's going on?"

"Didn't you hear? Grandpa Moisés collapsed. I need to get back home now," she said in between cries. Her chest was heaving, and her breaths were shallow.

He held her, and she didn't resist. She buried her face into his shoulder and sobbed into the sleeve of his t-shirt. He stroked her hair and kissed the top of her head.

"It's ok. I'll get you back home. I'll go with you. But what does all of this have to do with us getting married? I don't understand."

She pulled back and looked at him. There was a longing, a desperation in her eyes that made Luke's heart sink. Then she turned away.

"It's just too hard. You need to be here. I don't fit…I need to be back home helping my family. I need to run the restaurant after graduation…and now what if Grandpa Moi—"

"Ariana, stop." Luke cupped her face with his hands and looked into her eyes. "Don't even go there. He'll be ok. Don't make any

247

decisions now. Put this back on your finger. It belongs there." And he placed the ring back on her finger and pulled her in a tight embrace. She didn't move.

"I love you, Ariana. We'll get through this together."

Chapter 22

Ariana

Ariana sat in the History Department office and replayed the events from winter break in her mind like a video. She was still a ball of nerves from the last month. *I hope it was the right thing to do.* Everything had happened around her in slow motion that day on Luke's patio. She had stared at the back of the huge house as Luke had talked to her dad on the phone. Rebecca's words from the night before had charred her ears again. *What if she's right? Everyone is so nice, but do I* really *fit in here? What about Catalina? If I don't run the restaurant, who will? Everything she went through would have been for nothing.* Ricardo's voice had clamored in her head, "Aren't you going to go back to San Luis to give back to your community? You could make a huge difference there with everything you've learned here." And then her Aunt Gabi, "Nobody stays in San Luis anymore. These kids leave and never come back. It's going to end up a ghost town." The air had suddenly become thick, and her airways had felt like they were being choked off. Then, when she heard about Grandpa Moisés, that had set her over the edge. Reliving the memory again in her mind made her stomach turn.

He had lost a lot of blood in the ordeal, but she couldn't be more grateful that he was fine. *Who knew you could rupture your spleen from a fall?* She couldn't thank God enough. She had known being with her family was the right thing to do. The image of Luke's face when she had returned the ring was burned in her heart. But Grandpa Moisés's words had been the straw that broke the camel's back. When she had stood at his hospital bedside, holding his hand and hearing his plea, she couldn't refuse it.

"Mi'ja, come back home. I need you to take care of your grandma," he had said in a weak voice. "Your daddy needs you in the restaurant, too."

With a tear streaming down her face, she had squeezed his hand and said, "Of course, Grampo." She knew she would have to put her own desires aside, or at least on hold, and do what was right for her family—and for Catalina's legacy. *Besides, I'm not Karina. I don't have the time, the energy, nor the desire, quite frankly, to make myself into a supermodel. Or change my identity to fit in anywhere. I can be who I am at home…in my own little world where everyone knows me and I know what to expect.* She had pictured Rebecca's perfect, malicious little face staring at her on the sidewalk in New York. *You win. He's all yours.* The deepest part of her heart had crept up to her eyes and slid down slowly to her chin as she had kissed her grandpa on the forehead.

She had been numb when she had returned home from taking Luke back to the airport. Even her playlists had been dull and hadn't been able to ignite a shred of joy or contentment the entire ride home. She was happy to have made the drive on her own. She hadn't wanted the obligation to talk to anyone, and she had wanted to have the freedom to sob out loud if she had needed to. Then, as if things had not been difficult enough, a major Colorado snowstorm had left her crawling at a snail's pace, drawing out the whole experience that much longer. La Veta pass had been grueling and treacherous.

If she hadn't had so much adrenaline from her anger and sadness, she might have let her fear overtake her. She had prayed the rosary several times and then had cried and practically stopped to kiss the ground when she saw the San Luis city limit sign.

Thankfully after that, her parents had kept her busy from the moment she had arrived until she had to go back to school. They had participated in the *Posadas*[150] every night until Christmas Eve and Midnight Mass, even hosting one of the evenings at their house. They had prepared for days to welcome the procession of Mary, Joseph, the donkey, the musicians, and the devotees that followed to find posada in their home. They had provided refreshments for everyone. Ariana cringed slightly thinking about how she and her brother Carlos had worked themselves to the bone helping her mom make what she

---

[150] Reenactment of Mary and Joseph finding lodging

felt were an infinite amount of *biscochitos*[151] and *empanaditas de carne y de calabaza*[152] for the event. Karina had been working on scholarship and college applications.

They had hoped the goodies, coffee, and hot chocolate had warmed everyone up from their outdoor activities. It had been a taxing job and was enough to share with the entire town throughout the Christmas season and beyond, according to Ariana. With a hand on her hip, she had rolled her eyes, wiped her brow, and let out a heavy breath when they were finished. Yet she had found comfort in it. The memory conjured up the sweet smells of caramelized sugar and pumpkin. After three and half years of being on her own, these smells and tastes had become Christmas to her. The unique blend of anise, cinnamon, and sugar in the biscochitos were heaven on her taste buds. And as far as she was concerned, no one could touch the minced meat and pumpkin turnovers made from Grandma Aurelia's recipes. She sighed and smiled.

Then her thoughts trailed to Luke. Her heart flip-flopped as she sat back in her chair and envisioned what sort of new holiday traditions she would have loved to have created together.

"Ariana?"

"Yes?" Her History advisor's voice yanked her thoughts back into the History office. She walked in, sat down, and explained her progress and plans. Her advisor was pleased with her work and gave her some more theory ideas and tips for planning and organizing her time to ensure she would finish everything, including her Spanish thesis, by her deadlines.

Ariana walked out of the office and went straight to the library to get started. She began by first discussing her purpose for choosing this topic and how personal this project was to her and her family. Then she explained that she would have never known to pick an idea like this had she not been probed to look into her ancestry and DNA, stemming from her summer course in Spain. She wrote about how grateful she was to the generous, tireless genealogists and historians from New Mexico and Colorado who had delved into these ideas diligently to unknowingly pave the way for her to do her research.

---

[151] Traditional Southern Colorado and Northern New Mexican Christmas cookies

[152] Traditional Christmas turnovers made from minced meat and pumpkin

She quoted *Walkout* and wrote that she wanted to bring the past to life so that anyone who read her work would know that not only did these things happen but that their lives were real and compelling. That they were stories vital not only to her own family and heritage but for American history as well. It was more than worth telling. This history was part of the thread in the fabric of who we all are, and we are lost without knowing it. That there is wisdom in the old adages, '*You can't know where you're going until you know where you've been,*' and '*It's important to know where you've been so as to not repeat the same mistakes in the future.*'

She wrote for several hours, utilizing her notes and articles, until she was satisfied with her five-page introduction. A huge yawn came out of nowhere. She wiped her eyes that had leaked from the yawn and leaned from side to side trying to get some blood flow into her hips. It was late. She texted Luke when she got home to see if he was up. He immediately called back through FaceTime.

"Hi," he said. "What are you doing up this late?"

"Working."

"Me too…and thinking of you. I'm glad you called. How's school?"

She smiled and her tummy quivered. She wasn't sure how to respond with the way things were between them. Even though Luke wanted much more, he had honored Ariana's wishes to keep their relationship at the friendship level. He had promised to help her with her work around Catalina and Benjamín. He had told her that he couldn't tolerate not having her in his life in some way, and he had said that if it had to be solely friendship around the stories of Catalina and Benjamín, he would take whatever he could get.

"It's good," she said. "My advisor loves my ideas, and I wrote my introduction this evening."

"I'm sure you rocked it."

"Well, I don't know about that, but I think it's a good start at least."

She sat back on her bed and stared into nothing. She thought about what she had written thus far and how much more she still wanted to learn.

"What are you thinking about?"

"A lot of stuff."

"Let me guess. You want more."

"How do you always seem to know these things about me, Mr. Cohen?"

252

"You're a reflection of me," he said frankly. "I knew it when I read your first journal. That's why I knew you would be on the patio that night after your tours. I know how those can be, and I just…had to come and check on you."

She tried to keep her heart from swelling inside, but she loved how he knew her so well.

"You're absolutely right. These projects are just the beginning for me, Luke. I want to learn Ladino. I want to take more Sephardic studies courses, especially the historical ones, and go deeper into my ancestry. But more than anything, I want to tell *their* stories. I want everyone to know about people like Catalina and Benjamín and how amazing their lives were. Maybe someone else can draw inspiration from them or what they went through. You know, I got my own online ancestry account and I've continued researching my family."

"That's exciting!" Luke said. "Have you found anything new so far?"

"Well, I was curious about the woman married to Pablo Romero, specifically. Her last name was Mascareñas, and I found out that her last known ancestor was born in Lisbon, Portugal in 1590. I'd love to visit there and maybe look through some archives. I can't help but wonder if they fled to Portugal from Spain during the Inquisition, too."

"It's totally possible. Let's do it!" A huge, glowing grin took over his face. His eyes must have caught the hesitation in hers because the grin faded. "Come with me after graduation, Ariana." His voice was softer now. He looked down, ran his fingers through his hair, and then back at her. "Look, I know you chose to stay home with your family, but…" He blinked, and his jaws tightened as he formed the words. "We can still travel together at least, throughout Spain and Portugal and wherever you want."

An ache began to rise in Ariana's chest.

"I better go," she said. "I have an early class in the morning."

"Yeah, ok. Good night then."

"Good night, Luke." She put the phone down, sat at the edge of her bed, and buried her face in her hands.

That night, Ariana dreamed that she was cleaning an old, dusty, dim-lit room that was completely empty aside from its dark gray wooden floors and walls. Ariana noticed that a beautiful woman with long, curly hair and familiar bright blue-gray eyes was helping her sweep.

She turned to Ariana, smiled, and said, *"Mi'ja, eres suficiente. Sabes que el amor vive en tu corazón y allí en la parte más profunda encontrarás tu hogar."*

Then she became a light so bright Ariana had to squint until her eyes were closed. When she reopened them, she looked up and the ceiling was open. The sky was pitch black and filled with a plethora of stars. The two smack dab in the center in perfect view were the brightest. Ariana woke up with her heart racing, wondering what it all meant.

"I am enough? I have to write this down before I forget."

She had become accustomed to leaving a notebook and a pen on her nightstand and in her purse where she could easily access them to jot down thoughts and ideas that came to her for her thesis projects before she could forget them. She reached for the notebook and pen and began writing down the messages from her dream. "I will find my home in the deepest part of my heart where love resides."

She rubbed her eyes and peeked at her alarm clock, which was blurry at first. *It's 3:00 in the morning.* Ariana was stunned wide awake by this dream. *Could the woman have been Catalina? What were the two stars? What was she trying to tell me?*

Chapter 23

Luke

Luke threw his bag in the trunk of the Range Rover while he waited for Ariana to pick up the phone. *She's not picking up.* He pulled the phone from his ear and looked at the time. *Must be in a class or something.* He searched for his road trip playlist as he buckled in, set the car in reverse, and made his way out of the driveway, his neighborhood, and onto the highway. *I hope Jake's ready.* The blooming trees blurred past him, and he thought about how it was almost a year ago that he and Ariana had brushed hands in the bookstore. Her face from that day flashed in his mind, and his stomach tightened. He thought about the patio in Spain and San Luis and the flood of emotion that ran through them when she had accepted his proposal. His desires for her were a moot point. He had to respect her wishes.

At least he could still hear her voice and see her face once in a while as she finished her senior thesis projects. And as long as they had that connection, there was still hope to make her see that they belonged together. But for now, he had to focus on this job opportunity that could give him a foothold into his career while he attended grad school after his year in Spain.

As he rounded the corner to Jake's street, the phone rang. Her picture came up on the screen, and he picked up.

"Hey!"

"Hey! Sorry about earlier. I was meeting with my advisor."

"I figured it was something like that. How are things going?"

"Pretty well. He gave me some more literature sources in Spanish regarding unrequited love that I could reference in my story."

"Nice."

"How is work going for you?"

"We've been working nonstop. We're almost finished. The end of May is only a month and a half away."

"I know! Graduation can't get here soon enough. Is your dad happy with your work?"

"Yeah," Luke said. "I've tried to do everything I can on this project...to make him proud, since I know that this is it. You know, I've enjoyed working alongside him, Ariana."

"That's cool!" she said. "You're not thinking you want to continue with law, are you?"

"No, nothing like that. I'm just glad we had this time together. I think it's been good for us. I can appreciate how hard he's worked for our family over the years and to get the firm to where it is."

"That's great, Luke! I know what a struggle it was for you to make the decision to work with him in the first place."

"I know. I think we have a better understanding of one another. Now I think he understands why I'm not going to continue working for the firm. He talked to Rebecca's uncle the other day who has a friend in Boston that's doing some anthropology work. I'm heading up there now to meet with him. I'm going to need to line something up after Spain."

"Oh," she said. "Well, that's great." Her voice was flat.

"Are you ok?"

Jake walked out of his house with his suitcase in hand just as Luke drove up the driveway. He got out with his phone in his ear as he opened the trunk for Jake.

"Yeah, I'm fine. How long will you be up there?" she asked.

"Just through the weekend. I have to be back by Monday." He turned toward Jake and gave him a pat on the back. "Hey!"

"Who's that?" Ariana asked.

"Jake."

"Hey! Is that Ariana? Give me that." And before Luke could respond, Jake snatched the phone from him, ran to his side of the car, and hopped in. He quickly put it on speaker and said, *"Hola, mami chula, ¿Cómo estás?"*

Luke's jaw tightened. He jumped in the driver's seat, rolled his eyes, and put the car in reverse.

Ariana laughed out loud. "Practicing your Spanish, eh? Good for you!"

"You know it! When you coming out here again? You know my man over here is—"

"Jake!" Luke lunged for the phone and tried to pry it out of Jake's tight grip. It was tough to do while he was trying to drive out of Jake's driveway and get onto the highway.

"I don't know. That's a good question," Ariana said. "One of these days."

"Well, you better hurry up. *Hay uno aquí que 'sta llorando un río por ti.*"[153]

"Is that right?"

"Jake!" Luke yelled. He grabbed the phone from Jake and took it off speaker. "Sorry about that. Jake's obviously delusional." His face felt warm as he shot Jake a look that made him fold over laughing.

"You know I'm not, Ariana!" Jake shouted. "You should see how he's looking at me!"

"It's ok," Ariana said, giggling. "He's hilarious. It would be cool to come out there. But...I just—"

"Let's talk later," Luke said. "I'll call you after this trip when we can talk without interruption." He glared at Jake again. Jake choked on his soda, just about spitting it all over the dash if hadn't been for his arm covering his mouth.

"Ok," Ariana said. "Have a safe trip. Looking forward to hearing all about it. Say bye to Jake for me."

"She says bye," Luke said, eyeing Jake.

"*¡Hasta luego!* Got nuttin' but love for ya, girl!" He pounded a fist at his chest.

"He's so crazy."

"He's about to get kicked," Luke said. Ariana laughed. "I'll talk to you soon. L—Later."

"Bye," she said.

"You were about to say love you, weren't you?" Jake said. He wiped at his eyes that had leaked from all his laughter. He was truly enjoying himself. "You two need to quit playing games."

"Look, man, I'm just trying to respect what she wants."

"Well, you better figure something out, or you're going to find yourself just like your grandpa."

---

[153] There's someone here crying a river for you.

Luke was quiet. He knew his friend was right, but he didn't want to overstep his boundaries. He took a deep breath, turned up the music, and focused on the drive ahead.

They arrived in Boston late afternoon and drove up to the townhome complex near the marina.

"Is this it?" Jake asked.

"I think so." Luke pulled a piece of paper from his pocket. "Here's the address my dad gave me."

"I'm hungry."

"Me too."

They drove up and parked in an open spot in front of the address. Just as Luke turned off the engine, the door to the townhome flung open and Rebecca stood smiling and waving at them from the door.

"Did you know she was going to be here?" Jake's face whipped toward Luke with his jaw dropped and his brows almost reaching his hairline.

"Uh, no!" Luke said, annoyed bewilderment dripping from his words.

They got out of the car without their bags, looking perplexed as Rebecca shouted, "Luke! Jake! Come on in!"

"Rebecca, what are you doing here?" Luke asked. "I thought I was meeting up with your uncle."

"You are! This is their summer home where we'll be staying this weekend," she said cheerfully, grabbing onto his arm. "Come on! Sylvia's inside." Her eyes were bright and the look on her face resolute.

"Sylvia? I'm confused. What's this all about?" Luke pulled his arm from her grasp. They followed Rebecca inside, and the folding, exterior window walls at the far end of the space opened up to breathtaking views of the marina, creating the illusion that it was in their living room. A warm, familiar smell filled the townhome, interrupted by scents of coconut from a couple of candles Luke saw burning on the coffee table.

"Is that your Aunt Jane's cod chowder…and challah bread?" Luke asked. His eyes narrowed and he gave a half-smile at the childhood memory.

Rebecca glanced at Luke from the corner of her eye, her smug expression, slapping him in the face. Her neck twisted toward Sylvia. "I told you he'd remember, Sylvia. That's how much history we have."

Luke rolled his eyes. *What?*

"I hope you two are hungry," she continued. "Aunt Jane just brought it over."

"Hi, Luke! Jake." Sylvia screeched, shooting them a sort of naïve, yet knowing smile from behind the kitchen breakfast bar.

Rebecca straightened the white mini skirt on her gaunt frame—size negative zero supermodels had always been her idols—and combed through her sleek, blond ponytail with her hand, flicking it back out of her way. She blinked her jet-black eyelashes that sat under precise eyeliner and shadow, licked her cherry red lips, and grabbed for Luke's arm again to walk him over to the kitchen.

Still baffled at what was happening, Luke pulled his arm back and asked, "Where's the bathroom?"

"It's right over there." She extended a perfumed arm in front of him as she pointed to a powder room across the living room to the left.

"Thanks." Luke couldn't help letting out a cough.

"I don't know what you guys are up to," Jake said, pointing at the two of them and loud enough for Luke to hear as he walked away, "but this will not end well."

"What do you mean, Jake?" Rebecca asked. "We've been working really closely this spring. Just what we need to make it clear to both of us."

What is she talking about?

"So where's Pete?" Luke asked as he walked toward the kitchen from the bathroom.

"He'll be here tomorrow bright and early for breakfast at 8:00. In the meantime, we can have some dinner and take the boat for a spin on the marina, like we used to when we were kids. Uncle Pete has arranged for a friend of his to take us out."

Luke looked at Jake, who was drinking some sort of cocktail they had served him, and then back at Rebecca. *Is she serious? She can't be serious.*

"Look, Rebecca, I think there's been some sort of misunderstanding."

"Here, Luke." Sylvia, held out a wide-rimmed cocktail glass toward Luke. "Would you like a Cosmo?"

Really? "No, thanks."

"Let's go outside and talk." Rebecca threaded her arm through Luke's again. "The air is lovely out here."

Out of sheer curiosity, Luke followed her out to the patio to the oversized furniture. It was a crisp spring early evening, and the cool breeze eased the fishy marina smell. He could feel his jaws and neck muscles turning to rocks. This is not what he needed after the long drive out here and certainly not what he had expected. He closed his jacket around him and stuck his hands in his pockets to keep the cold out.

"So what is this all about?" Luke asked. He sat at the edge of an outdoor sofa that overlooked the boats bobbing up and down on the water.

"Luke, I never stopped loving you," Rebecca said. She sat next to him and licked her lips. *Did she have them...plumped?* Luke's face scrunched, confused at the yearning in her crystal blue eyes as she spoke. "I know things got weird in college for both of us. And I think we both needed to explore other options. We were *so* young. And I know you got engaged last winter, and that was cute and all, but the reality is, she left you, Luke. She was never good enough for you anyway." She lifted a hand to his shoulder and leaned in. "Besides, lately, since we've been working together...it's like we've rekindled a spark that—"

"Let me stop you right there, Rebecca. I'm still in love with Ariana." It ached in his chest as he let out the words. "I'm still trying to work things out with her."

"You can't be serious." She got up from her seat and stood behind him. She placed her hands on his shoulders and began trying to massage him. "Thing is...she's moved on, Luke. I thought she would have put up more of a fight for you. She doesn't know what you're worth...or she doesn't care...whatever. You and I come from the same place. We get each other. She could never understand you like I do." She paused. "Besides, look at this." She pulled up a photo of Ariana hugging some guy on her phone. "She's moved on."

"I have no idea who that is—" Luke's eyes were wide in disbelief as he stared at the phone that was thrust in his face from behind him.

"Don't look stunned. You're not the only one with contacts at DU."

He swallowed, feeling his heart drop to his stomach. His face was heating up, and his chest was tight. "You don't understand a thing about her." His breath was heavy now as he stood up swiftly, making

her arms drop and forcing her to take a step back. He looked her squarely in the face. "Look, Rebecca, I don't want to hurt you, but I'm totally serious when I say this. I'm not sure what you thought you felt over the last couple of months." His heart began to beat faster with anger, still he closed his eyes and took a deep breath. "I'm glad we've taken the company to the next level, but you and I both know it's not right between us. I don't know that it ever was."

"Luke." Her lip trembled, and her eyes blinked as they watered. "You…you can't mean that." Her voice got higher pitched with each word. "All those late nights in the office, the dinners, the times you offered to drive me home."

"I would have done that for anyone in the office. I have! I'm sorry you took it the wrong way. I *never* would have done all those things if I would have known that's what you were thinking."

"You two deserve each other," Rebecca screamed, making her face red and blotchy. She pointed at him. "You and that two-bit illegal Mexican…hood rat! Ugh! I don't care what she thinks she is…she will never—"

"What did you just say?"

"You heard me! She said she isn't Mexican, but what the hell is the difference anyway?" she shouted.

"When did you talk to her?" He was sure the neighbors around the marina could hear him now. But he couldn't help it. His index finger was in her face. "Rebecca, what the hell did you say to her?"

She breathed heavily through her nose, dabbed at both eyes with her ring fingers, and smoothed her skirt. Then, with an unexpected calmness, she said, "I think it's time for you to leave."

"Gladly."

"And you can forget about the job with Uncle Pete. He was just doing me a favor," she said as she studied her neatly polished fingernails.

"You are completely demented." Luke was filled to the tips of his ears in rage and disbelief at this utter waste of his time. His fists were clenched as he talked through gritted teeth. "And you know what?" He whipped back to her. "Ariana has more class and integrity in her little fingernail than you'll ever have. You can dress yourself in diamonds, gold, and all that designer crap, but you'll never be worth a quarter of the woman that she is." He walked back in the house, finding Jake knee deep in chowder and bread.

"Hey, we're out of here."

"But it's so good—"

"Come on, man!"

"Told you it wasn't going to end well." He shoveled a final helping of the chowder into his mouth as he leapt off the bar stool and followed Luke outside.

"I need to call my dad," Luke said as they jumped in the car just as Rebecca slammed the door of the townhome, yelling some absurdity he didn't care to decipher. "He couldn't have known about this. It would erase everything. I mean, what the heck was she expecting? That she would seduce me with childhood nostalgia and boating, and then what? Rekindle something overnight that was never there to begin with? She's out of her freakin' mind!"

"That's what I was thinking!"

"I have to call Ariana. When did they ever have a chance to talk?"

"Ariana?"

"Yeah. She said Ariana told her she wasn't Mexican."

"What does that mean?"

"I don't know, but I have to find out what." He swerved, just about taking the curb with him, as he rounded the corner. Everything was blurred, and his chest was pounding. He was beyond angry. He felt set up. Betrayed. Ambushed.

"Dude, are you ok? I can drive if you want. You just ran a red light!"

Luke blinked and looked at Jake, which snapped him out of his tunnel vision. "Yeah, man. I'm ok."

"Let's stop and eat somewhere so you could calm down and figure out what to do. You can't drive like this. Besides I'm still hungry. I didn't get to finish my food. You missed out. That stuff was good!"

Luke glared at Jake. He couldn't think about food right now. His stomach was in knots. "Fine. Let's stop there." He pointed to a restaurant up ahead.

They took a couple of seats at the bar, and Jake ordered a couple of shots of rum for him and Luke.

"Don't worry. It's all going to work out, bruh!" Jake gave Luke a reassuring pat on the back.

"Here you go." The bartender sat the drinks on the bar. "Do you want to keep a tab open?"

"Sure." Jake pulled his card from his wallet.

Luke tried to stop him. "Dude, you don't have to do that."

"Don't worry. I got this." Jake handed his card to the bartender. "Can we have a couple of menus, too, please?"

"Sure," responded the bartender, taking Jake's card.

"I hope she talks to me about it."

"Call her."

Luke slammed the shot, reached for his phone, and walked out the door.

"Do you want me to order anything for you?" Jake called.

Luke just waved his hand and let the door close behind him. The phone was ringing.

"Hello…Luke?"

"Hey! How are you?" He leaned up against the outside restaurant wall. His chest warmed at the sound of her voice.

"I didn't expect you to call me back so quickly. Did you get the job?"

"No. It wasn't what I expected at all. Is this a good time?" He heard music and some voices in the background.

"Actually," started Ariana, "it's not a very good time. I'm kind of…in the middle of something."

"Oh…well, I, uh…" He felt his blood starting to heat up. *What is she in the middle of? Should I ask her about the guy? No. Calm down. It's really none of your business. I* guess. He switched the phone from one ear to the other. "I have something important to talk to you about. Will you call me tomorrow, please?"

"Of course. Is everything ok?"

"Yeah…I just…need to you call me, ok?"

"Luke, I don't like the sound of your voice right now. If you need me to, I can break away."

"No, it's alright." He focused on the faint music and laughter of both men and women in the background. *That's not her family. Where is she? Is* he *there?* "Go ahead and get back to your evening. Just promise you'll call me tomorrow."

"Ok. I will. Good night, Luke."

"Good night."

He squeezed his phone in his hand, punched his open palm, and walked back into the restaurant, and joined Jake at the bar.

"Did you talk to her?"

"Yeah, but it sounded like she was at some kind of party. So we didn't get into it."

"Sorry, dude. Did you call your dad?"

"Not yet. I'll just talk to him at home."

"I got us a cheese pizza. You have to eat something."

"I guess I should. We have a long drive back."

"You want to drive back? Tonight? Are you ok to do that?"

"Why not?"

The adrenaline pumping through his veins could get him to Florida from here. He took another shot of rum and forced down a slice of pizza, giving him a stomach ache, and they got back on the road. The drive back home was quiet. Luke was *not* in the mood for conversation. Jake was in and out of sleep, and all he could think about was Ariana at that party—and that guy in the picture. He hoped she really hadn't moved on…like that. He didn't know how he would handle that. They were over halfway back home when Luke's phone rang. Ariana's picture came up on the screen. Jake shot up. He had been asleep. Luke and Jake looked at each other. He pulled over at a gas station off the highway.

"Do what you have to do, man."

He got out of the car and leaned up against the back. "Hello?"

"Hey, can you talk?"

"Yeah, of course. I'm so glad you called."

"I couldn't wait until morning. You sounded so—"

"I know. So, uh, Rebecca set me up."

"Rebecca? What do you mean?"

Her voice sounded more annoyed than his. "I'm not sure exactly what happened, but she set up the whole job thing with her uncle. She was waiting for me and Jake at his summer house and had this whole evening thing planned."

"Ooh, that little tramp! I knew she was going to do something like that! I was just waiting for you to call me one day telling me you were back together."

"Are you kidding me? I stormed out of there as quickly as I could. But she said something that bothered me. Did you guys talk at some point?"

"No, why?"

"She made some comment about you not being Mexican."

Ariana was quiet for a minute.

"Ariana?"

"I heard them, Luke."

"Who?"

"Her…and her friend at the holiday party. The night you proposed. They were talking in the bathroom. They didn't know I was there. Rebecca talked about getting you back and called me an illegal Mexican or something ignorant like that. So when I hugged her outside that night as we were getting in the car…it took everything inside me not to grab her by that fake blond…anyway, I didn't want to make a scene. Instead, I told her I wasn't Mexican so she would know I heard them."

"Why didn't you tell me?" The tightness in his throat was making it hard to swallow, and his blood was like a furnace now.

"I don't know. It didn't seem important at the time—"

"What are you talking about? We would have never kept her working at the firm if we would have known."

"And then after that…Grandpa Moisés. I just thought…I should leave it alone. It seemed to be for the best."

"For who?" He squeezed his eyes shut and his head fell back against the car.

"For my family. Catalina's legacy. For you. Your world. I wasn't sure if I would fit. You didn't need the burden of explaining me to anyone. I was trying to do the right thing for everyone."

"Everyone except…you." *And me.*

The passing cars on the highway highlighted her silence on the other end of the phone.

"Can I ask you a question?"

"Sure, what?"

"Why *don't* you say you're Mexican?"

"Luke! I thought of all people *you'd* get it."

"I do…kind of. I'm just curious. That area *was* Mexico, wasn't it?"

"Yes, but only for twenty-seven years. When my family came here, they were Spanish. Now I know it was culturally and nationally. We have Native American, French, Portuguese, Greek, and obviously Jewish roots, to name a few…that I know of. But they were all subjects of the Spanish crown. They spoke the language and practiced the customs. And you know about the religion. Luke, my Grampo Solomon was born a subject of the Spanish crown in Taos, New Mexico in 1819. Then, when he was two, he became a Mexican citizen. And when he died, he was an American, and he hadn't so much as moved an inch until he decided to come to San Luis in 1851, which was literally only sixty miles north. They were isolated, alone,

265

a buffer for the Northern border. They relied on one another as family for survival. That's why we call older people *mano* and *mana* instead of *don* and *doña*. It's short for *hermano* and *hermana*. Now I kind of think they wanted this. I think they wanted to be left alone so they could live as they pleased without anyone watching over their shoulders."

"And it worked…for a long time."

"Yup. Until Grandpa Moises's generation, everyone still spoke Spanish first. And it's the same Spanish from the sixteenth century, except now, with Anglicisms and other words here and there that they adopted from the indigenous wherever they were or from the French."

"French? Like what?"

"Well, *puela*, for example."

"What's that?"

"A frying pan. That comes from the French, and so does *veliz*, a suitcase. A *jején* is a mosquito, and I believe that's Aztec. Our language is different from Mexican Spanish. Our food is different. Mexicans are the first to point it out! The holidays we celebrate are different. The point is that the pivotal things that make up the Mexican identity, we didn't participate in—their Mexican Revolution, the battle of Puebla. In San Luis, we don't celebrate 16 de Septiembre, Cinco de Mayo, or Dia de los Muertos—or we never did until lately. Our most important holidays always revolved around the church, like Santiago and Santana. Our culture developed here in New Mexico, Southern Colorado, and the US. Aside from proximity, we are no more similar or different to Mexico than we are from Latinos of every other Latin American country. The only difference is we didn't have one. We're New Mexican. We're American, with a 300-year history of being subjects of the Spanish crown."

"Thanks for the history lesson, Professor Romero."

"You asked for it!" She laughed, lightening up. "Sorry. It's become my soapbox ever since my history thesis."

"Totally kidding. Seriously, though, I never thought of it like that."

"Not many people do. I didn't start thinking about all of this stuff, really analyzing it, until this year with what I've learned about having Jewish ancestors and finding out more about my ethnicity through the DNA testing. Get me now?"

"I'll be right there!"

"Luke!"

"Still kidding, sort of." Luke laughed. "Of course, I get you. Thanks for breaking it down. You are a beautiful person, Ariana, inside and out."

The awkward silence made Luke wonder if he should have said that. *It's true.*

"So, I had a dream about Catalina the other night," she finally said.

"Catalina?"

"Yeah. I can't think of anyone else it could be. I dreamt of a young woman with long curly hair helping me sweep the floor of a dusty, old wood-paneled house. She kept guiding me to sweep to the middle of the floor. Her smile was…incandescent, and her eyes were just like Grandpa Moisés's but luminous. She told me that I would find my home in the deepest part of my heart where love lives."

Luke felt her words flowing through his spirit, giving him chills; but "That's deep" was all he could bring himself to say.

"I know. I'm not sure yet what to make of it. It was probably just because I'm still writing their story."

"Maybe. How's it going?"

"Good. I'll send you a copy when I'm done."

"Can't wait." Luke felt the car move, making him stumble. He had almost forgotten where he was and that Jake was still waiting for him inside. *How long have we been talking?* "Hey, I better go. Jake's still waiting for me in the car."

"In the car? Where are you?"

"At a gas station on our way back home."

"You're driving home from Boston now? Lu-uke!"

"Yeah. It's ok, though. We're almost there."

"Be careful. Text me when—" she started as her voice got cut off. "Hey, I'm getting another call, but text me as soon as you get home."

"I knew you'd say that." He smiled. "I will."

"You better. I'll be waiting for it."

He got back in the car reenergized. It was something about her that moved him. Calmed him. That propelled him forward. He was buzzing.

"Wow, dude. Whatever you just had, I want some of that."

"What are you talking about?" Luke couldn't deny it. His gaga grin gave him away.

"You're like a different person. Why don't you just go out there and see her."

267

"I can't. It's complicated. It may take some time and creativity, but I need to do something better…bigger," he said, thinking of the party she was at, the photo, and the phone call she got while they talked. *Before it's too late.*

"Whatever you say," Jake said. "I can see the wheels turning. You know I'm here for you."

Chapter 24

Ariana

Ariana stood in front of her dresser and stared at the top drawer, debating whether or not to open it. She exhaled, pulled the knob, and grabbed the picture of her and Luke at the Palace Theater. She gazed at it for a second before holding it to her chest and throwing herself on her dorm room bed. She had hung up the phone with Luke feeling guilty. His words echoed in her mind. *"Everyone except...you."* If only she had been that brave. That noble.

The truth was she felt like a coward. She felt like she gave him up without a fight. She wasn't sure she would have been able to pull it off. To live in his world. To live up to the expectations of his family and his upbringing. Was she pretty enough? Would she be able to deal with all the Rebeccas of that world and not lose herself and become someone she didn't recognize? Yet, he didn't want Rebecca. He wanted her, just as much as she wanted him. Right or wrong. But with Grandpa Moisés's injury, it was easier to let *that* make the decision for her as much as it tore her heart apart.

She heard a faint knock at her door that made her heart thump. She sat up quickly and her head spun toward the door.

"Who is it?" She walked over and leaned her ear to the door.

"It's Liz. Open up. I saw your light on."

"What happened to you?" Liz asked as Ariana opened the door. "Everyone was asking for you. James, specifically, was wondering where you took off to. I think he tried to call you."

"I know. I just couldn't. She had been trying to get back into the social scene, and she knew James was into her. "It's just too much right now." She plopped herself on the bed with Liz sitting next to her, and she poured her eyes and heart out to Liz, explaining in detail everything that had just transpired.

"He loves you, Ana."

"I know. I love him, too. And I'm a horrible person."

"No, you're not." Liz put an arm around Ariana. "You're just afraid. She's lucky we don't live out there. That scheming, manipulating, *cabr*—"

"Liz!" Ariana smacked her arm. "I thought you were trying to be better about that *boca de lumbre*![154] She waved a finger in Liz's face.

"I am. But just saying."

"I know. I knew it. I knew it the first time I saw her through FaceTime in that freakin' fitted designer suit. She *is* lucky we're not out there. I would have loved nothing better that day in the bathroom than to wipe the floor with her." She fantasized for a minute and then shook her head. *What would that have solved? She would have milked it. It would have been her word against mine. I would have ended up looking like the stereotype.* "But either way, it's too late for me and Luke, Liz. How I feel doesn't matter now. I can't disappoint my grandpa. You should see how happy my dad is—all the plans he's making. The decision's already been made. It's just better this way. He'll find someone else, and so will I…eventually. And we'll both move on with our lives, and everything will be fine." She sliced the air with both of her hands.

"Only it won't. Who are you trying to convince? You can't get him out of your heart, can you? You guys are just going to repeat the same mistake Benjamín and Catalina did, *por tu maldita terquedad!*[155]

Benjamín and Catalina. "I better get some sleep. I have a long day tomorrow working on their story."

"Ok. I should get back home, too."

Ariana's phone chimed.

"He's home."

Glad you made it home safely! ☺ She quickly texted back.

"You better get to work on *your own* story, mujer!" Liz pointed to the phone as she hugged her friend goodbye. "Love you, girl. Trust yourself."

---

[154] Fire mouth!
[155] Because of your stubbornness!

On the last day her paper was due, Ariana awoke at the crack of dawn to upload Benjamín and Catalina's story to the class website and make a copy for herself. She stared at the computer screen for a minute. She couldn't help but sit up a little taller. She had read and re-read it what felt like a million times, running it by Luke to make sure she hadn't left anything out or misunderstood anything his grandmother had said. As a tribute to her, Luke, and Mari, she had ended it with a bit of magical realism, suggesting that Benjamín and Catalina had found each other as eternal shooting stars in the sky. And now, the final draft of her story, *El Amor Eterno de Catalina y Benjamín,* was finally finished. She hoped anyone who read this story would fall in love with them the way she, Luke, and their families had. With butterflies in her stomach, she hit send and emailed a copy to Luke, just like she had done with her History thesis, with a message saying, *I hope you enjoy reading about them as much as I enjoyed writing about them.*

Feeling a lump creep into her throat, she swallowed it away and called Liz who had been working hard to finalize the work in her final class as well. She had already heard word that she had been accepted to the CU School of Medicine and was planning on attending there in the fall. They had much to celebrate.

They went to the sports bar down the street and ordered dinner and a couple of mojitos. Graduation was next week, and Ariana would be boarding a plane with her family for Spain again a few weeks after that for the reception.

They were relieved, excited, and anxious all at the same time as they knocked glasses and said, "Salud!"

"Do you remember when we were in Mexico and you fell into the hotel pool?" Liz said with a giggle as she took another sip of her mojito.

"I remember you pushing me!" Ariana shot back.

"It was the only way to keep that guy from trying to talk to you."

"I know. I do appreciate you for that! Do you remember I waited for you sitting on a lawn chair at the beach?"

"Sorry about that. But Raul was *so* dang fine, though!"

"He-llo!" Ariana threw her hands out to her sides and leaned into the table toward Liz. "I fell asleep with a Corona in my hand and had to get a golf cart cab to take me home!" She waved a hand in the air as if pointing to an obscure hotel in Mexico and fell back into her chair with her arms folded.

"Love you, Ana!"

"Right. Hope he was worth it." Ariana laughed and rolled her eyes. She grabbed her drink and swallowed the last of her mojito.

They laughed and cried so hard, their sides ached. It was a mix of nostalgia and gratitude for all those experiences—the good and the bad—tugging at their emotions, knowing it had all come to an end. They were going to need to be ready for "adulting" soon—whatever that meant.

"What are you thinking about?" Liz asked. "As if I don't already know."

"Huh?" She forced her eyes from her glass and pulled her hair behind her ears.

Ariana suddenly became aware that it had been over a year already since the bookstore encounter with Luke. It seemed like a lifetime ago, yet she could still feel his heart beating against her own and his warm breath on her neck. She missed him so much, and every fiber of her being never ceased to remind her. She sucked at the ice in her mojito glass.

"You're staring so hard into that mojito glass, the ice has melted!"

"No I'm not."

"Haven't you talked to him?"

"No, not since I finished the first draft of Catalina and Benjamín's story a few weeks ago."

"Are you serious? Do you think he's moving on?"

"I don't know. Maybe. I did tell him to."

"Maybe Rebecca finally sunk her claws into him." She folded her hands, clawing the air and hissed like a cat.

"Shut up." Ariana sucked the air through her teeth. "I think that mojito's gotten to you."

She knew Liz was trying to make light of the situation, but a pang stabbed at Ariana's gut with those words. *Or maybe he just realized I'm not who he thought I was.*

"Why don't you just call him."

"I can't."

"You won't." Liz shook her head.

Graduation day was upon them soon after Ariana and Liz had gone out to celebrate. They had gone shopping for outfits the next day, and Ariana had been in constant contact with her mom and Aunt Juanita about her party, which would be held in her and Uncle Tomás's huge backyard. She wanted to make sure there was no detail left undone. Ariana fidgeted as her mom tried to get her hair and cap in place.

"Stop moving, Ariana."

"Sorry! I can't stand still!"

She was getting her cords when her dad came in her dorm room.

"*¡Apúrense!* You're going to be late, Ariana!"

"You look beautiful, mi'ja! I'm so proud of you." Her mom hugged her and placed the cords around her neck. "We're almost done, Joe. *¡Allí vamos!*"[156]

They walked Ariana to where her line was forming. The ceremony began shortly after with a speech from the class president. Then the keynote speaker spoke about walking in their destinies and following their dreams while hopefully contributing in a meaningful way to society. Ariana scratched at her chest through her robe and pulled at the collar. The air had become thick. Visions of the woman helping her clean the room swept through her mind's eye. She sighed. This had to be confirmation that being home was the right thing to do. Maybe she could get a Master's or a PhD at Adams State while she lived at home. *Home. San Luis* is *home.* Then Luke's face was distinct in her mind with his welcoming baby blues and sweet smile. Her palms began to sweat, and her heart began to pound when the person next to her nudged her. "Hey, it's time!"

"Huh? Oh, yeah!" Ariana's eyes shot to the right. Her entire row ahead of her had already stood up and had lined up outside the rows of seats toward the graduation stage, the board of trustees, and the college president. She had completely missed the last part of the keynote speech. She stood up abruptly, and her heel got stuck in the grass, making her trip and almost fall. She pulled at her shoe and moved forward, hearing some chuckles in the background. They moved through the list until it came time for Ariana to walk forward, shake hands with the president of the college, and receive her degree. When they read her name, "Ariana Angela Romero, Magna Cum Laude," she was still in a cloud. Her family screamed and hollered

---

[156] We're on our way!

with impressive volume from the audience, making her laugh out loud. She posed for her picture with the president and took her seat once again.

When it was over, Ariana found her family, and her cousins ran toward her and picked her up, lifting her high in the air. They were taking pictures of her with her degree in front of some of the historic buildings on campus when she saw Ricardo walking over.

"Congratulations! I'm so proud of you!" he said, giving her a bear hug.

"Thanks, Ricardo! I appreciate your help with everything— especially your class last summer." She swallowed hard and felt an unexpected knot rising in her throat. "It was...inspiring."

"I'm so glad you took the class and found your family, Ariana. That diary," he said shaking his head. "It's an unbelievable treasure."

"It is!"

"Are you excited about the reception?"

"Oh my gosh, yes! We're all so excited. I can't wait to have my whole family see what I got to see last year."

"I can't wait either. It's going to be a historical moment for all of us."

"All of us?"

"Yes, our team will be there as well."

Ariana's stomach fell to her knees. *Luke might be there?* She looked down and caught a glimpse of the tip of her gold heel covered in chocolate earth and blades of grass. "That's awesome!" She caught Ricardo's eye again and casually flicked her hair back. She hoped he hadn't noticed her sudden trembling.

"Yes! Well, it's wonderful to see you, Ariana. Congratulations again! See you in a few weeks!" Ricardo gave her a pat on the back and walked away.

She turned the other way and put her palm to her forehead. She could see her breathing rising and falling briskly through her robe. *What if he is there? What am I going to do when I see him?*

They headed for their cars and drove to Aunt Juanita and Uncle Tomás's house where a feast and huge cake were waiting for them. They had decorated the backyard in crimson and gold streamers, balloons, and a huge banner that said 'Congratulations Ariana' inscribed with the DU logo on each corner. In the kitchen, front and center on the island, Ariana found a huge graduation hat made for all her cards and a vase with two dozen long-stem red roses with baby's breath and a card attached to it. She gasped, and the room fell silent. She didn't have to think twice to know where those had come from. She felt her stomach knot up and the tears push at her eyelids.

"Mom, when did these get here?"

"They were delivered to the house this morning, Ana," Aunt Juanita said.

"I'll open it later." She sniffed and took the card.

"*Anda*, come and eat, everyone!" Ariana's mom waved her hands toward the food. "This is supposed to be a celebration!"

Right. Put on a happy face, Ariana. She quickly changed to shorts and a tank top and stuffed the card in her back pocket. As she walked back into the kitchen, Uncle Tomás had turned on the New Mexico music with Tobias Rene singing *Un Ratito*. Joaquin let out a grito that all the neighbors could hear, and everyone laughed, getting in line for the green chile, beans, mashed potatoes, salad, and homemade bread. Ariana grabbed her plate and walked out to the patio to eat. She couldn't listen to that song anymore. The lyrics were just too much.

She sat down and shoved a forkful of mashed potatoes into her mouth and squinted out at the yard that backed to the open prairie of the eastern plains in Aurora. *I should've brought my sunglasses.* The weather was perfect. They were grateful that last weekend it had snowed the last snowfall of the year—they hoped anyway. It was warm, and there were but a few puffy clouds in the sky.

"*¿Qué andas haciendo aquí 'fuera, hija?*"[157] Ariana's grandpa came outside and sat at the outdoor table next to her.

"Just needed some air, Grampo."

"Well, everyone is asking for you in there. They want to cut the cake."

Ariana laughed. She knew her grandpa had a sweet tooth.

"Ok, let's go."

They went back inside and tore into the cake and the other sweets her family had made. Ariana walked around and took in the familiar sights, sounds, and smells from the kitchen. Karina's graduation had been a similar affair. And now everyone had made the trip from San Luis to be with her on her special day. Uncle Tomás took Auntie Juanita's hand and spun her around, enjoying *Las Nubes* by Little Joe y La Familia. Uncle Steve stood on one of the coffee tables telling

---

[157] Would are you doing out here?

animated jokes while Tía Dianne yelled at him to get down. Poker was being played at the dining table. The family network gossip surmounted in cliques around the house. *Everything is perfect, except...*

Ariana's eyes began to blur as she walked around, and the sounds began to muffle. Her heartbeat was thumping loudly in her ears. She grabbed her drink and pulled the card from Luke from her back pocket and walked back outside. As she was walking out, she overheard her mom's middle sister Gabi talking to her grandma.

"Mírala, que relaje. Ta'via anda enamorada de ese gringo, que ni es católico. They don't even believe in Jesus!" Her eyes were wide and her hands in the air. *"Hubiera sido mejor quedarse con el Brian de la Margaret."*[158]

"¡Oh déjala, Gabi! Ni lo conoces. Es buen muchito."[159]

Sure, Tía, much better to stay with a cheater just because he's your friend's sister's son. Oh yeah, and he's a Catholic—supposedly. That makes much more sense.

Ariana's eyes met with her grandma's. She rolled her eyes and kept walking across the big yard until she came to the fence. She opened the card, feeling the blood rush through her veins.

Congratulations, Querida Ariana!

Magna Cum Laude, really? You have so much to be proud of. Thanks for sending me copies of your work. I read every word. Your History thesis was a perfect segue into Catalina and Benjamín's story. You described their lives just as I had imagined they would be. It means a lot to me that you put so much thought and care into their story. It's something both of our families will always treasure. I wish you the best in everything you do for yourself and your family. They're lucky to have you there.

I miss you,
Luke

---

[158] Look at her. What a shame. She's still in love with that gringo, who isn't even Catholic. It would have been better for her to have stayed with Margaret's son Brian.

[159] Oh leave her alone, Gabi! You don't even know him. He's a good kid.

276

Querida Ariana. She hadn't heard that name in such a long time. His name blurred as a tear fell directly on it, making the ink bleed. She heard music and laughter as the screen door slid open. She quickly wiped at her cheeks as her mom called, "Ariana, are you ok? What are you doing?"

Her head turned toward the house, and she walked toward her mom. "Nothing, Mom. I'm fine." Through the patio doors, Grandpa Moisés sat laughing at Uncle Steve who was whistling some joke about a *pajarito.*[160] His face was red, and he had to take his glasses off to wipe his eyes. *'Cómo 'sta loco, este,'*[161] she heard him say after clearing his throat. She smiled, took a deep breath, and filed her thoughts and feelings away deep in her heart. "I just wanted to read the card from Luke."

"Do you think he'll be in Spain at the reception?"

"I don't know. I'm pretty sure. He was part of the team. It's going to be weird to see him, Mom." Her eyes began to well up again.

"I know, mi'ja. But it'll be ok." She took Ariana's face in her hands. "You know it's for the best. Your dad and your grandpa are chomping at the bit for you to get started back home. And besides, if it's meant to be, it will happen. Ariana, like the saying goes, *'Lo que es pa' ti, nadien te lo quita.'*"[162]

"Thanks, Mom. I love you." Ariana wrapped her arms around her.

"I love you, too, baby girl."

They approached the house with her mom's arm around her to the commotion that was her family. Joaquin, Andrés, and Alejandro zoomed past them toward the fire pit with the guitar and some firewood. Ariana smiled. She knew they'd be out there singing into the wee hours of the night. The warm, spring evening was just right for it.

As she and her mom walked in, Grandma Aurelia was standing at the sliding glass doors waiting for them.

"No le hagas caso a tu tía, 'jita. ¡Esa entremetida de la Gabi siempre está metiéndose en 'onde no l' importa!"[163]

---

[160] Little bird.

[161] This guy is so crazy.

[162] Like the song says, 'No one can take what is rightfully yours.'

[163] Don't pay any attention to your nosy Aunt Gabi. She's always sticking her nose where it doesn't belong.

"Thank you, Grama." Ariana smiled and kissed her cheek. No matter how loud, obnoxious and crazy, or out of control the family "network" was, this was home…where she fit in.

Chapter 25

Ariana

After the long six-hour flight from Newark, Ariana and her extended family took a bus from the airport into Madrid and another one from Madrid to Corral de Almaguer and finally to El Convento.

"See, Dad! I knew you would love it," Ariana said as her dad took pictures outside his window.

The cameras on the phones had been going nonstop since they had left the airport. Ariana breathed deeply. She hadn't realized how much she had missed this place and the landscape. All of the memories from the year before came back in a blast as she looked around, taking in the floral hedges in the median and neatly trimmed olive groves just as she had left them.

"It's gorgeous, Ariana!"

"I'm so glad you're getting to see it for yourself! It's just like we used to talk about when I was a kid." She gasped. *My wish.* A vision of her kneeling on the pew in the church of Nuestra Señora de la Asunción last year in Corral de Almaguer flashed in her mind.

"It's exactly like I thought it would be," he said, glued to his window.

She smiled. Her wish had just come true.

When they arrived at El Convento, Roberto was at the front desk of the stone castle-like building, waiting for them and assigning each family their room. They dropped their luggage on the floor and slouched against the walls and the couches in the sitting room as they waited for their keys. It wouldn't be long before they would have to meet back in the dining room for dinner at 8:00 that evening.

Mari came out from the kitchen to greet everyone, and Ariana screeched, running to her and giving her tight hugs and kisses on both cheeks.

"*¡Mi linda Ariana! ¡Mi consentida! ¿Cómo estás? Gracias por cumplir con tu compromiso de regresar con tu familia.*" She hugged her and whispered in her ear, "*Ya te dije que lo ibas a encontrar si confiaras en el amor.*"[164]

"*¡Hola, Mari!*" Ariana squeezed her back and furrowed her brows, wondering what she meant. "*¡Es un placer de verla otra vez!*"[165]

She opened her eyes from hugging Mari to see Luke walking toward the reception area. When their eyes met, Ariana felt like time stopped. *What the?*

"Hi," she said in a breathy whisper as he approached, once again feeling like melted butter in Mari's arms. It was a good thing she was leaning on her hug for support.

"Hi," Luke said, beaming as he returned Ariana's gaze. She closed her mouth. *Oh my gosh, oh my gosh! What's he doing here?*

"*Y tú, hijo mío.*" Mari held Luke's face in her hands. Ariana stumbled to catch her footing as Mari let go of her for Luke. She embraced him and whispered loud enough for only Ariana to hear, "*¡Ya te había dicho que estabas enamorado!*"[166]

Ariana's cheeks heated up even more, and she fought the trembling that had erupted inside her.

He laughed. "*Yo no sé cómo sabías...ni yo lo sabía.*"[167]

Mari took both of their hands and squeezed them, addressing everyone and saying, "*Pasen, pasen. Todas las habitaciones están listas para Ustedes.*"[168]

"You guys should have really monitored all of this." Luke smiled and pointed at all of Ariana's bags on the floor behind her.

Ariana rolled her eyes. *Yeah, yeah.*

---

[164] My beautiful Ariana! My cherished one! How are you? Thank you for making good on your promise to come back with your family. I told you would find love if you trusted in it.

[165] Hi, Mari! It's so good to see you again!

[166] And you, my son...I told you were in love!

[167] I don't know how you knew...when I didn't even know it myself.

[168] Come on in! The rooms are all ready for you.

"Hi, mi'jo! It's so good to see you!" Her mom chuckled and opened her arms to hug Luke. "I know. I'm surprised they let us on the plane."

"Right? You probably barely made the weight limit!"

"He-llo! I'm standing right here!" Ariana threw her hands in the air.

"Luke." Her dad nodded politely and extended his hand.

"Good to see you, Joe." Luke returned her dad's firm grip and patted him on the shoulder. Ariana followed him with her eyes as he greeted all her family members, including her brother, sister, aunt, uncle, and cousins.

"'Jita, close your mouth," her mom whispered to her. She laughed and lifted Ariana's chin with her fingertips.

Ariana heard her mom as if from a distance. Everything was fuzzy around her with only Luke clear in her vision. *You've got to control yourself.* She blinked herself back into her mom's presence. She sucked the air through her teeth and tapped her mom's hand off her chin. "Really?"

"What's up, bro," Joaquin said coldly.

"Hey! Good to see you guys." Luke slapped Andrés on the back.

"Yeah." Andrés gave Luke a once over.

And when he got to Grandpa Moisés and Grandma Aurelia, he hugged them both. Then he turned to Ariana, whose eyes had returned to him like a magnet, and said, "See you at dinner?"

Those eyes. His mouth. "Uh huh."

Ariana swallowed and nodded, barely able to get the sounds out as he smiled at her. She felt faint as she watched him trot up the stairs. She stomped a foot. *Dang it.* She knew she had messed that up. The entire plane ride, she had rehearsed various scenarios about their possible interaction at the reception. She felt off balance. Taken by surprise. Deceived. *How could he?* She had pictured herself all dressed up at the reception, hair and make-up just right, talking to him casually, with her hand on her hip, flicking her hair—maybe even chewing gum—whatever, totally acting like she was completely over him. It wasn't that much of a stretch. But what she had just done couldn't have been more opposite than what she had wanted. Even after all this time, *everything* came flooding back with a vengeance. *His jeans. Her favorite spot.*

Her nerves continued to vibrate within her body. His presence was like sitting at the edge of the wide, rushing river that ran through her grandparents' property—calming and familiar, yet utterly unnerving if you got too close. And God forbid you fell in, surely you'd be taken away by the current. *Lord, you're going to have to help me get through this.* She gasped, suddenly reaching for the bun in her hair. *And me...a messy bun and no make-up...ugh!*

"You don't have to talk to him, Ariana," Andrés said, landing a protective hand on her shoulder.

"Yeah, what the heck is he doing here?" Joaquin asked.

"It's ok. I can handle it. Thank you guys."

"Whatever you say," Joaquin said. "Just let us know if you need us."

"You ok, mi'ja?" Her mom laid her arm around Ariana's shoulder.

"Uh huh."

"Did you know he was going to be here?"

"No, not at all."

Then she let out a sigh, grabbing for her bags, layering them on one by one. She had a system. Couldn't everyone see that?

As the families found seats at the various tables at dinnertime, the familiar aroma of Mari's food began to fill the room. Ariana smiled with nostalgia as she walked down the stairs. She spied Luke across the room with his parents. She linked her arms through those of her parents and said, "Mom, Dad, let me introduce you to Luke's family."

"Ok, mi'ja. Let's go," her mom replied.

Her dad grunted, following along as Ariana grabbed his hand and pulled him forward. She took a deep breath, straightened the skirt on her yellow sun dress, and walked over to say hello.

"Ariana! It's so good to see you!" Sofia opened her arms wide to greet her. "You look absolutely beautiful!" She leaned in and whispered, "I was kind of hoping we'd be celebrating a wedding here this weekend."

Ariana laughed nervously and hugged her back, saying, "Hi, Sofia!" *What do I say to that?* "Thank you. It's so nice to see you. Martin! How are you? Still making pancakes?" *Still making pancakes? What?*

Martin hugged her, laughing, and said, "Well, hello, Ms. Colorado. Of course, you know they're my specialty."

"These are my parents. Joe and Lucia Romero."

"Pleasure to meet you," Martin greeted her dad with a firm handshake.

"Same here," her dad said, clearing his throat.

"So nice to meet you," her mom said, reaching out to give Sofia a hug.

"It's a pleasure. We just love Ariana," Sofia said, hugging Ariana's mom back.

"We love Luke, too!" Her mom gave Sofia a knowing look.

Ariana nodded hello to Luke, whose eyes seemed to stick to her every time she made contact, and then she hugged and greeted Grandma Sara, Grandpa Isaac, Aunt Linda, Uncle Al, Nina, and Zach, taking the time to hold and talk to each of the kids. *They've grown so much since I saw them last.*

"He misses you like crazy, you know. He was devastated," whispered Nina as she hugged Ariana.

Ariana smiled at her, her heart pulsing throughout her body, and introduced her parents to the rest of Luke's family. She walked back toward an empty seat at their table, feeling Luke watching her, and she hoped her wedge sandals wouldn't catch on the carpet, making her fly into someone's lap. *That's all I need.* She sat down and pushed herself closer into the table. Her neck was hot, and her hands wouldn't steady despite her best efforts. She looked around the table at her family and exhaled. Miguel, Mari, and Roberto came out with their trays of food for each table. After each table got their delicacies, Miguel stood in front of the crowd and welcomed everyone with Mari translating after him.

"*Estamos muy contentos de darles la bienvenida a El Convento Real para un evento tan especial. Luke y Ariana son muy especiales para nosotros. Los queremos como nuestros propios hijos. Es un gran placer de conocer las familias de ellos. Felicidades por el honor que recibirán esta semana. Por favor, que disfruten su estancia aquí. Esta es su casa. Buen provecho.*"[169]

"So this is what you ate the whole time you were here, mi'ja?" her dad asked, taking in a healthy helping of the paella.

---

[169] We are very happy to welcome you to El Convento Real for this very special event. Luke and Ariana are very special to us. We love them like they were our own kids. It is such a pleasure to meet their families. Congratulations on the honor you'll be receiving this week. Please enjoy your stay here. This is your house. Enjoy.

"Yes! Now you know why I gained like ten pounds in the two weeks I was here!"

"I thought it was five. This is delicious," her mom said in between bites. "I wonder if she'll give me some of the recipes for the restaurant."

"I'm sure she will. You should ask her. She's the best!"

Ariana put her fork down. She was parched. She stole a look at Luke eating and laughing with his family. *I love that smile.* She couldn't drink enough water. *Maybe some sangria will calm my nerves.* She got up to the sideboard where the sangria sat and felt a familiar presence behind her. She began to fill her glass and turned to see Luke standing right behind her.

"Ha, you scared me." Her fingertips went to her chest.

"Sorry," Luke said. He chuckled and filled up his own with lemonade. "Uh, looks like you're overflowing."

"What kind of—"

"Your sangria."

"Huh?" She looked down at her glass as it began spilling over the top of the rim and onto the sideboard. "Oh my gosh!" She reached for the towel Mari kept in between the containers of the drinks and the desserts. They looked at each other and laughed.

"Meet me at the patio tonight?" Luke asked.

"Ok," Ariana said softly with her eyes fixed on his. Her nerves had faded. She was putty in his presence.

"I'll see you in about thirty minutes then?"

Ariana nodded as Luke touched her arm and walked away.

When Ariana got there, Luke was already sitting on their wrought-iron bench. She walked over to him, and he stood up and opened his arms to her. She leaned into him, holding him close, tears pushing at the back of her eyelids at how good it felt to be in his arms again. They sat down in silence overlooking the horizon. It was pitch black except for the few scattered homes she could see in the distance. The air was warm and humid. Only crickets sung in the darkness of el campo. She leaned into his chest and breathed deeply, taking in the fresh air and his familiar Christian Dior scent.

"Why didn't you tell me you were going to be here?"

"I knew you wouldn't come if you knew."

You're right. I wouldn't have come. "I wish you would have told me."

"I needed to see you outside of the reception," he said. "I needed you to see me. This is the perfect place to remind you of where we started."

Ariana didn't respond, and an awkward silence ensued until she asked, "How are things with your dad?"

"Uh, they're ok. Still a little tense. After he fired Rebecca, we had it out again about me finding my own way. I'm glad he didn't have anything to do with her little scheme, but he still can't get it into his head that I'm not going to be a lawyer. He still can't see how the work I love to do is worth anything, especially now that there's nothing for me to fall back on after my year here."

Ariana sighed and looked out onto the vast campo and its glittering lights peppered throughout.

"Trust me, I totally understand." She paused. "It's still just as beautiful as it was a year ago, isn't it? Just can't see as many stars tonight."

"It *is* beautiful." He gently turned her face toward him. "So are you…even with paella juice all over your cheek."

"Whatever," she said. She smacked his hand away and wiped at her face. "I do not!" *Oh man, do I?*

"You do," he said, chuckling. "Here, let me get it." His voice was soft and playful. His hand followed her cheek down to the side of her neck and through her hair. He leaned into her.

"Luke—" Ariana began as she felt a drop hit her forehead. Another hit Luke's cheek. They looked up at the sky and the raindrops began coming down faster and with more force. They laughed and bolted for the door. They crept down the steps at a brisk pace, Luke leading her by the hand, and they plopped down on one of the lounge chairs in the sitting room with Ariana landing on his lap. He hugged her, and they laughed until they caught their breath. In the short time it had taken for them to get to the door from their bench, they had gotten drenched.

His face was centimeters from hers, and she could feel his warmth mixed with the moisture from the rain on his face. *I want to kiss him so badly.*

"I better go get changed," she said in a whisper.

"Yeah, I guess I should, too," he said. "So much for that. I'll walk you to your room."

As Ariana was getting dressed for bed, she heard her phone buzz. Luke had messaged her a link to *Incondicional* by Prince Royce with the words:

> *Ariana, listen to this. Ours is a love that transcends time. It's never going away. Seeing you today proved it. I don't care what you do, whether you're in San Luis or New York or here, you'll always be in my heart. You're a part of me, and you always will be. Do what you need to do with your family for as long as you need to. Mi amor no tiene horario.*[170]

She shuffled into bed quietly, trying not to wake Karina, and placed her earbuds in her ears. She was glad she had downloaded that app to make her phone work here. She lay there, absorbing the beautiful mariachi music and every bachata lyric. She sighed. Any attempt at eradicating her feelings for Luke had failed miserably, and she was miserable without him. Still, she couldn't get past how it would all work or come together. She thought about his family and what Nina had said. *I miss him like crazy, too. He's right. It's been one thing to talk to him on the phone this spring, but seeing him today...feeling his arms around me...his hands touching my face. Nothing has changed. If anything, I love him more. How is that even possible?* Then she thought about Catalina, her dad and Grandpa Moisés, and kept trying to tell herself that being with Luke was selfish and uncertain. It wasn't the responsible thing to do. It was too late.

"What are you doing, Ariana? Why's your hair all wet? Where the heck have you been?" Karina sat up and questioned her sister with a yawn and rubbed her eyes, startling Ariana.

"With Luke."

"Ooh! I knew it! Did you guys get back together?"

"No. We barely talked. It started raining on us. But he sent me this." Ariana showed her the message and let her listen to the song.

"Just a matter of time." Karina smiled and snaked a little dance.

Ariana elbowed her sister under the covers.

---

[170] My love has no schedule.

"Ow! You know it's true!"

"Anyway. I have a lot to do with Grandpa and Dad at the restaurant. They're depending on me...and so is Catalina."

Karina rolled her eyes. "Stop being such a martyr. You have to follow your heart, Ariana. Besides, he's still *gorgeous*. And the way he was looking at you—"

"Shut up and go back to sleep!" Ariana whispered loudly, hitting Karina on the head with her pillow.

At breakfast the next morning, Mari had made *torrijas*, a type of Spanish French toast. Lucia loved it, and Ariana immediately showed her to the kitchen to talk to Mari about the recipe. While everyone was still eating, Luke announced that he had arranged for both families to tour the excavation site, Catalina's home, if they were interested. Everyone quickly walked out to the two vans waiting for them. When they arrived, it was still roped off, and the sign declaring it an official world heritage archaeological site was still in place. The air was humid, and the clouds in the sky were thick and gray, promising rain again. Mari had given them several umbrellas just in case. They stepped out of the van, and the crowd noise dropped to the silence of birds and crickets as their eyes fell upon the ruins of the home.

Ariana's heart skipped a beat, jogging the memory of how she had felt when she had walked through last year. This time, however, it took on a new meaning. This *was* her family's home. This was *Catalina's* home. She was connected to it, and it had tried to remind her the first time of who she was, where she came from. She saw it all with new eyes. The hole in the wall where the diary had fallen out. The tile floors and the jagged walls. She was swathed by that familiar feeling once again. How astonishing was it that she was walking through her 16x great-grandmother's home? That it was still standing was a miracle in and of itself.

She sighed, realizing what an incredible privilege it had been to write her and Benjamín's story. She was grateful to be living at *this* time. That it was *her* generation that had found it. All of a sudden, it occurred to her that maybe Catalina *wanted* her to write about her. Just maybe she wanted Ariana to learn more about her people, who Catalina was, her struggles, just as she had felt drawn to do several

287

months ago when she had begun her research. Now she had to decide which would honor Catalina's legacy more, staying in San Luis or sharing her story with the world. In any case, whatever she chose to do, she knew she was enough for the task. *Eres suficiente.* Now she understood. Her heart was warm. She looked off ahead toward the river and past the meadow and then at Luke. She took Luke's hand to follow her.

"Let's go to the river," she said.

"Ok, let me just make sure everyone knows what areas they could walk through and where they shouldn't be."

Luke explained to everyone the fragility of the home and how it could be dangerous to walk through certain areas. He showed them where it was safe to walk through and look at things, and he showed them the wall where the diary had fallen out. Then he walked off with Ariana and let them explore. They walked slowly at first, hand in hand through the meadow, and then Ariana let go of his hand and shot off running, looking back at him. He smiled, taking on her challenge, and chased her through the thick meadow filled with long grasses. It was damp, and Ariana was sure her shoes would be a mess, but she didn't care. She felt free. This river had been calling her since last year, and this time, she had to oblige.

Ariana was fast, and it took Luke a minute, but he finally caught up to her, taking her by the waist and holding her close as they reached the river. They stood there for a moment hidden behind the trees. A familiar warmth surrounded them. Still engrossed in that intense sensation, they found a large rock to sit on. Luke pulled Ariana to sit on his lap while he held her, and they watched the rushing water, listening to its calming hushing sound. It was peaceful and still, like there was no one else in the universe but them.

"This is where they used to come and spend time together," Ariana said, breaking the silence. "Wasn't his house right there across the river?"

"Yeah, this is where they spent their last moments together before he left. There's nothing left of his house at all now. I wonder what happened to it. Can you imagine? Benjamín fell in this water right here that night," he said as he pointed to the water, "preventing him from taking Catalina with him."

"I can't imagine. The frustration. The deep sorrow he must have felt."

"Yeah." Luke wrapped his arms tighter around her.

"I love that song you sent."

"I was wondering if you had got it."

"It's perfect." A golden butterfly floated passed them and landed on a tall blue wildflower near the edge of the river. "So pretty. Looks like the brooch on the diary."

"Ha, it does."

And then it fluttered over to them and perched itself on Luke's shoulder.

"Look at that! It likes you."

Luke laughed. "That's never happened to me before!"

"We should probably get back to the group," she said after the butterfly glided away high into the sky. She wished they could stay there forever. But the scent of his cologne, his warmth, all of it was…overwhelming.

"Yeah, let's go," he said as she got up to walk toward the vans.

She knew she would be lost in him again if she stayed any longer.

"But wait…Ariana?" He placed his hand on her shoulder.

The surprise of his gentle touch caught her off guard and made her lose her breath.

"Yes?" She slowly turned her head to look at him.

"I miss you." His voice cracked at the end.

She was all Jell-O inside as his words drifted through her ears and into her heart. His face was serious with palpable longing for her, and his blues eyes with their gold flecks shined bright against the navy of his shirt.

"I miss you, too, Luke, so much it aches in places I didn't know existed. But it's just not going to—"

And before she could finish, he pulled her close to him and pressed his mouth to hers. They melded into one another, their souls open with a sea of stars and night sky, overflowing between them. For a minute, they hadn't even realized it had started sprinkling. The wetness from their eyes mixed with the rain as it drip-dropped lightly over their faces. They clung to one another, kissing deeply, and Luke's hands entwined in her hair, and she held the back of his head with one hand and clasped the other on his back. It was like they had returned home, and they were exactly where they were supposed to be. *Home. En la parte más profunda de tu corazón donde vive el amor hallarás tu hogar.* And they were oblivious to the images of the shooting stars in the sky smiling and shimmering in the river dancing with the waves of the current.

"There are no words to describe how it feels to be here with you right now," Ariana said with her eyes focused on his when they finally broke away. "There's an emotion running through me, beyond comprehension, that I can't explain even if I wanted to."

"You don't have to." He kissed the tops of her eyelids. "I feel it, too." He lifted her face to him with his fingertips on her chin. "Marry me, Ariana. I love you." He looked to the ground, shifting his feet, and he took her hands. "I feel like I've loved you since the beginning of time. *This* is right, *we're* right…and my world is only right when you're in it. Marry me and stay with me here for the next year, please."

Ariana wiped at her eyes. His words were a mirror image of her heart. *My world is only right when he's in it, too.* She flung her arms around him. "Yes." She nodded, whispering in his ear through short, hollow breaths, "I love you so much…I will marry you."

He wrapped his arms around her so tightly that she could feel the tension in his muscles release as he sighed, relieved. She lay her head on his shoulder, and he held her head close to him. They turned to the river, hearing the droplets getting stronger and faster as they hit the water.

"We better go," she said.

"Yeah, it's going to start pouring any minute."

She was quiet as they walked rapidly hand in hand, thinking about all that she would be leaving behind staying here in Spain with Luke. She wouldn't be back home to San Luis for another year at least, maybe longer, and she hadn't been prepared for that. Her heart sank as she pictured her family, the restaurant, the mountains, and her beloved sanctuary at the top of the mesa. Then she thought about Luke and how without him, it was all…empty. She quickly tried to inscribe the memories of the last time she was there several weeks ago for Karina's graduation in her mind. She took in a deep breath. It was all happening so fast, yet she was confident in what her heart was telling her. It was ok. Who she was *was* enough. Once again, Catalina's sparkling eyes and smiling face emerged in her mind, sweeping with her in that old room. She knew what she wanted. She didn't have to operate on the guilt from her family or from anyone. She didn't have to become someone she wasn't or fit into someone else's world or mold. She knew her calling. She knew her worth. Most importantly,

she had found *home*. There was no place she would rather be than with this beautiful man walking beside her right here.

"Are you ok?" he asked, seeing her staring off into nothing.

"Yes." She smiled and stopped to put her arms around his neck. "I'm better than ok. I'm back in Spain with you. And I'm going to be Mrs. Cohen...sometime soon."

He held her waist, kissed her, and said, "I can't wait, mi querida Ariana."

Hearing that name out loud made her heart smile, and they walked back to the group more hurriedly, feeling the little droplets getting stronger by the second.

After a minute, Luke said, "Ariana, let's not tell anyone until I can ask your dad again and do it the right way."

"Ok." She smiled and leaned into him.

They got there just in time as the rain began dumping on the meadow and the ruins in sheets, making quick thumping sounds on the tops of the umbrellas. They all jumped in the vans with the kids shrieking in the background and drove back to El Convento.

"So what did you guys think of the ruins of Catalina's home?" Ariana asked her parents and grandparents.

"Mi'jita, it was amazing," Grandpa Moisés said, "to walk where my great-grandma walked and lived centuries ago." He paused and shook his head. "Thank you for bringing us here, Ariana," he continued, touching the hand that she had placed on the seat in front of her. "This is a once-in-a-lifetime experience, mi'jita. It's almost like you could feel their presence there. This is something I will remember forever. It has been one of the best experiences of my life." He looked out the window, blinking. "I wasn't sure I would make it here."

He hugged his wife and kissed her cheek. Aurelia blushed. "Of course you were going to make it here, *Viejo! ¿Qué tienes?*"[171]

"I never doubted it one second," Ariana added. Luke squeezed her other hand.

"I agree," Joe said from the front seat. "I was speechless, and you know that doesn't happen very often. Thank you for bringing us here, mi'ja."

---

[171] Literally old man, term of endearment for husband. What's the matter with you?!

"Did you guys see the trees across the meadow? The river flows through there. That's where Catalina and Benjamin spent time together." She put her chin on the seat in front of her.

"Yes," her mom said. "It's *so* beautiful. It reminds me of back home up in *Cañón* or *El Rito,* only it doesn't have the mountains in the background.

"Me too." Ariana sat back in her seat. She couldn't help but feel equally tied to this place. She glanced at Luke. *Yes, it's home. He's home.*

They arrived at El Convento just in time for lunch. Mari had more paella, several dishes with different meats, potatoes, and roasted vegetables, as well as Manchego cheese, olives, and bread with olive oil on each table. Joe sat at a table with a sign that said *Kosher* and began to grab a baguette from a basket at the center of the table. Ariana motioned to her dad with her arm as she passed him.

"Dad, come over here. That table is for Luke and his family."

"It is? What's the difference?" he said loudly, scooting out from his seat and following Ariana.

"Shh." Ariana pressed two fingers to her lips. "Eeeee, I can't take you anywhere. They don't eat some things that we do."

"Oh, well, I don't know!"

While everyone retreated to their rooms to change for lunch, Ariana and Luke stood by the doorway to the patio. Ariana could already taste the tender clams and mussels prepared only the way Mari could. Chocolate cake and churros con chocolate sat alongside the Sangria and lemonade. The smells were heavenly, and the humidity from the rain outside only intensified the aroma.

"I'll ask him during lunch, ok?"

"Ok."

Anxiety had begun to creep throughout Ariana's body. She hoped her dad would behave, but she knew he was going to be crushed. She prayed Grandpa Moisés wouldn't be angry or disappointed in her. She saw her grandma and extended family coming down the stairs from the corner of her eye. She let go of Luke's hand and said, "I better go."

He looked up and saw everyone walking toward the dining area.

"Ok. See you soon." He quickly kissed her forehead.

"Ariana, ven a'ca,"[172] called her grandpa in a deep voice from the library, startling her.

"Grampo! You scared me!" She felt her heart going a hundred miles a minute. Her hands began to sweat as she treaded lightly over to the library where her grandpa was seated.

"Siéntate."[173] He motioned to the other wing-backed chair on the other side of the end table next to his, and Ariana sat down reluctantly but gave him her full attention. *Uh oh. He saw me and Luke. Bring on the lecture.* She was trembling inside.

"Mi'jita," he began, "are you happy with all the plans we have for the restaurant?"

"Yeah, Grampo. What you and Dad want to do is exciting! You guys are trailblazers."

"Then you're ok with all the work it's going to take?"

Ariana sat still with her hands tucked between her knees and her feet crossed at the ankles. Her eyes shifted to the antique lamp on the table between them and she swallowed. "Of course."

Grandpa Moisés chuckled. "You've never been a good liar, mi'jita, and that's what I love about you. Remember when you ran into the fence with your friend's little motorcycle and you told me that the cows had done it trying to get out?"

Ariana laughed out loud. "Grampo! I was like ten years old. Why did you have to remind me?"

"I'm sorry," muttered Grandpa Moisés, hanging his head low.

"For what?" She twisted toward him.

"For making you do something you don't really want to do."

"I made my own decision, Grampo." She placed her hand on his that was rested on the table.

"No, you only said yes because I asked you to. *Eres tan jovencita. Tienes muncha vida…*I saw you over there." He pointed inadvertently toward the direction of the ruins with his lips. "*Yo los vide, a ti y al Luke juntos y…*it was wrong to ask you to stay home," he continued, shaking his head. "*Es que…*this is hard for me to admit, Ariana. *Pero, tenía miedo…*that I wasn't going to make it. But now I know *que…tenemos que vivir la vida con todo lo que tenemos…*without regrets." He lifted a fist. "You are so young, mi'jita. You have your

---

[172] Come here.
[173] Sit down.

whole life ahead of you. *Ya yo estoy muy viejo y*...all I know is that you have to do what you love. What makes *you* happy. *Y hazlo con todo tu corazón.* Ok?"[174] He finished, pointing at her heart.

"Ok, Grampo," she said in between sniffles, and she reached out to hug him. "I love you."

"I love you, too, hija." He lifted his index finger at Ariana. "Never tell anyone I said I was wrong, ok?"

"K." Ariana laughed.

"Because if you do, I will deny it ever happened." He sliced across the air with an open hand. "Now all you have to do is convince your dad. *¡Son iguales de tercos!*"[175]

Ariana laughed. "You aren't joking!"

She breathed a sigh of relief. She was so worried that she wouldn't have his blessing, and this...this was why she loved her grandparents so much. They had so much wisdom, yet they were so humble at heart.

---

[174] You're so young. You have so much life ahead of you...I saw you together...it's just that...I was scared...that...we have to live life to the fullest...I'm already so old and...and do it with all your heart.

[175] You're both just as stubborn!

Chapter 26

Luke

Ariana gave Luke a nod from across the room. He shifted in his seat, took a deep breath, and stood up to walk over to the table where Ariana was sitting alone with Joe and Lucia. He wasn't sure how this was going to go over, but he knew it was the right thing to do. Besides, he felt like he could do anything with Ariana by his side. His mind was still in the cloud of being with her in the meadow. It had felt like seventh heaven. He was glad he carried her ring with him everywhere—just in case. He had hoped being together here at El Convento and the ruins would remind her of what they had together and that she might at least agree to start seeing each other again, even if it was a long-distance relationship. He had meant what he had said about waiting for her as long as he had to. But, he never expected for his plan to work this well.

When he saw her with all her bags walking into El Convento, he knew. He had hated surprising her that way, but the way she had looked at him said it all. Then to hear her describe how much she had missed him at the meadow—it had sent him over the moon. And the humidity and warmth of the summer had nothing on the heat that flowed between them as their bodies wrapped tightly around each other. All of this, as they stood in the same place Catalina and Benjamín had spent their last hours together. It was as if they had been there with them in spirit—it was the icing on the cake.

He swallowed as he approached the table. His neck began to feel tight and warm around the collar of his shirt. He cleared his throat and sat in an open chair next to Joe. He could feel Ariana's energy as she watched him, giving him the cojones to move forward.

"Joe, may I talk with you for a minute? I, uh, have something I'd like to ask you."

"Aquí que vamos otra vez,"[176] Joe said in his deep husky voice. He threw his cloth napkin on the table in frustration. He let out a heavy sigh, slapped his hands on his lap, and turned to Ariana like this was her doing. "What's this about, Ariana? We haven't even been here two full days!" He turned and looked Luke in the eye and pointed at him with a thick finger, making Luke's neck jolt back and his eyes open wide. "Don't think I didn't know what you were up to when you planned to stay here, too."

Well, I guess I deserved that. I wish someone would open a window or something. He pulled at the collar of his shirt.

"Da-ad! Please listen to Luke."

"Joe!" warned Lucia.

Joe rolled his eyes and looked at Lucia, who was glaring at him. Luke smiled and winked at Ariana. *Love Ariana's mom.* He shook his head and paused a minute.

"Ok, Luke." He threw his hands in the air and sat back in his seat. "What is this about?"

"Sir, I...I'm not sure how else to go about this. I know we've been through this before." *Much harder to do in person, though.* "And I respected Ariana's decision. But being here in this place has shown us what I already knew. Nothing has changed between us. If anything, we love each other more. We belong together...and all this separation has taught us is that *that* will never change, no matter how long we're apart or how far we're away from each other." He paused and looked down at his hands. *You just have to do this, man.* And then he looked up at Joe again. "Will you please give me your blessing to marry Ariana?"

Joe's face was red and his eyes glossy. He twisted toward Ariana and leaned toward her. "Ariana, is this really what you want? What about everything we've been working for? What about your grandpa and all the plans for the restaurant?"

Ariana nodded and wiped the corners of her eyes. "Yes, Dad. I'm so sorry. I know you want me home. But...if I stayed home, I would be compromising. I love him."

Joe did a double-take at Lucia whose eyes were like lasers at him.

---

[176]Here we go again!

"Wha-at? I haven't even said anything!" He lifted his hands open-faced in the air.

He paused a minute, rested a palm on his lap, and stared at the floor. You could hear a pin drop from the silence in the room. Then he shook his head and said, *"¿Qué frega'o. ya no manda uno nada."*[177] His eyes met with Luke's, and he said, "Fine. Luke, you have my...*our* blessing," he pointed at himself and Lucia with his thumb, "to marry Ariana. And you better take *good* care of her...please." His voice cracked at the end of his words.

Luke wiped his forehead with the back of his hand. "I will make that my life's goal, sir. She means everything to me, and your blessing means everything to us." He leaned back into his chair, feeling the blood and oxygen return to the muscles in his neck. He couldn't wipe the grin off his face.

Lucia clapped and so did Mari and Miguel, who had been eavesdropping from the kitchen and crossing their fingers. They looked over at them and laughed. Luke stood up and Ariana jumped into his arms, shrieking and kissing his face over and over again.

He laughed, loving her kisses. She pulled away and walked over to her dad and squeezed him.

"I love you, Daddy. Thank you."

Joe hugged her back and then said, "Oh, get out of here before I change my mind."

"You did the right thing, Joe," Lucia said. She had finally softened the look on her face. "I know she's your baby, but would you rather have her home and miserable?"

"But what do we know about him or his family, Lucia? In San Luis, everyone has known each other for generations." He threw his hands in the air again. "And she *had* to find somebody—"

"Da-ad!"

"No empieces![178] They found each other, Joe. And he *is* standing right there. You *could* ask him...or his family, *hombre.* They're here, too, remember?" She gave him a good smack on the arm and poked at his chest. "Don't forget why we're here in the first place. *His* great-grandfather and *your* great-grandmother were in love centuries ago.

---

[177] Man! Can't tell her what to do anymore.
[178] Don't start!

Don't you think it's pretty special that these two families found each other again? There's no heritage or legacy more unique than that."

"Hey, you don't have to get all violent!" Joe rubbed his arm. "I guess you're right when you put it that way, Lucia. I love you." He gave her a quick smooch on the cheek. "Marrying *you* was the best decision *I* ever made."

"I love you, too, Joe." She laughed and hugged him.

He turned his attention to Luke and added, "Are you witnessing this, Luke? Are you ready to deal with it? You know she's just like her mom!"

Luke laughed and held Ariana close, kissing the top of her head. *Wouldn't have it any other way.* "On that note, I'm going to try this one more time." He got down on his knee again and pulled his great-grandmother's ring and looked up at Ariana. "Ariana, will you marry me?"

"Yes! Yes, a million times, yes!"

"Good, because I don't know if I'd have it in me to do this again," he joked, placing the ring back on her finger as he squeezed her, lifting her up in the air.

"I love you, Mr. Cohen."

"I love you, too." *Mi querida Ariana.*

Chapter 27

Ariana

Martin strolled toward Ariana and Luke who were already sitting in the dining room waiting for dinner. "So, I hear congratulations are in order once again, Ms. Colorado."

Ariana stood up and hugged Martin. "Yes, thank you!"

"I'm so excited!" Sofia added, squeezing Ariana. "So, looks like we may have a wedding here after all?"

"Me too! But I don't think so. We're only going to be here until next Sunday, and we're leaving to Madrid tomorrow. I hardly think there's enough time."

"You just leave that to me, Ariana!" Mari interrupted. "We can do everything next Saturday!"

"But there's so much to do. What about the money?"

"Ariana, ya sabes que sería un placer!"[179]

"Mari, le agradezco mucho, pero—"[180] Ariana replied, feeling a bit overwhelmed. "It's very sweet, but I just don't think we can pull this off in a week."

"Hablaremos con nuestros padres para ver lo que es posible y luego les avisamos lo que vamos a hacer,"[181] chimed in Luke. It was as if he could read her mind.

"Vale. Estamos a su servicio."[182]

"¡Muchas gracias, Mari! ¡Eres un ángel!" Ariana said. "So, what do you think, Luke?"

---

[179] Ariana, you already know it would be a pleasure."

[180] Mari, I appreciate you so much, but—

[181] We'll talk to our parents and see what's possible and then we'll let you know what we can do."

[182] Ok. We are at your service.

"It *is* our dream."

"I know…but…people literally take *years* planning their weddings. We have less than a week!"

"I know how you are about these things, babe." Luke put a hand on her arm. "But we do have everything we need right here. We have a caterer. A venue. Plenty of help. And all of the most important people in our lives are already here."

"Right! All we need are the special touches. We can shop in Madrid on Tuesday before the reception." Sofia's voice increased in volume and enthusiasm as she spoke.

Ariana was getting more tempted by the minute.

"I guess you're right. It took a lot of planning just to come out here for the reception, though. Let me talk to my mom and dad and see what we can do."

"About what, Ariana?" Joe asked as he and Lucia walked into the dining area.

"We're talking about getting married here, Dad."

"Coming back in a few months or a year?"

"No…Saturday."

"What the heck is the rush?" He threw his hands in the air, his voice rising several octaves.

"Ariana, that was your dream, mi'ja!" Lucia screeched and grabbed both of Ariana's hands.

"I know! Do you think we could do it? Dad?"

"I don't know why it has to be so soon, Ariana." He ran his hand through his hair.

"Joe! It was their dream to get married in the meadow where Benjamín and Catalina spent time together. When are we going to get the chance to be here again like this? *All* of us together?"

He shook his head and rested his hands against the back of a chair. Ariana shifted her feet waiting for his response. "Eeeee, Lucia! You should have been a lawyer!"

"Plenty of work at the firm," Martin offered with a chuckle.

Everyone looked at Martin.

"Just saying!

"Fine. Let's sit down and talk about a budget."

Ariana jumped up and down and embraced Luke.

"I don't know what we're going to be able to do, Ariana. So don't get too excited," her dad said.

"Aunt Rachel should be here. She can conjure an extravagant party out of nothing!"

"No se preocupan," Mari interjected, walking over from the kitchen. *"Ya están aquí. Y no van a tener que pagar por la pradera. Sería solamente la comida y las decoraciones."*[183]

"And the music!" Ariana added. "What's a *pradera*?" She turned to Luke.

"The meadow."

"Oh. I would have called it the *llano*!"

"Don't forget your dress," Lucia added.

They talked budget, decorations, music, ceremony, and all things wedding with Ariana, leading the way with her vision through the evening until they had all come to an agreement on everything and then turned in to get rest for their trip to Madrid the next day.

Ariana and Luke sat on one of the sofas side by side bright and early the next morning, waiting for everyone in the reception area, giggling and playing with each other's fingers when they heard a burst of laughter behind them. They turned around to find Joe folded over, his laugh almost an over-exaggeration. Ariana couldn't help but smile.

"What, Dad?"

"Nothing." He waved at her, unable to contain his laughter.

"Seriously? What the heck is so funny?"

"Well, I was just thinking," her dad said. He held his belly in between laughs like Santa Claus, "now that I looked at all your bags," he let out another laugh, "that there's a silver lining to this marriage thing after all."

"Geez." Ariana glanced at Luke. "I'm afraid to ask."

"All of this is going to be your problem from now on, Luke!" He wiped his eyes and pointed at all of Ariana's bags. "Good luck with that!"

"Seriously, Dad?"

"Wow," Luke said with a chuckle.

---

[183] Don't worry. You're already here. And you don't have to pay for the meadow. It would just be the food and decorations.

"I think he can handle it!" Ariana fired back. She balled up her napkin from her breakfast and threw it at him, making him duck and hitting her mom on the back of the head instead.

"Ariana!"

Her dad opened his eyes wide, put his hand over his mouth, and pointed at Ariana, *chungueándose.*[184]

"Sorry, Mom."

Her mom shook her head and smacked Joe on the shoulder.

After a successful day of wedding shopping in Madrid, the families arrived at the University of Madrid early and entered the large banquet hall where the reception would be held. Ariana found the welcome desk and led the families there for their name tags and seating information. Her eyes scanned the elegant room that was filled with tables adorned with white linens, colorful floral centerpieces, and place settings for dinner. At the far end, there was a podium with a microphone lifted on risers. Ariana paused when she saw the roped-off display of the diary on a small table with the brooch still attached and its casings sitting next to it. A warm sensation filled her chest. It was a moment in history, plucked from the past and positioned purposefully in the present time. Luke gently pulled her hand, forcing her to break eye contact and follow him to their seats. Both her and Luke's families were at tables next to one another, and the place began filling to capacity.

"Look, Ariana, there's Ricardo." She followed Luke's hand toward Ricardo near the front of the room.

"We have to make sure to give him the invitation to the wedding." She patted her purse.

"Yeah, let's not forget."

A tall woman with a red, pixie haircut and glasses stepped up to the podium and introduced herself as the president of the university. She welcomed everyone, letting them know that dinner would shortly be served, and introduced the director of the archaeological project under which Luke and Ricardo were working. After several sentences that the woman spoke, a translator standing next to her restated her words in English. A shorter portly man with a beard and receding hairline stepped to the microphone, pulling it down to reach his

---

[184] Teasing her

mouth. As he spoke, a server came by with bread and small plates with olive oil and spices and asked what beverages Ariana and Luke wanted.

"Bienvenidos a esta gran celebración honrando a uno de los descubrimientos más importantes conectando a España con América profundamente en una de sus eras más exitosas y tristes a la misma vez. La historia nos dice muy bien que una de las comunidades más adelantadas y fructíferas que eran los Judíos Sefardís en nuestro país fue maltratada horrorosamente, expulsada o forzada de convertir al cristianismo más de 500 años atrás. Hasta ahora no teníamos ningún otro dato que diera voz a lo que sucedió más que los datos de la Inquisición. El diario de Catalina nos da una luz dentro de la vida de su familia Sefardí en una manera vibrante que nos abre los ojos a la realidad de sus experiencias. Es un gran placer de presentar a ustedes los descendientes de Catalina Robledo Romero con una copia de este tesoro raro, las profundas palabras describiendo en detalle sus experiencias, sus alegrías y angustias escritas a mano como legado para sus familias."[185]

He paused as the group applauded. Ariana sat back in her seat to make room for the soup and salad plates that were being placed in front of her.

"Ahora, queremos honrar al grupo, más bien el equipo que trabajó sin descanso para encontrar este precioso regalo para nosotros y para ustedes."[186]

He called for the team from the University of Madrid and Ricardo and his colleagues from the University of Denver as everyone clapped

---

[185] Welcome to this grand celebration honoring one of the most important discoveries connecting Spain to the Americas in such a significant way during one of its most successful, yet sorrowful eras. History tells us very well that one of the most advanced and fruitful communities, the Sephardic Jews from our country were treated horrifically, expelled or forced to convert to Christianity more than 500 years ago. Up to now, we had no other document that gave voice to what happened other than the Inquisition records. Catalina's diary sheds light for us into the life of a Sephardic family in a vibrant way that opens our eyes to the reality of their experiences. It is with great pleasure that we present to you, the descendants of Catalina Robledo Romero with a copy of this rare treasure, the profound words she wrote by hand describing her experiences, her happiness and her anguish, in detail as a legacy for your families.

[186] Now, we would like to honor the group, or the team, rather that worked tirelessly to find this precious gift for us and for you all.

and watched them walk up. Ricardo took the microphone at the podium.

"It is an honor to be here with all of you tonight," he began, with the translator now switching to Spanish translation, "sharing this fantastic rare discovery with you, the descendants of Catalina Robledo Romero. However, no celebration of Catalina's works and life could be complete without honoring her counterpart, the love her life as he is mentioned in her memoirs, Benjamín Carvajal."

Ariana nudged Luke to look at his grandmother who was wiping her eyes with her hanky.

"In addition," Ricardo said, "no honor for our team could be complete without acknowledging the tireless efforts of his 14x great-grandson, Luke Cohen. Luke was onsite leading a group of students when we found the diary. We initially examined it together and were the first to read Catalina's heartfelt words, including those that mentioned his great-grandfather Benjamín Carvajal. Luke was a tremendous support and an integral member of this project from the beginning, providing countless hours of research and energy. He brought dedication and perseverance like no other."

Luke's dad glanced over at their table. He gave Luke an approving nod. Ariana smiled and leaned into him.

"Please give a warm welcome," Ricardo said, to the sound of applause from the crowd, "to my former student and now colleague, Mr. Luke Cohen."

Luke squeezed Ariana's hand and stood up, slowly making his way over to the podium. He lightly squeezed his grandmother's shoulder as he passed her. He hugged Ricardo, and they engaged in a short dialogue.

"It is my understanding," Ricardo said, "that one of the oldest known descendants of Benjamín Carvajal is also here tonight, Luke's grandmother Sara. Would you and your family please stand?"

All of Luke's family stood up, including, Sara, Isaac, Sofia, Martin, Linda, Al and Nina, Zach, and the kids. They smiled and waved as everyone applauded.

"This family is here in Spain not only to attend this unique reception but for another momentous and historic occasion that I have just learned about. Luke and Ariana Romero, a direct descendant of Catalina's, will be married in a few days, reuniting their families and bringing them back to Spain after almost five centuries." Ricardo looked directly at Ariana and said, "Ariana, will you please stand with

your family? Ariana's grandfather, Mr. Moisés Romero, will be receiving a copy of the diary as the oldest known descendant of Catalina's in Ariana's family."

Ariana held her breath and stood, feeling her face heating up. She hadn't expected any acknowledgment. The eyes and applause from the crowd on her made her hands shaky. She caught Luke's eye up front. He smiled and winked at her, putting her at ease. She returned the gesture and sat down just as dinner plates were being served.

Ariana was glad that Luke was getting the recognition he deserved for doing the work he loved. He and the team were given plaques and pins from the university and the archaeological museum. He also received a copy of the diary for himself and another one for his grandmother. As Luke headed back toward Ariana, he presented the diary to his grandmother with a hug and kiss on her cheek.

"¡Ay hijiko, munchísmas grasyas!" [187] she said, sniffling.

"¡Fue un plazer, Avuela!" [188]

During dinner, the president of the university stated that the diary, brooch, and casings included would now be a permanent collection at the *Museo Arqueológico de Madrid*. She explained that the display had been estimated to be worth hundreds of thousands of dollars. The brooch alone which had been dated to the late 1500s was an original made and marked by an unknown local artisan at the time. It was twenty-four karat gold, and the jewels were authentic. There had never been another made like it. It was estimated to be worth at least a hundred thousand dollars. However, to these descendants, especially Luke and Ariana, the collection was priceless. The president explained that it would also be traveling to Santa Fe, New Mexico; Denver, Colorado; and Mexico City in the fall for several months so that other descendants or admirers could witness it for themselves. Then she called each of the eldest descendants to receive their copy of the diary.

Ariana watched Grandpa Moisés stand and straighten the tie she had bought for him at Macey's for Christmas and walk forward as they called his name. His face had a glow about it, and his expression of pride was golden. Gratitude was an understatement for what she

---

[187] Oh, my son, thank you so much for this honor!

[188] It was a pleasure, Grandma.

felt that he was here, able to experience this moment. She swallowed the lump in her throat with a drink of iced tea.

After dinner, both families walked over to the display to get a closer look. They snapped photos of it and close ups of the brooch. Ariana felt the same enchanting energy that she had felt the first time she had seen it last year. She held Grandpa Moisés's arm as he wiped his eyes, taking in the display. She kissed his cheek. Grandpa Moisés took Luke by the hand and thanked him for his work and dedication that had brought this family treasure and legacy to light. Ricardo came over to meet both Ariana and Luke's families.

"Luke, Ariana, congratulations!" He hugged them both. "I might have known this would happen!"

"Thank you, Ricardo!"

"Before I forget," Ariana reached into her purse and pulled out the make-shift invitation she had made especially for him, "please come to the wedding."

"Thank you so much!" Ricardo held the envelope with his brows lifted and a grin. "I would be honored to be there."

"It would mean a lot," Luke said with a hand on Ricardo's shoulder. "After all, it all happened because of your class."

"That's right!" Ricardo laughed.

"Ricardo, is it?" Martin said as he approached, extending his hand to Ricardo.

"Yes," Ricardo replied and took his hand.

"Oh, Ricardo, this is my dad, Martin," Luke explained.

"So nice to meet you," Martin said. "I just wanted to say that," he looked at his feet and back up at Ricardo again, "that I was very impressed to hear all of those things you said about Luke."

"Well, every word is true. He's sharp and very dedicated." Ricardo turned to Luke. "That's actually another reason I wanted to talk to you, Luke."

"Oh?"

"Yes, DU is expanding our department, and I would love to offer you a position there, if you're interested."

A huge grin overtook Luke's face. "Of course! But I've already got commitments here in Spain over the next year."

"I know. I figured as much. It will take about that long to get everything underway," Ricardo said. "Your position will be there when you return."

Luke looked at Ariana. "What do you think?"

"Yes! Oh my gosh, Luke! That would be an amazing opportunity."

"Ok, then. It's done. I'll be in touch with the details." Ricardo patted Luke on the back and walked away. "See you in a few days!"

"Luke," started Martin. "Son…I'm sorry I've been so hard on you. Just want to say…that I'm proud of you. From the sounds of it, looks like you're a lot like your ol' man!" He placed a hand on Luke's shoulder. "Congratulations on the new gig."

"Thanks, Dad. It means a lot to hear you say that," he said and then gave his dad a hug.

Chapter 28

Luke

Luke and Ariana watched some of their family and the kids playing a ball game from a picnic blanket outside the courtyard. He outlined her high cheek bones and the shape of her nose and lips with his gaze. Her expression was content. This picnic was a much-needed break. It was Friday, and they had barely seen each other since they had returned from Madrid on Tuesday evening. They had been working nonstop on the wedding all week. Today, the sun was out, and the precipitation from earlier in the week seemed to be a distant memory. Ariana let out a heavy sigh and turned to him. Her eyes jetted to a loose thread in the colorful blanket, and her fingers pulled at it.

"What are you thinking? Don't tell me you're changing your mind." Luke landed a gentle finger under her chin.

She looked up at the sky with an adorable smile, tilted her head, and put her index finger on her cheek. "Well…uh…maybe." Her face quickly turned toward him. "Are you kidding me?" she said, laughing. "I was just thinking about how incredibly blessed I feel right now." She placed her fingertips on his cheek, which made Luke's chest flood with warmth. "You. Getting married here. It's the most amazing dream I'm fortunate to be living."

She grabbed his face with both hands and kissed him, then she jumped up to join the ball game. He smiled. *Me too.* Luke rested his elbow on the blanket and watched Ariana interact with their families, throwing her head back and laughing. He thought about what she was sacrificing to live with him in Spain for a year or more. He knew it would be difficult for her to be away from her family for such a long time. Heck, it was going to be difficult for him to leave his family as well. The kids were just getting used to him being around all the time. They would be that much older after their time away, and he was going to miss many more milestones. He stood up to stretch his legs.

"Just be good to her, bro."

Luke flipped around to find Joaquin's huge, heavy hand on his shoulder.

"Of course." Luke took a deep breath to slow his heartbeat.

Ariana ran up to the them, breathing heavily from their play.

Luke held her waist and kissed her cheek. He looked Joaquin in the eye, squinting, since the sun was right behind him. "I love this woman more than anything. I'll always do everything I can to make her happy."

"On that note," Joaquin said. He swung the guitar strapped around him from his back to the front. "I wanted to run this song by you, Ariana. I've been working on it since you asked me and Karina to sing for the wedding. I think it would be perfect for you to walk down the aisle to."

He pulled a pick from his pocket and began singing a remake of *Cariño* that he had adapted from the original version. Luke was surprised at what a nice voice he had.

"I love it." Ariana hugged him. "That's always been one of my favorite songs, Joaquin! Thanks for putting in all that work."

"I'm glad you like it. I'm going to teach Karina so she could follow me on her violin."

"Yeah, man," Luke said. "I like it, too. You're talented."

"Thought you knew," he said before laughing and walking away.

They both shook their heads.

"He just doesn't know how to take a compliment," Ariana said. "He's a pretty modest guy."

That evening, the rehearsal and rehearsal dinner were both held at El Convento. The local priest, Father Lorenzo, commissioned to perform the ceremony, was young and energetic—and, thankfully, spoke English. Luke knew how important it was for Ariana to get married through the church. Either way, it would have been next to impossible to find a Rabbi on such short notice, and making their union official was the most important thing as far as Luke was concerned. The priest looked at the ceremony outline that Luke and

Ariana had planned and welcomed the blend of religious touches they had both added to make their ceremony unique. They went through it just as it would take place at the meadow, including the music that Karina and Joaquin would play. Then they headed to the courtyard for the rehearsal dinner.

Luke held Ariana's hand and they walked through the open courtyard together. He smiled. He was pleased with their hard work. The strings of white lights around the top of the perimeter made the space festive yet elegant. The couple that sang for the end-of-class reception after Ricardo's class was playing music in one corner. They would be providing entertainment for the evening. Mari led Luke and Ariana to their table for two, and everyone else found seats while Miguel and Roberto served dinner. After a minute, Joe took a deep breath, stood up, and rang his glass. Luke braced himself. *What is he about to say?*

"Good evening, everyone," Joe started. "First of all, I want to say that it's been a pleasure meeting all of you. I want to thank you for making this trip first in honor of our ancestors and now…for everything you've all done to make this event a blessing for Ariana and Luke.

He paused and blinked before continuing. *A toast.* Luke's muscles relaxed.

"Most of you don't know that this process has not been easy for me. When I first saw Ariana and Luke together, I saw the glow around them, and it scared me. It's every father's nightmare from the moment his daughter is born. And as much as I've fought it, wanting to keep her close…anyone can tell from watching them…that Ariana could have searched the world over and not found anyone more perfect for her than Luke." He turned toward Ariana and Luke and lifted his glass. "May God bless you both and your marriage always. Everyone, please join me in lifting your glasses to Ariana and Luke. ¡Salud!"

Everyone clapped and said 'Cheers' or 'Salud', and Joe sat down, sniffling. Aside from his voice cracking a couple of times, he had done well. The back of Luke's hand went across his forehead, and he relaxed his posture into the back of his chair. He was grateful. He could only imagine how Joe was feeling inside. Lucia rubbed his back and kissed his cheek.

"You did great, Joe," Luke heard her say. "I'm proud of you."

Luke glanced at Ariana, who was wiping at her eyes with her napkin. He put his arm around her. That had to be tough for her, too.

Then they ate and danced with their families, savoring the last few moments they had together before they would be separated until late the next afternoon.

Ariana

Ariana awoke at dawn the next day with butterflies in her stomach. She sat at the edge of her bed and yawned, stretching her arms high in the air. *What did I eat last night?* She winced and rubbed her belly. The image of Mari's magnificent paella from the reception filled her mind and her senses, and her breath hit the back of her throat. *I'm getting married today!* A million goosebumps flooded her arms. Karina was still asleep. She rubbed her arms and rose cat-like, tip-toeing, to peek outside. The sky was clear, and the sun was just coming up, creating a peaceful hue in the horizon. She closed her eyes and said a prayer, thanking God for this day she had thought would never come, and before she could process the emotions rumbling in her tummy and her heart, voices and bodies infiltrated her room to help her get ready.

Karina worked on her hair and make-up, and Lucia and Sofia helped her get into her dress and shoes. She added her jewelry and studied herself in the mirror. She ran her hands alongside her dress. *Perfect for an outdoor ceremony in Spain.* It was bright white, strapless, and its slight sweetheart neckline drew attention to her face. The dress flowed long, light and airy with its delicate embroidered lace overlay from top to bottom and wide satin belt cinching her tiny waist in an elegant side bow. It flared slightly at the bottom in a trumpet-style, and it had a court-length train. It was contemporary yet timeless. She had already been to three boutiques and tried on dozens of dresses, and Karina had snubbed her nose at most of them until she had seen Ariana in this one. And when the attendant at the boutique had placed the veil on her head, it was as if Ariana was in the meadow by the river with Luke by her side. She had known it was the one.

A flash made her flinch. She tried to blink away the rectangular light that had invaded her vision. The photographer that Mari had enlisted for the event had been in the room taking pictures since the beginning when Karina had started on her hair. Everyone in the room was grabbing for tissues as the photographer captured the moment.

"Ariana," called her mom. She pulled something lacy out of a satin bag. "Come here, I want to show you something."

"What's this?" Ariana said before gasping.

"Your something new. I was…hoping this was going to happen," she said with tears filling her eyes. "So, I brought it just in case. I couldn't help myself."

"Oh, Mom, it's gorgeous!" Ariana whispered with eyes wide, and she gently pulled at the delicate fabric of the mantilla. "Where did you find it?"

"In Santa Fe." She placed it on top of Ariana's head. "I saw it after we went to the Santuario to do the walk on Good Friday, and I couldn't resist. I was still…well, I lit a candle for you two in the church. I knew how you felt about him, mi'ja. And I figured it would just be a matter of time. A mom just knows these things." She pulled Ariana's loose curls from under the mantilla.

"That's what *I* said." Sofia placed a hand on Ariana's shoulder.

She looked back at Sofia and smiled. Then she squeezed her mom and wiped at her eyes. "Mo-om, you're the best! I absolutely love it!"

Ariana peered at herself in the floor-length mirror again. It was a sheer floor-length veil that would sit flush on her head, pinned with a comb. It was bordered with wide, exquisitely designed beaded lace appliqué all around. The mantilla complemented the hairstyle she had picked that parted her hair on one side in the front with only a small section of hair swept up and pinned at the crown and teased a bit for some volume at the top. The front bangs framed her face in loose waves. The back was set in long, loose, curls, cascading from the crown all the way down with tiny rhinestones pinned throughout.

"Ariana, you are stunning," Sofia said.

"Absolutely beautiful, mi'ja," her mom added.

They walked out of El Convento, and Ariana was quivering. *This is it.* This moment had run through her mind countless times, and now it was actually happening. Planned in a week. A whirlwind. *Breathe.* When she boarded the van and had settled, making sure her dress was carefully tucked, she took a good sip of the water bottle Mari made sure she had before they left. Her breath was shallow and her hands were sweaty. Ariana carefully lifted her hair from the back of her neck and fanned herself. With her nerves and the heat, the air conditioner was definitely her best friend right now. She steadied herself with a hand on the seat in front of her. The van bobbed around through the bumpy, gravel road when she noticed the jagged edges of the open rooftop of Catalina's home were visible in the distance. She tried hard to keep herself from trembling. The image of Luke's face broke through the nervousness in her mind. The corners of her mouth turned up. She couldn't wait to see him.

When they got to the site, Ariana stepped out and she scanned the entire scene from left to right. The late-afternoon sun was still shining bright, yet it wasn't overpowering. Instead, it shone on the river, making it glisten. The trees and grasses swayed with the slight breeze. The seating was decorated with florals of red roses and baby's breath at the center and tulle hanging from the arrangement on the first and last seat, bookending each row. She pulled her lower lip from the grasp of her teeth, and a breath she didn't realize she was holding escaped her mouth. She watched it all in slow motion. Only the sound of her heart drummed softly in her ears.

Her dad helped each of the women get out of the vans, and Mari handed them their bouquets. Miguel pinned the boutonnieres on the men. Karina walked with intentional steps toward the altar, the side of her dress pulled in her hand. She set her violin in the front where Joaquin was already standing with his guitar, and then she headed to the back to stand with Carlos. Ariana's breathing was the sound of the ocean in a seashell against her ear, and her feet stood planted in the earth. The only things missing from the original plan were Liz and Jake. Karina and Zach were standing in as best man and maid of honor for them. Ariana made out the silhouettes of the priest, Luke, and his dad. They were already standing under a chuppah, which had been decorated with draped fabric and enormous bouquets of red roses and white flowers in each corner. She zoomed in on Luke in his black tux and white vest. Warmth swept throughout her body, and a grin took over her face.

The sound of her dad's voice startled Ariana, and her neck twisted toward his direction as he headed toward to the van to escort her down the aisle with her mom.

"Are you ready, mi'ja?" he said as he took hold of her elbow.

Ready? Nothing had ever felt more certain. She nodded and threaded her arm through his. They walked toward Lucia and stood behind the wedding party in front of the red, fabric-lined aisle.

Ariana watched as Carlos carried the rings up the aisle. She smiled as Olivia and Emma followed, prodded by Sofia, and threw red rose petals from white baskets, just as they had practiced several times. They were adorable in their flower girl dresses with red silk tops, puffy short mesh sleeves, and white skirts with thin red silk ribbons bordering the edges. Then Karina and Zach followed with Karina joining Joaquin to begin playing *Cariño*. Ariana waited for Joaquin's nod to walk down the aisle. The guests stood up and turned their attention to Ariana arm in arm with her parents. Her hands were sweating against the stems of her bouquet as they walked closer to the altar.

Ariana caught Luke's gaze. He shifted the weight of his feet from one to the other, and then the tear that came flowing unexpectedly from his eye made her heart pound, and one escaped from her own eye. Ariana's parents stopped at the altar.

"I love you, mi'ja." Her dad sniffled and hugged her tightly.

"I love you, too, Daddy."

Lucia tucked her arm in Joe's and led him to their seats. Luke and Ariana took each other's hands and stood before one another, grinning. He winked at her, and for a few seconds, as their eyes locked, everything and everyone else faded, and it was just the two of them again in the meadow in front of the river and the trees, enveloped by the bright sun.

Chapter 29

Luke

Ariana and Luke stood at the entrance to the courtyard, waiting for the DJ to announce the arrival of Luke and Ariana Cohen. The sun had begun its descent into the horizon, leaving its warmth surrounding the open courtyard. The stars would be out soon, and it would become even more idyllic. A breeze made the wonderful aroma of the wedding feast prepared by Mari and Miguel dance under their noses.

"It smells so good!" Ariana leaned in and whispered to Luke. "And look at the tables. Everything looks so nice!"

Luke squeezed her hand. He gave the room a once-over and chuckled. It was definitely Ariana's vision, but Aunt Rachel's touch was all over it. One side of the courtyard had been dedicated for dancing and the other for food and seating. Red roses with baby's breath for centerpieces were simple yet elegant in long, thin vases at the center of every table. And at the far end, they had placed the long buffet server. On the left side, it held three large glass beverage dispensers, one for water, another for lemonade, and the third for sangria. The cake sat right in the middle with other yummy sweets on trays on the other side. On the far right, there was an elegant red and black card box. And finally, next to the card box in the corner was a round table with a white table cloth where the families had already begun to place their gifts.

The DJ gave Luke a thumbs-up. He looked at Ariana and held out his arm. The twinkle lights illuminated the sparkle in her hazel eyes, and the courtyard somehow seemed brighter because of her smile. He felt strong. Content. On top of the world. His grin was permanently affixed to his face. Yet he felt like swarms of butterflies had taken over his body. From the first day he had seen her, he had wanted her to be his. And now that the moment had finally arrived, it was beyond what he had ever hoped for.

They entered the fairytale-dressed courtyard as everyone cheered and applauded. Mari, Miguel, Roberto, and a couple of other people they had hired began serving the appetizers and dinner by the plate. Luke and Ariana were led to a small table all their own.

Family members from both sides surrounded them like a rotating door as they ate. Luke barely touched his food. They congratulated them, brought them gifts and drinks, and told them about all the details of the wedding they had loved. Luke was getting antsy. He hadn't so much as had two minutes alone with Ariana yet. *The patio.* He waited for Aunt Dianne to hug Ariana and the DJ to switch songs. He eyed the crowd busy with their food and mingling.

He grabbed her hand and said, "Come on."

"Where are we going?"

"You'll see."

They dashed out of the courtyard and into the lobby.

"The patio," she said in between breaths.

He looked back, smiled, and nodded. They ran up the steps behind the office to their patio bench. Ariana pulled her train and gathered her dress.

"Wait, Mrs. Cohen…before you sit."

"Mrs. Cohen. I like the sound of that!"

"Third times a charm."

"What?" She let go of her dress and turned toward him.

He took her face in his hands and kissed her softly at first, then with a deeper, sweet desire, making her lose her breath. He held her close with his arms wrapped around her body and caressed her gently. She welcomed him and ran her hands through his hair.

"This is exactly what I wanted to do the first night we were up here together…last year, and then the other night before we got drenched," he said with his voice low and breathy as he pressed his forehead to hers.

"Is that right?" She rubbed the back of his neck with her fingertips. "Well, there's nothing holding you back now."

He kissed her tenderly again before they sat on the bench and intertwined their fingers. They looked out over the campo. The stars were huge and bright and seemed to be within arm's reach, just like they had been the first time they were together on the patio a year ago.

Luke looked at their hands with their rings, and he lifted them to his mouth, kissing her hand.

"I can't believe we're finally married," he said.

"Me either." She lay her head on her favorite spot. "You wanted me to plan my dream wedding, and it could not have been more flawless. Your mom, my mom, Aunt Linda, my Aunt Dianne, and Mari are miracle workers. I just wish Tía Juanita and Tío Tomás could have been here. But your Aunt Rachel? She is a party-planning queen from afar!" She sliced the air with her hand. "Who would have thought we could have pulled all of this off in a week! I loved every detail. Exchanging the rings. The vows. The unity candle. Our hands were so shaky, I thought we were going to drop it!"

"I know!" Luke said. "*My* favorite part was when you said I do. I'll remember your face saying that always. I wanted to steal you away right then and there."

She laughed.

"And then when I broke the glass at the end," Luke said, laughing. "I love how your dad yelled 'Mazel Tov!' louder than anyone!"

"I know! Did you hear that?"

"I think everyone in Corral de Almaguer heard it."

Ariana laughed and sighed. "This day was everything I could have ever imagined and more."

"It's still not over," Luke said with a sly grin.

"You're right, Mr. Cohen." She touched his face and pressed her lips to his. "There's still cake."

He laughed out loud.

"Right." He paused a second and gazed at her. "You know, you looked like…an angel as you were walking down the aisle. That dress is amazing. I was so nervous. My hands were sweaty, but when I saw you...something moved in me, like the first time I saw you in the bookstore, only it was more full, deeper than I could ever explain."

"I felt it," she said. "You calmed my heart as soon as I saw you."

He put his arm around her and breathed her in. She smelled sweet and sensual just like the first time he had held her in this very spot the year before, only now, they belonged to one another.

"Are you ready to go back?" he asked.

"No," she said with a groan, "but I know we should."

"I'm sure everyone is looking for us by now."

When they got back, everyone was still dancing to the music. Luke gazed around the room and stopped in his tracks when he saw his parents on the dance floor. He smiled and walked over to his dad. He wasn't sure he had ever seen him this relaxed and having so much fun.

"Nice moves." He leaned into his dad's ear and patted his back.

"Hey, you didn't think you got your dancing ability from your mom's side of the family, did you?"

They laughed and Sofia nudged him in the ribs with her elbow.

"Just saying," he said with a smirk.

When the song finished, two chairs were brought to the middle of the dance floor. Aunt Linda and Uncle Al called Luke and Ariana to come and sit. They began the tradition of reciting the seven blessings initiating a blend of Jewish tradition with *La Entriega,* which would begin right after. Aunt Linda, Uncle Al, Nina, Luke's parents, and grandparents each read a blessing and gave them an individual blessing. Then they poured wine from two goblets into one and gave it to them to share in the cup of blessing.

Joaquin and Karina brought their instruments to a spot next to them. Before he began, Joaquin explained that this was a traditional New Mexican marriage custom that afforded couples in the early 1600s through the 1800s the opportunity to marry when priests were scarce.

"In the lyrics of the song, whose name literally means *the giving,*" he explained, "the parents *give* their children to one another, the couple *gives* themselves to each other, and together they *give* their new life and marriage to God. And when I give the signal at the last part of the song, you'll have a chance to come and bless them and leave a monetary gift on the blanket if you choose to."

Luke watched Grandma Aurelia lay a thin blanket on the floor in front of them, and people started throwing money on it. He wasn't sure what this next tradition would look like exactly, even though Ariana had explained it, but he liked how his tradition was blending naturally with one that was important to Ariana and her family. Family members shuffled their way through the line to bless them, and the blanket began to fill as Joaquin and Karina played and sang their song.

When the Entriega was finished and the blanket and all of the treasure enveloped in it was put away, the DJ announced that the father-daughter dance was next. He began playing *I Loved her First*

by Heartland. Luke saw Ariana's eyes fill as she walked over to Joe, who was already complaining about his allergies, and pull him out on the dance floor. She gave him a tight hug and looked up at him, her eyes glossy. Her dad gave a her a squeeze and twirled her around. Luke wasn't able make out what they said, but he knew Joe had picked this song on his own, and he couldn't help but swallow the knot that had begun to form in his own throat from the lyrics.

They danced for a minute alone before Luke walked toward Sofia and took her out on the dance floor, too. And when the song ended, *Over and Over Again* began playing, and Luke took Ariana's hand. They glided around the space with his arms around her waist and hers around his neck through the first verse, and then the song blended right into the intro to *Tan Enamorados* by Luis Enrique. He kissed her and spun her around into position. And they salsa-danced the rest of their first song together as husband and wife, engrossed in the lyrics that spoke right to their hearts.

Everyone laughed and cheered at the unexpected change of the music. Uncle Steve and Aunt Dianne joined them soon after. Then everyone came out to the dance floor, couple by couple, including the kids, Ricardo and Mari, and Miguel. Luke didn't know when the last time it was that he had had so much fun. After the song ended, he took Ariana into his arms as they tried to catch their breath.

They heard a commotion with a group of people looking and pointing upwards. Their shooting stars zoomed through the clear, night sky. Almost immediately, the noise to fell to a hush as everyone watched the phenomenon. Luke gazed at Ariana who was grinning back at him. *It* has *to be Catalina and Benjamín.* He lifted her up in the air, spinning her around, and kissed her.

"How incredible was that?" Aunt Linda said from behind them, startling them.

"They're our shooting stars," Ariana said, still holding on to Luke's neck.

"What do you mean?"

"We've been seeing them since last year. First before we met here and then afterwards here in Spain and then in Denver. Mari told us that there's a legend that shooting stars are celestial beings looking out for us. We'd like to think it's Catalina and Benjamín."

"Well, you know, Luke, it *is* a common-held Jewish belief that our ancestors descend to attend the weddings of their family members."

319

"No," he said, "I didn't know that."

Ariana nudged Luke recalling their conversation in the mountains. "I think they're happy we got it right."

He smiled and kissed her forehead. "Finally, right?"

When the stars had disappeared, Aunt Dianne and Uncle Steve grabbed Luke and Ariana, taking their cue from the DJ that it was time for *La Marcha de los Novios*.[189] They led them to the back of the courtyard, pulling the wedding party behind them, women on one side and men on the other. It was sort of confusing at first since the space wasn't that big and Luke didn't know what he was doing. He stuck close to Uncle Steve and followed his moves. They danced and clapped to the music, with Aunt Dianne leading the women and Uncle Steve leading the men in spirals and circles, with the men and women meeting their partners together. Then, they formed a canopy with their hands, allowing everyone who had joined the march to walk underneath and back out again until everyone was dancing in one large circle.

Then Ariana and Luke were left dancing in the middle until Aunt Dianne and Uncle Steve led them to the cake when the song was over. Luke still couldn't believe that Mari had been able to call in a favor for this work of art at the last minute. The cake had three-tiers, which were all covered in white. Black icing in an intricate lace pattern covered the top of each layer as if it had been real lace fabric draped across the top. Large red roses hand-decorated out of icing sat at the top and in strategic places cascading down the sides of the cake. It was impressive; Luke hoped it tasted just as good as it looked. He reached for Ariana's hand to cut the cake together. He took a small piece of cake and brought it to Ariana's mouth, and she took it. His finger lightly grazed her soft lower lip, giving him a tingle in his stomach. Then she returned the favor. The cake was definitely as good as it looked, but it was his gorgeous new bride that he couldn't resist right now.

While everyone sat to enjoy the cake that was being served, Ariana danced in her seat, singing to a Spanish song that the DJ was playing. Her enthusiasm for the little things was contagious, and that voice…well, he adored every note—even the ones off-key.

---

[189] The Wedding March, another wedding tradition from Southern Colorado and New Mexico

Ariana

It was getting late. Ariana sat back in her chair and kicked her feet out. Luke had just scooped up the last bite of his cake. He sat back and put his arm around her. Her eyes panned across the room, watching their families devour the cake. Luke stood up and took Ariana's hand.

"Let's go," he said with a smile.

Her eyes narrowed, and she looked at his grin sideways. She took his hand and followed him out of the courtyard again. When they got to the door, she stopped.

"Wait a second." Ariana turned around to look at the party one last time. Her quivers were back. She watched her family eating the rich, dark chocolate cake with the delectable raspberry filling. She watched Uncle Steve dancing crazy in the only way he could. She watched the photographer and videographer capturing all the priceless moments. Then she caught her mom watching them. Her eyes were full, and she waved at her daughter and put her hand to her mouth. Ariana got a lump in her throat and waved back. Her dad came over and put his arm around her mom. He kissed the top of her head and held her as they watched her and Luke make their way out of the courtyard and up the stairs to the room that would be theirs for an infinite amount of time.

Ariana had picked up the key to room #7 from Roberto early the day before, and she had given it to Luke. Their bags had already been transported there. He stuck the key in the keyhole, and the door creaked as he opened it. He turned to Ariana and lifted her up in his arms to carry her over the threshold. She laughed and took his face in her hands, kissing him as they walked through the door. The heavy drapes, pink paisley wallpaper, and cherry wood furniture of her princess suite from the year before welcomed her back as if she had never left. Her eyes clung to every detail.

Lights had been strung up around the room. Several candles had been lit on the table and the mantle, filling the room with the subtle scents of jasmine and vanilla. Rose petals covered the floor and the bed. *The bed. This was different.* Sheer, white fabric had been delicately draped from each corner of the four-poster bed, enclosing them in a private, sweet, intimate space that protected them from the

321

world and belonged only to them. Luke let Ariana down on the edge of the bed and sat next to her. He traced her skin along the neckline of her dress with his finger and kissed her there, sending chills down her spine. She let her head fall back and exhaled as he continued kissing upwards toward her neck. When she lifted her head and opened her eyes, she noticed the display on the table behind him.

"Luke, look." She pointed to the table by the window next to her favorite comfy wingback chair.

He turned around to see what she was pointing at. They had left a plate of white chocolate-dipped strawberries drizzled with dark chocolate, a bottle of Spanish wine, two wine glasses, and a corkscrew. A large card sat on one side, saying *"¡Felicidades, Luke y Ariana! Con mucho amor y cariño,*[190] Mari, Miguel y Roberto. *"*

"Wow," he said. "I didn't know they would do all of this."

"I didn't either." She smiled. "They're the sweetest."

He stood up to open the bottle and pour a glass for Ariana and himself while she attempted to take off her strappy rhinestone-laden heels. Her feet needed the break, but her hands were sweaty and her fingers struggled gripping the buckles. She swallowed and wiggled her toes, finally breaking free from her shoes. When she lifted her head, Luke was there with a glass of wine and a strawberry.

"Thank you, Mr. Cohen," she said, her voice catching with her breath.

He put the strawberry to her mouth, and she closed her eyes, taking a bite. He ate the rest, put the stem back on the plate, grabbed for his wine glass, and sat next to her again.

"Here's to us, querida Ariana, my beautiful wife, and an adventurous journey through life together."

"To an adventurous journey with you, the love of my life! ¡Salud!" She rang his glass with hers. Her voice was vibrato, and the trembles still fluttered within her.

They took a sip of their wine, and he took their glasses and placed them back on the table. She stood up and met him halfway. She was eager yet hesitant. She placed her hands on his chest and pressed her hands into him. She slid them down, undoing each button until she had helped him remove the white vest from his suit. He kissed her neck and held her waist with his hands sliding from her back down to her hips. His embrace was determined but gentle. She wrapped her

---

[190] Congratulations, Luke and Ariana! With lots of love and affection

arms around his neck, and her quivers melted away with every caress of his hand. He kissed her deeply again and lifted her to the bed.

They held each other with tenderness, finally giving in to the electricity that had enveloped them from the minute their hands had first touched. They took their time delighting in one another all night until the sun began to peek through the openings in the heavy drapes in front of the picture window. Neither of them had known such pleasure nor such immeasurable love.

She awoke to a thin beam of light forcing itself through the drapes. They were still in the same position in which they had fallen asleep, his arm tucked tightly around her. She breathed in and smiled, not able to remember when she had slept so well. She rolled around toward him and looked at him asleep for a moment before kissing his forehead. He squeezed her close.

"Good morning, Mrs. Cohen," he said, kissing her back.

"It *is* a good morning," she said dreamily.

He leaned his head against hers. They lay there wrapped in one another's arms—reminiscing. His voice was soft in her ear, and his breathing tickled her neck. She could stay like this forever.

Luke took a deep breath finally and said, "We should probably go down for breakfast."

"I know, but—"

"They'll be leaving for Madrid pretty soon."

"You're right. And I *am* starving."

"I love you," he said and held her close a second longer.

"I love *you*, Mr. Cohen."

She kissed him, and got up to shower. She queued up her music, singing and dancing to the first song that came up on her playlist. He threw his head back against his pillow and laughed.

"What?"

"Nothing," he said, still laughing. "I love your voice."

"Shut up." She grabbed one of the pillows off the bed and threw it with impeccable aim at his head, making him jump up and chase her into the bathroom.

When they got down to the dining room for breakfast, their families were already there and practically finished with breakfast. They clapped as Ariana and Luke walked down the stairs hand in hand, making them blush. After a long, drawn out breakfast and helping their families pack the vans, Luke, Ariana, Mari, and Miguel drove them to the bus station in Corral de Almaguer. On their way back, Ariana leaned her forehead on the window and stared at the neat rows of olive trees along the rolling hills. There had been long hugs, kisses, and tears until the bus came and Luke and Ariana watched their families leave until they couldn't see the bus anymore.

"Can't believe it'll be a year before I see them again."

Luke put his arm around her and pulled her closer to him. "We'll make it a point to FaceTime them every week."

"Los vamos a extrañar mucho también."[191] Mari looked back from the passenger seat and wiped her eyes and nose with a handkerchief.

Ariana knew Mari had become quite fond of their families and had bonded with Sofia through the wedding plans and with Lucia through cooking.

When they arrived at El Convento, Luke and Ariana walked slowly up the stairs to the princess suite to finish the bottle of wine and open their presents. They sat down on the bed and spread out their gifts. Most of them were cards with money. Several other wrapped gifts were items that they could use for traveling or to make their small room feel more like home. Then they opened the gift from Grandpa Moisés and Grandma Aurelia. Ariana opened the beautifully wrapped box to find the heirloom menorah that Luke had asked about in San Luis.

Ariana sat up straight with her eyes wide. She let her fingers slide along the arms of the menorah. "I didn't even know they had brought it with them."

"Can't believe they gave it to us." Luke studied it. "We should have it appraised and find out how old it is."

"That would be awesome." She pressed the gift wrap into the box and held it up again. "This is a treasure. So cool they trusted us enough to have it." She placed the weathered menorah back in the box and noticed a card. "Hold on. There's a note with it."

> *Hita, we wanted to bring this to have it appraised, and we found out it wasn't from here like we thought. The guy told us it was made in the early 1600s, but that it was from Turkey. I don't know how our family ended up with it, but now it's*

---

[191] We're going to miss them a lot too.

yours. Your grandma said that Luke really liked it. We hope it
warms your new home with lots of love and blessings.
                    Congratulations! We love you both,
                    Grampo and Grandma

Luke and Ariana stared at one another.

"What does this mean? How the heck did it end up in San Luis?" Ariana jumped up to put it up on the mantel above the nonworking fireplace across from their bed.

Luke rifled through one of his bags and found the wooden paint box and set it next to the menorah. "I guess we're going to Turkey to find out!"

Throughout the year that followed, Luke and Ariana traveled through the southern part of Spain, including Sevilla, Córdoba, Ronda, Costa del Sol, and Granada. They kept in touch with their family through FaceTime and took courses in their fields of interest. Ariana found an institute in Madrid where she could take some Sephardic studies courses online, traveling once a month to Madrid. Luke took some online cultural anthropology courses through the University of Madrid as well and traveled there with Ariana when she went. They worked with Mari and Miguel through the week and toured on the weekends, researching and writing their way throughout Spain and Portugal. Ariana was still curious about her relative that had been born there.

In addition, Luke worked with colleagues on several archaeological sites he had set up and had begun research on what had happened to Benjamín's home. He was determined to find out whether or not any remnants of their former life had been left in the area where they once lived. Some of the archaeologists he had worked with helped him organize the area as an archaeological site. Ariana became more and more intrigued by the revelations she found in her ancestral research. She had chosen to follow Catalina and her new husband, documenting their voyage to the new world in a novel. Moreover, they were planning a trip to Turkey. But, most importantly, Luke and Ariana relished each other every minute as husband and wife.

325

By the end of the year, there was more brewing inside her than her first book. And the two shooting stars in the sky watched them from above, truly enjoying themselves. They rested, content knowing that their love and legacy had continued through Luke and Ariana, finally bringing their family full circle.

Epilogue

Benjamín,
Circa 1597

B enjamín pulled a damp handkerchief from his pocket and wiped his forehead and then his eyes. He stuffed the cloth back in his pocket and leaned over the railing of the deck. It was early afternoon, and the sun, at its strongest in the day, was beating down on his face. He squinted across the shimmering sea waves toward the horizon, and a smile curved upon his lips. He scanned the dingy clothes that had been given to him and his gritty hands and feet. He rubbed his wrists and twisted his hands, focusing on the scars from the ropes. A laugh, more like a grunt, escaped his mouth. *¡Estoy libre! Gracias a mi Dio que estoy libre.*[192] His hand patted the outside of his baggy breeches, and he reached in and pulled a sketch he had folded until it was small enough to fit in a hidden pocket inside. It was damp from the heat and its position against his body. He carefully unfolded it and stared at the image. Her sandy blond curls and blue-gray eyes lifted from the page. Her lips parted into a radiant smile that yanked at his heartstrings. A tear splashed against the sketch. *Libre, sí...pero ¿de qué me sirve si no estás a mi lado, mi Catalina?*[193] An ache filled his chest. He wiped his eyes again and put the image back in his pocket. *Volveré por ti. Te lo prometo.*[194]

---

[192] I'm free. Thanks to my G-d, I'm free.

[193] Free, yes...but, what good does it do me if you're not by my side, my Catalina.

[194] I will come back for you. I promise you.

Made in the USA
Monee, IL
19 February 2020

22040376R00194